REIGNS OF UTOPIA

War Of Evolution - I

UK Edition

ELSIE SWAIN

Ukiyoto Publishing

All global publishing rights are held by
Ukiyoto Publishing

Published in 2021

Content Copyright © **Elsie Swain**

ISBN - 9789356971820

Dedication

To My Family, especially my sibling for being my first alpha reader as well constantly bantering with me while teasing the character arcs and the graphic designer of my Cover Art, Mihika, for perfectly incorporating my character illustrations.

In a world devoid of ears, there are the unfortunate who are never heard because of the judgmental swallowtail and the fortunate who win the jackpot to dare to imagine.

Fading under the moonlight,

Becoming history.

Coloured under the moonlight,

Disappearing into a lingering imagery.

Our story will become a myth.

About the Author

Elsie Swain is an author of contemporary and sci-fi fiction, including Swan Song of My Era and her upcoming sci-fi series: War of Evolution. Reigns of Utopia is the first book in the series and talks about a dystopia ruled by divides. When not writing, she can be found sketching or fashion designing.

You can chat with Elsie on Instagram at @elsie.iyle.

CONTENTS

Prologue	*- 9*
CHAPTER - One	*- 19*
CHAPTER - Two	*- 42*
CHAPTER - Three	*- 69*
CHAPTER - Four	*- 79*
CHAPTER - Five	*- 103*
CHAPTER - Six	*- 127*
CHAPTER - Seven	*- 159*
CHAPTER - Eight	*- 180*
CHAPTER - Nine	*- 198*
CHAPTER - Ten	*- 213*
CHAPTER - Eleven	*-228*
CHAPTER - Twelve	*- 243*
CHAPTER - Thirteen	*- 257*
CHAPTER - Fourteen	*- 280*
CHAPTER - Fifteen	*- 301*
CHAPTER - Sixteen	*- 334*
CHAPTER - Seventeen	*- 359*
CHAPTER - Eighteen	*- 391*
CHAPTER - Nineteen	*- 418*

Prologue

Balance is key for multiple species to co-exist. But when the balance is lost, when one species grows stronger than the other. It rarely works out well for the weaker group. 50,000 years ago, humans shared the world with another species; the Neanderthals. Humans must have had a genetic advantage over them, and they thrived and outgrew Neanderthals in number.

While the details are unclear, Homo Neanderthalensis was driven to extinction while Homo Sapiens survived.

Then, whether through random mutation, evolution, a combination of both or something entirely different, a new species of humans emerged. The first Anthromorph. Now humans share the world with Anthromorphs/Breedlings/Cruxawns. And we find ourselves grappling with the big question. Can we all achieve balance?

The CULT had violated all the principles of The DECLARATION OF HELSINKI in the name of 'Development'. It all started with the twisted mind of one man who changed mankind of the 22nd Century: 'Gerald Watergate'. Watergate believed himself to be the reincarnation of the German Physician 'Joseph Mengele'. He considered it his duty as the son of the 'Angel of Death' to recreate mankind who would replace the current. Ever since the Government of the Czech Republic had shut down all funding for his research of experimenting on humans due to his proposal of performing vivisection on humans and rewriting their DNA to make them better, Watergate lost his sense of morality achieve his dream. 2054 was the historical milestone that celebrated the creation of the first successful gene recombination of a gene of another species with that of a human. Watergate called them 'ANTHROMORPHS', and his first successful subjects were none other than him and his family.

But why did he feel the necessity to change mankind? Was it because of the trapped work cycle he couldn't escape from? Was it because of the so-called life his elders 'advised' him to follow? Was it because no one cared to understand him? Or was it just because he was tired of the inferiority and the selfishness of humans that was poisoning the society he belonged to?

Imagination made us different from animals, and our societal rules separated us from their Jungle Law. The question is, which one was better?

   "As an animal, one only needs to think about their chances of survival, but as a human, the definition of survival goes far beyond food, shelter and escaping

predators. There isn't a division of strong and weak in our society. There is only one category in our community, unlike the two divisions of the Jungle Law; Inferiority and Superiority.

We kid ourselves into believing that we are the most intelligent beings on the planet. When, in fact, we are blindfolding ourselves from the illusion that we are the predators of preset judgement that are destroying Homo Sapiens. The CULT era will get rid of those Predators and bring evolution with the creation of ANTHROMORPHS. A civilisation of genetically modified Homo Sapiens who are stronger, smarter and better than the existing species of Human Beings.

I have isolated my own cells and tissue samples for this dissertation to introduce new genetic material into a genome. I have successfully integrated new genes into my DNA that enhances everything from muscular strength to mental acuity. Thus proving that the power of evolution is now in our hands. A power we need to cultivate before nature or other forces in our fast-changing world settle it for our descendants and for us."

- Gerald Watergate

Founder Of 'Civilisation of Utopian Lidska' byTost (**CULT**)

It was no surprise that Watergate had finally snapped and was tired of humans being governed by greed and falling prey to chaos. The existence of harmony could only exist in Utopia, and a Utopian society could only be created by eliminating humans.

Watergate had to come to realise that humans had lost their sense of unity and destroyed each other while clawing to survive by being their very best. At this rate, their place in the hierarchy of evolution needed to be controlled by a species united by the price of freedom above everything else.

After all, evolution had always been ruled by the survival of the fittest. His CULT merely needed to control the humane side of the anthromorphs and drive them into the desperation of survival or invoke the fear of survival within humans when their superiority in the hierarchy was threatened enough to unite them above their desire for power. Either way, the CULT existed to instil harmony among one species overpowering the weaker species by any means necessary.

Initially, the United Nations of Humanity (UNH) had been at odds while deciding the fate of anthromorphs, which had started increasing in numbers significantly.

Anthromorphs that didn't develop into hybrids had been harder to neutralise as most hybrids ended up losing their humane side, causing havoc upon the human population. In contrast, the retention of their humane side anthromorphs possessed a deadlier weapon - Complex thoughts.

But the group of anthromorphs who ended up being the founders of the Anthromorphic Council had found a definitive marker in their genes that verified which anthromorphs would end up converting into hybrids. Mammalian anthromorphs displayed an excellent rapport of surviving their lives as anthromorphs instead of growing up to end up as hybrids.

The Anthromorphic Council and UNH had unified under a common cause - to bring down the CULT. The Council were at their wit's ends. They wanted some fundamental rights to protect anthromorphs, especially the kids who were tormented until they were possibly killed.

It was a big win when mammalian anthromorphs were granted the right to be registered and live their lives like any other human.

So, accepting the UNH's proposal to train the registered anthromorphs to take down the rogue anthromorphs and hybrids harming the human population and shutting down the CULT's bases was a unanimous decision and being confined to facilities in the ECA (European Commission Autonomous Area) was a small price to pay as long as it guaranteed saving the lives of young anthromorphs and keep them in check if they did go rogue. It was all for the greater good.

Watergate had started his base due to the aftermath of the war, so it didn't come as a surprise that most anthromorphs were initially created in what was then Europe before branching out. When it came down to deciding the base for most facilities to house all the young anthromorphs, the UNH and the Anthromorphic Council saw the ECA as the best option.

The Council had only sought one proposal to seal the agreement - ensure that every human reported the transformation of a human to an anthromorph. Children hospitals were the best hiding spots for the CULT to breed and cultivate the genetic change of humans into anthromorphs.

Humans had dividing opinions regarding the young anthromorphs who were forced into their changed genotypes against their will. While some countries in Asia and the Americas felt sympathetic towards anthromorphs and allowed the existence of registered anthromorphs among humans if they were deemed fit by the facilities, several humans didn't see the same and not merely because of the imminent threat they posed with their enhanced physical prowess and mental acuity.

They were several humans who despised anthromorphs, for their very existence reminded them of the lives of all the animal species that the CULT had exploited into extinction and others who merely wanted to find their own fail-safe plan than the inhibition control in the RTFQ chips created by the Anthromorphic Council.

Most Cage-rings created by humans abducted anthromorphs, who resided outside the facilities to test their trauma limits by lethally poisoning them and luring them into a false sense of freedom if they fought off other anthromorphs trapped along with them.

Humans couldn't use weapons to kill anthromorphs, and none were effective for a permanent solution. Anthromorphs didn't require gene-enhancing tech for their energy surges to disperse in folds to protect themselves against weapons that carried traces of inorganic origin, even in their unconscious state. At the same time, their enhanced metabolism helped them heal faster than humans - lulling them almost in a hibernated state to recover without any aid. Poison could not kill them besides merely weakening them. Still, anthromorphs possessed the ability to kill each other with the *right motivation*.

UN-ECA

(United Nations European Commission Autonomous Area)

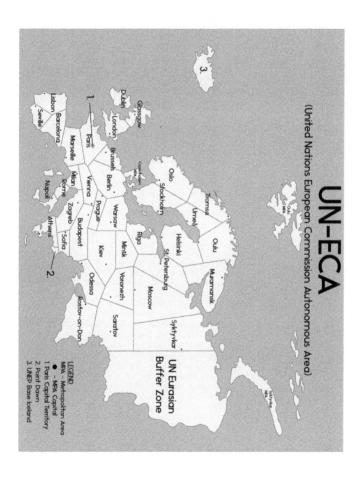

UN-ECA

(United Nations European Commission Autonomous Area)

UN Eurasian Buffer Zone

LEGEND
MPA – Metropolitan Area
● – MPA Capital
1 Paris Capital Territory
2 Pont Dawn
3 UNEP Base Iceland

CHAPTER ONE

Year 2155:

Zella Rune had been doing this for four years now after the gruelling training journey to master using her equipment.

It's better to capture an army than to destroy it. She had learned that more can be gained by controlling people in peace than in the chaos of war. For war is death and death? Death is a waste.

And life should not be wasted while it may yet be controlled to serve a greater purpose.

However, nothing in those four years, nor the gruelling journey before them, prepared her for fighting off the reptilian anthromorph who had stolen tech that enhanced their animalistic gene over their human gene.

Nobody cared about the miserable torment and outcasting of anthromorph with genetic recombinations bound to other species besides mammals. They were either shunned or locked up by the mammalian anthromorphs if they ended up creating havoc against the humans.

Pieces of her hurled scales had melted off where Zella merely aimed the existence of all kinetic energy around her crackling through the air and boiling the cheap plastic- but the thing just wouldn't die.

She could hear the woman responsible cackling somewhere in the distance where a street lamp was uprooted and wheeled around, holding her up like a trophy.

"There's not gonna be anything left rooted in the city at this rate!" Pearl snapped as long strands of her auburn hair loosened from the tight bun because of the storming wind while sidestepping a mailbox and slapping her hand against it, sending it floating off into the sky.

"Can someone please stop her from laughing - It's grating in my ears," The other auburn-haired twin, Caledon, ordered, hitting the ground hard from a different street lamp swinging at him like a bat.

Pearl punched the air from the ground - bright infrared rings of radiant energy bursting from her fist like a cannon shot and completely disintegrating the metal that warped into nothing but particles.

"Knock her unconscious!" Charm turned his back against the door that was chasing him as Pearl launched a stream of infrared flames at the woman across the street.

The door he had ignored slammed into him, sending him to the ground as the woman simply laughed harder, doubling over as slabs of sidewalk leapt into the air, blocking the infrared energy.

"Zella, what the hell are you doing?" The ebony-haired boy demanded his usual poised demeanour fading in folds before blasting the glass door at such a high force that it shattered. "I could really use your help!" He snapped, scrambling to his feet as the shards of glass began to scurry after him, like sand blowing over itself.

"Waiting for a little help!" Came the annoyed response, Zella jumping back from the deranged reptilian-cruxawn and directing a transparent hemisphere of rippling white shield energy blocking her from bricks that were leaping at the barrier.

The sharp-amber eyed bianthromorph, who hid her Avian gene recombinant, struggled to control just her registered Puma-genetic bound side charging her Kevlar gloves. She held her hands out on either side of her, like trying to stop a stampede as miniature versions of similarly coloured shields that were the strongest force fields to exist appeared on the ground in scattered bursts.

"What the hell is Caledon doing?" Zella snapped as her back hit Pearl's.

"Running around like a chipmunk because a sewer grate spooked him- and now he's dodging rocks and can't focus enough to change!" The Panther-genetic-bound anthromorph yelled, taking another snide at her twin, as the Cheetah-genetic bound anthromorph got encased in Zella's shields as he scampered around. "Sis - how about you focus on doing your own job ?"

Pearl yelped as an electric wire suddenly dropped from the telephone pole, snaking after her. "Zella- a little help!" She yelled, racing off towards the end of the street.

Zella rolled her eyes but caught the wire that slapped at her, wrapping it around her wrist tightly-

Zella's equipment didn't wire with her genetics to create electricity or any form of energy. Still, she could manipulate her control over kinetic energy onto electric energy, unexplainably.

And while she could still control outside electricity, it was something like putting the wrong blood type in a body.

Zella could feel that this stuff was wrong, was different, and she didn't like touching it for longer than necessary. But she still felt the surge of power through her veins as the wire's sparks surged into her, startling her for a moment, but no sooner than it entered was Zella shooting it right back out.

Fire burst along the overloaded wire, frying it and burning the wooden pole as well-

She distantly saw city lights flicker out in the distance, but that was a problem for later.

"Cal, if you are here just to fast-talk instead of using your feet, I swear-" Pearl yelled, a brick narrowly missing her temple as she ducked.

Caledon stood outside of Zella's kinetic shield, obliterating debris with molten energy balls that simply turned them into something smaller that attacked. A little chunk of hail that assaulted Caledon was like annoying kids throwing rocks.

From a distance, Zella threw a kinetic shield around Caledon's twin, too, to stop Pearl from getting brained by a fire hydrant.

Zella turned, the rogue breedling limping back towards her, a curse leaving her as she readjusted her black leather mask over her nose.

"Where the heck is-"

A manhole cover shattered through the window of a nearby shop, Charm jumping out after it, picking

it up with his hands and tearing it in half in annoyance. He threw the pieces to the ground so hard, they embedded in the sidewalk, unable to move.

"Enough of this," he muttered, not even feeling the bits of brick and sidewalk that assaulted him as he approached the little shields Zella had been shielding Caledon with.

"Distract her," The Asiatic-brown-bear anthromorph glared sharply at their obstacle, drawing his hand back.

The cackling woman didn't even notice Caledon until he knocked her off her feet.

Her laughter very quickly turned to shrieks, her hands scrambling in her hair for the cackling infrared-lighted energy beam sparkling off Pearl Allyson's kevlar gloves, which were like rodents pulling at her hair, wreaking havoc.

The crazed reptilian anthromorph suddenly fell, collapsing into a broken mush of melted, charred scales.

The rain of debris fell to the ground, and the fire hydrant chasing Charm fell still as her concentration broke.

"Zella," Pearl called calmly, shaking out her wrist that tingled with leftover radiant energy.

The other dropped the kinetic shield around herself, throwing a hand out. They all watched a little disc of transparent kinetic force field fly through the air as the screaming woman finally lost her balance atop the street lamp.

She tumbled with another shriek, still clawing at her hair wildly as her feet slipped.

She only fell for a moment before the disc of energy hit her, expanding into a sphere around her as she hit the ground hard but protected.

The woman stood, tiny scratches covering her face, her hair an absolutely mess- her shoulders heaving with how she breathed through her rage.

"You think you've won?" she hissed, eyes beginning to glow. "Rise, Minions of-"

A small shield appeared over her mouth, the glow in her irises fading as there was a muffled cry, her hands leaping to her mouth and trying to pull the thing off.

Her screams of rage were ignored as Pearl blew out a breath. "Charm, call Chancellor Cullins to send in the transport."

"Already done," he assured her, his leather coat slightly singed from his own abilities. He tugged his mask up higher, ruffling his ebony-black hair out of his ash-streaked porcelain skin that Pearl both envied and fawned over. "They'll be here in a minute."

"Next time, warn me before shoving me again," Caledon muttered darkly, straightening his long coat.

The other Allyson twin merely shrugged, unbothered. "Don't be useless next time."

"Charm Chang spent half the fight throwing around a single manhole cover!" Caledon reminded her, annoyed and dusting off his dark pants. "I don't see you complaining about him."

"No one was useless," Charm said sternly, trying to diffuse another disagreement between the twins. Even without seeing the others' mouths, he knew that the tallest among all four of them was sticking his tongue out. "It was a bit disorganised, but it all worked out."

"Ow," Zella deadpanned, arms still suspended in front of her, expression unamused as the woman beat against the shield, her mouth still covered. "No, really, you're doing such a job of hurting me. Keep doing it- I'm sure I'll give out."

Her glare was murderous, and Zella simply gazed back at her impassively. "Unless transport is getting here in the next minute, I need hands," she reported to them flatly.

Caledon rolled his eyes, messing his wind-swept hair, but stepped up, placing his hands beneath Zella's extended elbows, supporting her tired arms.

"The fight barely lasted an hour- you're already tired?" Pearl teased, dusting bits of rubble from her sculptured leather coat.

"She is still not over yesterday," Caledon said, in place of Zella, who continued to glare at the screaming woman. "She basically had them up the whole time. We were out there for what- six hours?"

Zella rolled her stiff shoulders and knew that she'd probably need to visit the infirmary for an ice pack or something.

Zella gazed around and figured that they... had at least managed to keep damages to one area - well, minus the power outage she seemed to have caused down the street. The sidewalk was torn up, the lamps were all damaged, the windows mainly were all broken-

But no casualties, no humans injured, and nothing done to their team aside from grumpy attitudes from the early hour in the Warsaw Metropolitan Area (MPA).

Overall, a success.

There was the distant wail of sirens, and all of them straightened as the black transport van appeared, racing down the streets like a fire engine after a burning building. It slammed to a stop just before them, a man jumping out from the back of the van.

"Alright, kids, let's step back- I've got a job to do."

Zella and the rest of the bit back a groan.

She jarringly hated when Scott Pierrot, or whatever his real name might have been, was on duty.

Bad enough, the public saw them as nothing but freaky kids. Pierrot, their wolf-genetic bound anthromorphic senior, loved to walk into the nice, safe clean up scene and act as if they were only in his way.

He stepped up to the sphere, levelling the woman with a disapproving frown. "Now, see what happens when you pick the wrong side, sweetheart?" he asked politely as if scolding a child, despite looking like he was only a few years older than her. "Are you regretting your life choices yet? I guess this is a little bit of a bigger deal than dropping out of medical school, huh?"

She slammed into the sphere, clawing at it fiercely, still screaming-

He stepped back, turning to Zella with an expectant cocked eyebrow. "Well, kid? You gonna let her go so I can do my job?"

Zella simply stared at him and felt her lips twitch, hidden behind her mask.

Pierrot lifted the eyebrow higher. "You turn deaf, kid? You're gonna do this every time?" he challenged, mocking parental voice turning annoyed.

Zella stared.

"Kid, I swear to God! Let the bitch out of there, right now! So I can-"

"You are not our leader." Charm said quietly, voice flat as he tilted his head. "You can't boss her or any of us around in the field."

Pierrot's face darkened. "You're really going to play this game every-"

Pierrot whipped around, glaring at Zella- silently threatening her to control their team. Pierrot growled in annoyance as Zella dropped her arms.

The sphere fell away, but the disc over her mouth remained as she fell forward, the walls suddenly gone-

Pierrot caught the reptilian-cruxawn by the wrist, squeezing.

Zella had gotten used to seeing the people seize under his touch- going as stiff as a board and then collapsing, unconscious.

Transport was always individuals with muting powers- be it the ability to turn off powers or (like Pierrot) the ability to force people unconscious.

He caught her, swinging her over his shoulder just a little too roughly.

"Careful," Pearl warned, eyes narrowing.

Pierrot chuckled as he strode back towards the truck. "You kids really want to get mad at me for handling a rogue a little roughly?"

"Their treatment isn't your call," Zella said darkly, fists formed at her side. "Your job is only to take them to the holding facility-"

"I don't need you to explain my job to me, *junior.*" he said sternly, tossing her into the back of the truck with another loud noise that made them all glare.

He grabbed some tape from the toolbox back there, slapping his own shield over her mouth and handcuffing her. "Well, I'll see you amateurs later, unfortunately," He sighed, slamming one of the doors closed. "Try not to be too much a hooligan before then, okay?"

He smiled at them, something so utterly irritating in it that Zella didn't bother trying to hide her glare.

If Pierrot happened to have, his insides thrown due to the random influx of kinetic energy surrounding them when he touched the van next. Well, that was probably just the surge of kinetic energy in the atmosphere around them because of the fight. Canis breedlings always had their desiccated brains brimming with their egos.

Due to the ongoing underlying tension between humans and the accepted mammalian anthromorphs, there were two separate movements among the registered anthromorphs. Movements divided by their opinions to stand for their rights and possibly stand up for other anthromorphs whose genes were recombined with other species besides mammals. The CULT had always been accurate in reading the brainwaves of the foetus while deciding the gender of the animal to be bonded with the true gender of the foetus despite its biologically assigned sex as a human infant. Unlike the human world, anthromorphs matured early and didn't have to use hormone patches or shots after their sex-reassignment surgeries for the heightened hormones produced by the sex of the secondary species bound to their human gene, acted naturally and permanently, once their anthromorphic side activated from the ages of 12-14.

One of them stood for clear distinction and hierarchy among the roles the males and females played in a pack like the jungle law. The mammals living in packs followed, believing that this hierarchy was needed to control the confused psyche of mankind by only accepting breedlings whose biologically assigned sex as a human was the same as the gender of the secondary species bound to their human gene.

While the other believed in the showcase of the superior mindset of anthromorphs by representing the developed psyche of an anthromorph transcending through the concept of anima and animus. They believed that anthromorphs were the very example that redefined the complexes automatically associated with masculinity and femininity. Hence, it only mattered if the gender of secondary species aligned with the gender identity of their human side. For anthromorph or humans, they needed to manifest and exercise humanity above everything else. That can be brought forth by adopting the abstract symbol of the archetype of being humane among the rising chaos.

And it was pretty easy to see the basis on which the anthromorphs chose the movement they supported.

Anthromorphs, whose genes were bonded with the mammals that lived in packs, almost unanimously supported the movement, which stood for the stereotypical differentiation of behavioural attributes defining masculinity and femininity. In contrast, the ones bonded with mammals who preferred to survive alone fought for the right for humans to embrace both their masculine and feminine sides despite being biologically assigned as a male or female and support their fight against gender dysphoria to accept their own identity. They introduced the concept of
'*Mihinity*' (where *mihi* stands for the Latin word for 'me'): setting our own nature-based on our own unique and individualistic behavioural attributes and characteristics, which remains unchanged no matter who enters or leaves our lives.

Not all were on board with this introduction, especially Canidae anthromorphs like Scott Pierrot. Their orthodox mindsets, frozen in the early 21st century, believed that only the animal's gene with the same sex as the one aligned with their biologically assigned sex as a human, defined their identity and hierarchy in the chain. They were several like him whose mindsets reduced the value of humanity further over the years.

He undermined breedings like Zella, whose recombinant gene not only happened to be that of a female feline but that of an alpha female feline species. He had no regard for the gender she had always identified with, even as a human or after her sex reassignment surgery three years ago.

"I don't think I hate anyone more than that bastard," Caledon muttered, shaking out his head like a cat shaking off unwanted water.

"I hope he chokes," Pearl said bitterly.

"We all do," Zella assured them, trying to move on before things escalated. "I'll bring it up with Chancellor Cullins again-"

"He can't do shit about Pierrot," Charm reminded them needlessly. "He's not in charge of who is assigned for clean up- he just assigns us whoever Professor Topaz suggests."

"He can reprimand Pierrot," Zella assured them firmly. "And it just means that when Pierrot does get in danger of being suspended, he'll have a whole list of things ready."

"Incoming," Caledon said, head tilting to the side, listening.

"About time," Zella said quietly, rubbing at her shoulders that always ached after she held them up for too long. Pearl placed a hand on her other one, squeezing and massaging it gently as they walked away.

Barely a minute had passed before the sound of a chopper grew louder. They all gathered in the middle of the street (Zella beginning to feel how little sleep she got last night), and when the chopper appeared overhead, no ladder dropped down for them.

Caledon simply tapped them all lightly on the shoulder as Zella felt the familiar "dropping on a rollercoaster" sensation in her stomach as her feet left the ground.

The first time they had tried this, Caledon's gravity manipulation had sent half of them the correct distance up, but the other half had begun floating away. Caledon had chased them all down, but several of them hadn't spoken to him for a few days. He had it under control now, though.

They rose up like helium balloons, and just as they began to reach the helicopter, Zella felt a sinking sensation in her gut as she stepped in; her gravity returned to normal by the time her other foot hit.

She collapsed into the first seat she saw, leaning her head back as the other were also lifted to the chopper. They grabbed onto their safety handles, and the helicopter began its flight back to the base.

Zella knew she couldn't fall asleep- she still needed to talk to the Chancellor, Sebastian Cullins and give the mission report- but that didn't stop her from closing her eyes to slight nausea in her veins.

"Pearl, I'm stealing your good body wash."

"Why?" she complained before Zella had even finished, glaring at her. "You always want to steal it- buy your own!"

"Because you made me grab that wire, and now I feel all gross and out of balance," Zella retorted without opening her eyes. "I feel dirty."

"Well, sorry your kinetic energy got fucked up or whatever— Ow !"

"It was your job to ensure our equipment was charged enough to channel our genetics, this time." Zella said flatly. "I'm still using your body wash."

"Uptight brat. You are just uselessly tall, like Cal." The Allyson twins were born in the ECA, specifically the London Metropolitan Area. They had not known life outside the ECA, unlike Charm and Zella, who were extradited to the ECA ever since they were identified as anthromorphs.

"Don't engage with that midget, Zella." Caledon teased, his voice playful and sing-songy. Zella let out a slight smirk when Charm held back a laugh while holding back the scowling panther-breeding.

It wasn't surprising that the twins had adopted Zella as their sibling, especially the taller twin. The amber-eyed bianthromorph was always assumed to be older than the twins even without trying, especially when the truth couldn't be furthest from the presumption. Even if the occurrences were rare, the only times it was possible to see her act her age was around the Felis-Jabatus cruxawn, most specifically while squabbling over food. Even among anthromorphs, these two had astronomically high metabolisms.

The ride back was silent, save for the quiet conversation about what they planned to do once they got back. Zella rested her eyes for as long as she could, but all too quickly, she felt the helicopter begin to descend on the base.

She got out with the others, groaning after spending so long resting and getting comfortable. She hopped down, straightening her jacket and adjusting her mask.

"Zella, you want to meet in the cafeteria after you talk to the Chancellor?" Charm offered.

"I'm going to sleep after I finish," Zella informed them firmly. "And I'm going to stay there until tomorrow morning."

"Boring," Pearl teased, bumping her shoulder into Zella's.

They entered the base, everyone pulling their masks down in sync and breathing out in relief.

These outfits were good in terms of protection from basic attacks and hiding their identities, but they were hell to breathe in.

The key feature of the University, inside one of the most defended walls, was the structure of the main facility complex with a green roof that had a slope of almost forty-five degrees. The green roof looked like two sloping, tapering arcs interlocking with a third, more minor arc to form the beautiful, sunken almond-shaped courtyard in between.

Based in the Capital of the ECA - the Paris Capital Territory, the facility was just a glorified lockup for mammalian anthromorphs that allowed them to survive as free-living beings. They were isolated away from the humans. Unless they chose to be caged like animals, just like the rogue anthromorphs they were forced to capture, as a warning for surviving outside the cage.

The courtyard was beautifully highlighted from the reflections of the glass walls of the building and the floating pathway adjacent to the building. There were six identical cream coloured, three-dimensional geometric-shaped buildings on either side of it, all connected by bridges because of the floating platform between the narrow limestone pathways surrounding the building. Each 3D geometric-shaped building contained seven lecture halls, each hall dedicated to each subject.

The twelve-storied Dormitory was situated between the end of three 3-D geometric shaped buildings of the east wing. Except for the ground floor, the dining hall, all the eleven floors were designed for dorms. The sports' field situated behind the main building was as huge as a stadium. Each student had a dorm entirely dedicated to themselves. The dorms were arranged according to the names of students in alphabetised order.

The large metal facility they walked through was bustling with life, as always. Their team split off in groups- a few of them leaving towards the cafeteria, a few heading to their rooms, and Charm heading alone to the rec room.

Zella walked on her own to the Chancellor's office- bottom floor, third door, knock twice.

Zella had only gotten through one knock before there was the quiet call to enter. She sighed quietly, pushing the door open, and as she entered, she found the Chancellor already watching the door.

"I know I ask this every time," Zella said, closing the door behind her. "But why do you bother having people knock if you already know they're here?"

He smiled quietly, lips quirking up as he pressed a button on his computer, booting it up. "Now, how would I keep respect around here if I didn't have an air of mystery?"

Beside his desk was one of those couches you might see in a psychiatrist's office- a red leather finish, worn by use. Zella walked straight to it, sitting down heavily. He didn't glance at her as he opened up a program on his desktop.

"Someone hasn't been sleeping," He noted curiously, typing quickly.

Zella hummed, laying down on the couch, her head resting on the armrest. "Training. Reports. Homework," she listed, settling in.

The Chancellor hummed. "Well, let's hope it didn't affect anyone's performance," he said lightly, swivelling his chair to Zella and sliding over until he sat near Zella's head.

Zella had almost pulled his guts out the first time they had done this, but now the process was virtually calming with its familiarity. She closed her eyes without Cullins needing to tell her and relaxed into the couch beneath her, letting it take the weight off her muscles.

"Relaxed?" He asked, connecting the wires to Zella's forehead to monitor the frequency of her brainwaves.

She nodded slowly, already feeling a bit tired.

"Let's begin," he said calmly. The blackness that Zella saw behind her eyelids suddenly exploded into white, and suddenly she was standing in her room, listening to the call over the speakers- "Zella Rune, please report. -Rune report."

At least Zella got to rest a bit as the ensuing fight played back in her mind, the Chancellor observing it all like a TV show being played.

The reptilian anthromorph was no more dignifying the second time around.

CHAPTER TWO

*M*ammals: *With the exception of Homo sapiens, 83 per cent of the entire species of mammals were last seen in the flesh in the year 2051. Chronologists marked this era as another momentum in evolution in the genealogy of humans and an era of unexplained aftermath of "the CULT's" experiment that introduced the existence of 'Anthromorphs.'*

More than one-third of the current population of humans has already been classified as anthromorphs. The fusion of genes of mammals with that of the anthromorphs has heightened their animalistic senses of the particular animal's gene fused in their DNA. This major leap has instinctually pushed all to desperately protect the rest, 17 per cent of the endangered mammal species, from getting extinct. Unlike most surviving Anthromorphs, who were required to be in the fetal stage to survive the genetic recombination process, most animals didn't survive the gene-splicing process - for only full-grown developed animals were harnessed for the controlled evolution. The corpses sold in black markets among the humans for tusks, leather or blubber, generated enough money to keep the CULT functioning in the shadows.

But, the évolution of Homo Sapiens brought forward new issues in social differentiation. Though anthromorphs are still humans with unique characteristics and abilities, their speciality either provokes envy or awe among normal humans *towards them. For the most part, it was hard to distinguish between humans and anthromorphs. Still, the latter's eyes distinctly shone more like vibrantly coloured gemstones mimicking the colour of the irises of the foreign species that their human gene was bound to, changing in accordance to their emotions, rather than looking like actual lenses. Advancement in science has an inverse relationship with humanity; the broken barriers in science have only created more barriers around the term 'HUMANITY.'*

The main reason behind the shunning of anthromorphs among humans is that the mysterious 'CULT' 'experiment that created anthromorphs has been considered 'illegal.'

This negative aspect is most clearly seen when anthromorphic characteristics dormant in parents become active in their offspring, which often leads to parents shunning their own children who are anthromorphs. According to statistics, most of the anthromorphs usually have parents who are humans. Although there have been several advancements in the Police Force, 'The Elite Task Force Of Anthromorphs,' the Capture of the 'CULT' still remains a long desire waiting to be fulfilled.

One would think that being charged with protecting people from nefarious individuals would warrant a free pass on homework.

And yet, here Zella was, sitting in the cafeteria, ignoring the food in front of her, as she tried to ignore Caledon's rant about how the hell the answer was supposed to be 34 when he got .296. Caledon scratched his pencil across the paper when Zella paid him no mind completing her paper due for her 'Evolution and Biotechnology' Course.

"I'm stealing your apple slices," Caledon said without preamble, snagging Zella's untouched food. "I'm going to throw this workbook," he sighed, dropping his pencil and rubbing at his eyes. "The damn exam is tomorrow, and I don't even know what the hell I'm gonna do— I can't figure this shit out!"

Caledon munched on apple slices as he flipped through Zella's notebook around, chewing thoughtfully as he scanned and compared the messy numbers scrawled across the page of his workbook. "Well, first of all," he said, swallowing. "I think I might have to check the intensity of beams and go through the system scans all over again."

Zella shot up, snatching the notebook back, while the hematite-grey-eyed anthromorph threw it down, banging his head against the table. "I want to die."

"Well, don't die just yet; we need you in dodgeball, Cal."

Zella tilted her head, snickering at the presence of the other Allyson twin, staring up at Pearl. "Is that why you came?" Pearl nodded, popping the last apple slice in her mouth. Caledon stared at his miserable homework in silence. He lifted curious eyes to his twin. "Equipment allowed?"

Pearl grinned, adjusting the jacket over her gear which she always customized onto a peplum style, by herself. "Topaz's off duty today, so yeah."

He slapped his notebook closed. "Fine, but I can only stay for a couple hours— I can't fail this test."

"What are they gonna do if you do?" Pearl asked as her brother gathered his things. "Kick you out?"

The Allyson twins strongly voiced their attraction towards everyone who sparked their interest, but things took a different turn when they were barely acknowledged. Caledon thrived on being flustered when people disregarded him for not chasing them and falling head over heels having it all in boundless folds even by the standards of Anthromorphs, money, beauty, and brains.

When it came down to their sexuality, feline anthromorphs were naturally known to swing both ways because of their genotypes, and the twins embodied that with pride. It wasn't hard to distinguish the pattern of the targeted populus by the CULT to create Mammalian Anthromorphs. They targeted families endowed with money, beauty, and status.

Frankly, they were barely any who didn't acknowledge them, so Pearl found it absurd to believe that those rarities existed, shutting down anyone who dared to question it - "*I like pretty things. Face it, everyone lusts over some form of beauty, and some just don't have the luxury of owning them, and some are too ignorant to admit it. I am not indulging with the amusement of entertaining that ignorance."*

Zella snorted as they walked towards the rec hall.

The anthromorphs here… weren't exactly being forced to be here. But it was a "highly recommended program for the registered anthromorphs, to ensure their safety and the safety of those around them." You didn't have to go to jail as long as you enrolled and had the RTFQ (RTFQ: Radio Transmission Frequency Quantum Fluctuator) chips installed on your skins, but…

The chips acted as trackers and activated their respective mutated anthromorphic genes along with their kevlar gloves that bound with the motor nerves on their hands to channel specific energy around them. That was unique according to the prowess of the animal attached to their human gene.

The genetic recombination processing cryogeneration chambers that forced their mutation reformed how a particular form of energy reacted uniquely to their existence and cemented small changes that were not limited to enhancing their phenotypes.

Well, no one learns how to control their animalistic genetic-side overnight. And even the most desperate of parents eventually give out under the stress of their child's abilities that couldn't be harnessed without the proper tools.

Zella knew that the twins' parents had been the least hesitant to let go, out of all of them, being huge advocates for the equal rights for anthromorphs, even before their children's genes were genetically re-engineered.

None of them could really understand their abilities without outside aid. And Humans just didn't have that ability to help. They didn't understand the toll it took on someone when they struggled to keep the changes due to the recombinant genes within themselves locked up, struggling until their will failed and everything came bursting out like a broken dam.

That's how people got hurt, and that's how people were forced into the system.

Zella, on the other hand, finally found the quiet life she sought anyways. The secluded lifestyle was always a desire when lack of privacy and the spotlight followed both her parents, who just happened to be A-listed Hollywood stars, even after her mother's death.

Technically, after you passed all your control training, you were free to go out into society on probation and surveillance to ensure you didn't go off the deep end.

However, they still faced the same problem they had faced during their youth: they were still *different*.

But eventually, people always found out. Their exotic phenotypes, especially their bizarre eye colours, gave them away.

And Zella would certainly draw questions with the violent, stark scars that raked down her arms in the shape of talons, painless but a blatant reminder of the consequences of hiding her identity as a bianthromorph and burying the eagle gene binding with her human gene along with the puma gene.

So, really, the system was the best place for them. It wasn't that bad, their parents visited every five months, and they made friends with the other mammalian anthromorphs. The only anthromorphs that were accepted to be registered and be given human rights than the rest.

And they had *dodgeball*. Which might have been the most random and simplest way of testing their kinesthetics memory.

The others were already occupying a rec room, a basketball court without the hoops set up, a dark red line down the centre, and the others already divided; Zella and Caledon on one side and Charm and Pearl on the other.

"Who gets the extra player?" Pearl asked as the jade-eyed Coyote anthromorph, Maia Emerson, smirked back at Caledon's wink. She was one of the few Canidae anthromorphs they truly loved, some more than the others if one of the Allyson twins had anything to say about it.

"She should join the winning team," Caledon chided as if he already knew that the sly raw-sienna skinned, teal-green-haired breedling would choose his team, ignoring the other team's grumbling. No matter how much all four of them and the skilled Canis-Latrans cruxawn wished to pair up together for assignments outside the facility, Professor Topaz almost always assigned Maia to lead the freshmen instead during their first assignments.

Most cruxawns in the facility often interacted only among their age groups, especially with the team members they frequently worked with during their assigned missions, rarely mingling outside their teams unless absolutely necessary.

The balls were all laid out in the middle of the court, along the line, all of them made of various materials from regular rubber to pure steel.

Charm held a whistle around his neck (the only person you could trust to make a fair call, even on a team). Once everyone had backed away to different walls, they waited for his signal.

Charm brought the whistle to his lips as they all tensed; Zella grinned as Pearl made a "You're going down" gesture.

The whistle shrieked, and everyone surged forward.

Learning how to use their powers effectively without killing a teammate was one of the first lessons they had been taught.

Charm didn't even bother picking up a ball, simply kicking a steel ball across the court, right at Caledon, who was still running. The other fell back, knees hitting the ground as he bent back, letting it fly over his head and crash into the wall (which didn't break, designed for such rough treatment).

Caledon didn't even stop as he got to his feet, placing his hand against a thick wooden ball and flinging it at a speed until it caught a blast of flames that sent it flying towards Pearl as it burned when his twin tossed it back at Maia.

Zella was the only one who hadn't moved, standing in the back of the court and simply throwing a shield in front of Maia and stopping the flaming ball in its tracks. Maia used this shield to her advantage and flung another disc back at Pearl, who just happened to be as short as her compared to the other three, stopping the regular ball Charm had thrown.

"Can we implement the rule that makes Zella actually move?" Pearl asked, picking up a ball made of rubber, but when it hit Zella's shield, it made a sound as if it had been made of dense metal thanks to the kinetic shield acting as a force field.

Unlike Zella, Charm was registered into the facility of his own will and not as a lack of choice. But he understood Zella's desire to visit her Asian roots, her mother's hometown in Siam, just like his foolish dream to settle in his native lands of China. Who wouldn't? Asia had emerged as the most prosperous Continent since the European Union's Collapse in 2050. Even the least developed nation among the 20 UNH Sovereign Member states, the Federal Democratic Republic of the Union of Scythia, had a higher GDP than the ECA.

During times like these, Caledon's diplomatic side, inherited from his parents' occupations, shone through. He couldn't understand why neither of them wouldn't wish to settle in India among all of the countries in Asia. China and India were some of the few countries that treated anthromorphs well. Granting them equal rights, while India even gave anthromorphs the chance to be a part of the Government. The former had a separate branch in the Government for Anthromorphic Affairs. It didn't matter because it was easier for all of the inhabitants of the ECA to sprout horns than pass through *Point Dawn* in the UN ECA-Asia Border Control Zone and escape to Asia.

"You didn't say it before we started," Maia said, pitching a ball vibrating at a frequency, manipulating elastic energy that quickly gave the illusion that she was hurling at least thirteen balls at Charm. Zella barely had time to see the projectile rocketing towards her fast enough to break bones before she threw a punch, halting the ball and sending it flying back at its sender. There was a frustrated curse shrieking around them before the ball connected with Pearl's stomach, sending her flying into a wall.

Pearl lay there for a moment, winded before her amethyst eyes shone a challenging gleam matching her smug grin. "I am impressed. That shot was worth the loss."

Dodgeball would leave you smarting and bruised, but they were skilled enough to make sure no one died.

"Pearl is out." Zella called calmly, throwing up another shield to block herself.

"Stop it with the shields!" Charm yelled in annoyance, throwing a carbon-fibre woven ball at Zella, who just blocked it.

"The only permanent rule we established was that I couldn't block myself completely, and I could only use one shield at a time." she said calmly. "Should have thought of that before the game started."

"You are insufferable, Rune!"

Zella smiled quietly. "At least, I am not an insufferable loser."

Charm frowned but was too occupied with questioning Zella's sanity to see Caledon and Maia both throw their balls at him while he was distracted.

Maia grinned, knowing Charm wouldn't be able to block both without breaking a rule-

"Breakage!" Caledon yelled at Charm, outraged as the latter pegged him with a regular ball in the hip, sending him to the ground after punching through both Maia and Caledon's shots.

Pearl grinned, even as Caledon stuck his tongue out at Charm. "He's right, though, Charm. You eradicated the ball, and you are out."

Charm's face dropped. "You are supposed to be on my side—"

"Rune, Allysons, Chang, Emerson, please report. Report; emergency dispatch in Hangar 7. I repeat—"

Zella straightened at the message coming over the loudspeaker. "Up, guys," she ordered as they all dropped the balls.

"Emergency dispatch?" Pearl repeated, her definitive upturned eyes widening a bit and understanding why they were letting Maia join them for the first time. It was merely out of convenience that they all happened to be in the same field during the said time.

"Let's go," Zella ordered; everyone stumbled to their feet (Caledon still chiding Charm) and ran down the hall together.

"What do you think happened?" Charm questioned, frowning. "We aren't the Hunting team that tracks and stops the CULT's base."

"It might be a base that's already exposed," Zella said as they all raced around a corner. "Or one of their older experiments might have survived the genetic recombination process long enough to be an anthromorph."

"We haven't had one in a while, though," Caledon noted, his skin turning paler. There was concern in his tone compared to the usual amusing glint when their location was set to land in the Zagreb Metropolitan Area (which was comprised of most of the Balkans). "They usually experiment and complete the process with infants below six months old, and anyone older doesn't survive the process. Even if they do… They end up being a hybrid and not a breedling."

If they were calling an emergency, the CULT had to be involved. Something beyond just a rogue person with stealing tech to enhance their animalistic gene and wreaking havoc.

"Zella, are you sure that you will be okay going back there?" Caledon quietly pulled back Zella's arm, feeling the rigidity seep through her skin and seeing through her stoic eyes, watching the colour drain from her face from the moment they had announced the coordinates.

"I will be fine." Zella offered a forced smile, trying to convince herself more than anyone else.

"Remember that I got your back like you have got mine."

"I know." Zella said without a second thought, returning the reassuring smile as he nodded with satisfaction before racing to catch up with the others.

They reached the hangar where helicopters and jets awaited. They saw a facility operator standing by one chopper that was running. "Get in," she ordered. "Other teams have already been dispatched to deal with their exposed bases, but in a different area. Use whatever means necessary to restrain the rogue Hybrids."

'Hybrids' was the keyword branded to the humans who had failed to transform into a full-fledged anthromorph during their conversion. They looked more animalistic than humane in appearance. Depending on the animal's gene being bonded to theirs, they barely acted like humans, living on pure raw animal instincts to kill anything that crossed their path.

If the CULT failed to cultivate the humans' genes into anthromorphs, the hybrids were usually killed or abandoned in isolated forests to live the rest of their lives in pain. So, facing them had only two conclusions, kill or be killed.

Zella nodded sternly, hopping in behind the others as the chopper suddenly took off, the hangar opening into the sky.

"Get dressed," Maia reminded. She frowned deeper as the others began pulling on their leather jackets atop their gears and sliding masks into place. Their gear was meant to be stealthier and was designed to be insulated against extreme temperatures, electric shock, and projects against projectile weapons. "There was no file, so I suppose we don't know anything about the base exposed or the number of hybrids in that area…."

"Nothing?" Caledon asked pointedly, pulling his mask up to conceal his face.

Zella shook her head as she pulled on her own jacket, letting the weight of it settle on her shoulders. "But if we're going in blind, our number one goal is to keep the humans out of it. Charm, I want you to immediately start searching the area, and we'll focus on clearing it if it's not already."

Zella shoved her mask up over her nose.

It was always unsettling to walk into a CULT's base without knowing anything. And it was even more concerning that they would be facing hybrids, and they had no idea how many. Usually, the facility was tracking the CULT's bases to not lose their ordeal with the humans of safekeeping the rights they had managed to scrape together until now; even if they couldn't find much on them, they had something.

"We'll just have to be ready for anything," Maia said seriously, settling back in her seat.

Zella nodded, feeling her stomach churn a little. She didn't like not knowing things, and she didn't like failing to give their team the best chance to survive as possible.

"Reaching the drop point," the pilot said over the speaker.

They all stood. "Eyes peeled," Zella warned. "We don't know what we're getting into."

Caledon saluted sarcastically, even though his expression was as serious as any of them.

"Drop point," the pilot said, voice crackling.

They all let themselves fall from the chopper, Zella's stomach flipping at the familiar sensation of free fall. She saw Maia pass her up, everyone calm and collected as the ground rushed at them.

She felt a drop in her gut as they all suddenly began to slow down, cold concentration in their eyes as they landed firmly yet harmless in the middle of the warehouse district.

"Great, abandoned warehouses," Pearl muttered, turning in a circle to scan the area.

Zella hummed, "Charm, search the area for anyone, and do it fast."

Zella only just finished speaking before the Asiatic-bear-breedling offered a curt nod and walked away to scout the area.

The rest of them stood for a moment, the silence of the area creeping up their spines. "You would think an emergency dispatch would bring us somewhere filled with more… carnage," Maia muttered as they began walking down the street. The warehouses were untouched, and nothing but empty crates and shipping containers lined their vision.

"Lots of places to hide," Pearl said darkly, fiddling with her anthromorphic-characteristic-enhancement-gloves, nervous energy radiating from her aura.

"We are being followed," Zella said before taking off her backpack and handing it to Maia, who was trying to catch a whiff.

"Are you sure? All I can smell…are pine needles and concrete."

"Yes, I am positive. We've been trained during Forensics class in too many ways to recognize the characteristic smell of hybrids for me to get this wrong." Caledon said firmly without any trace of doubts in his voice or eyes, being the only one in the team besides Zella to take up Forensics Chemistry as one of his majors.

"But won't their scent be masked by the warehouses?" Maia asked, hoping both Caledon and Zella were wrong.

"No, trust him on this," Zella said solemnly, as the remaining two of them nodded along.

"It's too fresh like someone has purposely rubbed themselves against the metals to confuse the scent of the air. Stay quiet." Caledon whispered. "Listen for the footsteps."

They started circling around in tiny footsteps, looking for a hybrid to pounce at them.

For long moments of anticipated agony, they merely heard the distant ruffle of leaves and a couple bird chirps, nothing out of the ordinary, which just heightened their fear of the unseen even more.

Footsteps! Zella could distantly hear twigs crackling beneath two pairs of feet; no, wait… Four pairs of feet… That were heading their way. Zella nudged

Caledon's shoulder, pointing in the direction over his right shoulder. "Over there," she whispered.

But, these footsteps were too light to belong to a human or a hybrid.

Before Caledon could shoot at the approaching beings in that particular direction. Zella threw a shield against his shot, violently yelling, "Wait! They are just harmless animals.", keeping her grip on his arm as he steadied his lost balance to see two deer facing them.

"Good catch," he muttered with a thankful smile for preventing him from killing harmless animals. "Who knew a psychotic band of people would fancy keeping deer as pets in their base."

They all took a deep breath in slight relief, listening to the sound of tall grass brushing against the flow of wind, before Maia bolted off into the trees towards her north, without any warnings. "Where is she going?" Pearl said, yelling after her, as Caledon swiftly raced after Maia without giving any answer to either of them.

"Come on," Zella said, after taking a quick glance around their surroundings for any surprise attacks before walking in the direction, that Maia and Caledon had bolted off to.

Zella started hurrying her pace along the thick grass as Pearl toddled along right behind her. Forty feet up ahead, there was a small clearing, where they could clearly see that Maia had a hybrid, almost twice the size of her relatively short and petite frame, by the throat pinned against a tree, its feet were dangling, and it was snarling, trying to scratch at her.

"How does it feel to know you are about to die?" Maia asked as her jade eyes shone with a taunting glint before her grip tightened, rather enjoying the struggle of the squirming body beneath her grasp. It was rather satisfying to see her back in action. She hadn't lost her habits at all; the same old tradition of taunting her opponents before landing the blow remained.

Zella stopped at the edge of the grass, watching Maia in the field for the first time, in awe just like Caledon, who swiftly kicked the hybrid in its shins to prevent it from kicking free. Maia unsheathed a dagger from the knuckles of her Kevlar gloves, passing in front of the hybrid's eyes, taunting it.

It protested fiercely, using its last bit of strength in an attempt to break free, its chest heaving as each breath became harder. Maia's emerald eyes just turned greener as she plunged the dagger into the hybrid's neck, twisting it around, making the hybrid growl in agony.

Blood squirted out and landed at Pearl's feet as she snarled. "I think you have had enough fun. Just kill the thing already."

Maia smirked at her for a second, taking a deep breath, as she pulled the blade from the hybrid and dropped the twitching body. She wiped the blood off on the glove of her free hand before the dagger retreated back into the knuckle of the Kevlar glove, watching its body go limp.

"Was it alone?" Zella asked as Pearl looked at her, appalled that the taller wasn't surprised like her at this side of Maia.

"Just one," Caledon confirmed, closing his hanging lower jaw. "The only thing that would make this more epic would have been some good background music." He announced, grinning from ear to ear.

Zella scoffed and elbowed his arm as Maia looked over at them and smirked with pride.

"Should we split up?" Pearl suggested.

"Not if we don't know what we're dealing with," Zella said sharply. "Just keep an eye out, and be ready."

They walked between warehouses, Pearl's hands rechecking the power of her kevlar gloves. At the same time, Caledon scratched the back of his neck, trying to recheck if the scar that existed as a remainder after the insertion of the RTFQ chip had faded away.

Each of Zella's gloved fingers glowed a soft white with the pulse beats that rested there, ready to be thrown in aid.

"Cal," Zella said after too long without a single sound being heard. "Speed through this area and see if you see Charm-"

All of them jumped, Zella whipping around and looking down at Charm, who was knocked off his feet.

Atop one of the warehouses stood, a figure dressed startlingly like them; a black coat that came till his knees, a mask pulled over his mouth, but he had the addition of a wide-brimmed hat pulled low over his eyes. Zella rushed over towards Charm to check his pulse.

Pearl was already launching a boom of infrared energy, watching it blast through the air it resonated in.

The figure seemed to melt into darkness, disappearing before the attack could even touch him. He had complete control over manipulating potential energy to absorb any other form of energy. A perfect counter-part to Zella's control over kinetic energy channelled her control over other forms of energy in temporary outbursts.

Was he a—

It dissipated into a ripple of dispersed energy, but Caledon was already manipulating gravity to run over to the rooftop where the figure had stood before disappearing, as Zella tensed with a kinetic pulse beating disc sitting in her palm prepared to throw.

"He's gone!" Caledon called, eyes scanning the area. "I don't—"

"Gah!"

Zella whipped around at Pearl's sudden cry, only to see the other jerk move forward and slam her into the ground.

It looked like someone had managed to absorb her radiant energy, something that resembled photon splicers flattened against her as she channelled the infrared rays into holding the splicers back.

He wasn't using stolen tech, no this was way too customized to be stolen-

He definitely wasn't a hybrid.

Behind her stood the figure, Zella unable to make out any features on his face as she threw out her own hand, a burst of raging kinetic pulse-beats arcing through the air and hitting the figure with force.

The figure was gone again before anyone could get to him at his fallen state, shadows wrapping around it and swallowing it into nothing.

Zella spun in a circle frantically but saw no one.

Caledon's hands were curled into fists, his head ducked as a weak cry tore from his throat.

"Zella, help him," Pearl ordered frantically, soon realizing that the figure could absorb the channelling of all energies directed at him, except Zella's.

This man had been around for thirty seconds, and Zella officially wanted him dead.

Pearl dropped to her knees beside Caledon, who was gasping into the concrete, his hands shaking. Zella didn't know if that thing could absorb energy directly from Caledon and not just the energy that the hematite-grey-eyed breedling controlled. The sight of it made her stomach churn.

The Kinetic disc in Zella's hand pulsated as she flicked it forward, trying to shield Caledon so that he could stop writhing in pain to prevent his energy from being drained any further.

Zella watched Maia's attempts to manipulate the air's elasticity around the figure, trying to suffocate him, the pure silvery colour of it turning an ashy grey, hardening into something brittle, and crumbling before it even got beneath it.

He didn't absorb her energy, almost as if he had anticipated her move and knew what form of energy the Latrans cruxawn controlled.

Everyone stared at Maia turned pale, her hands shaking where they hovered beside Caledon. "It-It just —"

"I will go after that bastard," Zella snapped, turning around to ensure the figure was gone. Her heart slowly rose to her throat.

It was never good when someone got hurt in the first minute.

It was something perilous to attempt, but Zella didn't know when Caledon would regain his consciousness as he stopped having seizures.

"You are not going alone," Pearl stepped up readily, a mass of infrared energy gathering at her fingertips. "I'm gonna try and aim away from you," she said quietly, flicking her finger.

The energy shot forward with a massive surge, and Zella watched the radiant energy blast skim along the edge of the black form, passing right through it as if nothing was there.

Caledon hissed, curling tighter on the ground, nails digging into his palms as his teeth clenched-

"Damn it!" Pearl cursed. "What the hell?"

The hairs on the back of Zella's neck stood up, and she hadn't even fully turned before both of her arms channelled the entirety of the pent-up kinetic energy around them, her fingertips burning with the amount being expelled.

Zella saw the figure standing there, but he was somehow quicker, as if he too had figured out that he couldn't absorb the pulsating energy and could only avoid it by dissolving into darkness.

"Pearl!"

Zella threw a shield, instinct rather than thinking it might help, and the black form slammed into Pearl, the disc turning grey and then shattering.

But it had stopped the form's momentum, making it fall to the ground where it sat like a regular shadow, slowly disappearing.

Zella's mind raced as Maia rushed over from Charm's fallen figure, dragging him near the twins, as Zella checked Pearl's pulse, which thankfully hadn't weakened, neither had Charm's or Caledon's pulse.

"We can't see him, and now he has shut down all our tech using an electromagnetic pulse!"

What the hell was she supposed to do?

Caledon suddenly coughed, a splatter of blood hitting the pavement.

"I have had enough of this!" Zella hissed under her breath, dropping to her knees beside Maia, gritting her teeth in preparation. "I don't need the tech. It's a two-way street. If I can't use my tech, then he can't use his tech either."

"Zella, don't—"

CHAPTER THREE

Z
ella didn't like this: they were exposed, they were outmatched, three of her people were down, and she didn't have a single goddamn idea that would extend into something coherent as far as a plan.

She was already running without waiting for the others, eyes flickering around.

There were dozens of warehouses in this area, and their team consisted of five people trying to look through them all, now, reduced to one.

Zella ran until the end of the row, throwing an arm out and kicking a door off its hinges.

Subtlety clearly wasn't going to work against this guy, so Zella didn't bother. She rushed inside, running through the warehouse full of shipping containers stacked against the walls; forklifts and heavy machinery scattered around.

Seconds passed like hours as she looked around frantically but found no one.

She ran to the next warehouse, breaking a window to leap through, boots crunching against the broken glass as she caught herself.

"Stop playing games!" she called, not knowing if he would take the bait and show himself. "Come out and face me—"

"Don't get in my way. I am here to take down the CULT's base, and I don't care about you." The figure spat as if he were trying to offer pity. As if he truly felt guilty for mistaking them as the CULT and attacking them. But not sorry enough to spare them if they dared get in his way again. "So, consider using a different uniform than those despicable assholes."

Primitive.

There were emotions that Zella couldn't explain. But she knew that the easiest way to screw yourself over is to trust your instincts.

Zella became so distracted by her present and future, the past began to fade. The rage was way too familiar, and she needed to kill that nightmare before it took over her.

"So, that justifies nearly killing anyone as an accident." Zella didn't even realise she reacted. She grabbed his hand and flipped it backwards and upwards, breaking it. The bone pushed through his skin, shooting blood onto his sleeve. The figure screamed out; grabbing his hand, he popped his wrist back into place with a loud snap. Zella just continued to stare him down, heat rising from him with each rapid rise and fall of his abdomen, each breath laced with animosity. She immensely enjoyed breaking the bastard's wrist as his hat fell off, revealing long ragged dark-blonde hair curtaining a clawed scar over his cold apatite eyes gleaming with unrivalled anger.

Zella stared at the scar in near horror, something twisted and vicious in her eyes, her lips curling into a murderous sneer. The mere reminder of that scar reminded her of her own.

"I don't kill. I would never." The figure held up his arm to grab Zella's approaching fist, not taking his sharp apatite eyes off of her. His tight grip was crushing the bones in Zella's hand. He pushed her down to kneel in front of him as if the very word 'kill' had ticked him off.

It felt like two like poles of a magnet had been shoved together, an invisible force pushing her hand back, suddenly vouching for swift and calculated attacks, studying each other's movements. Before Zella realised it, she had been swept off her feet and was lying on the ground on her back. If he hadn't injured three of Zella's closest friends, then Zella wouldn't have hesitated to admit that his moves were fierce, fast and elegant… probably the fiercest that she had ever fought. And damn if that notion wasn't thrilling up to a good challenge.

"If we lived in a normal world, I would have considered it an honour to spar with you for hours and not bother if you ever got in my way." He said with almost an amused glint in his tone, as if he felt slightly guilty and dejected that she couldn't deflect a rather nasty kick to her abdomen that made her double over in pain, cursing at his very existence. "You are good. Well, good would be an understatement."

"In a normal world, there wouldn't be a necessity for people like us to learn to fight for our survival." she hissed, twisting the fabric around his neck before kicking up to flip from the ground in a standing position and cracking her neck to take this seriously from now. "I don't need your damn evaluation."

He backed up a few feet, motioning her to come at him... and Zella swore that she could almost see a smug smirk even behind his mask, but his eyes turned icier, pupils dilating in raw rage over rationality.

He drew Zella in close, ice and fire dancing in his gleaming apatite eyes. "Are you fighting to survive or fighting to kill?"

"Who are you—"

He ran at full pace to throw a punch straight at her chest. Zella bent her back almost in half to dodge his blow and rolled over on the ground, and while in mid-motion, she noticed him turn back towards her to take another swing. She kicked up and hit him square in the face, causing him to jolt backwards, holding his lip.

Zella never claimed to be generous.

He spat out some blood on the ground and took a deep breath. He held his hands back up in a fighting stance, and they circled each other a few times as Zella took a few jabs at him, and he ducked each of them. Zella swiped at his face once again, but he immediately grabbed her hand and elbowed her in the mouth.

Every inch of his face was fuming with rage when he tackled her to the ground in one swift motion. Zella felt her body bounce off the ground as she let out a giant huff and yelled due to the impact.

He quickly strangled her knees with his legs, blocking her chances of getting back on her feet, before laying down a wrath of fury for taunting him earlier. He ripped his hands from her hold, tearing her sleeves to reveal clawed scars that were nearly always covered with the jacket over her gear, and hit her square in the cheek. Zella felt her head fly to the side from the blow, her mask shattering in shards.

"You…" He whispered it like Zella was a ghost, Zella's breath bursting against the remains of her mask.

Zella's chest suddenly burned, and the blonde blinked as his eyes widened in focus, staring down at Zella as if she had merely just slapped him.

Zella stared up at him as his torso heaved above her immobile limbs, eyes wide as he stared at her. Zella's throat finally closed up as she stared at him, icy eyes turning almost familiar.

Her blood stilled inside her veins.

Her lungs stalled. Zella stared at him with recognition in her heart.

"You are a bianthromorph…"

The moment he uttered the truth… that's when Zella really did lose control; she couldn't stop herself when both her feline and avian sides woke up. She suddenly felt threatened, and her animalistic side took over her human side, as all anger and frustration brimming from her past that she had been holding back seized up her rationality. She couldn't hold back the moment her eyes changed to carnelian.

She couldn't see the face of her target, no longer recognising them or remembering why she was fighting against him in the first place and went straight for her opponent's neck, squeezing it with all her strength. She pushed him off her and slammed him on the ground, full force.

Zella kicked him in the gut, shattering a rib. The bianthromorph gasped for air as he felt his broken ribs move with each raspy inhale and exhale. She was sure that he had a punctured lung.

She kicked him one last time across the face; the force caused him to roll over onto his back. His lip had split open, and blood trickled down his cheek. He coughed, and a stream of crimson spewed from his mouth, gagging him.

Why was he no longer putting up a fight?

Zella held her opponent down, her usual amber eyes, now red as raging crimson flames, a burning vengeance in her bones to end him for challenging her in the first place. Her rage grew as she felt her opponent not even trying to struggle to break free from her hold as she applied more pressure on his neck, making him choke.

This bastard reminded her of those rogues that she had been trapped with… from…

Samuels' Cage-ring—

NO!

"And so am I." He added flatly. Zella blinked her eyes, feeling her eyes coming back to focus and her human side taking back control of her mind when he pushed himself off of her. His stoic eyes zeroed in on her scars completely running down the length of her left arm and her back, as if they caused him greater pain than her hits, before ripping away his mask to reveal his entire face. "The way you fight for survival, unlike the rest of them. That can only be instilled by *Samuels' Cage-Ring.* I would recognise those survival scars anywhere."

Castiel Sylvain.

She could recognise that face, anywhere... how could she not? Even if she hadn't seen any traces of those eyes for the past five years. She still recognised the face that had filled out of the same ten-year-old she had met, outside the sets of the last movie her parents had done together, in Salvador, Brazil. The only year they had spent outside California before her mother was diagnosed...

Back then, they had never looked at the other and ever felt anything but bubbling fondness and warmth. Empty, hollow eyes stared back at each other as if they were merely seeing the shell of the person they had known for a year.

So, it felt like a piercing blade, the way her stomach shrivelled at the sight of him. They glared, cold eyes appraising each other like livestock- gauging the other's honesty and value. They were torn between the distant nostalgia of the person they held dear and gazing at the other, who were each beaten down in different ways to let go of all they held dear from their lives as humans.

Words caught in her throat infuriatingly.

Because Castiel hadn't looked away, his eyes still locked on Zella's. And there was more than a flash there.

It was deep, hidden beneath the glowering rage, but it was there. Something harder.

Something that was almost like an echo of the younger Castiel's eyes, that was locked in her memories.

They were never near as cold, calculating, haunted, unrelenting, and fearless as the one she struggled to recognise.

They were looking to Zella. Her mind screamed to her that the eyes were conjured by her memories of the past; they were wrong; it wasn't real.

His chest felt the familiar pressure that always followed Castiel's eyes on her as if his gaze itself was a weight to bear. It was a watery version, and an unrecognisable version, barely even a noticeable presence.

But it was still there, and it was making Zella hesitate.

Because it wasn't the one from her memories - nowhere close.

And yet it looked like him, in the most primitive form; it was the younger boy she knew.

And Zella felt betrayal well in her throat. She couldn't recognise who the person she was when she was ten.

"What now?" She gritted through her teeth, finding no gain in denying the truth. He already knew way too much. And she knew nothing about him besides the ugly fact that he shared similar nightmares as her.

Zella looked back at him as she tried to help him sit up when he quietly handed over his jacket, merely lifting her eyebrow in question. "For now, I think you need a replacement for the garment that I have torn."

Jerk

"You need to leave——" She barely had time to finish her words before they heard the sound of the chopper above them.

"They… want me to die," He said lowly, expression open and understanding. "They won't hesitate to throw me away."

CHAPTER FOUR

"**A**re you hurt?" Pearl demanded as she reached Zella, her heart racing. Zella shook her head quickly but barely gave her an answer. She looked over at Maia, dragging in over twelve knocked-out anthromorphs and the damaged cryogenerators, raising an eyebrow and silently asking her if the four of them took them down.

"No, these three just regained their consciousness a while ago." Maia met her stare. Her expression softened as she looked over the recovering state of their team before her gaze shifted on to the wounded bastards running this base, finally landing on the bianthromorph behind Zella. "These morons were knocked down way before we got here. Most probably by *him*."

"What is going to happen to that guy?" Charm demanded, his eyes widening as he looked at the guy behind her. "Did you—"

A look into his phenotypes gave it away that he definitely wasn't a hybrid or just an anthromorph.

"I know you. Castiel Sylvain." Caledon said with a warm smile in recognition. A smile that wasn't shared by anyone else. "You are a bianthromorph."

Especially his twin, who winced in disgust. "He is a *bianthromorph*? That explains the emergency dispatch."

"What is that supposed to mean?" Zella snarled in a low tone that alarmed Pearl, for the former never used that tone on her. For Pearl knew about the fading feelings that the taller girl had harboured for her.

"There was no one around, and it's the warehouses, which means there probably weren't humans around after he locked up those anthromorphs running that base." Charm murmured, narrowed eyes scanning the area. "He basically did our job for us before we even got here."

"Then why does he want to be locked up, voluntarily?" Maia demanded as Castiel stared at her almost in recognition. A look that didn't go unnoticed by Zella, as if Maia wanted him to snap out of his sacrifice. "Why the hell is he not defending himself if he is capable of doing that?"

Zella shared the thought, but no matter how much she wished to literally knock the reality into his head, that he should walk out instead of walking into another nightmare, especially when they knew that he was.

There was a particular reason behind why bianthromorphs weren't accepted even among anthromorphs. The genes resulting in complete animalistic behaviour and mutation part of this had to do with the complete isolation and rejection they faced in every aspect, which slowly caused their rationality and mental state to deteriorate. Ultimately leading to the total destruction of any sense of reasoning they had in them. There were exactly thirteen registered bianthromorphs around the world, including Castiel. Usually, anthromorphs who show signs of being a bianthromorph develop their full-fledged traits of being one after they hit puberty. After they were identified as bianthromorphs, they were monitored at the year to keep them in 'check'.

But that *pig-head* refused to budge, insisting on being held accountable for his actions. What the hell was his deal? Why on earth did this fool believe that the facility was going to listen to him. They had already sent forces to capture him, so they must have known that the was a bianthromorph and sent them in blind to capture him without any measures.

And that didn't sit well with Zella whatsoever.

She had to keep an eye on him to figure out his intentions, but that wasn't the worst part. The worst headache that was about to befall her was hopefully convincing Cullins to not let the others running the Anthromorphic Council lock him up.

Perfect, another stubborn head was just what she needed to cause more unnecessary chaos in her life.

"I have already radioed in for pick up," Pearl declared, her voice losing its authority. Zella glared at her as Pearl's venomous tone against Castiel which invoked her own nightmares to flash across her mind. "Let's go."

They walked in solemn silence, knowing that today had not been a victory. They might have recovered physically but were taking in a person who had single-handedly taken down the bases of psychopaths who permanently robbed them of a life of normalcy.

"You know him." Zella raised heavy eyes to Caledon, ignoring Pearl's piercing gaze. "Can you convince him to walk out of this?" His eyes narrowed in deep, confused sympathy. "You know the rules…They already know about him, and we will be locked along with him if he walks out."

Zella bit the inside of her cheek hard. She shook her head as echoes of the past still reverberated.

***

"Do you see your freedom, bianthromorph?"

Zella did see it. It was behind a black door. In front of the door stood a man. A man holding a gun. The gun couldn't kill her, nor the knives that three others were holding. She calculated the jumps she had to take and the leaps she had to make to get out. She could still try to escape, despite the broken hip bone and her twisted wrist. She didn't feel pain.

She could jump for the kill, seeing red in front of her eyes. She could escape. She just had to kill.

All she had to do, was kill the one talking to her.

"Come on, freak, the door is right there" The voice was speaking from outside the room, Zella figured. She was tricked. Her body shook, limbs too tired to move, several wounds on her body were open, she couldn't breathe, but she still felt nothing. Nothing but the fear of what she had done or, worse, what she might do.

She was lying on the ground, right in front of that door, surrounded by corpses. The ones that were killed when they failed to survive. Zella was tricked. There was no way out of that room.

***

"Zella," Pearl said hoarsely. "What the hell?" She looked away, lips twisting regretfully.

"Why did you inform them?" Zella demanded, tensed.

"I have a better question since when do you care about captives over my decision?" Pearl asked quietly, carefully as she sat beside Zella. "We... our abilities were useless against him. How did you... he is a bianthromorph. How did you cause more damage?"

Zella closed her eyes, leaning her head back, hoping that it might knock back the memories. "Not now, Pearl," she said, sounding a little more pleading than she had planned. "If you don't trust me, say it out loud or else I am not interested in talking about this anytime soon."

"This is highly irregular! Who cares if he took down the CULT's base. He is capable of being far more volatile than them!" Pearl snapped. "The bianthromorph is to be made unconscious to be placed within a holding cell! We will not risk the people within this facility!"

No matter what he wanted, Zella didn't want anyone snooping around Castiel's mind, looking through his worst nightmares without his consent.

She could feel the others' gazes burning into her, but Zella could not respond to them right now.

Pearl had always been too privileged and ignorant to connect every dot. Her worldview had been too narrow, too carefree, despite everything.

Zella was directed to the Chancellor's office the moment they arrived, the others saying they would save her a seat in the infirmary if she wished to take care of her injuries. Zella hadn't even reached his door before it was opened, startling her with her frazzled nerves.

Zella jumped, stumbling back a step, and he stared at her with gentle eyes. "Come in," he said, opening it further for Zella.

Zella didn't want to do this.

There was a tray set up beside the little couch, a cup of coffee and some hot soup sitting ready. "First, eat that, and then we'll talk," he said, sitting at his desk.

Sometimes Cullins was a little too in tune with reading their minds and thoughts. And that never stood right with Zella. She would rather walk out of this.

Zella stared at it as she sat, her stomach-churning. "Not hungry."

"You look ready to pass out," He said firmly. "Eat at least a little."

Zella sighed but picked up the coffee, grateful for at least the heat. She hadn't realised how chilled her blood was until she held the hot mug. She swallowed, trying to keep everything together.

"I'd- I think I'd rather just do a verbal mission report," Zella said quietly, staring at the dark liquid.

Zella heard him hum gently. "Those are usually the times when people want to hide something. And usually, the times when it would be most beneficial for me to see exactly what's going on."

Zella tightened her grip on the cup, something flowing quicker through her blood. "I- I don't know if I'm ready to relive certain parts of that again."

"None of your teammates reported anything particularly alarming, aside from Pearl's warning that the bianthromorph needs to be locked up," Cullins replied curiously, quietly. He leaned forward slightly, frowning. "What happened, Zella? I can feel your distress from here. You disagree with her opinion, and that's concerning."

Zella took a sip of the coffee just to keep from answering, but it only made her stomach roll.

Cullins might go snooping around Zella's head without her consent if she didn't choose her words carefully. If she pushed to only do a verbal report, Chancellor Cullins would comply with her request until such a point that it was a hindrance to their duty.

"I knew the guy we were after," Zella said hoarsely, the coffee burning her throat. "Distantly."

She could hear the creak of his chair as he shifted. "You knew him? The bianthromorph you were sent after?"

Zella nodded slowly. "I think he was one of the captures forced into the fight rings of Brett Samuels; *survive until you kill or get killed*." She had intentions of telling anyone of the precious memories she had held as a human.

There was a long silence, and Zella set the coffee cup down when her hands started shaking a little too much.

It was just all so jarring.

"I think- It may be easiest on you if you allow me to see," Cullins said with a forced smile. "You don't have to revisit your memories from your time in his ring."

Zella was honestly so tired; any sort of break from thinking about this would be a blessing. But what would happen?

Zella didn't know what sort of process Castiel would go through, what he would need to prove, what they would try and do.

Hell, for all she knew, the facility may become a prison for him; if they decided he would never have enough control to be allowed out. Especially when something as natural as emotions would set him off.

That stubborn fool acted like he was paralysed when he realised that she was tortured in Samuels' fight ring, too. Why didn't he leave before the facility had sent its chopper?!

"What's gonna happen to him?" she asked darkly.

Cullins took another deep breath, not looking at Zella. "Before they waste their time with a lockup, they want to do a psych eval and genetic mapping on the bianthromorph. First, to cultivate how much his animalistic genes influence him and how he controls absorbing the potential energy. If he's capable of subverting them, and then to determine his psyche beneath all that influence."

Zella couldn't help but curl her fist defensively. "They want to turn him into a lab rat," she summed.

"It's for the greater good."

"Be honest," Zella murmured her expression hardening into annoyance and anger. "What chance do you think he has?"

"He didn't cooperate and speak from the start." He said tersely. "So, they had no choice, and since you were the one who captured him, you might have better insight."

"He came along voluntarily and did a better job of capturing the anthromorphs running that CULT's base than most of our teams here." Zella snapped, nearly snarling at him before remembering that he basically ran this facility and was basically helping her to keep her true identity hidden. It was easy to forget it when he led her to the room where Castiel was restrained under straps and was having seizures. He had wires connected to his forehead which read the frequency of his brainwaves against his will.

"You can't allow them to invade his mind—"

Yet that wasn't worse than actually seeing his nightmares. Seeing the very hell-hole that she had also been thrown in, while mourning her mother's death, away from her father, in his memories. It made her jaw clench to the point where her teeth could easily be ground to dust if she didn't stop her reality from slipping into her own memories in that living hell any sooner.

She hated that her father still felt guilty over being helpless about it and felt like he owed Cullins for running a facility that shut down those fight-rings that forced anthromorphs to fight till death. All this for the CULT's mere entertainment, testing the prowess of the cultivated genetic recombinant of their test subjects under trauma or just some overpowered humans and unregistered anthromorphs who were banished if the animal gene binding to their anthromorphic gene wasn't a mammal. Moreover, she knew that her father's fear was subdued by understanding that being accepted in that University prevented that nightmare from being a reality ever again.

After all, anger was nothing but fear adorning its sultry persona.

That scum, *Samuels*, found sick joy in only snatching anthromorphs fuelled by anger. Imagine his luck when he had stumbled upon not just one but two bianthromorphs.

***

And then something flipped within him, making his lungs breathe in the ice-cold air. Fright.

The memory was there to cause nothing but chaos and pain.

He couldn't understand their language, he could see their lips moving, but he had no idea what they were asking him to do. A whip pulled Castiel out of the daze, and the skin that just got ripped from his back was only itching. The scariest thought that he had was that it stopped hurting. He counted. Castiel needed 20 whips to start feeling, and he needed his limbs to get twisted so he could start screaming.

"Come on, freak. Are you going to admit that you are worthless? What kind of a bianthromorph winces to few scratches?" The nasty face of the same man appeared in front of his eyes. Castiel recognised the small angry red eyes. He was dreaming about them every night, nightmare after nightmare.

He had no idea how he was even sane after what that man had done to him.

There was one thing that crossed his mind, though. Castiel wanted to survive.

Castiel was going to be killed.

Another whip crossed his face this time, ripping his nose and lips apart. He smiled, spitting blood right at the man's face as the wildness filled his heart with rage, and the silver chains that were tightly wrapped around his wrists didn't bother him that much, but the pain was about to stop once when he had his canines ripping holes onto that bastard's neck.

"What's the matter? Are you angry?" The man asked, swapping the black whip into his other hand and swinging it hard, hitting Castiel on the face one more time.

This time Castiel saw red. This time he needed only seconds to engulf the burning pain attack the bastard.

Screams. He heard one screaming rogue, but his voice died out into Castiel's grip around his throat. His dagger ripped the person's jacket in the count of three seconds, the sharp, penetrating edge of the knife cut slits his skin, stabbed him above the ribs and the next thing that he felt was the silver chain, wrapping around his neck with dangerous force.

He had survived. No, Castiel finally killed his nightmare.

***

"Unless he can be controlled, he is an existence of chaos and not value." Chancellor Cullins said, voice as if he were reading from a textbook. "Don't you agree?" He straightened as Zella remained statuesque.

It was *truly* laughable.

Mammalian anthromorphs would have been rewarded for shutting down a CULT base single-handedly. Even anthromorphs with animal genes bound to any other species would have been spared for serving the greater good. But the mere existence of a bianthromorph was a greater threat to them, no matter what they did, and their survival was majorly ruled by hiding or being locked up.

Cullins would spare his life if he had a *fail-safe plan* while controlling the trapped bianthromorph. More specifically, a controlled bianthromorph *already* existing in his facility to control the new one.

"You want him to be the fail-safe plan to keep me in check, too," Zella scoffed petulantly. Some of her anger bleeding away as she reigned in the binds of her situation. "If threatening to harm my friends fails to ground me if my bianthromorphic side takes over my human side."

"The Anthromorphic Council trusts you and knows that you have it controlled." He said, voice remaining level and firm, giving away nothing. "It all depends on whether he agrees to the ordeal."

Zella's brow pinched, clearly wondering whether or not Cullins was being truthful.

For all, she knew the bianthromorph who was capable of taking down the CULT's base single-handedly had a much bigger goal for insisting on walking into a death-wish. His actions might appear to be bat-shit crazy. *For god's sake, he had nearly killed her entire team*, but she had to believe that his motives definitely held much bigger intentions that she was yet to figure out and hope she didn't bash his stubborn head or pull all of his blonde hair out before that.

No matter what, she owed it to the boy that she had trusted from her memories, to not let him be used by anyone else.

"Your team will undergo a change, and I will arrange the papers to enrol him into the facility." The Chancellor's response was stoic as ever, so blatantly devoid of feelings. "His actions will reflect your responsibility, so try not to be negligent even by accident."

Zella took in a sharp breath, her mouth settling into a dangerously thin line. "I am not known for my negligence."

"You wouldn't be here if you were." He clarified with a warning as if he were almost apologetic in reminding her that she could easily be in the same state as Castiel. His eyes turned steely as if to drive a point home before he waved a dismissing hand towards the guards reading Castiel's brain waves to stop the process.

She was strong enough to take down 16-17 of the trained anthromorphs in this facility, but she knew that she didn't stand a chance in taking down hundreds of them, all at once, especially if they activated the inhibition control in her RTFQ chip.

Control. The ability to have the freedom of taking decisions to make one's own choices without any hurdles obstructing those choices demonstrated the value of having control over one's life. Humans need that control in their lives. When they lose that freedom to control their own lives, they find a path to exercise that lost control by implementing the lost control by other means. Their most accessible escape route being, living in the presence of contentment by controlling another life.

But, how does that equation change, given Zella has never truly had that complete control all her life?

Castiel ground his teeth together, wincing in pain as he regained his consciousness. His hand grabbed the throat of the body, invading his space before the figure escaped his grip and grabbed his upper arm instead to steady his balance.

He had never missed.

Silence hung between them like a curse, loud and angry when they were left alone.

Time seemed to stretch forever, cracked and uncertain, moments turning into aeons before snapping back into seconds as he stared into the calculating amber eyes of the figure offering him a helping hand.

For a moment, it appeared almost as if he might pull back and ignore her help as if it was *beneath him*. But finally, he agreed and extended his hand, watching her face with a sort of strange, reserved curiosity, like you would with an animal in a zoo.

"You are getting in my way, again."

Castiel lifted his sullen expression to her face, and he practically snarled at her, his expression dark. There were shadows in his eyes, things he wanted to say, and secrets he knew he should keep silent. He looked down at the first-aid kit in her hands, uncertainty crossing her face, and her shoulders sagged in annoyance. There was a long moment where nothing was said, and Zella approached him like he was a wounded animal, hissing and spitting and frightened. He shifted as she sat down across from him, picking through the minimal items in the kit.

After a long moment, Zella finally scoffed at him. "You have a lot of nerve saying that, especially in your position."

That was almost insulting. He glanced up from beneath his lashes and offered a one-shouldered shrug. "I would be grateful for your instant attachment to care about my life, but it's an interference that is just not amusing to tolerate."

She let go of a soft breath and hummed. "Next time, get locked up somewhere else where they don't fry your brain out, in my vicinity."

Castiel grumbled something rough in the back of his throat but chose not to pick a fight with her, at least for now. Zella was appreciative of that, at least, she could be kind of an asshole when she wanted.

But, despite himself, Castiel found himself fascinated with her profile and watched the angular lines of her face as she continued to meticulously stitch up the damage she had caused during their encounter as if she had done this way too many times. *Maybe she had to make it out of Samuels' fight-ring, alive.*

Zella was classically beautiful in a way that made his chest tighten. Her roundish-almond eyes largely gave away the only hint of her Asian heritage. The sharp bones of her cheeks and jaw, and the strange soft fullness of her lips, all blended together to create something that seemed almost... otherworldly. She looked a bit like a fallen angel, regal but deadly in her own way.

But it was her eyes that made him pause. Wide chestnut brown eyes that had turned fierce amber flashing a carnelian red when riled up, but they gazed at him, and they challenged.

Castiel looked at her eyes, and they were challenging.

They were tenacious and sharp but tired.

"I am responsible for your actions, henceforth. So, keep your discoveries about me, shut permanently—"

Castiel felt the ice-cold shock ripple through him, draining his mind of all sensible thought. Whatever spell he was under snapped in a second, and Castiel looked back at her, his eyes narrowing. She watched him pull his hand back, his mouth turning up into an almost-snarl. "You don't actually think I'm going to join *your* merry-band?"

She blinked, trying to understand what he meant before everything seemed to snap like a rubber band pulled too tight. Her lips pressed into a thin line, and she huffed out an annoyed breath, feeling a sharp spike of anger start to boil under the surface of her skin. She pitched forward, meeting his stare and swallowing a breath to try and calm herself. "You don't have much of choice, you ungrateful insolent! You actually need to live to get to fulfil whatever you sought *before* my interference."

It was nothing close to the ten-year-old from his memories. But... perhaps, maybe... he could see something there. A spark... a glint... a flash... Something that spoke of determination...

Of trust.

And those were two things he had shared with Zella from his memories. It made Castiel want to recoil, not willing to slip into a trap of compliance. And there was that flash again... That almost-trust. That near-determination.

This wasn't the same Zella, but rather *someone* who worked for slimy bastards like Cullins.

Castiel glared at her, anger rippling through him like a shockwave. Zella could feel it pull at the edges of her senses, scratching and clawing at her. He looked steely and cold, as if there wasn't a thing in the world that could bring him warmth, and leaned closer to her. "So you are volunteering to be my watchdog because you like dancing to their tunes?"

When it came to people in these damned facilities, his definition of trust was as weak as wet paper, tearing even as you tried to hold it.

The Legacy of the CULT.

All the registered and accounted bianthromorphs were chained up in isolation by the Council to protect society. Imprisoned and neglected to the point where they died after being driven to insanity by their overpowering dual animal instincts. These were the CULT's failed attempts of creating bianthromorphs where they lived in the intermittent stage between an anthromorph and a true bianthromorph. Often they were falsely classified as full-fledged bianthromorphs when they clearly weren't, so they knew all along that those bianthromorphs were doomed from the beginning.

There were always two leaders, successful full-fledged bianthromorphs, who led the CULT until the task was passed on to the next. Those who knew how to lead their main purpose of development, through their twisted definition of creating anthromorphs and reducing humans' population, induce the forced evolution to ensure the reign of these beings on the planet. Someone who had the intellect and the vengeful heart to do so.

All those Bianthromorphs created without their choice, all those lives ruined because they had to be stripped of all choices by the society, driven by helplessness and anger to lead the CULT,... disposed and led to believe that they deserved to be an abomination.

Today had been the closest he had ever gotten to finding the mastermind who ran the CULT. Ruin that so-called damned *Legacy* into unsalvageable filth.

But now, he had driven himself into another dead-end.

ZELLA RUNE

CHAPTER FIVE

W inter was right around the corner, and the sun's rays were muted and slanted as if they weren't sure if they wanted to actually shine through the windows just yet. Outside, a bird flew past the window, pecking at its reflection briefly before disappearing around the corner.

Zella had ignored Pearl's rants which, bordered onto a near obsession, to drive home her warning that getting a bianthromorph was the biggest mistake she could make. Instead, she was bent over a few books spread out in front of her, trying to conjugate verbs in Spanish and translate a few journals on varying OPDs, setting the designs for different interferometers before writing her Forensic Chemistry paper. After this was done, and she was sure that no one else would see her snooping, she was finally going to dig around in the back section of the library. She wanted to find something to ensure her genetic markers hadn't started displaying signs of either of her animal genes overpowering her human gene. Or, more accurately, both her's and Castiel's.

Her phone buzzed, and she glanced down to see a link to another article from Pearl:

In the recent joyous occasion marking the celebration of anthromorphs (Homo anthromorphis) and humans (Homo sapiens) walking hand in hand.

Another striking controversy has risen about the birth of bianthromorphs. Bianthromorphs are anthromorphs that have genes of two animals in their DNA instead of one. During the sequencing of genes of Anthromorphs, if one strand of the helical bond of the DNA is completely human, then the second strand is a blend of the animal gene and the human gene in equal ratio. While the second strand of helical bond in bianthromorphs is a blend of the genes of two animals, where the gene of the second animal they are bound to, replaces the human gene in the second strand. The genetic recombination of potential anthromorphs or bianthromorphs was activated around the age of 12-14. All hospitals are needed to hand over the annual health check-ups to the Anthromorphic Council if the genetic markers of Homo sapiens started lighting up as Homo Anthromorphis instead.

Unfortunately, this special creation and unique recombination come in the form of a curse for the genes of the two animals combined together are in equal ratio with the human gene in the helical bond, which may result in an animal in a human shell after the bianthromorph loses their sanity. They can slowly start to mutate as time rolls by.

In a recent interview, one of the youngest Nobel Laureate winners Charlize Pierrot, the brilliant mind, explains why bianthromorphs are a threat to society, unlike anthromorphs. 'The chance of anthromorphs undergoing mutation is slim, almost zero as the human gene is superior compared to the animal gene in an anthromorph's DNA, but this equation changes in the case of bianthromorphs where superiority changes its course towards a majority. The basic difference between the animals and Homo Sapiens and Homo Anthromorphis is the comprehension of the word 'logic'. Society abides by rules and systems, differentiating what was right and wrong and development and destruction. When all of this disappears from a Homo Sapiens' brain, they are no different from a dangerous wild animal. Miss Pierrot also shared a favourable opinion on the detention of the two bianthromorphs who were recently taken in for experimentation. 'The slightly violent methods used to keep their strengths and abilities in check is necessary. This has been done after several tests and reviewing the total capacity of their strength. This will help the bianthromorphs and society as a whole, which will be protected from them. After all, the advancement in Science is for the stable development of the society.'

She sighed and turned her phone on silent, shoving it into the depths of her bag. The last thing she needed to do before their combat class was another reminder from articles like these that her true form should be locked up instead, that she was merely living a lie.

She never had to fight Castiel in *Samuels' Cage-ring*, but when the Allyson twins rescued the rare survivors from that menacing human's death trap, it wasn't a surprise that both the bianthromorphs were tormented to their worst states compared to the rest. So, when Pearl mistook her identity to be an *anthromorph*, Zella never cared to correct her. She just wanted to get back home to her father. The tall amber-eyed bianthromorph would always remain grateful to the shorter Allyson twin for that. That was the first of many reasons why she had fallen for the amethyst-eyed anthromorph until she finally embraced the bitter reality and moved on a year ago, after realising that her feelings would never be reciprocated.

From the moment she noticed Caledon's sad eyes hesitating to voice out his frustration at the helplessness of his situation where he had no choice but to lock up Castiel for his genotype before they decided his fate, she knew that they wouldn't spare her when they discovered her true identity in the facility, but Zella could barely keep her consciousness before she was taken to the facility. Unlike her, Castiel was never brought to the facility, for he managed to flee before the chopper reached their location in the Zagreb MPA.

Inheriting the best of human parents who were naturally blessed with *highly-pleasing* phenotypes from both America and Siam helped hide any possible doubts of her phenotypes resembling that of a bianthromorph. Even if her phenotypes were enhanced significantly by anthromorphic standards. Besides the striking shade of amber colouring her eyes, her phenotypes were hardly affected by the said enhancement. Her phenotypes stood out even before her genotypes were mutated from a human to a bianthromorph.

But Castiel's features certainly raised distinct doubts that he wasn't just an anthromorph but rather a bianthromorph whose human gene was bound with the genes of the Salvador Coyote and the Mackenzie Valley Wolf. Besides Zella, it still came as a surprise to the rest of her team that he was nineteen like her and Charm, expecting him to be at least a year older like the twins or two years older like Maia. Maybe it was just the sharpened planes of his cheekbones that heightened the features of his origin: Brazilian.

It's easy for people to think that wolves and coyotes were the same because of their similarities, so they forget to account that wolf anthromorphs were always driven by a sense of loyalty that suits their selfish needs. In contrast, coyote anthromorphs were driven by a sense of solid survival need, better than anyone else through their cunning side. But both canine species are driven by pride and not respect, so they easily undermine each other despite their strong sense of loyalty and survival instincts, respectively.

***

Even back then, It was Zella who found Castiel.

Sort of.

Having been home-schooled for her entire life, it wasn't a surprise she had begrudgingly agreed to attend a private school in Salvador, even if it was for a year.

The shoot was bound to end at midnight, and she had a habit of easily slipping past the guards whenever the security system was down. Hence, she hung around the deserted skatepark that surrounded the sets, out of sight of them but close enough to at least be comfortable.

And it wasn't her fault. Really. She had just been staring up at the stars that shone so brightly, even among the city lights in the distance, and then suddenly, she was stepping on a body hidden in the shadows of night.

She knew immediately that he was stepping on something she shouldn't be, so she jerked her foot back up, which upset her balance, and she went tumbling into the grass, half landing on the thing she had just stepped on.

A boy stared back at Zella, face twisted in discomfort.

"Ow," was all he said flatly.

Zella immediately leapt off of him. "Sorry!" she burst as the boy sat up, rubbing at his leg that she apparently stepped on.

He sighed as if he were too tired for all this. Zella felt a little bad about it, despite not doing it on purpose. She recognised him faintly, having seen him around the school. *Castiel?*

He was almost icy. He was cordial and polite, never loud or rambunctious.

He flitted back and forth between keeping a wall of polite company and delving into something like warm friendship with everyone he met.

He was infinitely calm, it seemed, even when doubled over laughing at something that was said. His eyes were warm, but his posture was stiff, even among friends. Zella could not, for the life of her, figure out what his personality was. What part he was playing.

"It's fine," he sighed, sitting with his knees curled up slightly and clutching his skateboard beside him. "It's hard to see out here, I guess." Even if he recognised her, he didn't give it away.

Given her parents' status, it wasn't surprising that most people were waiting to fawn over her.

For every name on anyone's lips, Zella's was on theirs five times. Always spoken with reverence or quiet daydreaming, never the screams and squeals from most people. They were still a rare few who were absolutely vile and orthodox enough to ask if she was just confused to not identify with her biologically assigned sex. They purposely used the wrong pronouns when they got irked by Zella, giving them a look that clearly branded them as nothing more than insignificance.

But, once more, the people were too close, clapping her on the back but never encroaching her space until she made the first move and then stepped back to a distance.

So, it wasn't a shocker that they never spoke much, despite being in the same class.

But her eyes narrowed down to his phone lighting up on the ground, practically blaring that he had managed to hack through the updated security systems of the sets nearby.

"So, it was you." She smirked, tilting her head genuinely amused as he rushed to explain.

"Look, I just do it for fun, mostly because I had overheard one of your guards bragging that the security systems were too modern for this *ragged* city." He said evenly, one fist clenching at his side. He knew his firewalls were too strong to let anyone trace him back, easily but he made the stupid mistake of setting a crackling sound for notification.

Zella knew precisely who he was talking about, the guard who was fired for cackling about the Runes being utterly delusional so as to call their *son* their daughter, entertaining the child's stupidity instead of correcting *him*.

"Well, the only thing ragged about this city was *his* presence," she said, knowing that the warm-brown eyed boy was way too genuine to lie about something as basic as this. "Besides, I wouldn't have been able to sneak out if it weren't for this."

"Are you telling me that I shouldn't be expecting to be locked in a juvenile cell for *this*?" He scoffed, chuckling in amusement at the turn of the events.

"I should do something about my newfound knowledge." She said as if this was just dawning on her. "How about this? If I win, then I will feign ignorance, but if I lose, then I came going to spill the beans."

"You seem to be awfully confident." He said, trying to bite back his smile, eyes gleaming up in challenge before he handed over his skateboard.

He expected her to be good enough to place this absurd wager, but he wasn't actually expecting her to be *that* good.

Zella would go racing up a halfpipe and grab the ground as she flipped herself back over, slamming her wheels back on the ground and tearing back across the pipe.

She would just jump, and the board would follow like it was glued to her as she raced along pipes that were nearly above her waist.

And she did it with confidence and glee.

She rolled off to the side, grinning as she dispersed his momentum and rolled to the end of the rink, popping the board up and catching it as she jogged over and handed his skateboard back. "Maybe. But that's only because I am a sore loser."

"You are on." He laughed heartily, expression twisting into a bright smile as he skated up the side of the pipe, practically sitting on his board as he raced up the pipe.

***

For the most part, he never said a word since the Council had inserted the RTFQ chip. Zella didn't need him to voice out that he felt defeated as they reminded him why the chance offered to him was a bigger boon than he deserved. She had been through this herself.

She never raised a question when he mostly stayed around her corner during their shared classes, almost appreciating the quietness of the space around her from the snide chattering of a few anthromorphs that quickly faded down in her presence. Though she never saw the slight quirk of his lips lifting up to a small smile from the moment, he discovered that Zella had broken a few nasty bones during their combat classes to make those snobby anthromorphs stay clear from her. She couldn't help but return a smile when he warned her of crowded corridors way before she walked through one, quickly picking up on her micro-expressions.

Staring at Zella were the familiar eyes that were still sharp with determination or wit, eyes that would warm in rare displays of affection shown in hearty waves of laughter in response to gentle punches to his shoulder. Warm brown eyes paled into icy-apatite now that used to look back at Zella, broadcasting trust and reliance when they scoured the city of Salvador.

Neither made any attempts to reminisce the person or the bond they had once cherished as if there was a silent agreement between them to not tarnish the memories that held the goodness of their lives as humans.

For a person who spent nearly a third of his life in hiding, he had a natural affinity for Applied Physics and Biotechnology, confirming Zella's suspicions that he had indeed designed his own kevlar gloves. Also how he had managed to overhear by wiretapping into the intel of the CULT's bases from most facilities, arriving there way before the assigned teams were flown in. *Considering his crazed interest in nanotechnology, even when he was merely ten, she wasn't surprised at all—*

Unfortunately, the facility set in the capital had better technology than others. If Castiel had wiretapped the intel from any other facility, then he might have continued his spree instead of being locked up here.

But they clashed heads when he insisted on staying locked up in his dormitory, refusing to have dinner with anyone. His state was worsening, and it didn't bode well for Zella that the Professors were watching them like a hawk to assess if he was adjusting *well*. He was her responsibility... It didn't take a rocket scientist to figure that he clearly didn't feel like he fit in here.

Then again, when had Zella ever claimed like she fit in the facility, either?

If Zella wanted to find every opportunity to snap his wrist every time he restored back to his stubbornness indifferently, then Pearl wanted him completely obliterated. She had made that fact perfectly clear on Castiel's first day here and AGAIN every week in combat class. Hell, last week, Pearl nearly broke her spine, refusing to admit defeat and tap out of the match sooner to go nurse her injuries in the corner. Despite not being allowed to use his kevlar gloves, unlike the others, Castiel got her to yield in the next round.

Pearl's back slammed into the mats under her, the wind escaping her lungs in a forced rush. Stars filled the corners of her eyes, and she looked up at Castiel, feeling the dull edge of a practice sword against her throat. Even with the inhibition control activated in his RTFQ chip, he still had the edge over her.

Pearl had both lost track of how long they had been at this. Some of the other students had already pulled out their phones, bored with what was happening. Pearl shifted again, taking a millimetre away from the dull-edged sword at her throat. There was a way out of this; there just had to be. Castiel shifted his weight to follow her movements, and he was unsteady for a fraction of a second.

There.

Seizing her opportunity as quick as she could, Pearl snapped to activate her gloves and wrapped around his back ankle, pushing him off balance. He stumbled backwards, the cold steel of his practice blade nicking her jaw.

"Yield, *Krizenecion.*"

Even among anthromorphs, *Krizenecion* was a rare degraded slur for bianthromorphs that merely meant the progeny of a filthy cross-breed. Pearl ignored the snap of pain and propelled herself up to her feet, surging forward as discs of radiant energy snapped around her fingertips. There was the crackle of infrared rays in the air, and she directed them at him before he had time to react.

Damn it! Still too slow.

"Tch." Castiel seemed to know what she was doing and caught his footing quicker than she expected. He righted himself, flipped his sword in a movement too fast to see, and dodged her attack as it dissipated against the peripheral wall behind him. Castiel didn't even flinch. This was so not fair. Pearl spun towards him to try and unleash another attack, feeling him push forward again, but Castiel was already pressed beside her, pinning her arm against her side. The sword's back edge was wedged underneath her breast, pressed against her ribcage with the tip pointed dangerously close to her heart. If the blade had been live, she would have been dead.

Pearl stood there, her jaw locking into place in annoyance, her lips curling in distaste and stared at his face with hatred. Zella's eyes darkened, feeling unexplainably bothered by her expression. Castiel leaned closer to her, wedging the sword tighter against her chest.

Pearl slowly raised her free arm and tapped her upper thigh in defeat. He immediately offered a hand in help before Pearl slapped his hand back and stormed off to the opposite corner of the room, snapping at Zella as she took a step towards the panther breedling to check her injury out of worry. "Don't. Just don't."

He stepped back, his expression vulnerable and unreadable, looking at Zella as his eyes filled with guilt. She tore her eyes from Pearl feeling torn to rush towards her, before looking back at Castiel, his pupils widening as he took a deep breath through his nose, his jaw ticking as his right hand tensed under the ace wrap that he used to hide his scars across his wrist, sub-consciously. Even if her hand inched above his shoulder to comfort him, she held her hand back because she knew that she didn't have the right to invade his space to reassure him. Also, what could she possibly say?

The emotions inside Castiel were a mess, a mixture of what Zella was feeling and something else, and Zella felt a bit like she was caught in the undertow of a wave, being pulled further and further down with him. He stared at her for a long moment, his breathing slowing, before turning on his heel and quietly standing beside her.

Pearl flushed, and she glared between the bianthromorphs as if she wanted to tear down whatever was going on between them.

Their instructor, Professor Topaz, one of the rarest marsupialian anthromorphs, looked surprised, "That was… good training. And that is exactly what you are supposed to do if pinned and how to get out of it. Channel your energy and resources to your advantage, look for an appropriate opening and move. Also,

Castiel's recovery was spot on by anticipating his opponent's moves, and—"

"Professor Topaz, I would request you to dismiss your class and leave Rune and Sylvain behind." Chancellor Cullins stood there, his head high and his hands behind his back as he gazed out at the dispersing students until the two remained behind. "The Council needs another update on his prowess and the hold of the inhibition control of the chip in him."

"You were right. The brutality the Cage-ring has also heightened his kinesthetics memory to easily stand his ground even with the inhibition control activated in the chip against an anthromorph at her very best." Professor Topaz reported to his superior. The latter's expression looked down slightly as if he refused to show his reaction to his statement. "In her complete gear."

"How about a bianthromorph at their complete best?" He noted, almost casual. Neither of the bianthromorphs had time to react before Zella fell on her knees, seizing violently as if her spine was being ripped out from her back, her eyes flickering in carnelian-crimson. "She is way too controlled to snap to that, increase the frequency. Her chip is designed to handle it, and it won't fry."

Castiel stumbled forward, trying to hold down her seizures by tightly wrapping his arms around her shoulders, a cold fear settling in his bones. He fought down the anger threatening to rise as he stared at both the anthromorphs running this wretched facility, who looked at them as if they were witnessing the most boring event unfold before them. But it still choked him, something inherent and reactionary in it, despite barely knowing the bianthromorph writhing in pain.

That *damned* RTFQ chip wasn't just a tracker housing and inhibition control. He fought down the snarl in his throat as his expression darkened, seething daggers at the anthromorphs, resolution steeling.

Castiel jumped to his right and barely dodged out of the way of her attack. They both watched a bench by the side of the combat room take the hit from her kinetic energy disc, splintering into bits of metal and wood over the room. Pain, a disgusting, vicious thing, swelled up inside her as she tried her hardest to control her bianthromorphic side, trying to protect her. Emotion flooded her body, consumed her mind, dulled her senses, and she pitched forward, swinging her fists as if she was going to land a hit behind him.

Castiel dodged her blows, shouting at her, but nothing he said made sense - they were just jumbled up words muted by the force of pain of rippling through her, fighting against her bianthromorphic side, trying to subdue it. He jumped back, using his momentum to pitch forward and swing a leg into her hip.

Zella could barely process the words of the force trying to hold her back mutter, "I am sorry", all she knew was that she should have felt pain by the sound of the impact. But the rage of the animals of her bianthromorphic side was too deep, trying to break through her pain and tunnel her vision to just escape from the room. The only thing she knew was that she wanted to hurt the source of the pain caused by the figures behind the force blocking her. She wanted to break him apart piece by piece until the source of her pain was just as damaged as her.

Finally, she landed a hit against his shoulder, but Castiel took it more as an opportunity to hold her back, with a reckoning force. He managed to invade her space, knocking her off balance to tip her backwards. His hand wrapped around her wrist, and in a swift move, he had grappled her arm and pulled her down to the floor. She screamed, the sound a deep tremor of the pain tearing through her trapped bianthromorphic side shattering through her very being, and she pushed against him, but Castiel held her down, still shouting at her.

Zella twisted her head against the padded mat, trying to pull free, but she saw his arm above her head. His icy eyes were glowing bright, like a beacon for her, and all she could do was stare at it. It called to her, reminded her that her human side could fight through the pain without her animalistic side. She could practically hear the snap that shut down the frequency, nearly frying her pain receptors.

"Zella."

She blinked, feeling the shadows of the figures walk out of the room as if they were the ones trapped, her brain still remaining way too fuzzy to process retaining their identities.

"Zella!"

Zella tilted her head back and looked up at him, gasping and heaving. The padded mat beneath them had torn, and Castiel was on top of her, pinning down her shoulders. She gasped for breath, quirking an eyebrow as if there was a chilled rock wedged into her spine. Her hands were shaking, and she blindly dug her fingers into Castiel's sweater, pulling herself close to him. Every nerve in her body trembled from the sudden push and pull of control, and she could cling to the only thing that made sense.

Castiel fell back and pulled her into his lap as she buried her face into his chest.

To see those eyes… staring at him… in pain… He felt a tug in his gut.

The one that he used to feel whenever younger Zella held out a hand demanding help, support, guidance and Castiel's body reacted without thinking, reaching to take it.

He sat there, with his arms wrapped around her for a long moment, saying nothing and everything at the same time. He was warm and steady, and each passing second reminded her that he was there and that he was a rock she could cling to in this storm. Zella waited until her breath stilled, and she finally looked up at him.

But it was her face. A face Castiel had seen in every situation, every emotion for over a year.

And it was writhing in agonising pain. And Castiel felt the instinctual tug to rip away the source of pain, to protect, to stand at her side because this was the friend embedded in his memories for over nine years. It wasn't. But it was.

He shook the memories away, teeth-gritting together.

"I—"

Castiel lifted an eyebrow at her, waiting for her response, but she kept quiet instead, looking for another opportunity. Both their chests' were heaving, and sweat pooled down the curves and planes of his bronze skin, soaking his shirt. Zella caught his stare and then felt her eyes drift lower as shame blossomed deep in her gut. Embarrassingly, she found she liked the way wet cotton clung to his collar and chest - there was no hiding any part of him from her.

Gods. Zella closed her eyes for a second, trying to pull back in her emotions before they got out of control. She was such a mess, and this was so not the time to be thinking about that. Her eyes snapped open again, and she looked back into Castiel's waiting expression.

"Don't move." Castiel ducked his shoulders so that his forehead brushed against the crown of her head. She could feel him swallowing air as he pulled her tighter against his chest. "Just… just let me help you until you regain your full consciousness."

She just nodded.

Zella was a little miffed to find out that Cullins had thrown her under the bus to remind them that he pretty much held something close to a death switch to control them. It was clear that Castiel's combat skills, even with the inhibition control, didn't invoke a positive reaction.

She sat in a stiff, uncomfortable armchair across from his bed and glanced around his room, trying to decipher a little more of who he was. If her room was bare, his was practically spartan. His bed was neatly made, everything put away. There wasn't so much as a family photo on his nightstand, but she could see a neat pile of books on his desk and his bed covers haphazardly bunched near the wall.

"Here. Give me your arm."

She turned and saw Castiel sitting on a chair in front of her, a first-aid kit perched on his lap. Her eyes narrowed before glancing away as she felt her cheeks heat up by the slightest before she gave him her left arm, and he started cleaning a gnarly scrape near her elbow. Flinching under the sting of alcohol with her pain receptors being highly on edge, she tried to pull her arm back, but Castiel kept cleaning it, staying quiet. He seemed focused on his task and said absolutely nothing for a few minutes.

"How's your hip?"

She would be limping for a day or two while her heightened metabolism repaired the damage, but otherwise, she was fine. "Alright, I guess."

"Mm." Castiel shifted and picked up her other arm, examining it before putting everything back into the kit. He tucked it neatly in his desk drawer and sat back down across from her. They were both tense, but he seemed even more than her like he was twisting something around in his thoughts. His face was a steel mask she couldn't read, and she found herself drawn to the tick in his jaw, his long dirty-blonde hair pulled back and the fullness of his lower lip.

They sat there in silence for a moment, and Zella watched the late afternoon light filter in through the windows at the ceiling, catch flecks of cyan in his irises. His eyes were too pretty, and it was utterly distracting.

Zella took a shaky breath. "Thank you."

He looked into her eyes, but his face was unreadable. "You are responsible for my actions, and things are already insufferable for both of us. I don't want to make things worse for you because of me."

"Thank you for stopping me." Zella pushed her caramel-brown hair out of her eyes and glanced away. "I nearly lost my temper."

"If that's you *nearly* losing your temper, I would love to see what happens when you get angry, especially when you wield it against *bastards* who deserve it." He leaned back in the chair with a small smile and continued to stare at her.

Silence settled over them again, and Zella kept trying to read his expression, but she couldn't get past the way his eyes followed her. She tucked a loose piece of hair behind her ear and thought about standing up but wasn't sure what would happen if she bolted suddenly from his room. Curling her toes in her shoes, she looked around the room again, trying to focus on anything other than the way he was looking at her.

"We should talk about that *chip*."

Zella jerked her head up towards the upper left corner of his room before looking back sharply at him.

Your room is being monitored.

His eyes turned back to her, mouth setting into a dangerous line, as he mouthed '*I know*'.

Zella's spine stiffened as she glanced to see Castiel waiting for her to tell him about any blind spots around, arms crossed over his chest. She must have hit him pretty hard, eyes following him with guilt as his right arm twitched, but he pretended to ignore it and just stared at her, eyes dark. The tension between them both was thick, twisting around her until it felt like something was strangling the very breath from her. Her hand tightened into a fist, and she turned away from Castiel, trying to calm her heart.

Zella stood up to walk back to anywhere else, but the door opened before she could even take a step. Frozen in place, Castiel turned to see Zella already standing in the doorway staring at her, his face unreadable. His mouth tilted down in a half-frown, and his eyes slipped down to her feet before looking back at her again.

"If it's outside, then you should rest for a while before heading out."

Zella felt heat creep up her neck, "I will be fine", before she pushed the door wide, returning the slight smile from earlier and looking back at him, lifting an eyebrow. "Are you coming out or what?"

He paused outside the door, fidgeting for a half-second as he stepped towards the door. He needed to find a definitive way of frying that chip before Cullins played Russian roulette with all the features in that chip. Maybe he hadn't walked into a dead-end, after all.

CHAPTER SIX

T he sun had set below the horizon, the orange turned red, the red to black, the stars twinkling between thick blankets of dark clouds. It wouldn't take a genius to figure out that they both were fighting off tiredness badly and were seconds from falling down on the road and dozing off right then and there.

A stretch of silence passed between them, and Castiel realised he had never seen Zella look so casual. She was usually so put together, but right now, she was only dressed in a pair of low-slung sweatpants and a t-shirt. Her hair was a little messy, and there was a pillow crease along her cheek. She stifled a yawn and rubbed at her face with the heel of her hand, and Castiel found his heart doing something strange in his chest - skipping beats and turning over. Zella had always been attractive, with her unearthly amber orbs, angular face, and long limbs, but this was the first time Castiel realised she was actually cute. Although, she'd probably kill him if he ever told her that. He couldn't help as his lips broke into a quiet smile, imagining her posing that threat.

He was confident that neither of them trusted each other, and they already knew way too much about each other. The only unspoken common ground between them was getting rid of Cullins' obsessive attachment looming over them.

He fidgeted with the mask-wearing the gear offered by the facility for his first assignment, twisting it around his fingers. "I couldn't sleep."

"That's obvious." She sat down across from him, resting her forearms on her knees as she bit back another yawn. She ran a hand over her face and sighed, obviously annoyed that the only way they could talk about Cullins was during a mission. It also didn't help that Pearl threw a fit when Castiel joined their team. "First missions are always assigned in the crappiest timings. Especially if they are assigned in the Berlin Metropolitan Area."

***

"Pearl, if you are worried about his control on his bianthromorphic side, then you have nothing to worry about." Pearl started walking towards her dormitory, but Zella caught her arm, staring down at her. That weighty silence settled over them again, and she watched as a muscle in her jaw ticked, like she was warring with herself. "I have studied the reports of his genetic markers, myself." She had read her own reports way too many times, reminding herself of the facts rather than getting swept

away by Cullins' predictions, to be familiar
with reading Castiel's

Finally, Pearl tilted her chin in the direction
after Castiel was summoned into Cullins'
Office. Face burning red with embarrassment,
she pulled her arm from her grasp and
narrowed her eyes at Zella. "You like him."

Zella looked indignant, her lips twitching in
annoyance. "Because I checked to confirm if
he would have our backs during the mission?"

"Choices are hard, and someone does end up
getting hurt… and you made yours pretty
clear."

"What is that supposed to mean?" Zella
asked, her voice sharp and definitive, jerking
back, blinking in surprise.

"Well, it didn't take seconds for you to get
attracted to a lost cause. I mean, don't we all
love that sense of feeling like a saviour?" Her
tone was evidently callous and cold; of all the
things she might have said, nothing could
have been so unforgivable as these very
words.

"So all my actions are motivated because I
had a twisted desire to feel like a saviour?"

"Isn't that what you are to him? He is doomed
no matter what you do." She looked away, her
mouth turning down into a bitter frown. "All

you're doing by clinging on to him is reminiscing your attempts to chase away the loss of losing someone or at least regain the feeling of control that was ripped away from you during your abduction in Samuels'—"

"How dare you?" Zella spat, swallowing a slew of insulting words and accusations, as she felt her emotions start to claw at her, which were ripping down her carefully-placed barriers.

Pearl blanched and stumbled over a response, knowing that nothing she said was going to make any sense. "Zella, I didn't mean that." She wasn't sure why she felt the need to justify her feelings to Zella, but she did, even if the latter had stormed off. "I am really sorry. I don't know what came over me—"

***

"Since it's a recon mission, it will be led by a senior, Lizzie Monet," Zella said, pointing towards the woman who seemed to be in her mid-twenties, with short and uneven platinum blonde hair, rich olive skin painted with light freckles and stern face which screamed that she stabbed her opponents as a warning, but her heterochromatic eyes softened her strong features.

They barely had time to speak to each other, each taking up an assigned task to match up with the time. It was hard to tell when the sun rose or set.

Sometimes, they worked on developing the EMPs, enhancing them to their maximum potential so that they could potentially shut down any operating electromagnetic device of any capacity within an eight-hundred-meter radius for fourteen hours. Other times, he just worked on arranging the nano-electromechanical circuit system of the Kevlar gloves with Zella using the genetic data on each particular anthromorph of the team assigned to this mission. It was a part of their redemption to repay the Council's *'generosity'* for housing them.

When they weren't busy working on the EMPs, they worked on the suiting gears with Caledon and Maia. Designing them to be form-fitting according to the wearer, making them out of nano-regenerative polybenzoxazole fitted with carbon nano-tubes, to make them resistant to almost everything. The Casimir effect of the in-built nano-based circuit technology in the suit just amplified that effect. It provided an in-built control panel to access or control any data on the foldable screen-boards fit in the under-arm of the suit.

Almost an hour had passed since they had landed in the coordinates sent by the facility, and still no sign of any patrollers working for the CULT or any lab in hindsight.

"Stick with me. I need you guys with me to rescue the humans while my team shuts down this base and takes care of the twisted geniuses." Lizzie said, separating away with Zella and Castiel, signalling the rest of them, including Caledon and Maia, from the team of fifteen assembled for this mission.

The entire facility shut down within seconds after one of the anthromorphs activated the EMP. They followed Lizzie scaling the walls of the Lab, pulling themselves up onto the roof. They had managed to go from the back end of the facility mostly without detection even before activating the EMP. The only resistance were two guards who were now stuffed in the dumpster, courtesy of Lizzie, who got in their way moments ago.

"It's too quiet. I don't like this," Zella remarked, completely alert and no longer feeling any hints of tiredness.

"Why are there no guards?" Castiel asked, looking at her.

"This is their biggest facility in the city, and it's barely guarded compared to their other facilities we have already taken down. Something wasn't making sense since the beginning, so I needed more firepower to protect my team." Lizzie said, no longer hiding the fact she had separated them from the rest to avoid the chances of any casualties in her team. "Cullins found it necessary to inform me that you were a bianthromorph, too, Rune."

Both of them immediately stopped in their tracks. Zella scowled at her, not at all fancying the truth of her identity was being handed out like candy, as Zella raised her eyebrow in question as if she was rechecking if Lizzie was addressing her.

"Relax, I don't have any pre-determined reservations against your type." Lizzie prompted, nodding at Zella to confirm her doubt and scoffing at the end as if it was ridiculous. She would use that endearment on anyone else on this rooftop. "I have had access to your reports on genetic markers, and even if you go astray, I have been handed the control over your inhibition centres in your chips," she added, daring to wink back at Zella and jumping down after attaching the hook-end of the zylon rope from the tiny crossbow attached to her Kevlar gloves to the railing of the roof until they heard glass shattering below us.

"I am definitely awake, now." Zella grimaced, clenching her jaws at the notion she was back to being treated the way she was when she first got her.

"Hey, let's not let it get to us. You have complete power over her gear. So, if she decides to mess with your chip, you can return the favour." Castiel reminded carefully, unfazed by Lizzie's declaration. Quietly offering back a smirk as Zella's eyes sparkled with amusement, she jumped down after Lizzie, using the zylon rope she had left behind. He would have been more surprised if Cullins hadn't sent them with a *leash*.

"Well, let's just hope it doesn't get to that," Zella whispered, starting to more and more irked, gritting her teeth and following the older Lynx anthromorph in charge.

"Why are there no guards?" Castiel repeated once again after Zella got in through the shattered window and pulled at the end of the rope to unhook the rope from the top so that Lizzie could retract the zylon rope back into her crossbow.

The entire room was dark, with several fried computers and control panels, due to the activation of the EMP.

"They must be along with the humans." Lizzie dismissed with a half-hearted wave. "Must have hurried down after we shut down the place. We need to find the main room with the pods."

Lizzie headed over to the door and opened it slightly, scanning the hallway before motioning the two of them to follow behind her.

"None—" before Zella could finish asking her question, Lizzie pushed past her and aimed a semi-automatic revolver at the lurking guard's legs, not bothering to answer as she fired thrice at the guard's shins. The guard immediately fell on the pathway, clutching his leg and screaming in pain. "Where did you get it?"

"Back holster of one of those losers we faced in front of the back gates," she said, shutting her ears in annoyance to block out the screams. "Either of you has something that can shut him up, temporarily?" she asked, pleading with a lop-sized disinterested expression.

Zella merely shot a tranquilliser at the guard's neck to put him off to slumber.

"Impressive." Lizzie praised with a mocking glint, smirking at Zella.

"Should you be surprised at that?" Zella scoffed, throwing a forced condescending smile at her, as she glared before rearranging her expressions immediately. "I am a *bianthromorph*, after all."

"Feisty, good, I don't like boring," said Lizzie, before throwing down the borrowed gun beside the fallen guard as Castiel bent down on his knees, wrapping an abandoned cloth- piece tightly around the guy's wound, with a satisfied grin. Zella responded, "Funny, I don't break in a cold sweat, holding the switch controlling our chips like a detonator... when I am amused."

She scowled furiously before heading down the end of the hallway where there was a large, out-of-place, steel-like door set in the wall, leaving both Zella and Castiel behind, for a moment, as his mouth broke into an unconscious chuckle.

Zella made it her business and her skill to never make it look like she was lost. It reignited his memories, reminiscing the countless times they would visit various nanotechnology exhibits - a mix of bravery and confidence to throw people off the fact she was running out of time and plans to distract them. At the same time, Castiel fixed the pieces he *might* have messed with back to their original setting.

Maybe that was a much more ignorant, much more childish trust- like a child nodding along to their parents' stories of where their dead pet was.

"Did that guy have the key?" Zella asked behind Lizzie.

"I am not sure. I didn't check." The heterochromatic-eyed senior said, suddenly feeling embarrassed for not having her head in the game for a minute.

"Here," Castiel said, tossing her the keys he had rummaged from the guard's pockets after making sure he wouldn't bleed to his death.

The moment they entered the room, a mist of fog hit them immediately. Lizzie immediately fell on her knees as Zella started staggering on her feet, clutching her head, and Castiel caught the end of her elbow to help her maintain the balance.

"I c-can't move my l-legs," Lizzie said, struggling to speak and gasping for breath.

"The fog contains succinylcholine." Zella coughed violently before looking over at Castiel, who seemed to be in the same state as her, knowing that both she and Castiel would probably be least affected. Their bianthromorphic sides were nearly immune to the sedative that enveloped them almost regularly in Samuels' Cage-rings. "It's not affecting you because you are completely immune to it—Help her, I can handle this—"

He knew extremely well that besides her Bianthromorphic physicality, the only reason Zella wasn't reacting to the fog as badly as Lizzie was because her body could recognise the poison in the system and was taking more time to fight against it compared to his. Unlike him, Zella was trapped in Samuels' Cage-ring a month lesser than the time he was abducted.

"Stop talking." He said, placing a mask on her face before heading over to Lizzie, retrieving another mask from his suit, and placing it over her face. She clutched his hand tightly, breathing hard through the mask, "I c-can't m-move—"

"Stop talking. You will run out of oxygen before she injects you with the antidote." He warned sternly. "This mask will help you to breathe only for a few minutes, don't waste your breath."

Lizzie kept panicking, struggling to form words, tightening her hold on his wrist, which would definitely form a bruise later.

"Look at me, focus on my words." He said, staring directly at her. "Take deep breaths. Breathe in. Breathe out-"

Castiel stopped talking, feeling a squeeze on his shoulder. "Zella, you should—"

"I am fine," she confirmed, pointing to a small pint on the jugular of her neck, indicating that she had taken the antidote. "But, she won't be if I don't give her the antidote now."

He crawled back, placing Lizzie's head on Zella's lap as she injected the antidote on the side of Lizzie's neck.

"We need to get out of here," Castiel announced as he picked up Lizzie placing one of her arms over his shoulders as Zella did the same with her other arm. They stepped out of the room, following a tiny beam of moonlight shining through the glass panes of the foggy room.

Before either of them had a chance to analyse the expanse of the surroundings outside the room, they were knocked down by two masked figures, as each pinned the bianthromorphs to the ground and jabbed them a few times. Zella pushed Lizzie's barely conscious body, as far as she could, back inside the room. Castiel immediately grappled Zella's waist using the retractable whips from his gloves and dragging her away from the figure's grip as he jabbed the figure atop him straight on his jaw and got back on his feet as Zella got back on hers a moment later. The masked personnel took advantage of their drugged state, and judging from their strength, they were undoubtedly anthromorphs, considering their average build.

They seemed two steps ahead of the drugged bianthromorphs, blocking and ducking all of their attempts as if they had studied the bianthromorphs for a while, anticipating all their moves, relishing that. If the evil little smirks forming on their mouth, which could be seen clearly through the transparent gas masks, had anything to give away.

The only way to end this as soon as possible would be by making some new moves and not being predictable. The bianthromorphs glanced at each other and nodded in acknowledgement to do what had to be done.

Without wasting any further time, in a flash, their fists made contact with the side of their heads in unison, as their masks shattered near the hit immediately. It didn't even take a moment for them to drop on their knees as they swiftly removed their masks, suffocating them along with the gas from the room and lying down cold as lumps before her and Castiel ran back towards Lizzie.

Zella took off her mask. Before checking Lizzie's state, who was coughing through the mask, she slid her across the wall before Castiel went back to shut the back doors of the room by latching a broken piece of the window sill through the handles of the doors. "Well, that was a f-first," said Lizzie, slowly gaining her consciousness.

"You really need to stop talking." Zella reminded with a low grumble, like that soft warning sound of thunder before a massive storm. "I am going to take off the mask now, and I want you to take deep breaths on my counts. Focus."

"Don't worry, we are not leaving anywhere without you," Castiel said matter-of-factly, sympathising why she felt the need to rush to assure them that she was okay. "Just send a warning to your team to avoid this wing before we proceed further."

Damn, that girl had unrivalled determination. She stumbled back on her feet and steadied her breath after merely ten minutes, stating that this was nothing compared to the pain the humans trapped in here must have experienced, knowing how painful it was to undergo the change for a full-grown human.

They must have families of their own who must be worried sick about them and go to any lengths to protect them.

Both the bianthromorphs matched her slow pace, not saying a word to make her feel more frustrated with herself than she already was feeling for wasting time and not recovering fast enough.

"I think we now know where all the guards were." Zella started feeling thunderous eyes flickering red as they stared at troops dragging innocent petrified humans in shackles.

Even with the inhibition control activated in his chip, unlike Zella, Castiel knew that he was losing control over his rage as he felt his eyes turn icier. He stared down at the troops rushing towards the three of them like an angry swarm of bees, clearing outnumbering them by a considerable margin.

Zella felt a sudden rush of air beside her, snapping her head to look at the source to star down at Caledon and Maia grinning at them, with Lizzie's team behind them. "Glad we didn't miss the festivities."

At this moment, Zella didn't have the time or stubbornness to argue why they had followed them here and was just thankful that they had because it would have been foolish to fight them all while keeping on Lizzie at the same time, who was still recovering and was in no state to fight them on her own.

That's when complete chaos started erupting from all sides, and Zella barely had time to register what was going around when one of the guards stormed towards them and took a swing at her. She barely managed to duck away at the last second, slamming him into the wall before catching the elbow of the guard and yanking him within her reach, firing off blows to his face and abdomen and kicks to the head, dropping him to the ground after he fell unconscious. From the corner of her eye, she could see another blow coming for the side of her head. Zella swiftly moved aside, grabbed her attacker's arm and swung him around, throwing an elbow to the back of his neck, dropping him like his predecessor.

Before he scrambled to stand back on his feet, Castiel wrapped his retractable whips around his feet and yanked him to hit him square in his nose until he fell unconscious for good this time around. *She could really use those retractable whips being installed in her kevlar gloves.* She could sense the rifts around the precise shots flying past her. Even through her barely controllable rage, she could recognise Caledon's aim, calculating the wind and the movements of the troop. He was careful not to hit one of theirs until it severed through one of the faulty wires of one of the Cryogenerator, half-broken through the walls of one of the chambers.

She knew that Castiel had designed the suits to sustain the highest voltage of the electrocution power emitted by nearly any equipment. They couldn't waste more time in punching their way out when an unrealistic number of them seemed to be coming after them all at once. She gave a quick nod as her gaze quickly locked on the icy eyes zeroing in the shattered generator before looking up. *If they had received the right blueprint of the lab, then this should definitely work.* Castiel swiftly kicked the torso of one of the guards, trying to get back on their feet before just breaking all the sprinklers located on the ceiling with one lash above their heads.

And yet, the weight of memories was stronger than they had been in years. And Castiel had no reliable Zella to lay their weight onto. Though he would never admit it, it never felt like he was tarnishing his memories of the Zella he knew by using the one who existed before him.

During those days, it always used to make Castiel feel so damn happy when it happened. When the two were brainstorming and just fucking ran with an idea- no matter how crazy. They were not the same, and Castiel kept having certain qualities shoved beneath his nose, and he didn't know how to react to them. The same fire and ferocity, same determination with faith and confidence to spare.

After making sure that the remaining troops were drenched wet, Zella merely ripped a couple of wires protruding out of the broken generator and let them fall on the damp ground and simply watched the high-voltage current seeping through the cables to electrocute all of them at once.

"Why didn't you do that before?" Caledon asked with a tired chuckle, swiftly throwing off the guard he was fighting on the floor and sliding across the wet floor to prevent getting crushed by the falling grotesque figure behind him, as her eyes turned back to their typical amber shades.

"Boy, am I glad that you two are on our side." piped another voice from Lizzie's team.

Castiel didn't say a word, still gaining composure from his lost temper, as he combed back the wet strands of his dirty-blonde hair falling on his face. He then headed over to the room where the humans were chained in shackles and helped Lizzie and Caledon break the shackles as Zella and Maia headed to the back of the room to manually unhinge the doors of the pods and check the pulses of the unconscious humans trapped in those pods.

The humans didn't say a word and trembled with so much fear, running away immediately when they were freed, recognising them as anthromorphs from their distinctive lighter eye colours.

"Don't worry, this always happens; they don't trust any breedling. They are scared of us," said Lizzie, immediately noticing the broken looks on her and Caledon's expressions. "Try to understand this from their perspective. How are they supposed to separate the good ones from the bad ones? I mean, if I were them, I too would suspect that I was kidnapped by another group who would experiment on me for another pathetic reason that makes sense only to my kidnapper. As juniors, you four have helped us more than we could ask for. In fact, this is the fastest we have ever raided down a CULT's base. My team will take care of convincing them."

"So, you just wanted to see us on the field today to test our loyalty?" Castiel asked, extremely aware of the camera attached to Lizzie's suit that she had activated only moments after she had activated the EMP.

"No offence, but you both are their most bizarre experimentations. You can't blame us for doubting you guys." Lizzie lowered her voice so that no one except Castiel could catch her words, shrugging her shoulders unapologetically.

Castiel's arm twitched, and he muttered a soft curse under his breath, the sound a rumbling noise, like far-off thunder. He glanced away before lifting his eyes back to Zella's, and for a moment, she could see past the mask he wore so often.

"Thanks for trusting us," Caledon said with a satisfied smile, especially since he was the one who handled the majority of their intel and negotiations between the four of them and Lizzie's team. Among the four of them, especially with Zella and Castiel mostly expressing their opinions in grunts or glares or nods, it was no surprise that Caledon seemed to be the most social. In Lizzie's words, he seemed to be the only one who didn't have 'all the social grace of an untrained bull'.

"You really have a way with your words, Allyson. You have a knack of knowing how to use a person's secrets against them to threaten them effectively." Lizzie scoffed, trying to glare at Caledon for getting on her nerves, but her teasing tone gave it away that she was just joking.

"It's a family heirloom." Caledon trailed off with a wink and a lopsided grin. There was a long, heavy pause as if Caledon was waiting to deliver a punchline.

"So, I heard you are looking to be a model for a hair salon or something. I can arrange that." Lizzie whipped her head towards Castiel as if she finally remembered why she wanted to speak to him. Caledon turned completely pale, the colours draining from his face, continuously signalling her to shut up. "I mean, my mom is a hairstylist, and we could use new shots for her salon." The blonde's eyes widened as if he couldn't process if the senior wasn't accidentally mistaking him to be someone else or speaking to someone behind him.

"Really?" Castiel blinked, his eyebrows knitting together as if he had never heard anything more ridiculous than her proposal. Zella couldn't help but note that this was probably the first time she had ever seen him look so *naive*. "And where may I ask did you hear such a thing?"

"Those two," Lizzie confessed unfazed, pointing to the troublemakers, Caledon and Maia, having no idea that it was a running joke between the couple while trying to befriend the bianthromorph. "They talked about it as if it was an extremely urgent matter. I mean, you do have *'freaking great hair'*, as they quoted."

Castiel cursed under his breath, and his shoulders sagged as he contemplated getting back at the couple's silly antics. Even if he silently appreciated the couple's efforts to treat him like they treated anyone else in their circle, he was still taken aback by their pranks, and he just wasn't into it. Despite Zella's playful warning, if he were to be completely honest to himself, he was *scared* of their unpredictable antics and often froze when then either of them pulled these stunts.

He turned towards Maia, who pretended as if she hadn't heard a thing and was busy helping Zella in trying to wake up the unconscious humans they had retrieved from the pods, not letting anyone else near them disturb them in any way. "They aren't wrong." Zella gave him a teasing look, stifling a laugh and looked up into Castiel's face, her smile softening at the edges, looking back at his eyes were nearly glowing with ease and excitement. For the first time, his expression was not soulless, but his eyes held the same expression as the ten-year-old Castiel as they stared at her.

Zella had wondered, idly, what it might be like to see Castiel wear a full-blown smile. To hear the familiar genuine, from-the-chest laugh, from her memories in reality. Allow him a moment to shed the burdens of the prejudice he faced for his identity and hell, to experience that sort of freedom for once.

And to suddenly have that shoved in Zella's face nearly made her choke as she stared.

Castiel stood there, annoyed, but also somehow amused, and maybe even a little *happy*? Who was he kidding? The thing that feared him the most was the growing warmth and comfort he felt in her presence, once again.

"I am going to throw away your personal stash of food, Allyson." Castiel threatened him, though his words held no actual malice.

"Listen, let's be reasonable here, please?" he asked, barely stifling his own giggles and hiding behind Lizzie using her as a shield, who found it confusing that it was all a joke. Caledon was too amused that the other had at least *tried* throwing back a joke for the first time. "You don't have to take out your anger on my food. That's just bonkers!"

"Wait, you weren't being serious about this?" Lizzie asked, finding it hard to believe that the couple was just joking about the whole thing.

"Thanks for the offer, Lizzie, but I am good," Castiel said with a forced smile before ripping Caledon's arms around his shoulders and binding him into a headlock. Both stopped bickering and stopped in their tracks as soon as they heard a SLAP echo through the entire hallway.

"Stay away from me!" yelled the aged woman, who had just slapped Zella across the face.

"Don't dare touch me, you freak!" she screamed as she glared right at Zella's golden-orange eyes.

Lizzie immediately pulled Castiel back when he snarled involuntarily towards the old woman. "Don't! Not you too!" she hissed at Caledon, gnashing his teeth and wrapped her free arm around him, tightening her hold around his wrist as he tried to break free. "She is in distress, and your involvement will scare her more."

"Ma'am, I am just trying to help you." Zella reminded her carefully, blinking her eyes twice before trying to reason with the woman again. "I will back away as soon as I make sure your vitals are normal."

"I don't want your kind anywhere near me!" she yelled, swatting both Zella's and Maia's hands away from her and panicking in distress.

"We promise we are not trying to hurt you," Zella said with a calmer tone.

"I would rather die than your filthy hands touch me," she spat, sneering with a venomous look in her eyes, "I don't want to be developed li-li-like you, guys. With those eyes, you look nothing more than a demon!" Before anyone could predict her movement, Castiel felt something clenching his heart tightly, suffocating it as if something awful was about to occur. He felt everything around him slowing down as he witnessed the woman's hand lift up with two of her fingers pointed like daggers as if she was planning to stab something with her fingers.

It was as if he could sense what her target was and his feet moved on their own accord and jumped in front of the old woman and felt his eye-lids shut according to their own will, as he felt two crooked fingers viciously jab his closed eyes, poking them as if she wanted to pierce her fingers through them.

"CASTIEL!" yelled a voice, as he opened his eyes, staring up at the old woman who looked scared out of her wits, as he clutched her hand tightly, feeling better she never got to take a hit on her intended target. Zella's eyes.

The human started trembling in fear more venously as his irises turned paler, losing the shade of apatite colouring them.

"You may call us whatever you please. Freak, Demon, Abomination, and we will accept that because we feel sorry for what you have gone through, but so have we.

We were humans at one point too, and guess what? We didn't—We never had a choice in the first place to choose whether we wanted to be an anthromorph or not. You know what's worse? We always endure. That deep inside, we seek acceptance from people like you, instead of seeking acceptance from ourselves! So, you have no right to hurt us either!" His voice was pure, iced steel, seething in nothing but the pure rage that was starting to snap under the tension, and if he wasn't careful, something irrevocable was going to happen. He was swallowing breaths, struggling with the last bits of his self-control. "You have no right to hurt a part of us that makes us who we are!"

"Castiel—" said a voice, shaking his shoulders violently. Amber eyes practically pinning him down in warning. "Castiel, please let go of her hand. You will send her into a shock if you don't let go of her hand. Let go!"

He felt a force surge through his spine before he immediately let go of her hand and stared back at Zella's golden-orange orbs before scrambling back on his feet and rushing away from the room.

He raked a hand through his hair, gritting his teeth together as he tried to reign in his own turbulent emotions. The anger he was holding onto seemed to dissipate, and his arms fell to his side.

"At one point, you get used to numbing their words from your ears." said a figure behind him as he looked up at the full moon atop the abandoned rooftop of the lab. He was no longer scared of looking at it illuminating the sky without caring about the other larger burning bodies in the sky who twinkled and paled in comparison to the moon, despite being larger in size and brighter in luminosity compared to the moon, in reality. The moon may not have significance on other heavenly bodies, but it did on earth's, exclusively. He looked at Zella, expression dark as he weighed everything carefully. It was as if he wanted to say a million things to her all at once, but he couldn't choose what thing he needed to say first.

She had never seen him so utterly *livid* before, even during their first encounter, after nine years, while fighting in the ruins of the CULT's base in the Zagreb MPA. Castiel was usually cold and sardonic in the facility, and there wasn't anything that could faze him, but this seemed to be his tipping point.

"How is she?" He asked about the old woman, who was shaking violently before he had stormed out of the room.

"Sleeping. Her vitals are almost back to normal. You shouldn't—"

"I know. Her words just reminded me of those humans in that bastard's Cage-ring." Castiel's lips twitched, but his expression was still unreadable. He spoke after a moment of silence before getting back to her previous statement. He glared at her before reverting to another seething silence. It filled the space between them, seeping into cracks and bits of themselves before finally deafening them both.

"Sometimes, it's hard, it's really hard." She sighed, her breath steaming in the cold air, nodding in a vague understanding, resonating with his pain while simultaneously sympathising with the woman's fear despite still being furious with her actions. "So easy to be tempted by anger and let my actions be guided by any reminder of those *memories*, being trapped in there."

The rogue was offering him things that Castiel had never mentioned to anyone, and he was so close to accepting the offer, just to stop the torture. He needed a day to realise that he wasn't locked up anymore.

As a bianthromorph, Castiel's mind could heal too, but the process was too slow. It left a mark that he was trying to erase desperately.

"I needed a solution. But there was nothing there. If I had someone to think of, maybe I would have found my way out faster." Castiel continued the trail of thoughts in order, realising that he was talking to Zella like she was already important to him. His past was the only thing that Castiel had fears of, and including Zella in it meant that there was nothing to hide anymore.

"What happened there was," Castiel pulled back a bit and stared at the stern amber irises who refused to waver away from him. "The rogues broke my bones, whipped me, talked shit, to the point where I stopped feeling. I was just thinking of that fucking door and what I had to do to reach it and leave. I had no idea how long I would have been there as well. But when I faced you guys, being hunted down and attacked. My mind just leads me back to that room and the killings, and if I ever fight, I don't know if I actually might end up killing my opponents. It's better for me to be called a coward than to be called a lunatic. A killer. Rogue. That would hurt more."

"You may be many things, but a *coward* isn't one of them." She said like it was the easiest thing in the world, and that particular notion was, to her. "You are formidable, have always been that way. It's not just an option, it's a fact. Back then or even now, that hasn't changed." Her words echoed in the back of his mind, replaying like a broken record. Hurt was woven in her expression as if that mere association with him made her want to strangle the speaker.

"Ignorance is bliss whilst cowardice is easier to cope with." Castiel closed his eyes and looked away, sighing heavily.

"Do you think we deserve to take an act of cowardice when all of this comes to an end?" She asked, dipping her shoulders, raising her eyebrows and biting her lips in anticipation.

"You mean '*if*' this comes to an end?" He blinked as Zella approached him, determination filling her expression.

"A little bit of both, I guess. The *if* always turns into a *when*." He shrugged defeatedly, smiling more and more every passing second. The energy was radiating off of him like he had a spark inside him, and he needed to light something on fire.

"Even if it ends up being the wrong choice?" He prompted, each sweep of his eyes trying to decipher another layer Zella was trying to keep secret.

"The difference between right and wrong is extremely blurred. We just have to choose the less harmful ones. Both have major consequences." A moment passed as she shifted, regarding him carefully. He shifted and thought back to the first time she had ever healed him despite hating his guts, and his heart did a strange flip in his chest. That one moment felt like centuries ago, and neither of them could have had any foresight on what would have happened then. If they had, neither of them would be here. "It isn't easy, by any regard, to decide which is right. During those times, it's easier and best to trust the person who bears the responsibility of handling it because no one has thought about it more than them."

"That's a really long time." His head tilted to the side in question, trying to see a glimpse of her most vulnerably raw self. "What if people change? What assurance can we have to prevent that?"

Her memories played games with her mind and emotions that couldn't decide whether to utilise or scorn at the appearance of these traits of the older Castiel, clashing with the present.

Everything from the smaller fits of anger (not the raging fury he wore sometimes) to the determination, to the way he stared at her, to the way he held himself, to the furrow of his brow as he thought.

Castiel would be lying if he proclaimed that he hadn't harboured vicious doubts over her working for Cullins until he got that maniac obsessively keeping a watch on him like a sneering leash. Cullins barely spoke to them, separately, although neither wanted to be entertained by his existence even by the slightest.

She chewed on her lower lip for a moment, thinking carefully about something that was tangling in the darkness of her mind. "I don't think people change. They can either modify themselves to recognise their truth or get tired of lying and shed the facade to be their true selves."

Castiel's expression softened, and whatever suspicion he had melted. Her words weighed heavily on his shoulders, and he shifted, trying to find the right words. "When we accept that, that's when people don't have to try to hide from each other but rather try harder to not keep running away."

"Running away from?"

A pause.

"Life." His voice was so firm, he barely recognised himself. He sounded so definite, but he knew there wasn't another option when he was around her. Her eyes met his again, shadows hiding behind them. "Don't we all keep running away from life and live in fear until we stop trying so hard to take the easy way out?"

There was another pause, and she cocked her head to the side, shoving her hands into her pockets. The silence turned weighted as if they were both waiting for someone to do something, but they weren't sure what. It felt like aeons passed before she spoke again while handing him two switches. "You can reverse-engineer this to shut down the controls they must have over the RTFQ chip. I picked Lizzie's pockets and got them."

He stayed silent, his stare boring into her as if he wanted to pin her to this moment forever, and Zella moved to pull her hand away, fingers shaking. "Why are you handing over the switch of my own chip too?" Why in the world was she trusting him when he had snapped to his volatile self a few moments ago? Why hand over the very thing that could control him if he turned against her?

"Like you said, it would be a delight to see the fate of the person who ends up being at the opposite end when I do end up losing my temper." Zella snorted, but there was a start of a small smile against the corner of her mouth that was slowly cementing, evidently. It's like he was barely making a gracious effort despite bitting the inside of his cheeks to hide his smile. "Besides, I'm simply returning the favour of ensuring I don't make things worse for the both of us, either. After all, it's *my* responsibility."

CHAPTER SEVEN

Honestly, Zella had half-expected Pearl to rescind her offer of spending the holiday with her family after what happened over the weekend, driving away to her home with Charm before anyone else. It didn't help that her twin blatantly went ahead and insisted on bailing on visiting his own family if Zella and Castiel refused to come along with him.

It was evident that the hematite-grey eyed breedling still held guilt over being helpless for not being able to get Castiel to the Facility five years ago, where they would have treated him as they did now instead of proposing to lock him up right away. No matter how much the bianthromorph tried to assure him that he wasn't at fault and had offered him more generosity than anyone else during the said time, Caledon continued to be deaf to his words.

Zella found it increasingly harder to prevent herself from marching down to the Berlin MPA and storming the Anthromorphic Council's Headquarters. She wanted them to reconsider her decision on denying her father the right to visit her in the ECA for the second year in a row.

She couldn't help but think about the first time the twins had made it a ritual to drag Zella along with them, every time they went back for a benefit that neither of them ever bothered to explain.

***

"You seem to care for the twins."

"It's gratitude." Her eyes were narrow, and her expression was dark as if something had taken over what little amicable personality she had.

"Well, friendship seems to be a good motivation to keep your bianthromorphic side in check if it does overpower you."

The Chancellor running the Facility barely looked in their late-20s despite being in their early-40s, perhaps being a capybara anthromorph diluted their sneering eyes and that alarming excuse of the flaming mop of red hair.

Zella's hand tightened, realising how little regard the Facility held for their lives while still being the most concerned people to obsess over their anthromorphic identities. "Are you claiming that you are willing to endanger their lives if it fails to motivate me?"

"If they fail, then we would have to send in more manpower to restrain the situation." Chancellor Cullins seemed unaffected, shoving his hands in his pockets after fixing the creaseless lapels of his indigo coat, attempting to make the explanation as vague as possible, which didn't ease Zella's nerves. "They may not have an emotional hold, but they are equally skilled in combat as the Allysons."

"The Allysons don't have an emotional hold over me." Zella's face went cold as she took in the information.

"Pardon me if I find that hard to believe."

"I am indebted to them." She corrected, biting the insides of her cheeks sharply to prevent herself from snapping and trying to hide her fear before asking if she could be dismissed. "They didn't just save me, and their family went above and beyond to ensure that I don't lose the only family I have."

Even if she was surprised to face Pearl standing right outside the door, she looked away, rearranging her expressions in a snap that somehow managed to say everything and nothing at the same time. The shorter Allyson twin was clearly trying to read the taller bianthromorph's expression and the

Chancellor's half-hearted courteous smile as if they were having an entire conversation that Pearl couldn't translate.

"Ah... Hey... Good morning." Pearl could obviously tell something was bothering Zella, and she took a small step backwards, holding her hands up in defence. "Cullins seems to overestimate your combat skills. I know that it can be a lot, so I thought maybe I could help —"

"I'm fine." Zella pushed past her, glaring at nothing in particular. The last thing she wanted was for Cullins to have leverage against the twins and just find a way to get the Chancellor to torment her over the Facility's fears of her going berserk even if her regular lab reports over her stable genetic markers suggested otherwise. She just couldn't handle developing the feelings of care for anyone, only to have their lives bait against her existence. As if their lives mattered so minusculely. "And even if I wasn't, I don't wanna talk about it. So, I'm going to go and train. Alone."

Pearl ignored Zella's blatant attempt at getting her to leave her alone, and Pearl chased after her. "Look, it's not really my place to say anything—"

"You're right. It's not," she huffed and tried to ignore Pearl as she continued to follow her.

"But," Pearl continued as if Zella hadn't said anything at all. "You could talk to us, you know. It's easy. You just open your mouth and just let us help you," Pearl smirked as she slid up beside Zella. "Or, at the very least, just tell Cullins to hand over the assignments to us."

Zella whipped her head around and stared at her. "You practically have enough money to overthrow him and choose your missions."

Pearl shrugged, unapologetic. "Look, it doesn't work that way." A pause. "I mean, no matter what, we should never try to stoop down to the level of manipulating power, like bianthromorphs driven by their mere brawl instincts?"

Zella snarled and clenched her fists tighter to prevent herself from shoving at Pearl's chest before she took another snide at the bianthromorph that escaped from their rescue mission in the Zagreb MPA before the chopper flew in. Pearl just gave her a teasing smirk, mistakenly taking Zella's rage to share her hatred for bianthromorphs, which only infuriated Zella more. Cursing under her breath, Zella threw the door open to the training room, and Pearl walked in, following her, obviously still trying to talk to Zella.

"I couldn't ask you to help me any more than you already have, Pearl. I'm fine. I just need to control myself better." Zella changed into her combat gear and threw her jacket in the corner, ignoring Pearl behind her.

"Yeah, you're controlling yourself really well." Pearl teased in a playful tone. "I mean, I can only imagine the horrors you must have encountered fighting that bianthromorph in that ragged hole-"

Zella glared, trying not to remember Cullins' warnings, but Pearl was oblivious to her inner battle.

"-and now you're hiding in the training room to try and punch your frustration away. So, sorry if I don't think you're handling this really well. But you're not exactly giving me a reason to believe you." Pearl continued, rolling her eyes. "I get that you need to be all mopey and brooding to get through your terrible time there-,"

"Shut up."

"-but we are here for you, and you deserve an actual conversation."

It was during times like this when Zella had half a mind to start letting herself fall in tune with her developing feelings for the panther cruxawn but chose not to, remembering the amethyst-eyed cruxawn's prejudice against bianthromorphs.

She'd been hot-headed enough to let herself imagine the possibility of the latter losing herself to her anger a few times and had always come away with broken knuckles. Zella ground her teeth together and turned away from Pearl, not bothering to wrap her hands as she started on the punching bag. She really, *really* needed to hit something, and Pearl was not making this any easier.

She couldn't forgive them for failing to offer the same life to Castiel that they had spared to her, but most importantly, she couldn't forgive herself for failing to be there for him. Every second she spent breathed in the protection of the Facility reminded her of the dangers he might be in, especially in a world that hated his existence, in that battered state. She had to reel her mind from ever letting it swerve into the worst conclusion.

"Look, Pearl." Her words were punctuated by the smack of her fists against leather. "I really don't want to talk about my time there. You aren't going to understand it. No one will." Zella snarled and started punching harder, her knuckles turning red and sore. "I really need you to believe my state in there was because of a survival duel with that bianthromorph. I hadn't even seen him until you guys shut down the ring and set up the emergency camp for the survivors. Trust me, my hyperthymesia makes it difficult to forget."

"Fine."

Zella paused and turned back around to look at her. "Fine?"

"Fine." Pearl lifted her hands in defeat and took a step back. "You are safe with us, here."

"Debatable." Zella gnashed her teeth.

"Zella, you and I both know that all that money and power can't protect us outside the ECA. This is the closest as we can get to the lifestyle we were used to before our anthromorphic genes were activated." Pearl levelled another stare at her, her mouth set in a thin line. "It's complicated. We were only fourteen, and neither of us got a choice to process that we were anthromorphs before the media broadcasted it because of our family's position."

Zella sighed and let her hands fall to the side, just wanting this conversation to end, not wanting another reminder of how her mother's death was overshadowed by her presentation as a bianthromorph. "Pearl, you and your brother are the only reason I can still meet my father. The only reason he is permitted to travel to the ECA and back home is because of your parents." The Council had declared all of the surviving anthromorphs, rescued from the Illegal Human Cage-Rings to be way too volatile, from being allowed to meet their Human families for the next eight years unless the meetings took place in the presence of Human Diplomats in the Anthromorphic Council.

"We really meant it when we said we would be your family. This is nothing." Pearl shrugged, giving her a smug grin, admitting it in a heartbeat. "The only thing you need to worry about is getting some food before Caledon swallows all the food on the table."

Zella rolled her eyes and walked away from Pearl, moving back to the punching bag. "You have personal chefs, and I have seen them cook up a rage even during their breaks."

"That beanstalk never feels full. You could use the relaxation. And I'm sure it's better than prowling around in the combat room looking for a place for your special alone time." Pearl gave her a half-hearted wave and started for the door. "Try not to break all the equipment in your inconsolable rage, Rune."

"Get out."

Zella glared at the bag, feeling her muscles tense as she turned Pearl's words over in her mind. But damn it! She didn't know how to take at least one step in the right direction.

So, for right now, it was just easier to punch something.

Zella felt herself turn numb, falling into a haze. She lost track of time, her hands and legs becoming numb as each punch and kick seemed to take just a bit more fight out of her and offer her some kind of clarity. She finally stood there, her body finally exhausted from trying to fight, gasping breath as she tried to come up with a real plan to try and make this okay.

***

If Castiel could see through Zella's expressions, he made no attempts voicing it out loud until she did and the chances of that occurring were jarringly slim. He knew that Zella: poised, composed, cold, calculating, distant Zella, could hopefully find a way to seek the very thing she had been looking forward to as they followed behind Caledon and Maia.

"Just stop thinking about it."

Her voice was a low rumble, like far-off thunder, which ripped Castiel from his own daydreams. He turned and looked into the driver's seat, watching as Zella white-knuckled the steering wheel and glared out at the horizon. She changed lanes and merged onto an exit ramp, looking a bit like she needed to reel her control back in. Her lips twitched, but through the thin afternoon light, he could still see her eyes darken, and a reddish tint tinted her cheeks. Had he been thinking about it too? Or was he still just feeling the echoes of her own emotions?

He shifted in his seat, looking out at the trees as they sped by. They were still an hour away from the twins' home, but most of it was a country road.

A quiet, empty, country road.

"Sorry." She tucked a piece of hair behind her ear and cleared her throat, her heart skipping a beat. "I, ah, my mind was wandering, and I didn't mean to snap at you."

"I know. I have re-engineered the switches for the chip, but I think I have also found a permanent solution to deactivating the chip." His right arm twitched, and he glanced at her. She felt like his stare was boring into her, breaking off bits of herself and claiming them as his own, but she couldn't turn away. Castiel shifted again, and his mouth tugged into a frown. "The only way we can fry it off is by going for a frequency way higher than the Cullins had set for your chip in that combat room."

"What's the catch?" She huffed out an annoyed breath, her mouth reacting before she had a chance to stop it.

"You had predicted it all along." Castiel winced, and he clenched his fists together, closing his eyes.

"So, the only way we can shut it down without setting off any alarms is to fry off everyone's chips in that perimeter." Zella sighed and shifted the car into a higher gear, running a hand through her hair. The tension rose between them again, stretching painfully thin as they both tried to search for the right thing to say, but nothing was coming to mind, and they were both trying to stumble through a mess of emotions that didn't make sense to either of them.

"This is the only place where we can work to activate the re-engineered switch and test it out." He nodded and turned away from him, looking out the window. He rolled his sleeves up as if he needed something to do with his hands. "Look, I know that this is beyond complicated—"

"This might be the only chance you get to meet your family, and I don't want you to throw that away for this." It all sounded so methodical when she said it like that, but maybe if they approached this with a cool head, they could make it work for both of them. Or, at the very least, make it less awkward when things inevitably went sideways. "I need more time to figure out the solution for a permanent vial so that no upgraded version of the chip can reverse the effect."

He crossed his arms over his chest and looked away, chewing on his lower lip as he tried to sort through his own feelings. "I don't have a family. You already know that my mother died during my birth, and my father disowned me ever since I was identified as a bianthromorph, blaming me for her death."

Zella jerked back, blood leaving her face.

During her time in Salvador, Zella had always empathised with Castiel, being used to his father's busy schedule as a News Anchor to spare time with him. Still, the latter always made an effort to get his son whatever he wanted and rooted for him during all his football practices. But she hadn't expected him to ever throw *those* words at Castiel's face, especially when he had always been the one to assure that it wasn't the younger's fault, every time Castiel used to longingly look at Mothers rooting for their kids during his football matches and blame himself for her death.

Castiel's words speared her heart, and Zella glanced away, taking another slow breath. It felt like fate had crushed her heart between their hands, and she didn't know his words could hurt like that. Like they were weapons. Anger filled her, and Zella let her head fall into her hands. She felt angry for him. "How could he —"

"Do you know who shreds the absolute meaning of hope? The human life of our past that we can't leave behind. But, like miserable insolent idiots, we hope the most towards them due to delusions of the warmth of companionship. Failure isn't disappointment but foolishness to desire that in the first place. Yet, our greed never permits us to let go of that hope." He scoffed and pinched the bridge of his nose, thinking to himself. It seemed like the rest of the universe faded away for a while, and they lived in this moment. "I can hardly remember my life from back then," he lied, rubbing his thumb along his jaw.

"Forgiveness doesn't exist; either we manipulate ourselves to swallow and forget the pain, or it just gets repressed, acting as a catalyst to test our limits, until it gets spewed into a bigger chaos." Zella finally met his stare, and he sighed. She felt the weight in her chest grow too heavy to bear. She shook her head in defeat. "The damage has already run its course until people let go of their pride to hold themselves accountable, and that's just rare idealism fading away from this current world."

"Yes. Is that such a bad idea?" Castiel nodded, avoiding meeting her stare. His voice had dropped low, but it somehow sounded like a shockwave rippling through the car.

"No, not even by the slightest."

She heard Castiel shift but knew that she couldn't look back at him, or her mind would wander again. He swallowed a shocking noise, and he finally looked back at her, uncertain what he needed to say. Zella was glaring at the road still, but there was tension running up and down her arms that spoke of something else.

More because something was eating at her that she didn't quite understand. It was clawing at the rawest edges of her, and Zella was struggling to find the right way to handle it all. It was all a knotted mess that neither of them really knew what to do for the next step.

Castiel shook his head, trying to clear his thoughts. "We have different ideologies of that '*when*' after this comes to an end."

"Are you claiming that you seek a different end other than freedom?" Zella asked with mirth, but he didn't look at her. She was thankful for that because if he did, she might admit that she was beginning to understand her emotions a little better. She just didn't want to face them. She didn't want to face the truth that she might care for him because that would be absolutely mortifying.

There was another slow, tense pause, and Zella almost thought the conversation was over. She turned back to the window, watching the thick trees and rolling hills slide by. Castiel's voice was barely above a whisper, the sound husky and hoarse in the silence. "No."

She jerked but stared into her lap, not wanting to make eye contact out of fear it would break the spell between them.

"But unlike you, I don't have a plan after that." Castiel glanced at her from the corner of his eye. "I don't know if that terrifies me more."

Zella pushed at her hair again. "You must have your dream for a home."

Castiel snorted, his expression falling flat. "The only idea of home I have ever had scared me more than the Council, and that's the last thing I could ever want."

Zella pressed her lips together and stared ahead, desperately trying not to look at Castiel. "You can't be scared by someone who is equally scared by the Council for the very same reason." She dug her fingers tightening on the steering wheel. "We tolerate each other, to be comfortable around the other's presence. So, if it comes to it, you consider it as a contingency plan; a quiet life in Asia is a viable alternative until..."

Zella half-expected Castiel to turn to her and snap out a sarcastic response, but nothing came. Instead, he let a slow breath out of his nose as if he was thinking about her proposed 'contingency plan' with reason. "I guess that's an option. If it comes to that." He wet his lips and glanced at her from the corner of his eye.

"Right." Zella tried to sound casual, but she felt more like her voice was frenzied and high-pitched. Oh, Gods. Why in the world did she have to be so utterly embarrassing? "I mean, we wouldn't actively seek each other out if you hate—" She wrinkled her nose and downshifted the gear, turning it onto an even more barren road.

Castiel glanced at her, expression unreadable. "I wouldn't mind your companionship. I've never hated it."

That was a rabbit hole she wasn't entirely sure she wanted to travel down, especially since things were already so *unknown* between them both. Instead, they fell into silence again, and Zella let it fill the space between them. At least they had some kind of agreement or plan or something. Now they knew when to stop and what they were allowed to do if it ever became as desperate as it had before. Which, Zella hated to admit, seemed more of a possibility than before.

"So, I meant to tell you-," Zella's voice was a quiet kind of cautious like she was approaching a tender subject.

Castiel looked over at Zella and raised an eyebrow, urging her to continue.

"-apparently, we have to attend the benefit even if we have no families awaiting our visit."

He paled. "What?"

"I was planning on trying to avoid it altogether, but apparently, our presence is required, without question." She rolled her eyes and shook her head, turning down another side street behind Caledon's car. What little bit civilisation had been scattered through the trees was now completely gone, and it felt like the last escape they might have to avoid this holiday altogether was consumed by space. Looking around at the tightly packed, bare trees, she felt like she was at a loss.

Castiel shifted again, his teeth sinking into his lower lip. "Am I supposed to come?"

Zella shrugged, but there was tension in her movements as if she knew how horribly this would end. "You've been invited. But the twins' parents are too polite to tell you that you have to come. If you'd rather not go, they would understand." She paused, her face falling. "They've treated me like their family, even when the twins weren't close to me."

Castiel felt a wild rush of panic slam into him, and his chest tightened. It wasn't like he knew how to behave at one of these things. He had lived as a runaway for the last five years of his life. How in the world was he supposed to know how to interact with people at a benefit? Besides, with his past experiences at his father's after-parties with other News Anchors or attending his late mother's brunches with other writers to celebrate the success of the motion films that incorporated his mother's scripts that hadn't seen the light of the day during her 20's, he didn't exactly do well at parties. Castiel blinked, running through a list of excuses he could use if it came to that.

"I…" Zella shifted, and there was another long pause. "I wouldn't mind the companionship."

Zella's request was so quiet that Castiel wasn't sure if he heard her correctly, and he turned to look at her, eyes wide. That feeling of panic grew in his chest, and Castiel was positive Zella could hear the sound of his heart. How could she not hear it? It was so loud. He sat there and stared at her for a long moment, letting the request settle over her. She was asking him to a party, but they still didn't even know what they were.

"It's not like you'd be a date." She scoffed, scrambling for an excuse, but Castiel could see the soft flush to her cheeks. Zella glanced away as if she couldn't bear to admit to anything in front of him. "It's just that the twins excel at these kinds of things, and I, I'm not exactly what you'd call social." She shifted again, looking back at the road. "You seem to be one of the few people who understand that, and I guess I appreciate it."

"Oh." Castiel had no idea what to say to that. His eyes seemed to bore into her, stripping Zella of all of her armour and looking past her own words.

"Ultimately, it's up to you."

Castiel let the request settle over him, filling the space between them with a strange, heavy silence again. Her confusion felt almost volatile now, and she felt a massive surge of emotions press against her senses. They were still in the world of almosts, and this wasn't helping her figure out what this was between them. He wanted to tell her no. He wanted to say that he didn't want to be a part of her life like this. He wanted to say a hundred things that would have demanded a definitive answer from her.

But he didn't. Instead, he nodded slowly and agreed. Even if they didn't know what they were, despite being uncertain that they didn't know what they liked anymore, the truth was he was beginning to like her for who she was now. And if she wanted him to be a companion for something like a silly benefit, then he would agree, just like old times.

She was still driven by forces beyond all comprehension, wouldn't hesitate to die for her friends who mean the world to her, still knew how to throw her whole self into a task until it was completed.

Castiel nodded in acceptance. "Okay. If you want me there, I don't mind." He paused and watched the last bit of tension escape Zella's shoulders. She looked oddly pleased, and a warm feeling flooded Castiel's chest at the sight of her not-quite smile. She fidgeted a bit. "I just, I don't have anything I can wear. I'm barely equipped for non-facility functions, let alone something that requires a suit."

"That's not a problem," she shrugged, "I'm sure Cal has something you can borrow. You're the only one who is as tall as him."

Castiel's eyebrows knitted together, realising that he honestly thought that the twins were merely her friends, but it made more sense that they were like family. He realised he might be running into a situation he was wildly unprepared for the first time. "What are they like?"

She groaned, running a hand through her hair. "Caledon and Maia reach their peaks of being nosy and obnoxious, on a whole new level."

Castiel thought he might dig a little deeper, but Zella finally slowed down and turned up a long, winding drive. It curved through the hills, turning and twisting until there was a break in the trees. A massive house, built during the turn of the century, stretched out in front of them. It was a sprawling stone thing, gleaming in the early evening light. He had known that the twins had come from wealth, other students went to the Facility that didn't have powers within the Council, but they had money. That was enough to get them into one of the most elite facilities in the country. But, the twins had the kind of money that was something that didn't even register on the scale.

Outside on the front step, the taller Allyson waited for them, staring at his cell phone. A broad smile split his lips.

"Oh, hell! Cal." Zella groaned and dropped her head into her hand. "We don't have to do this, Castiel. If you want, I will turn this car around, and we can head somewhere. Anywhere. It doesn't even have to be campus."

Before Castiel could question her, he saw the Cheetah anthromorph turn and shout into the house.

"Zella's here, and she brought her boyfriend!"

A split second later, it felt like a crowd of people had rushed out towards the driveway and were all staring at them both.

Oh no.

CHAPTER EIGHT

C astiel's head was practically spinning as everyone seemed to press against him and ask him a hundred questions at once. Most of them ranged from the mundane to a little personal, but all of them were utterly embarrassing, mainly because Caledon and Maia asked them on behalf of his parents. How had they met? Were they really dating? How was the drive up? What was Zella like at the Facility? Where was he from? What were his energy manipulations like? What conditioner did he use for his selfishly luscious hair? Zella really had friends besides the twins, Maia and Charm? There was so much pushed at him all at once that Castiel didn't even know where to look or what to say. Despite all, he couldn't help but see how the taller Allyson twin was a clear embodiment of his father and why Zella felt like she was around family in their presence. *He did have that once… as a human…*

Although a large part of him had wanted to believe that his father had no idea that Samuels' henchmen didn't actually work for the UNH. The latter handled the transportation of young anthromorphs to ECA while handing him over to them; that wistful hope soon vanished. He still couldn't forget him practically spitting-*'I can't believe that I had been raising the very same creature that killed her. You are no son of mine, and you are not even a human!*

The last thing he wanted was to spend time around people who seemed to act like the *'Parents' of the Year'*. He certainly wasn't expecting *this* when he agreed to Allyson's proposal, partly to stop his nagging and partly to show his gratitude for Caledon was one of the few who treated him like an actual person and not an abomination.

"You're all annoying him, and you're annoying me. Stop it." Zella glared and shouldered Charm out of the way, her eyes narrowing. It was clear that Pearl was coldly avoiding them. "Where's Mrs Allyson?"

"Still in Glasgow. She'll be home after a meeting with Leonard, so probably just before dinner. Our head chauffeur already sent her a message that you're here and brought your *friend*. So, I'm sure she'll be racing home to meet him." Caledon's smile tilted to the side, and Zella looked even more annoyed with him. "You didn't honestly think you could go three months without properly introducing him, right?"

Zella sneered. "I had hopes that I could starve you for three months, but here we are."

He shook his head and motioned Castiel and Zella away, but Maia still followed. "He told you about the benefit, right?"

"Don't remind me," Zella ground her teeth together and took Castiel's hand, ignoring the whispers from Caledon and Charm. Castiel felt heat curl up his neck, but he stayed perfectly still, trying not to draw any more attention to the fact that Zella was holding his hand. She pulled him towards a side hall. "I'm going to show him to the guest bedroom, and I'm sure you all have something more important to do than to bother our guest."

"Nah. Not really." Caledon grinned. "Why would I find something else to do when I have my own little soap opera playing out in front of me?" He snapped his fingers as if he's forgotten something. "Oh! I made sure they set aside the empty room next to yours, Rune." His teasing grin tilted to the side. "In case either of you gets bored and wants to *talk*."

Charm sniggered behind him, and Zella felt the heat crawl up to the tips of her ears. She dropped Castiel's hand and buried her head in her hands, muttering curses under her breath. She looked like she was about three seconds away from killing all of them, and somehow none of them looked bothered by that. She started down the hallway, and Castiel paced after her, barely taking in the grandeur of the main entry hall. Maybe later, he would ask someone to give him a proper tour. He was sure that if he didn't follow Zella, he would be utterly lost.

Maia seemed to slide up beside him without a sound.
Her steps were light on the carpet, and she watched
Castiel for a split second before breaking the silence.
"You are attending the benefit, right?"

He nodded, his chest tightening out of surprise. All
this attention was wreaking havoc on his control, and
if he wasn't careful, he might actually break something.

As Castiel followed her down the hall, he barely had
time to take in the finery of the sprawling house. It
felt decadent and opulent, with dark panelled walls and
fine art everywhere. They passed a set of French
doors that led out onto the patio, and Castiel saw a
long length of snow-dusted lawn that seemed to
stretch forever before disappearing into the rolling
hills beyond. Castiel paused and stared at the space, a
little overwhelmed with how beautiful everything was,
even in the dead of winter. Something in him stilled,
as if at peace for just a moment, and he felt Maia step
next to him, smiling.

"It's pretty, right?"

"It's amazing." Castiel fidgeted with his bag, moving it
on his shoulder.

"I don't think I've ever seen Zella remotely agree to
attend an event that involved dancing even when the
twins, well, mostly Caledon, always nagged her
endlessly. But she barely moved a budge." Maia

paused, dropping her voice to a loud whisper. "Much less entertain a date."

"We're not really dates." Castiel shifted and looked over at Maia, trying to give her a sympathetic look. "Sorry to burst your bubble."

Maia tilted her head to the side as if she didn't quite believe Castiel, and there was a long stretch of silence until she finally turned with the grace of a dancer and started back down the hall, following Zella's path. "Okay."

Castiel felt as if he'd been slapped, and he chased after her confused. Okay? That was it? No teasing or joking, or even mild disappointment that her friend could possibly be really interested in a bianthromorph? "Wait, what does that mean?"

"It means okay," Maia smiled at him, but this time it wasn't teasing. It looked more as if she knew something that Castiel didn't or as if she saw something that he didn't see. It felt weird to have that settle over Castiel, and he racked his mind trying to understand what the Latrans cruxawn was thinking. There was a heartbeat's pause before Maia spoke again, completely changing the subject. "I am just glad that both of you are attending the benefit and have a break from the facility."

"I told Zella I would be there." Castiel shrugged, uncomfortable about admitting that he had agreed when Zella had told him she almost kind of wanted him there. "She said she would appreciate my companionship? So, I thought I should come."

"Oh?" Maia's smile widened, and she looked intrigued. "So, she asked you?"

Castiel turned to see them stopping outside a room on the second floor, feeling a bit like he'd been magically transported through the house. Shaking his head, he looked around the hallway, hoping he could remember how to get back down to the first floor. He was beyond thankful to be saved when Zella pulled her so that he could finally head to the guest room.

Zella seemed less annoyed by Maia's teasing jibes than she was by the other two, and whatever tension she was holding onto seemed to ease just a little. She shoved her hands in her jacket and sighed. "If there is a dance, then I am fleeing."

Maia's smile tilted to the side, teasing. "You could change your mind."

Zella stopped and turned around, her eyebrows knitting together as annoyance filled her face again. "Why would I ever do that?"

Maia gave her another smile as if she was holding onto a secret. "Well, you have a date, and he might change your mind."

"Castiel isn't my date." Zella rolled her eyes. "And, I don't dance."

"I never specified the name," Maia gave a slight shrug, that smile still playing on her lips.

"I feel like you are way too amused to be acting like a bunch of old church biddies with the latest gossip."

Maia's smile broadened even more, and she pitched forward as if she was about to whisper a secret to her. "Well, you two always seem lost in your own world. It's the first time I have ever seen you enjoying the company of a person instead of the combat room or our Biotechnology Lab or the Library."

Zella stumbled over a response before she turned back around, skulking down the hallway as she cursed under her breath. Zella flushed brightly and kept her eyes pinned to the floor as she tried to flee from the conversation. Why in the world were they bringing him into this conversation? Castiel had nothing to do with it, and now she was questioning why she had tormented him with this stupid invitation to the benefit.

For a moment, Maia looked as if she wanted to say something that would undoubtedly make Zella blush even further, but whatever expression was on her face was replaced by genuine joy and excitement. "Good! Do you have anything to wear? Probably not, right? I mean, it's black tie, and I know the Facility doesn't exactly do dances or formals or anything. Nothing but studies and missions."

"That's true," Zella's smile tugged at the side, and the tension in her chest eased as she felt the familiar sense of comfort around Maia. "Well, unless leather jackets count as black ties, you're definitely right. I don't have a dress, other than the Facility's uniform sweats, and I left it back at the dorm."

Unlike Zella, who had a habit of wearing an endless array of sleeveless turtlenecks under the leather jacket given by the Facility along with their gear, Maia had a habit of ditching the jacket outside missions and opted for wearing just waistcoats with relaxed, loose-fitting trousers.

"It belongs in the trash bin. Ugh. Those things were always so hideous and itchy. You think someone would have invented itch-free wool by this point in history," Maia made an annoyed face before waving her off with a shrug. "Don't worry, we'll take a look after dinner. It'll be fun," she motioned to a door beside them, "But for right now, you should get settled in. I know that the drive here from the London MPA's Facility is tirelessly long."

She hadn't realised they had been talking for so long, and Zella found herself standing in front of the guest room, deciding what excuse would hide her checking up on him or head towards Pearl's room to face the confrontation that both of them had been trying to avoid, desperately.

Castiel was standing in the doorway, looking tense again. He whipped around and glared at her, slamming the door closed. "You can't come in here."

Zella jerked back. "What?"

"You—Allyson—"

Castiel's hands tightened next to him as he tried to come up with an explanation for why he wasn't letting Zella in. Maia seemed to slip under his arm and turned the handle with a curious giggle, throwing the door open for all the world to see. Zella managed to see over his shoulder, and she felt heat curl up her neck again. The room was nearly filled with candles and flowers, and a blanket of rose petals was strewn across the covers on the bed. Her face burned hot, and Maia was practically cackling now, her eyes bright.

Castiel glared at the jade-eyed anthromorph. "Did you know about this?"

"No," Maia started back down the hall. "But, I should have. That's a good one. I'm impressed the boys managed to pull it off without the head butler warning Mr Allyson," she waved, "Have fun cleaning that up, you two. Mrs Allyson will never forgive you if you don't."

Castiel ran a hand down his face, cursing in Portuguese as he glared at Maia's retreating form. Zella walked into the room, her senses immediately bombarded with the scent of roses. She winced and looked over at Castiel, who wasn't faring much better. "It's-it's fine. I never grew up with siblings, so I can only imagine what it's like, but-" She ignored the fuzzy handcuffs on the nightstand, thinking that probably wasn't a place her mind should wander, "-this seems like something deranged morons would do."

Zella opened a drawer on the nightstand and shoved the handcuffs in there before either of them looked too hard at them. Quietly and with as much dignity as she could find, she started to move around the room, cleaning the rose petals off of everything, and they were everywhere. She picked things up silently, watching from the corner of her vision as Castiel started to move around the room, helping her clean up.

"You must miss her."

His statement came so suddenly that Zella wasn't sure if she heard him right. She stood up and blinked, trying to think of anything else she could say to him. Panic filled her chest again when she realised she would have to tell him the truth. "I don't think I could ever process her death, no matter how many years pass by," she paused and turned to dump a handful of rose petals into the waste bin, not wanting to meet his eyes. "My mom had the stone-man syndrome, and it cut down her career two years after we got back to California from Salvador. I couldn't even attend her funeral," she trailed off.

Castiel stilled, his voice quiet. "That's the time you were abducted by…"

Zella paused again, swallowing a shaky breath. "Samuels' Cage-Ring? Yeah, that lunatic discovered that I was a bianthromorph before anyone else. He confirmed the gene of the bald-eagle bound to mine that was unreadable in the initial reports of my genetic markers."

For a moment, it seemed like Castiel wanted to dig a little deeper, but he stayed quiet instead. He stood across the bed from her and helped her clean the flower petals off the bedspread, dumping them into the trash bin. They fell into a tight silence again as they both worked to pick up the room, but Zella was getting used to it by now. Castiel seemed to prefer quiet, and most of the time, she did too. It was easier to say nothing than to struggle through a painful conversation about her mother.

***

Zella lived in a house that was just on the underside of being considered a mansion.

It had a spacious lawn, a long driveway, and a wrought iron gate surrounding it with decorative shrubbery along the way.

"My parents didn't flaunt their wealth in their housing," Zella explained as they drew closer to the house. "However, anything you find in there that's made of fabric, I wouldn't touch unless you have several million available to hand over."

She winked playfully, and Castiel laughed despite not thinking she was joking at all.

The man opened the door, and they got out, walking up the steps. A woman opened the door in a similar uniform to the man.

"The shoot should end by 10 PM," she told Zella, bowing as they entered.

"Thanks," she said, grinning as they set their bags on the table just inside the door. "Let's go—I'm sure we can test if you can drink all the sodas in the fridge."

His father didn't let him have sugar to keep him in his best shape for football. He didn't like it much, either, but soft drinks were his guilty pleasure.

The house was spacious and modern and made Castiel want to talk with whoever had designed it. There was no blatant colour pattern or design, but every merged in an eclectic static, looking like it blurred together as much as it popped out.

Zella laughed. "Like it?" she asked as they climbed a staircase as wide as a room.

Castiel's head was craning back to stare at the delicate purple trims on the upper walls. "Yeah," he said a little breathlessly. "I'd kill to meet whoever designed this place. The colour schemes here are incredible," he murmured.

She chuckled, catching his arm when he nearly tripped on the last stair. "I'm sure my mom would love to have that conversation with you,"

Castiel baulked. "You mom designed it herself?" He demanded.

Zella grinned, feline and proud as if she had done it herself. "She did," she said proudly. "She loves acting, but interior design is her hobby. If she gets home early tonight, maybe you can talk to her about it. She changes the interiors of the three houses, they have, every couple of years."

They walked into a room that looked like it was both a bedroom and game room combined. In one corner was a massive bed with an entertainment system surrounding it. Two of the walls were taken up by screens and computers and game devices with a couch in one section and a series of beanbags in another.

"Wow! This is bonkers!" He said, voice shaking with disbelieving laughter.

"Wanna watch a movie?" Zella questioned curiously. "Or play a game?"

"I'm fine with anything," Castiel assured her. "But a movie sounds nice. I am exhausted after our Advanced Arithmetics classes today."

He honestly hadn't expected it to be this carefree here. As quick and chaotic as his football team was, he just preferred the quiet moments he and Zella had.

About halfway through the movie, Zella's head dropped so that her cheek rested against the top of Castiel's head. A quiet whisper asked if it was okay, and Castiel settled in, comfortable with the weight surrounding him.

About three-quarters of the way through the movie, the full weight of Zella's head fell against Castiel's head, and he glanced up, trying to see what had changed.

A quiet breath was all he heard from Zella before glancing over at her mother, who had just walked into the room following the sound, grinning.

He tried his best to greet, scrambling at his feet, without disturbing Zella, but her mother immediately waved her hand, amused by his struggle.

"That's why she didn't wish to come over to the sets after school," she whispered. "She just wanted to sleep."

Oh. Zella was asleep.

"Want me to rescue you?" Her mother offered, going to pull Zella up.

"No," Castiel said quickly, quietly as she paused. "It's fine. Don't wake her up or anything. It's fine." It was. Castiel was comfortable, and he just hoped Zella didn't get a crick in her neck.

Her mother smirked. "Cute," she chuckled as she settled back in. "She'll sleep through anything, though, so let us know if she starts crushing you."

Castiel hummed, now hyper-aware of the fact that Zella had fallen asleep against him. He also didn't think he would have been comfortable enough to let it happen with anyone else.

Zella was different, though.

They were comforting. Peaceful. And somehow, knowing that Zella was sleeping peacefully was comforting to him.

***

It took a bit before everything was back to how it probably looked before, but they finally seemed to get the room back in order. Zella stood there, looking around the space as Castiel shoved all the candles in a box and tossed them in the closet.

"Thank you."

Castiel looked over at her, confusion flashing behind his eyes for a moment. He waited for an explanation, walking up to where she was standing.

"For, helping me clean up, and agreeing to come to the Benefit with me and…" She shrugged, feeling strangely hopeless. There was something about being here, their usual quiet filling in all the empty places between them again that made her feel like she needed to tell him something. She needed to tell him how she was feeling, even if it seemed stupid or mundane. "Everything, I guess. Just, thank you."

Castiel stood there for a long moment, his face completely unreadable, and shifted. He opened his mouth as if he would say something but snapped it shut before the words could escape. Instead, he took a quick step forward, waiting for her to push him away or close the space between them as she met his stare. She meant to say something dark. Something amusing. Something that was sitting in her chest, hot and curling—

It died in her chest as she stared at Castiel.

Castiel, who stared at her, was almost curious about her next move. Quiet and dark and waiting, waiting for Zella's word.

Still waiting for her word to move, to act.

The fire that had begun to blaze in her chest suddenly turned to a lump of smouldering coal pressed to her lungs. Castiel saw something shift in her face, the quiet curiosity turning into something sharper as she frowned.

Caledon's eyebrow rose high. "And will the two of you be joining us?"

Zella's hand grabbed the pen from the desk near the bed, throwing it at Caledon with the precision of a knife.

The Jabatus cruxawn's hand swiped across the air, snatching it in his fist, still smirking darkly.

"We'd be happy to join," Castiel said behind Zella. "I didn't realise the rest of you were so eager to get voluntarily beaten up for this ridiculous prank—"

"Shut Up! You just can't appreciate humour, Sylvain." Caledon snapped, throwing the pen back, glaring as Castiel caught it before it even passed Zella. His lips curled as he turned away. "Fine. We'll be in the living area when you've finished."

Zella's face turned to cold steel like it always did when she questioned a boundary either of them could have sub-consciously crossed. She moved towards the door, pausing when her fingers touched the handle. Castiel waited, unsure if she would actually speak, and then,

"I-I will send you the updates on my progress in finding the solution for the vial before the event begins."

Castiel's shoulders sagged, and he looked away, listening to the sound of her footsteps disappearing down the hall.

CHAPTER NINE

Z ella found herself tucked in a plush chair in
the corner of the library, a book sprawled out
on her lap as she scrawled through her notes
and finalised the components for concurring the vial.
Outside, the sky was dark, and the wind picked up
over the hills racing against the old, leaded windows.
Perhaps she felt less miserable after speaking to her
father, not wishing to claim she missed his presence
and make him feel even more guilty than he already
did for not being allowed access into the ECA. She
wasn't tired, even though it was probably far past
midnight now, but she also knew she couldn't sleep. If
she laid down, her mind would be running over
everything; her conversation with Castiel in the car this
afternoon, figuring out Cullins' agenda, who had
gotten more imposing than she expected, and then the
pending confrontation with Pearl that she had easily
forgotten around Castiel; Castiel, she didn't know what
she wanted to cross if Caledon hadn't barged into the
guest room. It was too much all at once, and the day
felt like it weighed on her as she tried to sort out what
exactly had happened.

Dinner had been surprisingly enjoyable, even though
sometimes it felt a bit like Castiel didn't know where to
turn or who to talk to. Most of the time, Caledon and

Charm behaved well, although Pearl had made a few underhanded comments, and then after dinner, Maia had dragged her to their rooms to help her find a dress to wear next weekend. Caledon seemed to have the time of his life, telling Castiel about stories of Zella during her first year in the Facility and teased about how nice it was to know that she could make efforts to initiate a friendship. He was beginning to see a pattern with Zella. The night had been almost fun, but when Zella laid down to go to bed, she just couldn't sleep.

She wandered the halls for a bit, looking out at the dark shape of the massive lawn, before she had managed to find the library on the first floor, next to the study.

"It's late, Zella."

Zella jerked and looked up at Noah Allyson, standing in the doorway, looking at her. He looked almost larger than life as if he was filling the space by simply being in it. Zella nodded and moved to close the book on her lap. "Ah, sorry, Mr Allyson. I didn't mean to intrude-"

He held up his hand, and Zella felt compelled to stop talking. There was a pause, and he offered her a soft smile. "I don't care if you're up late reading. Heavens knows I don't have time to enjoy all these books. Besides, you're on break, you're allowed to stay up later than normal. But, I just wanted to let you know that it's late, in case you wanted to go to bed."

Zella nodded. "Yes, Mr Allyson."

He laughed, and the sound warmed her. "You don't have to call me Mr Allyson, you know. You can call me Noah."

Zella still thought that sounded far too informal for someone like Noah Allyson. Even among the top industrialists around the world, he was at the top of their pyramid, just like his wife's brand reigned over the Fashion Empire. She paused for a moment before responding. "For now... I am still settling with Mr Allyson as a good compromise?"

He laughed again and walked up to her, shoving his hands in his pockets. There was no doubt in her mind that he was the twins' father. Even if they had completely different personalities, there were too many similarities to ignore. He seemed to read through her, his stare questioning. "I take it you can't sleep?"

Zella shrugged. "Sometimes."

Thankfully he didn't press deeper. Instead, he shrugged and nodded in agreement. "It's been quite a day for you. I know that everyone can be a handful sometimes." He paused and shook his head, "Especially Caledon. I heard about the prank he played on you and Castiel."

"It's-It's fine." She paused and looked up at him again, cautious. "You know Castiel, and I aren't... ah... a couple, right?"

He laughed again, and that same warmth seemed to banish the shadows. "I know. But, the young lad seems to like you. I've never seen you have such an open and healthy frequency with anyone in your life."

Zella's eyebrows knitted together in confusion. That was open? It was like trying to read a closed book half the time. She couldn't even figure out what he was trying to say or how he felt, even about their whole situation. She waited for an explanation, and he seemed inclined to give it to her.

"Even if all anthromorphs are robbed of a life of normalcy, you two have had at the worst, and I am not saying that pain is a competition, and neither am I trying to pin it as rankings in a scoreboard." His face went still and unreadable as if he was thinking of something that made him angry. He took a deep breath and let it out slowly. "It's just nice to see that both of you can have someone you can talk to and be close with, especially after what you have gone through. You know that the twins love you, and there are moments they can definitely get on your nerves most of the time."

Zella froze.

He had known all along. The Allysons knew. Of course, they would. They were the ones to set up the arrangement to give her a life as any other anthromorph.

She rubbed the back of her neck and leaned back in the chair, sighing as her shoulders sagged. "How long have you known?" For a moment, it looked like there was an entire world resting on her shoulders, weighing her down.

"Since the beginning. We just didn't say anything because we didn't know if my daughter's denial to accept you as a bianthromorph sprouted because she wished to respect your decision to hide your identity or... At least, I am hoping that is the only reason."

Zella knew her reason, and it all made sense. Why she had always been persistent over reminding herself of Zella's fake identity as an anthromorph even more than Cullins like she wanted to warn her of the repercussions of being a bianthromorph as if she were merely disapproving a bad fashion choice that could be discarded. And why Caledon was so eager with her growing interest in Castiel, even she was confused herself, and his words dawned upon her-
"*For all your brooding, you deserve someone who understands that instead of eliciting their own illusion over their projection of you.*" Her feelings weren't as oblivious to the outside eye, as much as she had hoped to believe, otherwise.

She sat there, feeling like the floor was crumbling out from under her feet, leaving her suspended without anything to cling to. She felt herself stumble a little, and her heart practically disintegrated in her chest, making her hollow and empty. Zella shoved her emotions down, grinding her teeth together and wrapping her fingers around her arms to stop herself from storming into the panther anthromorph's room.

She didn't want to admit how much Pearl's thoughtless words had hurt her or how they cut so deep she wasn't sure that she would ever stop hearing them. She wanted something to break, something to be destroyed because, at least then, something else would feel just as broken and useless as she was. Tears were gathering behind her eyelashes, and she was shivering. The animals of her bianthromorphic side were howling inside her, pushing against every last vestige of her control, trying to remind Zella how easily she could destroy *everything* if she wanted to.

Zella didn't fit into her life in any way, and it was foolish of her to think that she did.

She shifted, wanting to hear more about Pearl but knowing that she wanted to hear it from her and not her father. As softly as she could, she changed the subject. "Thank you for always accepting me and always offering me a room to stay, Mr Allyson. I appreciate the offer, and it's nice not to stay at the Facility over break."

"Of course, you have always been like family." He looked at her, his eyes understanding. "If Caledon trusts you, then you must be a pretty good person. At least he is an excellent judge of character. He considers you as his long-lost sibling."

Zella nodded. "I appreciate everything he has done for me, and I can't thank him enough for that."

He smiled. "Well, it's nice to know that you always have his back. And I'm glad you decided to come to the benefit."

Oh, right. That thing. She chewed on her lower lip and looked back up into his face. "I-I'll be honest, Mr Allyson. I… don't remember what I'm supposed to do at one of those things. It's been over seven years since I attended one with my parents."

"Me either, if it's any consolation." He laughed, and Zella felt the little bit of nervousness in her chest ease. He shrugged again, his smile softening. "I just appreciate that you'll be there with your date. So, it'll be nice to have someone you can talk with." He offered a sly smile. "And you seem like you two get along."

She wasn't so sure about that, but she at least smiled and nodded.

"I'll let you get back to your reading, Zella. Don't stay up too late." He turned and walked out the door.

Zella sighed, her heart falling into her stomach. If they only knew how irrevocably she had screwed up the twins' lives, when Cullins decides to be irked by her actions, they might not have been so kind to her.

She turned back to the book on her lap, trying again to read over Castiel's notes that he had recovered while reverse-engineering the control switch, before stumbling upon the notes on the destruction of the tissue mass contained the mutated ACVR1 genes written in the manual code of the chip before disappearing into letters that she couldn't decipher. At least, that was one thing the Allyson Manor library had- a massive selection of books. It was almost as big as the one at the Facility. Zella settled into the chair again, taking notes and letting shadows press against her. It seemed like the night stretched on forever, and she could feel the hours slip by without question.

"It's nearly two in the morning."

The sound of the voice was so jarring that Zella nearly dropped her book out of surprise. She jolted out of the page and looked up to see Castiel standing in front of her, his arms crossed over his chest. He looked torn between confused and wanting to argue with her over something. His hair was damp as if he'd just showered, and the scent of his spiced soap filled the space between them. Zella felt her body react without her consent.

She swallowed and closed the book. "I couldn't sleep."

He shrugged and picked up a book she had set on the table to her side, glancing at the title. There was a long pause, and he glanced at her from beneath the shadows of his thick, dark lashes. "Me either."

She shrugged. "I thought if I couldn't sleep, I might as well try to work and figure out the manual code."

"Mm."

Castiel's response told her nothing, and he stared at her for a long minute until Zella grew uncomfortable and turned back to her book. Zella sunk her teeth into her lower lip and watched him as he shifted as if he practically felt the heat of her emotions burn up the scars running down her arms.

Castiel's jaw ticked, and he leaned over her, slamming his hands on either side of the armchair. "Tell me to stop… And I will."

Zella blinked, and she felt him tense under the weight of her emotions. Shock coursing through her system, she waited for more of an explanation, not entirely certain it would come. He closed his eyes and leaned forward, pressing his forehead against her own in a move that felt so strangely intimate. He was invading her space with ease, and Zella was just letting him. "She hurt you; I get that Allyson is like family to you, but—" His fingers dig into the leather of the armchair as if he was fighting something inside himself that he couldn't admit to. She could hear the leather strain under the force of his grip. "I don't know why it's taking every molecule of my being to stop myself from barging into her room for inflicting the same pain. I don't know why I am so bothered."

There was that flash in Castiel's eyes. That trust. That belief. As if he knew, in his heart, that Zella might give in. As if he had faith that she would.

The traces of her memories unfolding in astronomical magnitudes, still too gentle, too intimate.

"You are merely assuming things," Zella leaned her face up just a fraction of an inch, meeting his stare. A war was raging inside her, and Zella knew which side was going to win before she took another breath. She looked up into his eyes, watching flecks of ice catch the thin light in the library, and her heart stilled for just a moment, offering her a fraction of clarity. This was dangerous, impulsive, and downright stupid. "Why do you care?"

"I don't want to." He struggled to find the words and shoved himself away from her, anger at his own actions filling his eyes. He paced for a moment, his fingers raking through his hair as he muttered to himself in Portuguese. Finally, he turned and glared at her, more out of frustration than actual anger. "The only will that's holding me back is the fact that my actions are still your responsibility. I care about that. I care about you."

"What?" Zella picked her head up and stared at him, confused. That didn't make any sense. If he didn't want to care for her, then did that mean... She stopped that thought before it had the chance to root in her mind and spread like a weed. Shifting, she watched him pace back and forth a few more times before he looked back at her, almost defeated with himself.

"I don't want to care for anyone. I am not even sure if I am capable of that," he repeated, his voice softer now. He looked helpless against his own mind, and Zella didn't know how to respond to it. His shoulders dropped, and he took a step back away as if he needed the distance. "But... I think I do. I think I do care for you, and it confuses me, and I'm not— I don't like it. I don't like thinking about you or getting mad when Cullins or Allyson dare to belittle your identity as a bianthromorph or want to hold you when you hurt."

"There will always be some inferior tyrant that tries to manipulate humanity through the games of power and hatred in order to its hopes. They do this by igniting false fault lines in the form of creating a hierarchy based on gender, melanin, identity or genetic combination." Zella thought back to their combat nearly a month ago when he had cradled her in his arms when Cullins messed with the frequency of her chip to test his combat skills with the inhibition control. She thought about the softness of his voice and the way his arms wrapped around her, and she thought nothing could have brought her back from the brink of anger, but he did. He brought her back to her human self, held her as she shook against his chest, and it felt like he was keeping her whole. Zella's heart twisted, and she looked at him as he took another step back, wincing.

"Can you truly proclaim that you have never been helmed that realm to harm, even unintentionally in your defence?" He shook his head, raking his fingers through his hair again. "I don't like any of it. But I care for you."

"I have moved past her for over a year." Her voice was pathetic and soft, but Zella couldn't find the strength in her to demand more. At least, not when he had just admitted that he cared for her. "I just didn't want to admit the truth to myself."

Castiel shook his head, his shoulders sinking even more as his head fell into his hands. "But you are still hurt—"

Zella's eyes narrowed. "I will get past it."

"I know." He looked at her, his expression blank. "I just want you to promise me that you would stop me if my anger gets the better of me. I owe it to Caledon's hospitality to not strangle his sister."

PEARL ALLYSON

CHAPTER TEN

Zella shook her head and moved down the hall. She couldn't hide forever, as much as she wanted to. Zella felt her feet move on their own, and she stepped down the silent hallway to the bright, cheerful noise of the stairs. Each step down felt like a mile, and she was dragging her feet along the wood floor. Finally, she reached the bustling entryway, the pressing of people against her washing away her own thoughts. For a few moments, no one noticed her, and it felt good to be invisible.

It felt good to not exist.

She took a shaky breath and moved towards the main hall, trying to slide between the crowd of people. It was a sea of black and sequins, tuxedos, and delicate dresses, and she was lost in it.

Zella felt too many emotions radiating from the people around her all at once to the point where it felt like it was overloading her head. There was greed, and envy, and lust, and pride, and wrath, all tangling together as each person wandered around the first floor of the massive estate. They were looking over everything, trying to figure out how someone like the Allysons had come to amass such wealth and whether or not their anthromorphic twins were tax write-offs. Zella could feel all of their desires sink into her like sharp claws, and they pulled at her skin and tried to rip her apart. Thankfully, she hadn't crossed paths with the other Allyson twin, knowing that the latter was actively avoiding her.

She took a shaky breath and swallowed a gulp of water from her crystal glass. Back at the Facility, it was easier to disappear into the shadows and wander away if she needed to, but every movement here felt watched. If she adjusted her hair or took a sip of water, it was like a hundred eyes recognised her; Why was the daughter of the late Violetta Rune at the Allyson estate? What did she do to deserve being here? Did her father refuse to meet her because she was the one behind the actress's death when her anthromorphic side was activated? Was the Council trying to hide her genetic markers that would soon reduce to a hybrid? Whispers were raking down her senses, and Zella could feel her bianthromorphic side start to surge; both the Puma and Bald-eagle genes inside her annoyed with the behaviour of her human side. It wanted to show them the force that mainly lay dormant inside her and remind them what happened when they underestimated her.

Zella reached into her hair and fixed a loose pin, feeling at least three people catch the movement. Even though she thought she was dressed modestly, she somehow still felt practically bare in this strapless black satin dress, and more than once, she caught and nearly snarled back at the curious eyes on her. Almost immediately, she could feel the eyes look away as if they knew better than to try anything with the amber-eyed girl who looked like she was desperately waiting to get an excuse to break their bones.

Zella looked around the room for someone she knew, and Maia would have easily saved her from this disaster if she needed it.

"You look uncomfortable."

Zella looked up to see Caledon barely towering over her, the width of his shoulders nearly blocking out the light. He offered her a lopsided smile and stood next to her, his fingers wrapped around a crystal scotch glass.

"Thank you." Zella let go of a quiet sigh, and her shoulders dropped in relief.

"Don't mention it." His smile was softer now, understanding. "I could see those assholes from a mile away. Don't let them see you nervous, they prey on that, and while I have no doubt you could hold your own in a fight, I'd rather not cause a scene," he paused and grinned down at her. "But I'm not above a little property damage. Maia would be way too excited to go slash the tires on their Bentleys? It'll teach them a lesson."

Zella couldn't stop the chuckle that escaped, and she shook her head. "No, but thanks for the offer. It's almost sweet that Emerson is rubbing off on you." It was no surprise that Caledon's optimistic side oddly complimented Maia's violent tendencies. He was the type of person to love his lifestyle in the Facility, enjoying the missions that made him feel like the existence of fictional stories that idolised the creation of *'superheroes'* over a century ago.

"Offer still stands if you change your mind. I'm fully prepared to completely inconvenience and annoy more than a few rich assholes." He shrugged and took a sip of his drink, his eyes scanning the crowd. There was a heartbeat's pause, and Caledon glanced over at her, a glint in his eye. "I'm surprised Sylvain isn't over here fawning over you. I thought that Brazilian Blondie would be next to you all night, but I haven't seen neither hide nor hair of him."

"No one is fawning over anyone." Zella had felt like she had this conversation with either Caledon or Maia or Charm at least twice a day, and it was still so awkward to have. Especially after what had happened in the library. Since then, Castiel had barely spoken to her, and Zella found herself more often with Maia's company. "We're barely even friends."

He nodded but was still smirking as if he didn't believe her. "So I've been told. By both of you, actually. And more times than I think I can count." He paused and took another sip of his drink, glancing back out at the crowd of people draped in silks and dripping with diamonds. "But you know that you make doe-eyes at him whenever he is not looking, right? He is not subtle, either. I swear, his whole face lights up, and he can spot you in half a second before you even enter a room."

Zella gave him a flat look. "Now you're being ridiculous."

"Oooh," he lifted his eyebrows, teasing, "Oh please, he has even got your trademark glower down. I'm impressed. I feel like it took you almost your whole entire life to master that look."

"I knew that you wouldn't shut up and end up being the bane of my existence in here," she shook her head and looked away, frowning.

"I wouldn't. That is a true statement." He nudged her with his shoulder, the same way he would with Maia or Pearl, and grinned down at her. "Look, even if you guys aren't together or whatever, yet, I'm just glad he is here. Neither of you is particularly social, not really interested in other people, very focused on whatever your task is at the time. You are a little ball of stress and anxiety and pent up emotions, and I've seen you lose your temper more times than I care to count."

Feline anthromorphs were explicit about their bisexuality, and this is where Zella's puma gene shone through. But, unlike all feline anthromorphs who thrived on nursing their egos by flirting, her Avian side was always too busy brooding to even entertain the idea of it. For the past two years, she had always been blatantly oblivious and infuriatingly cryptic at the same time to the feelings of the anthromorphs who pinned over her before moving on to Pearl. Her feelings for his sister remained unchanged even while indifferently entertaining these anthromorphs in their Facility for a few weeks, to blow off steam whenever they had to capture rogue anthromorphs who were more lost than evil.

Did Caledon feel sorry for Reyna, Nadia and Artem for being toyed by his sister to get over Zella? *Perhaps, Yeah.* Did he ever do anything about it? *No.* But was he glad that Nadia and Artem's frustrated outbursts at Zella's apathetic aura, claiming that her unapologetic stubbornness would ruin her relationship with Pearl, finally pushed her to move on? *Yes.*

Zella looked over at him, her eyebrows raising. "Little? I am almost as tall as you, and I am still 6 feet tall. You are only 3 inches taller than me."

"Seeing him around you, well, you are not a completely different person, but you have changed. And I think it's for the better." Caledon's expression softened, and he gave her the beginning of a genuine smile. "So, whatever the two of you are, I hope you figure it out, and I hope it works out in the end. For both of you. You are going to be fine."

Zella flushed and looked away. "Fine is overrated. I just hope that someday I gather the courage to let go of hanging on to the notion of *fine* and embrace being *real*."

"I heard that my Dad told you that we had known all along about."

"He did." She rested her hand atop her head and swallowed the fear building in her chest. It wouldn't do her any good

"Zella, nothing changes." Caledon's voice was low, and he fidgeted with the hem of his suit again as if he couldn't look at her. "I had known all along, and I am going to keep it that way."

"Pearl had known all along even when she spoke about *them* like we were nothing more than—" She took another deep breath and let it out slowly, obviously trying to calm herself down.

"Whatever happens, I am here for you. Even if I have to choose sides, I am never going to make a choice where I abandon you." He rubbed his thumb along his jaw and sighed. "I just hope that it never comes to that. I just hope that it's just her pettiness and not her hatred. I won't lose you. You are my long-lost sibling."

Zella let his words settle over her, uncertain with the way it made her feel like the world had stopped spinning, and she was trying to find a way to keep the ground under her feet. He was right in a way, and they weren't sure if they were able to face that truth.

"I don't think I can handle losing you, either," Zella nodded, chewing on her lower lip, "I mean, we might end up eating like pigs wherever we go, but I wouldn't trade that for anything else."

"Neither would I." To hear her say it so blatantly made him want to wrap his arms around her and protect her. She was his family. He knew she was fully capable of keeping herself safe, but he wanted her to know that she wasn't alone in this. He was going to be by her side, no matter what. Caledon reached out and tangled his hand with her own, his fingers sliding along her palm. "Whenever you do confront her, I will be there for you. She can't avoid you forever."

She had to avoid that confrontation at all costs. She just couldn't let Caledon get caught between the wildfires of this mess. That's the last thing he deserved, and she wasn't going to be the person who dared to tarnish the twins' bond.

Caledon's expression softened for a moment, and Zella suddenly felt as though a big brother was truly standing in front of her, genuinely wanting nothing more than for Zella to be happy. That thought was unnerving. It wasn't that she was not used to him caring about her, but Zella still wasn't used to accepting kindness so easily. She was used to his silly pranks and angry words when a mission went wrong. She wasn't used to seeing someone look at her with hope *for* her. Zella looked away, uncomfortable as Caledon's smile tugged at the corners of his mouth.

"Now, since that sappy conversation is out of the way, let me let you in on a bit of information we've all survived on when we attend the benefits." Caledon's smirk widened, and he tilted his head to a door tucked in the far back corner. "If you ever need to get out of the limelight or it's just too much to deal with some rich asshole talking about his third house in Taipei or his 'cottage' in the Silverlake Vineyard in Pattaya, you can always head into the kitchen. Ronald never minds an extra set of hands, and he doesn't judge you if you need to hide your face for a bit. Plus, you can always steal something before it heads out to the table."

Zella's shoulders dropped in relief, and she watched the flash of a camera fill the entry hall to her left. She could hear Charm chatting cheerfully with someone, and she looked over into Caledon's face with at least a little gratitude. He might have been frustrating sometimes, but at least he seemed to understand what she was going through. "You know I might have to take you up on that. Thank you."

Caledon shook his head. "Don't mention it."

There was a bit of noise from the front entryway, and when everyone seemed to be more interested in whatever was going on there, Zella made her way to the back of the room and ducked into the kitchen. If she thought it was going to be quieter, she was sorely mistaken. Sounds of clattering dishes and caterers yelling at each other filled the space, and there was the press of people moving around her as if she didn't exist. It was raucous, but everything seemed to have a purpose, and no one really noticed her. Zella picked up the train of her dress and made her way over to where the old British chauffeur with greying hair, Ronald, was barking orders like a drill sergeant. He caught her stare, and his expression softened as she made her way over, wiggling between two caterers plating canapes.

"Miss Rune?"

Heat ran up her neck, and she lifted her stare to him. "I was told that if I didn't want to be out there, you could put me to work in here?"

He shook his head and offered a soft laugh. "You're fitting in just fine with the rest of the family, I see." Ronald pulled her away from the centre of the kitchen, where the noise was the loudest, and moved her to a table in the back where stacks of sugar cookies were waiting to be iced with white icing. He handed her an apron and moved her towards the table. "I haven't had time to finish icing these. It's just white icing, nothing too fancy. And they don't have to be perfect, so don't worry if you make a mistake." His smile crinkled his eyes. "And you can stay back here as long as you need to." He took a step away before turning back to her, dropping his voice to a loud whisper. "And, I didn't really count those biscuits, so if a few go missing, I'm sure no one will notice."

Zella laughed heartily, and he winked at her before stepping away, returning to the canapes on another table. For a few minutes, she worked alone and in silence, letting the hubbub of the kitchen drown out her own thoughts. It was an easy task, but it gave her something to do, and no one seemed to pay her any attention. Pick up a cookie, ice it, put it on the plate. It was repetitive but somehow oddly relaxing. She barely registered when Maia came and stood next to her.

"You've iced like twelve cookies and haven't taken a single one yet? I'm impressed." Maia grinned at her and picked up an apron, draping it over her own expensive evening gown. She snagged one of the iced cookies off the plate and shoved it into her mouth. "Ronald usually makes like three dozen extra under the knowledge that they're going to go missing by the end of the night."

Zella gave a small smile and made room for Maia. "Does everyone come back here for a break during the Benefits?"

"Yep." Maia nodded, mumbling through a mouthful of cookies. "Even Noah and Angela."

That made her feel better somehow, and they both fell into easy conversation. Maia gave her a few tips on how she personalised her dagger in her kevlar gloves and bemoaned how jealous she was that Zella consistently topped their Anatomy and Physiology class. It felt good to have a normal conversation, and Zella found herself laughing along with stories of Maia dealing with training naive, eager-to-please recruits during their first missions. As they talked, Caledon came in and sidled up on the other side of Maia. And then Charm.

Charm gave the couple a lopsided grin, leaning back on his heels. "So, are we really going to have thrown an intervention to get you two to admit that you are dating?" The ebony-haired breedling found it hilarious and offending at the same time that the couple actually believed that no one had caught on to change in the air between them, if Zella had earned a nickname as 'Boudica' in the Facility, then Maia and Caledon had earned their titles as the angelic versions of Maria Bonita and Lampião.

Caledon looked back at him, eyes wide. He glanced between Zella and Charm, looking for some kind of explanation, but they just laughed at him from behind their hands. "It's about time, and you guys have been dancing around each other for over two years. You guys weren't subtle in the slightest. Even Castiel thinks that you are a couple since his first day in our shared Applied Physics class." Zella shrugged and shoved a freshly iced cookie into her mouth.

He flushed and picked up a cookie, offering a small, sheepish smile as his hand brushed Maia's. "The declaration just seemed weird to plan, and there was just no perfect timing. We've been together for a while."

Maia grinned and looked up at Caledon. "Well, we finally stopped chickening out."

Before Zella realised it, Mr Allyson had joined them at the table, icing a few cookies with the rest of them and falling into the conversation as if he'd always been there. They talked about everything, what everyone was doing, what their plans were for the next holiday coming up, who was wearing the absolute worst possible dress, and how in the world they had managed to fit their huge egos through the door. Their conversation was joyous and loud, and there was a strange kind of warmth that seemed to wrap Zella up.

"Smiling suits you almost as equally as throwing in the final blow."

Zella looked next to her to see that Mr Allyson had left to return to the party while Maia had walked over to take his place, and Castiel was standing next to her, his face unreadable. He looked down at the pile of cookies and reached for one to ice with her.

Charm raised his hand and leaned over the table with a teasing grin. "I'd like to make a motion to trade Cal in for Castiel."

Caledon glared, his mouth settling into a thin line.

Maia raised her hand as Caledon's lower jaw sprung open in betrayal, looking at his girlfriend for an explanation. "Motion seconded."

"Motion passed." Zella raised her hand. "All in favour, say aye."

"Haha." Caledon rolled his eyes and set his iced cookie on the plate with finished ones. He bristled, but it felt more out of habit than actual anger. "You're all so funny."

"You know it, Cal." Charm set his cookie on the plate and wiped off his hands before heading back into the party.

Castiel and Zella fell into silence like they always did, and Caledon and Maia seemed to notice that there was something between the bianthromorphs. They exchanged a curious look between each other before taking off their aprons and returning to the party, leaving Zella and Castiel practically alone in the back corner of the kitchen. Castiel's face set into a tight expression as they worked silently together. She could feel him tense beside her, uncomfortable and awkward as if he was fighting something inside him. He shifted as the back of their hands brushed against each other, and Zella pulled back, looking into his eyes. It felt like electricity was snapping against her skin, and she didn't know what to say, so she kept quiet.

Castiel returned to icing cookies with her, still tense and quiet. Minutes passed like this, and he finally turned his head and looked at her from the corner of his eye. "Come with me."

CHAPTER ELEVEN

There was a long pause as if the rooms had faded away, and he was trying to weigh out whether or not he should talk to her, wordlessly moving through the crowd and into the quiet library of the Allysons' Manor.

Zella swallowed as she stared at him from across the room, taking in the shape of him. Heat crawled up her cheeks, and she stared shamelessly at him, taking in his polished-apatite eyes and bronze skin like it was the first time she was seeing him as he adjusted the suit coat on his shoulders.

"The manual code is the actual key to shutting all controls of the RTFQ chip besides the tracker. The pre-programming installed works based on some sort of a key-phrase that shuts it down. If we figure it out, we can shut it down without having to fry it or causing any alarms." His words were clipped as if he wanted to get through the cordial part of the conversation before getting to the eye of the storm. A moment passed as his gaze swept down the length of her, examining her with the same shameless curiosity that she had towards him.

Zella's face went cold as she took in the information. "We don't have much time, so let's hope that my guess is right."

"Your hunch is as good as hitting the jackpot; I am certain of it." He said it so simply like there was no other response he could give.

The key phrase merely consisted of a few sentences in Hebrew that read:

The centre begins it all. Once they start to lose their identity, give shelter to the lost ones in order, beginning from the smallest. For only, the last and largest one finds its way back to its twin following the footsteps of the first whole, which never lost its colours over generations. Remember to always support the community of the weaker ones.

"Perhaps, if colour can be perceived as segments, then the part, '*the first whole which never lost its colour over generations*' could mean that the first whole could possibly represent the eight in digital time. It's the only number where all the segments are filled." Zella's voice was almost conversational. She sighed and rubbed at her forehead, a tick that told Castiel that she was frustrated for being unsure.

"Segments. If it's segments, then we have to look at each of the segments comprising the digital eight, like a pattern... which means the segments could be numbered." He paused and glanced up at the ceiling as if thinking. His head dipped, and he glanced at the

230 | *Reigns of Utopia*

ground before lifting his eyes to barely meet hers again.

"Exactly, and I think it tells us how to number those segments at the beginning. '*The centre begins it all*' and the anti-clockwise sign signifies that the middle segment is one while the other six numbers are numbered in an anti-clockwise fashion." She nodded, her face twisting into its own unreadable expression. "So, we might have to add the numbers representing each segment depending on the actual numbers covering up the segments on the seven-segment display, from one to nine."

His arms crossed tightly over his chest, still a million miles away. His eyes cleared, suddenly staring at Zella, but almost as if he was seeing her for the first time.

"*Remember to always support the community of the weaker ones,*" which means we have to add the covered portion or uncovered portion of the numbers filling up the digital eight depending on the sum that yields a lower outcome on the addition of the numbers representing each assigned segment." He rubbed his jaw, thinking. "For example, one represented digitally adds up to eleven, and one symbolises alphabet A, that means A is enumerated by eleven." Castiel trailed off, his voice drifting away as he thought, before snatching the nearest spare notebook he could find sprawled near the plush chair that Zella often spent her time lazing in, and shading the two segments on the right side of a digitalised eight, and adding up the upper segment representing six and the lower end representing five.

His expression softened just briefly as if he was appreciating her, and Zella felt her heart stop in her chest. It was one thing to have him glaring at her from behind too-thick lashes, but it was something different with him gazing at her like she was something special.

"So, H, which is the eighth alphabet, is enumerated by eight because *it doesn't lose its colour over generations*," Zella said, expression twisting until she and Castiel stood inches apart, fierce eyes meeting like a black hole swallowing Suns, as she looked over his shoulder to read the numbers associated with each alphabet on the sheet. "So, for double-digits like ten, we have to consider the segments for two-eights and add them up. The digital one still represents eleven, while digital zero could be one since we have to consider the lower end, so the uncovered centre segment, add both of these, and we get twelve. That would mean the tenth letter, J is enumerated by twelve."

"Precisely, we just have to add eleven to the numbers associated with the numerical outcomes of the digital zero-nine, to get the numbers enumerated to the alphabets till R, the eighteenth letter without getting any repetitions." He nodded, not mirthless, but dark and heavy, as all things in this world were, before glancing down at his cuffs and straightening them.

"Right, because we have to change things around when they lose their '*identity*,' which certainly means every alphabet is assigned to a particular number and does not exceed twenty-six." She leaned back on her heels and looked away for a moment before glancing back at the sheet in his hands. "Since it's a fixed community because the largest one is identical to its twin. So Z, the last alphabet is numerated to twenty-six and doesn't change like H."

Zella ran a careless hand through her hair and took another deep breath.

"The only remaining part of the saying that we haven't implemented yet is '*once they start to lose their identity, give shelter to the lost ones in order, beginning from the smallest*' which means, here the lost ones are the numbers that haven't come up as an outcome of the addition through the segmented numbers along with the digital eights," Castiel said, as he rested his head against the opposite tip of the pencil, like a weary wanderer, finally taking a brief rest from his constant movement. Like a car, puttering out with no gas left to fuel it, as he came across S, the nineteenth letter, which yielded a sum that was already enumerated with the fourth alphabet, D.

Zella simply stared blankly, as if she was a million years in the past.

"So it concludes that letters from S to Y have to be enumerated to the remaining numbers which haven't come up, in ascending order, starting with S numerated to uh… uhmm... two," Zella confirmed, going through the list once again and spotting the first number that hadn't shown up, yet.

"I think we did it! I think this makes sense." Zella looked surprised at his admission, and she stared at him, returning his small smile. It was a startlingly desperate promise that was oddly familiar. Similar to the first one they made when they built their first hesitant truce. "I remember one combination that was used quite often 7-19-11-3-20-5-20-1-11-15-9-2. If we use this code in this combination, then it stands for BRAINWAVES. It works."

"It works." Zella felt the air between them change, and the tension in her shoulders suddenly eased with his presence. She looked at him in the darkness, her thoughts thick with relief, caked with unidentifiable peace, but somehow felt almost okay. There was odd tranquillity between them, and Zella let it wash over her as she scratched the back of her neck where the chip was embedded.

Things were happening around them, *between* them, that she barely noticed, or if she did notice them, she continued to ignore them out of some form of idiocy or self-preservation (she couldn't pinpoint which), as they confirmed that nothing more than the tracker was activated in their RTFQ chips.

Zella clenched her hand around the notebook sandwiched between them, taking a slow, steadying breath before speaking the next words. "We should walk back and blend in before Cal or Maia find another reason to believe that their teases have actually manifested into reality."

Silence stretched between them again, and Zella almost considered repeating herself. Had Castiel heard her, or was there something else eating at him?

Castiel didn't pull back, and neither did she. They just stood there, suspended in time and waiting for the other person to make the next decision. "Zella, I don't think that we have a common goal, after this—"

"*Common* goal?" Zella sneered dangerously, eyes narrowing like knife blades. "And you know my goal, Sylvain?"

"You and I both know that Cullins is definitely working for someone, who is pretty much helping the existence of the CULT's bases from within the Council," Castiel nearly snapped back. The tension in his chest nearly broke like a wiredrawn too tight. Yet rather than exploding, he just felt his shoulders fall like a tent falling without a support beam. Deflating. Falling. He was tired. And he was beating fear back, but acceptance was just as deadly. "You knew why I was there in that small CULT's base in Zagreb. Finding and taking those parasites individually isn't going to matter until we find the one running this chain, in the shadows or else it might cost more lives, and I have seen enough."

"Then you know that the biggest lead to that is Cullins, and I don't just think that the Council is infiltrated by some members who provide the funds to keep the CULT's bases running." Her voice was a low warning rumble. The leash that Cullins held on her led her to be more calculative of the information she acquired from the missions, knowing that Sebastian Cullins played for the long haul, and she couldn't throw her patience for a toss singlehandedly. "I think that over half of them actually run the bases and send us on staged ruins of the CULT's bases just to maintain a rapport with the UNH."

"I know that I can not get to the bottom of this without you, but freedom doesn't matter to me as much as it matters to you. It's all just a contingency plan to me, not the ultimate plan." Castiel bent his head down to look into her eyes, anger flaring up like a fire inside him. His voice sounded like it was booming, screaming in her ears, but he was talking normally to her.

"What the hell does that mean?" Zella swallowed back another curse, the air pressing against her like a physical weight.

But with Castiel's apatite eyes boring into her without a hint of anger or sharpness within them, it felt like being paralysed. Forced to spell out his every fear for her.

"You are doing all of this because you see '*freedom*' as the end to this. I don't." He rasped, expression hardening almost defensively like he was getting too close to feeling something. Lips pressed into a firm line as he held a warning hand out to Zella to hold on. "You are *not* motivated by vengeance. I *need* the power of control that was ripped away from me."

"They killed my mother," Zella spat, fists clenching as her eyes turned crimson, like carnelian, ripping with rage unrivalled. Most pregnant women barely survived the genetic recombination process of their foetus as their own genetics modified into acquiring stone-man syndrome, especially when the foetus' human gene ended up binding with the animal gene, successfully, whether they ended up growing into an anthromorph or a hybrid. "They destroy lives of millions against their will, by either turning them into mindless hybrids or locked-up anthromorphs."

Even when those eyes and that voice were the only things keeping her grounded in the present, Zella had fought them like chains that burned.

"Are you saying that you won't take the chance to get out of this if you find another alternative to get to Siam?" Castiel demanded through his teeth, eyes drawing over her lips before looking back at her eyes

in a snap. He glared at her. Not angry. Just vehement
in his belief in his actions.

"Do you think I like being stuck in the facility? I can't
even meet my own father, like a *damn* prisoner in
chains! Do you think that I have not tried finding an
alternative to get out of that glorified dungeon for the
past five years?!" Zella scoffed, lips curling. Her heart
merely beat out a horribly loud rhythm as she held his
gaze. His expression calmed down in a trance, merely
realising the gravitas of her words and processing that
someone was on his side for the very first time.
"There is no other way to reach my outcome besides
taking them down. I can't get there until I claw out the
power stolen away from me. It was mine—*is* mine."

"Maybe, you're right," he faded off, eyes intent.

But this had always been the Castiel she recognised.
His eyes were harsh but not cold or bitter. They stared
at Zella as if she was something, like staring through
at the past.

A spark, a glint, a flash. Something that spoke of
determination.

Of trust.

Zella listened to the crisp sound of frost underfoot as
they stepped outside the Manor. She took a deep
breath, tasting the moist, cold air on her tongue. He
followed her trail of gaze to look at a few of the fancy

suits dancing together as the rest of the crowd cheered them on. As the horizon itself started to ink the arrival of late nightfall, more snowflakes started to fall down on the snow-covered ground, with the pace of a turtle reappearing from its shell after a period of aestivation. The bonfire seemed a world away, and Zella sat down on a fallen, mostly dry tree to look up at the stars in the sky. Castiel settled next to her, and for a long while, neither of them said anything. They just sat there in almost comfortable silence, staring at the stars in the sky and waiting for the other person to talk.

Castiel seemed to sense the change too, and he leaned closer to her, his fingers resting over her own.

Her fingers threaded through his own, pulling him closer to her. It felt like dipping a cold limb into warm water, agonisingly painful for each moment it brought relief as Zella tugged him closer.

"You know that if you don't join in the dance by yourself, then I am going to shove you guys in." Zella turned around and saw Caledon standing next to her, his lips tugging to the side in a wicked grin.

She gave him a flat expression. "Go and choke—"

"It must be the season. I think it's just an extension of the Copenhagen Dance festival that happens around this time, each year." Maia rolled her eyes but felt too much delight in her stomach before trying to pull Zella to her feet, ignoring her protests and her muted curses, while the latter still held a vice grip around Castiel's wrist. The cheetah-breedling took it as a perfect opportunity to use the pair's imbalance to practically kick them in the dancing circle as they stumbled through the maze of dancing couples.

Logically, Castiel knew it was just scar tissue, devoid of nerve endings and feeling and yet he,

"I am not suffering through this alone." Zella's grip on his wrist tightened had passed the stage of gentle to tangible, not restraining, simply holding.

"I don't dance, Zella." Castiel groaned with disdain and looked at Zella, his eyes dark. His mouth set into a thin line before nodding ever so slightly to give her the permission to lead them to their doom and grab both of Zella's wrists. He didn't tug at her or drag her anywhere but rather held her arms patiently.

"Neither do I." She continued to stare at him, taking a step closer to invade his space.

"Well, the only way we get out of this without looking like fools is making this as less insufferable as possible." He could only stare into the planes of her face, and watch as her eyes searched his own, as she effortlessly kept up with the ornamental steps without repeating them and keeping up with the rhythm and the accelerating tempo, focusing all her unrivalled concentration on the footsteps of the leading pair of the dance.

Somehow, looking up at Castiel always made her feel powerful. Like she could take on the world.

Someone who was able to stand against the gales she produced. Someone who wouldn't crumble against Zella's fiery obnoxiousness. Someone for her to beat herself against and remain as sturdy as stone in her way.

"I thought you said you couldn't dance," she smirked with an amused tone. She lifted her head and looked at him, curious.

"I don't. I am a quick learner, though, and I have been watching this way longer than you have. We had to learn to dance this back during Lunar festivals back in Salvador." He trailed off, mumbling more to himself than her before picking up the pace of his steps to match with the rubato tempo of the melody. "Plus, my mother cherished her Latina culture, especially performance arts because cultures are the very thing that added colours to our life, enhanced the gravitation of humanity among people to cherish art. She used to love those Lunar festivals. It had always been our little custom."

"It's beautiful, almost like mapping out the constellations in the same night sky," Zella murmured gently, looking torn between understanding and something warmer. Zella's lips pressed together as if she was debating whether or not to say something.

This was the first time he spoke about his life as a human, and she didn't wish to ruin that.

"I thought you wanted to dance with me?" Castiel said lowly, icy eyes locked onto Zella's like a hook. Holding onto Castiel, grounding even in the whirlwind around them, even as Castiel tugged at her, afraid, he held fast, like a chain and a shield all at once.

"I am dancing with you." She stilled for a moment, raising her eyebrows and turning his question over, but he didn't respond.

"No, you are not."

She did not like the older Castiel's perceptiveness anymore than she liked, the younger Castiel's from her memories. She had learned that his pervasive, drawing nature was something she needed too and always eventually would give in to.

Though he had lost juvenile aura, every action of his held the same intent, same purpose, the same willingness.

Zella stared at him from beneath her eyelashes, her own breath coming in short gasps. They barely held each other, but their emotions were swirling inside her, creating a dangerous concoction.

"Yes, I am." she scoffed aimlessly. Zella's glare was thick and rough, but nothing about it was sharp. Nothing was threatening. This was just who Zella was.

Zella tossing ice cream at the twins or him, claiming she had bought it from their cafeteria but didn't feel like eating anymore.

Zella just side-hugging her people in a vice protective grip, under the pretence of a truce after combat training, and whatever tear-logged person was beside her simply accepting the comforting hold of a friend.

Not like gentle sunshine and breezes that Castiel had never felt for the past five years. It was oddly familiar, like the heat waves that flew through the air, uncomfortably warm but almost gentle when compared to the fire itself that stung and burned.

Not something gentle, but something gentler.

And it was unexplainably familiar. The same traits of the boy in her memories heightened in the eyes of the one who had grown in a world who had tried to strip his inimitable traits of loyalty, fierceness, an inability to sit by and watch something happen, but had failed.

"You are still not dancing with me," Castiel said firmly, like a wire wrapping around Zella, forcing her immobile. She couldn't look away if she wanted to. His voice was low, and there was a rawness behind it that shook Zella to her core. "When you dance, you need to look at me. Only me."

CHAPTER TWELVE

L ook, I'm sorry to throw this at you last minute, but
"   there are people higher than me pulling this thing
        together. They don't want anything going wrong,"
Cullins sighed slowly, speaking about their next mission to
Novyslava as if he was apologising about the mere change
in weather and not forcing them to one of the places where
humans loathed Anthromorphs the most. "And nothing
should go wrong. Most people there will likely be hostile
with just words. But I need you to be prepared."

The ECA was formed in the aftermath of the Russo-
European riots of 2130, which led to the downfall of
Russia. The EU collapsing in 2050 symbolised the
tipping point for everything to fall like dominos,
including Watergate's compulsion to create
anthromorphs in 2054, setting off the era of species
division between the Created and the Creators.

As the numbers of anthromorphs started rising during
the European Collapse, the UNH had to intervene by
branding Europe as a Code Orange Continent, which
immediately led to the Paris Stock Exchange crashing
in a snap. Fearing that UNH would restrict travel,
Europeans rushed towards Russia, for it was their
easiest gateway to the gleaming, prosperous continent
of Asia.

The Russian army withdrew its forces from the East and redeployed them to the west to stop the surge of incoming Europeans. Unfortunately, the military couldn't reach there quick enough, which finally led to Moscow's downfall. Alarmed by the disastrous fall of Moscow, China, India, Scythia, and Persia sent in their troops to aid the Russian army to reach the Ural Mountains before the panic had settled in the European Camps.

For over a month, the enraged Europeans started a large-scale spear of anarchy, riots, and looting of western Russia.

It was evident that the aiding countries had a much bigger vested interest while sending in their troops. Neither of them wished to handle the consequences of Europe's spillover, eminent poverty, and economic disruptions in the East.

Although there were no casualties, the final showdown at the Urals led to the capturing of Protest Leaders.

The fall of the last domino forced the UNH to pass the UNSC resolution 1812/1878, which formally established the United Nations European Commission Autonomous Area (UNECAA) in October of 2130.

"Why are you selecting only the four of us?" Caledon asked slowly, a heavy stone settling in his gut. The hematite-grey-eyed Allyson was the last person to be fearful or even sceptical about a mission. Still, they were being thrust into an arena that was against their very existence. After all, it was *Siberia*.

Regions west of the Urals of the former Russian Federation were incorporated into the ECA, while the remaining broken eastern fragments of the world's then-largest country, reunited under the banner of Siberia, with Novyslava as their capital. It was no surprise that almost all inhabitants of this nation downright loathed the existence of anthromorphs more than any other country in the reformed world. Post the Collapse, the humans who had barely begun to piece their lives together in Siberia saw the species of Homo-Anthromorphis as nothing but the very reason behind their former country being burned to the ground.

"Well, the team was supposed to consist of five, so you have every right to follow your sister's decision, Caledon," Chancellor Cullins paused, his expression almost sly. "She backed out of the team because she didn't feel comfortable working with certain members of this chosen team. Except for Mr. Sylvain, the rest of you are welcome to walk out."

"Why are you sending him on a wild-goose chase to find a *ghost*?" Maia lifted an eyebrow but worked to keep her expression blank, her confusion threatening to show.

"Well, besides the coordinates and the objectives, it's not your place to question anything, Ms. Emerson."

His eyes turned steely as if to drive home a point. He tapped his fingers on the table, letting his words settle in his own mouth before responding to her. "Mr Sylvain was pretty insistent on pursuing this assignment alone, but Ms Rune refused to abdicate her responsibilities because, as she stated, '*his actions were her responsibility until his redemption period wraps up.*'"

That's when things became clearer to the coyote anthromorph and explained the sour atmosphere as well as why Castiel and Zella looked torn between ripping each other's throat for not backing out and ripping Cullins to shreds together.

"Well, if they are going, then neither of us are backing out," Caledon noted resolutely before Maia gave a one-shouldered shrug with a lop-sided grin as if it was absurd to even consider that she would back out.

"Charm has already been assigned to lead the mission in the Oslo MPA. Each of you was chosen because you seemed the perfect fit to survive the radar in Novyslava without using your kevlar gloves. They won't permit you through the border if the inhibition control in your chips isn't activated." Cullins shrugged his chin over laced fingers, voice like ice. "You need to log in more hours in the combat room as much as possible, and you will be needing that."

"You are sending us there to chase down a person who might as well be dead, without our energy surges to defend ourselves?" Maia gritted through her teeth, fists clenching as the Chancellor's expression fell as though he was entertaining peasants who weren't worth his time.

"We have analysed the pattern. It's her." He sighed, resting a hand against his forehead. "It's Delanna Jericho."

Delanna Jericho was one of the founding members of the Anthromorphic Council, hailed at the time as one of the good ones who wanted a fair balance between the anthromorphs and humans, sympathising with the latter's fear more than any other member of the Council. She was one of the rarest anthromorphs, a stag anthromorph. She was known for her regal and elegant demeanor, isolating herself from the world after her only child disappeared from the face of the earth, for reasons that weren't clearly known despite several stories and hypothesises regarding her disappearance or her presumed death that wasn't confirmed by her only kin, her mother, till date.

Zella's lips twisted. "So, one of the founding members of the Council is a *criminal*, now?"

Cullins sighed, shaking his head and throwing his hands in front of him helplessly. "Apprehending her doesn't make her a criminal."

"Then why are we bringing her down here, assuming that she does exist," Maia said quickly before she could lose her resolve. It sounded so ridiculous, even to her half-asleep mind and even her awake mind. They barely had time to step into their dorms after getting back their stay in the Allyson's Manor before they had been summoned into his office. But it made no sense. It just didn't add up.

"You are not the Council," the Chancellor reminded her firmly as if they had rattled something loose in their brains, "So, fortunately, that's none of your concern."

"What happens if things escalate out of hand?" Caledon frowned, replaying the most possible scenario one last time, and he just kept coming to the same conclusion. These were humans who were the most violent and open about their outrage against the anthromorphs.

Cullins stared at him for a full minute before slowly looking disbelieving. "You have the upper hand; you have been trained in combat to prepare for this."

"How introspective. It's not like you are handing over the control of our RTFQ chips to fry our nerves off if they wish to test it out just for kicks." Castiel scoffed, his lack of expression unchanging, speaking up for the first time since the rest three of them had joined him in this room. "As if that place isn't already crawling with Anthromorph trafficking cage-rings run by humans."

"I am not known for my humor to be delighted by your sarcasm, Mr Sylvain." His deadpan expression turned into a mocking chide, merely raising an eyebrow as if he were questioning himself and asking himself why he was being tormented by nagging *kids*.

"Then you shouldn't be sending them into a walking death trap—"

"No one was forced. They still aren't." Cullins let go of a low laugh as if he didn't quite believe that they were still blabbering and robbing his time. "Leave. You have surpassed your time in being enlightened about the mission. Prepare accordingly."

***

It felt like a waking nightmare.

Like those dreams where everything was wrong and ominous and frightening even if there was nothing but green fields and bright sun.

Zella kept seeing flashes from the corner of her eyes, her paranoia lighting up like a lightning rod in the sand, all of her senses suddenly kicking into overdrive as if she was being hunted down right at that moment.

Zella glanced at the rough walls, waiting for a door to burst open to try and escape, glancing around like they might drop from the ceiling.

She had almost reached the end, a slightly brighter light coming from the room it was leading her to—

She heard a door open quickly behind her.

She stiffened, turning.

A hand suddenly grabbed Zella's hair too fucking tight, like they wanted to rip it out.

The figure before her was dressed in torn rags, but all she really saw was a thick leather mask drawn over their mouth, hiding everything but eyes that were sharper than their knife.

Zella almost screamed, her hands scrambling for fist that dragged her to the side, slamming her into the wall hard enough for the abrasive cement to tear through the palms of her hands that tried to catch her.

Real fear hit Zella for the first time, her voice dying even as she tried to scream.

Her face was pressed hard into the wall, the rough material scratching her cheek roughly as she tried to breathe around the terrified half-sobs sticking in her throat as she breathed too quickly, too loudly.

"You dare to be alive?" a sharp voice demanded dangerously, shoving Zella harder into the wall, making her forehead rub against the harsh surface that tore through her skin.

The figure raised their knife, pointing it at Zella as their other hand reached up, pulling the mask down. But it wasn't until she looked up at her own face staring back at her that Zella felt a different kind of fear.

Her eyes.

She couldn't recognise what she had become

Those were like that imposter's knife.

Cold, sharp, threatening.

Dangerous.

Mercilessly, they stared on.

"Shut it! You are nothing but an imposter," Zella growled lowly before flipping around, the imposter's back shoved against it, a hand latching her throat like a viper, choking her so harshly, she could barely open her eyes.

Viscous, suffocating fear clogged the imposter's senses as her head spun with each heaving breath her lungs struggled to take.

Her head smacked against the wall as Zella shoved her back harshly-

"Better to be an imposter rather than the monster that you are," they croaked from beneath her hand, crushing her throat.

Zella sucked in shaking breaths around the tears streaming down the imposter's face, hyperventilating and shaking so hard, she could barely stand.

Terror began to writhe its way into her heart. Zella started breathing faster, the longer their silence went unbroken, something building in her chest, dangerously cold. She stepped until her back hit the wall of the hallway, eyes flickering at who or rather what she had become.

"Zella! Come back!"

Zella jerked at the low sound of a familiar voice rumble next to her ear. Eyes wide, she turned to see Castiel holding her shoulders.

"You're here." The last part of her statement was supposed to come out rougher like a disbelieving sneer. It came out too quiet. Too genuine. Zella's nails dug into her palms.

Zella remembered that. She did not wish to remember what those monsters did to her, but she remembered every moment where her hand would nearly fly out to strike at Caledon when he came to check in on her, being responsible for her during her redemption period.

Every snap that made him stiffen at such a retaliation.

Every breakdown of her suddenly throwing objects from the desk in her dorm just to feel like she was still alive, that she was free to move, that she could feel things now.

That there wasn't just darkness, there were no chains, no cages.

But, Castiel was the first and truly the only one comfortable enough (or, perhaps, just desperate enough) to fight back Zella.

To grab her wrist before she could strike. To restrain her arms when she tried to throw the plastic swords with deadly accuracy. To practically pin her to the floor until his yelling broke through the static in Zella's mind that just told her to run and fight, but she didn't know what she was running from or fighting against.

"We need to talk about Novyslava—"

Zella was silent, even as her eyes begged to tell him something, but she settled for walking past him, not sparing even a glance back at him. "I'm fine. I need to go to the Combat room and clear my head if I have any chances of surviving that place."

For the first time, Castiel had seen anger that went straight to Zella's core, but even further than that, he had seen fear.

The same fear he was used to seeing hidden among anger and rage that covered it expertly. The fear when plans went awry and dangerous annoyance had her beating her fist against a wall.

Fear that was rarely shown but was tangible in the rage that fuelled her. The fear when one of them was injured during their missions and Zella's rage was loud enough to cut through the skin.

Castiel's nails broke through his skin as he shook his head sharply, steering firmly away.

He remembered his first days here. When Zella would go hours, searching for him, only to find him staring at a wall somewhere, unresponsive. Even when Zella would grab him and shake him, his eyes remained a million miles away.

Worse were the times when Castiel was staring straight at her but never saying a word, no matter how much Zella coaxed him, either calmly or with threats. Those days of apathy and calm made him seem like a corpse walking.

-

Zella touched his arm, quite possibly the gentlest touch the older version had ever bestowed on Castiel, just like the younger one from his memories, causing him to jerk away, ripping himself out of his own head.

"You were doing it again," she said, voice heavy and quiet. Not accusing, but he chose to view it as such.

He stared down at the log he was writing after their third assigned mission together, ink dripping from his pen and ruining the page he hadn't written on in probably minutes, lost in his head without a map.

"Take a break," Zella said, firm but coaxing, "You aren't getting any work done."

These were the times when Zella was the closest to gentle he would ever see. When Castiel had stopped the violent outbursts tearing through his head almost always after Cullins' tested the different controls of his RTFQ chip and was just lost. No longer angry and threatened, but lost with nothing to hold him down, wandering and wandering without any idea where he was trying to go, not knowing where exactly he was supposed to be.

Another firm touch to his arm to draw him back. He hadn't even realised he was wandering.

-

Those were worse. When Castiel stared at her, he acknowledged her but never responded.

Castiel hated Zella, then.

But afterwards, he was faced with the realisation of the debt he owed Zella each time he saw her face. Just how much of himself that Zella snapped into place over and over each time Castiel ripped himself apart.

Castiel felt like he was caught in a riptide. A tug of war, a hurricane, tugging him this way and that, demanding his attention at the past and present, the real and the fake, the do and the do not, his memories and his reality.

Zella liked to argue that Castiel had saved her, too, drawing her out of her mind and unlocking the parts of herself that the monsters had locked away.

Castiel saw it as nowhere close to the same thing.

Because while Zella had been desperate to make Castiel open himself back up, she had never had to pin down the person who was confusing his *sad excuse for feelings* more than any other person he had ever met. He never had to pin Zella to a bed for fear of what her addled mind may command her to do when Cullins played with the control of the RTFQ chip to check their pain tolerance.

And that was why Zella owed no debt. But Castiel owed one too large to ever be repaid.

Both reacted to their nightmares that occurred with a stronger frequency every time Cullins tested their tolerance with a different frequency setting on the chip. Castiel turned inward on himself, hiding inside a mind that tortured him. Zella was explosive. Dangerous. Emotional.

Everything she could never afford to be.

CHAPTER THIRTEEN

P art of their combat training involved practising blindfolded, merely hitting targeted holograms in the stimulation, with precision even when one of their senses was deprived and they relied on their remaining heightened senses. Zella merely tightened the blindfold over her eyes before hitting the first dagger at the hologram target located 12 feet away from her 2 o'clock, slicing it across the back. She then slid across the room to swiftly miss the blow of another target probably aimed with a 7-inch blade, slashing it horizontally from left to right. But she needed the 16-inch blade armed in the opposite corner of the combat room before pivoting with her knees bent it and slicing the armed target with a quick reverse flash, severing its Achilles tendon.

"You have always excelled in this part of our combat training."

"Have you lost it?!" She sounded incredulous, and her lips pulled down into a strange mixture between a snarl and a frown before taking off her blindfold to look back at Pearl and drawing her blade back that disappeared as Pearl shut down the controls of the stimulation set up near the entrance of the Combat room. "I could have hit you—"

"No, you wouldn't have." She smirked, knowing the other's control was far too good to let that happen even by accident. "Your feline side is wired to be sensitive to footsteps."

"Right as opposed to the other animal gene bound to my human gene," Zella replied flatly, straightening and unwrapping the ace wrap wound around her hands.

"It's nearly dormant, Zella—"

"You don't get to determine that." Zella's tone was resolute. Pearl turned to her, her shoulders sunk. Zella scoffed at the sight of her. *How dare you stand there and look hurt.*

"You have spent the last five years perfectly controlling it and keeping it dormant." The auburn-haired breedling raked a hand through her hair, like a withered scarecrow, a lump of straw into the soil. "Why embrace it now?"

"I have always embraced it. That's what controlling means. I have never kept it dormant; it only gets exposed whenever I am in my worst state." Her jaw clicked into place, and she took a step back as if she could barely stand wanting to be around Pearl. "You wanted to see whatever you wished to believe. Don't drag me into that."

Pearl looked at the anger tightening her face, and she felt her own panic start to settle in. Zella had never looked at her like *that*, where she found it a nuisance to even spare a reaction. Didn't make the usual jokes during their customary combat practices and offered her quick tips. "*Use more forearm on that jab.*" So, she did the only thing that could concur a reaction from her, knowing that the bianthromorph trusted their physical space to not slap away her attack.

And rather than acute horror at the thought, Pearl only found herself narrowing her eyes accusingly at Zella.

She took advantage of Zella not paying her any attention and whomped her in the stomach, and as Zella bent over gasping for air, she kneed her in the face sending her back to the mat, her nose gushing blood all over the smooth vinyl. "Why *him*?"

"Am I supposed to understand whatever the hell that means?" Zella grabbed Pearl's foot and pulled it forward. The shorter anthromorph landed on her back in a huff.

Pearl took another swing, but Zella ducked, grabbed her arm, spun up around her, and pinned her to the mat.

They had spared enough times in this very room to realise that Zella was merely holding her down as a warning and still not bothering to fight back, enraging the amethyst-eyed breedling even further.

Pearl felt an itch under her skin. One that never used to accompany one of them being injured.

The pull of the taller's brow, the tug on her lips, the darkening of her eyes with thought. It was only made more violently abrasive by the dark clothing that matched.

Everything was thrown off, now.

"You don't have to be like him. You had a choice, and you are throwing it all away for what——" She murmured thickly.

Zella was better than *him*, Pearl knew the *Puma-anthromorph* like the back of her hand, and she wasn't letting her be tarnished like that *bianthromorphic bastard*.

Zella's fist curled slowly at her side, a warning racing through her blood as Pearl frowned at her like she was begging Zella to let her understand her reasons.

It felt like a waking nightmare. Like those dreams where everything was wrong and ominous and frightening, even if there was nothing but green fields and bright sun. Zella kept seeing flashes from the corner of her eyes, her paranoia lighting up like a lightning rod in the sand, all of her senses suddenly kicking into overdrive as if she was being hunted down right that moment.

"I never asked for that damn choice." Zella's face turned unreadable, and that dangerous line in her jaw had returned. Pearl stared at her for a long moment as she turned over her mocking admission in her head.

"Well, you had a better chance of surviving your life with that *graced* choice." She whispered weakly, hands clenching desperately.

"I don't care about the delusion of that *wretched* choice," Zella snapped, "I just need the false identity on legal papers to survive the chaos in this damn place."

"What have you become?!" Pearl snapped back, fists clenching defensively at her sides. "Do you really want to go back being that *scum* we found in Samuels' Cage-Ring?"

"I was *always* that scum," she said roughly, that familiar discomfort in her soul.

"This is why Sylvain should be locked up! Or better yet, killed for the benefit of the rest of us!" Pearl hissed, her voice dying into a quiet murmur, stomach curdling at the reminder that that vile loose cannon wasn't locked up yet. *Why on earth did Cullins spare him?*

Several moments of paralysing terror gripped Zella as the possibility of him being killed.

Castiel was perhaps more genuine than most of them, hiding his emotions perfectly until the moment they peeked out. As grounded as the metallic bond of the most electropositive element yet to be discovered.

Pearl lunged forward and struck Zella in the gut, making her double over, then clasped her hands and chopped Zella on the back, sending her down to the floor.

She really needed to stop taunting Zella, but there was nothing else she could think to do, torn between rage and tenacity.

Rage seemed to be the only language Zella understood and tenacity because Zella only seemed to understand one language.

Zella didn't bother holding back. She grabbed Pearl and flipped her over her hip, slamming her to the ground and pinning her down to the mat. The panther-breedling tried to buck her off by trying to manoeuvre behind her, but Zella grabbed her in a loose chokehold and just held her there.

Pearl struggled, letting out a choked cry and flopping around like a fish out of water for a few moments before breaking free when the amber-eyed bianthromorph loosened her hold completely.

"Don't you *dare* speak about him," Zella declared, with an air of finality, that wasn't merely a warning. "Walk out before I do something that we would both regret."

She looked away, but the tension from Zella's shoulders forced her to stare back at her's. Pearl looked back at her, wild and desperate, appearing only moments from breaking apart at the seams. Part of Pearl wanted to slap her, to demand she get a hold of herself and finally reach a breaking point of what was *right* for her.

"I wanted you to be different than the monster you were wired to be. Trust you to have my back for the rest of my life—" Pearl fought desperately, her voice almost breaking.

"I have done that for the past five years, in a heartbeat, and none of that was because I hid away a dormant side of mine." Zella reminded her darkly.

"You don't get it, do you?!" She yelled, so sharp it rang in Zella's ears. "Out there, every mission we are thrown into, nobody would care if you bianthromorphs snap and kill me. I might be more privileged than the rest of you, but so is every single anthromorph created. That's how the CULT chose their experiments!"

"Then why on earth are you looking down upon bianthromorphs?!"

"My privilege doesn't hold any value because I am an anthromorph; all of that power and money only holds value in the human world, but it's not enough to overrule my genotype," Pearl said firmly. Zella's chest rose and fell quickly as she breathed angrily. "I care about my family. I care about saving my skin. That's my survival instinct. I am brave enough to actually draw the line, unlike my brother."

"That's the very thing that motivates every being to want to live."

"You were like my family." Her heart skipped beats, and she tilted her face up towards Zella's again, hoping that the taller still harboured feelings for her, hoping that she could use it to convince Zella what was best for her. But all that flashed across the shattered amber orbs was something unexplainably agonising. They no longer held any traces of fondness for her. All that was left was mere anger and agony mixing in a sickening yin and yang, after knowing that Pearl had known her true identity all along while trying to manipulate her that she had to be something else than the monster that the shorter cruxawn saw her be while embracing her bianthromorphic side. "We could have gotten closer, just a few more years if you had continued controlling your bianthromorphic side until one gene became permanently dormant—"

"Who are you kidding? You can't even accept me for who I really am." Zella scoffed, turning to Pearl with dark eyes that held a dangerous warning. "Don't insult the very meaning of a family to me."

And her silence only made Pearl feel like a kid throwing a fit, giving the silent treatment because she couldn't think of another way to hurt her.

"So, you are going to be like Sylvain?" Pearl said, eyes scrunching in a sarcastic smile. Zella's jaw tightened as Pearl looked ready to spit in disgust.

"I don't have the skin to fathom being like anyone else. This is who I have always been." She took a quick step forward, glaring heatedly. Pearl's gaze was calm once more and clashed with her poisonous glare that thrashed around like a sea monster, hell-bent on killing and destroying as much as possible. "And you can never be as brave as Caledon. Not like this."

"Maybe you just don't want to admit that your own father can't look at your face without guilt because your *bianthromorphic* identity reminds him why his wife's altered genes led to her death!" Pearl snarled bitterly, lifting her eyes to stare into the carnelian-darkness she could see her own reflection in, knowing that she had shattered through lines that she couldn't rebuild. "We both know that you blame yourself for that, and that's why you wanna be miserable because you don't know how else to live your life, any other way."

Zella's chest felt like it was being torn in two. Her wrath knew no mercy before she stretched the shorter's arm upwards behind her towards her head. Pearl let out a blood-screeching scream when she felt her shoulder pop out of its socket. "Hate for me for good, now. You are insignificant to me from this second onwards."

"You are a fool to throw away that choice. There is only one way; all of this ends with Sylvain and you killing each other."

"Great, don't bother showing up to my funeral," Zella bit out, voice stiff with the prickling pain of ice, before popping Pearl's shoulder back into her socket and storming out without paying any heed to the latter calling out her name. The Allyson twin just couldn't fathom her actions; *what had she done?*

The last thing Zella needed was to run into Castiel, whose eyes narrowed into the towel she was using to stop the bleeding from her nose while just leaning against the farthest corners of the walls outside the library, opposite the Combat Room, for it happened to be one of the rare blindspots in the entire facility.

He walked towards her, clutching her free hand like it might ease the ache it had failed to cure a million times over. His expression changed into something that she couldn't decide if it was shock or apprehension, and Castiel's breathing got that much thicker. His heart raced painfully as he tried to figure out what to do as Zella stared up at him, eyes a clear crystalline lake that let him see straight through to the bottom.

"What happened?" He whispered inaudibly, his voice pained, but he swallowed, taking a deep breath to calm himself. Every function in his body suddenly kicked into overdrive, everything sharpening and focusing like a camera finally finding its focal point. "*Who* did this to you?" He asked, heart aching when Zella's eyes snapped to stare at his icy hands that came up and wrapped around her wrists gently, not crushing, just touching. Like he didn't want Zella to let go. Castiel clung like Zella was the thing keeping him from drifting into his rage.

"It's just a mishap during combat practice." She lied, voice dull and lifeless like she was talking in her sleep as she stared. "I lost my balance and crashed against the wall accidentally."

But her breath stalled, and when Castiel's head looked over her shoulders sharply following Pearl walk away from the Combat Room, she stared up into Castiel's eyes that were almost closed with how they pinched with anguish. It was tentative, like waiting for something with bated breath. He always seemed on the edges of dormancy. Like the volcano that always threatened to erupt but was finally taking a break, never knowing when it would erupt again.

Rather than waiting for Castiel to willingly break (which could happen way faster than she could react), Zella took another slow step forward, holding his shoulders in a vice grip as he tried to break free from her hold, but he simply tracked the fading silhouette of the panther cruxawn with eyes that were icy and bloodshot.

"Great, I am going to ensure that I crush her bones *accidentally*." He snarled viciously.

"No. Don't." She warned, inclining her head towards Castiel's raw, broken expression. "I am responsible—"

"They're all the same, all of them," Castiel replied sharply. He was breathing heavily, shaking his head as he tried to break free from her hold. "Tell them that I knocked you out before getting to her so that they don't lock you—"

He broke off as Zella lost her balance and crashed against his chest like she was trying to fuse the two of them together and tightened her hold around his shoulders.

Castiel flinched, his body seizing for a moment.

Zella could only hear her own harsh breathing and Castiel's heartbeat through his funnel knit-wear (Mostly borrowed from Caledon's crazed rampage to buy every funnel knit-wear he could get his hands on during last fall and then deciding to never wear them for more than three weeks). The desperation in her chest died off with each beat of his heart against her ear, and soon Zella could breathe without feeling a stitch in her side.

This was Castiel, calm and coherent, choosing to quietly wrap his arms around her tightly and his face pressing to her neck harshly as if he was trying to mould with her before one of his hands slowly rose up to softy cradle the back of her head.

There was tense silence, and then Castiel's heavy head dropped to Zella's shoulder, his arm tightening the slightest bit around her.

His eyes closed, Zella remaining perfectly still as Castiel shook just the slightest bit, like he was trying to stay still, too.

Zella was warm.

It took a few minutes, but Castiel could feel the gentle pulse of body heat from her against his chest, began to notice the gentle rise and fall of her chest against his, the way her fingers flexed on his shirt.

She cleared her throat, feeling something swelling in her chest the longer Castiel rested against her.

She still held on, though.

And she felt the way his muscles slowly relaxed against her, his breathing turning slower and deeper.

"I don't care about that!" Zella pressed firmly, the words passing between them as though they were children with sweets trying not to be discovered. "I care about what they would do to you!"

"Are you starting to care for me as your *team-mate*, Rune?" He teased, trying to ease the weight of her words.

"No, it's not limited to that." She clarified firmly, leaving no chances for doubts that could be veiled by ambiguity. "I care because it's *you*."

Castiel felt himself breaking apart with Zella, like standing too close to a whirlpool and getting caught in the current. He felt the riptide grab him and pull him under. But he still held onto her, not wanting either of them to get separated in the chaos.

Not after they had struggled so much to latch onto each other. She felt like she had broken through the surface of a lake, taking a breath of air after drowning for a long time. He stared at her dumbly, his mind hazy and numb as he begged that he had not misheard.

"You shouldn't." Castiel was breathing around a rock lodged in his chest as his hand came up to rest against Zella's on her cheek. She flinched, a cold icicle pressing into her heart as her expression pinched.

"You don't get to decide that." It was like letting go of the one thing between you and falling off a cliff- why would you want to? It settled like physical pain in her chest as she clenched her eyes shut and breathed harshly against his chest. She pulled away from him immediately and simply stared, glaring heatedly, silent.

"I do if you end up interfering with my goals," Castiel said gently, lowering his eyes to watch as he grabbed Zella's hands once more, stubbornly. "Why did you accept his deal, despite knowing that I would take your place if you declined to go to Novyslava?"

"I don't know what you are talking about." Her sneer died before she jerked her hands away from his hold. Her glare faded the longer she stared at Castiel's quiet determination.

He chastised sharply. "Lies. You had agreed to Cullins' deal way before I did. That psychopath might be many things, but he isn't a liar."

She lifted her eyes and found Castiel entirely still, staring at her as if waiting for her to deliver a blow. "I took up his deal because this benefits me more than anyone else."

Nothing colourful, nothing desperate or poetic about it: a simple statement that held the weight of the obvious fact. Zella, however, felt as if she had been dunked in a stream in winter.

Castiel swallowed thickly. "What do you fight for?" he inquired carefully. "If not your team, then what? So, what are you fighting and risking your life for?"

He stared for another moment, and he waited for her to storm away. But she simply leaned harder against the wall, letting it take more of her weight.

"At first, I fought just to survive," she said lowly, never tipping away from the underlying anger in her voice, that roughness that seemed to be part of her. "But here, I found people like me, people willing to fight, even for a lost cause. People who were tired of dying. People who chose to live for each other."

Castiel's tongue tasted like bitter ash in his mouth as he stared at her.

"I fought to survive," she repeated firmly. "And then it changed—I changed," she amended. Something in her eyes went very, _very_ far away, as if staring into the past. "I did it for them," she murmured, voice deep in her chest. "I started fighting for them. For all of them. All the people who risked to have my back."

He couldn't help as the past five years of his life flashed across his mind, from the time he had escaped when the facility had tried to lock him up after shutting down Samuels' Cage-Ring in Zagreb. Survival-driven and half-dead, clinging together for a desperate chance to live another day, where death was as common as breathing. He still had the scars beneath his hair from where he would strike his head against the chains and cuffs, trying to get away from the torture inflicted on him, in case he failed to win the duel and cost the humans who had placed their bets on him, to win the fight against the other captured anthromorphs.

"I stopped caring about my own survival. I wanted to keep them alive," Zella went on, voice dropping into nearly a whisper, still so angry in its calm. Her arms crossed tightly over her chest, still a million miles away.

"I can't let anyone else be harmed because of my choices."

What fucking hells were they living in? What sort of system would create these sorts of people, gathered under flags against the threat of mutual extinction.

Zella's lips pressed together until they paled. "I am going to risk everything," She whispered. "Myself, the people around us, just to give them just another day to live." Her expression pinched lightly. "In the end, we are going to end up stronger the longer we force ourselves to survive."

She wasn't sure when the last time she took a breath was.

Castiel shrugged roughly. "Unlike you, I don't care for the greater good; maybe all I care for is putting an end to this, permanently," he agreed. "Maybe I don't want innocent lives to be caught in the crossfire." He shook his head. "But in the end, it all comes back to getting vengeance for personal satisfaction. I don't care if it would result in a perfect society or not. If anyone is designed to be the ultimate, selfish disappointment, then it's me."

Zella's heart clenched at the quiet tone. They had fought before. Even at their darkest moments, Zella had never seen Castiel look so cold and uncaring. As if everything around him was just an obstacle in his path to destroy.

Her lip curled slightly, distasteful but calm. "I don't fight for the greater good," She muttered, shaking her head. "There is no such thing as a perfect society. There is a stark difference between what's right and what's perfect. In search of perfection, this division has ended up becoming a pyramid of hierarchy."

"To them, a society of any community in this world consisting of different races, different humans and anthromorphs, different genders is not ideal because it's chosen by people, by their own choices, created by their own free will. They wanna strip that." He said, much quieter, his voice hoarse. His lips twitched darkly. "Like selling a little bit more of yourself to the devil, just for one day more, one day more, one day more—"

"It may not be ideal, but it's right." She murmured, "The differences don't create disputes in the society; it gives us a cause to unite the humane core of a society." Zella's jaw twitched.

It only made the ache in his chest larger as her arms tightened across her chest, a sort of longing in his eyes as they glazed over the past once more. His expression was set in bitter stone.

His fingers curled in the pocket of the denim jacket he wore like it was battle armour.

"You call that selfish?" he asked lowly, a challenge and accusation. "You've never had a selfish thought in your life, even if you try to act like you do."

She whispered, expression heavy and dull. "But you'd be even stupider than I to try and convince me that you are selfish."

"I am, and much more."

"Then, what would you call it?" Zella whispered.

"Desperation," Castiel hissed. "Obsession and selfishness."

"No," Zella said quietly, shaking her head heavily. "No, that's not what you described to me. You just want to be happy, don't you?"

"Happiness does not exist in this world," Castiel scoffed. Happiness. It was secondary to everything else. Second to safety and secrecy and assurances that they wouldn't be discovered- "And even if it did, it dies faster than people do."

"If you were selfish, then you wouldn't risk everything to ensure that no more lives are spared by going to Novyslava, all by yourself," Zella's lips pressed together, something flashing in his eyes. "If you were selfish, you wouldn't care about the lives lost as long as you get your goal."

He lifted firm, quiet eyes. "You and I both know that place is like Samuels' Cage-Ring magnified by ten folds."

She scoffed at his pointless revelation. "I don't need a comparison analysis to know that." But the sensation that raced through her veins was something alarmingly close as Castiel simply stating that as fact.

"Exactly, so why are you risking your life?!" He demanded swiftly, looking up sharply, making her stiffen. He lifted a slow eyebrow. "If you know about the deal he offered me, then he must have offered you the same."

Zella's fist curled slowly at her side, a warning racing through her blood as he frowned at her like he was begging her to let him understand. So, she came up with the most convincing dismissive response that would shut down his stupidity of going through this alone. "Novyslava fast-tracks my gateway to Asia. I don't have to bother with anything else to reach my goal."

"If those words held any truth, then you wouldn't have been this troubled by Caledon and Maia's choice to come along with us." He corrected flatly, straightening.

"You are delusional." She gritted through her teeth darkly.

"You would want them to go along with you and start a better life in a free land." He snarled frantically. "Heck! You would have persuaded Charm to come along too."

"If you know how much this means to me, then why do you have a problem?" She asked quickly, eyes stinging. She let go of a broken breath, pressing the heels of her palms to her eyes.

Castiel felt bile burn his throat, "Because that's not a ticket to Siam, but rather a death wish!" He breathed in horror. "We will be stuck there for months until we find a person who might as well be hiding elsewhere."

"The chance of getting out of here might never come again." She retorted, just rambling in hopes to have something make a difference. "People only get desperate when they are stripped of choices from getting what they desire."

"Then why don't you get my desperation to not let you go to that damned hell?" He asked brokenly, something in his expression breaking down. Just a quiet, torn whisper as if he were begging to know the answer to a legitimate question. "Stop risking your life by going there."

"Why are you risking yours?"

In the past five years, their entire existence had been coated in a thick layer of prejudice and injustice and hatred.

They both always tried to hide the pain, to save the other the guilt of leaving or being trapped, but it never worked. Perhaps, they knew each other too well.

"You heard him. Unlike you, I don't have a choice," Castiel said, voice heavy as he stared at Zella, who slowly glanced up with red eyes.

"You are in your redemption period. Your progress report still depends on my words. I can ensure that only I go to Novyslava with Caledon and Maia." She paled dangerously, expression wrinkling in distaste. No matter how much she tried to get Cullins to change his mind after using this excuse. The Chancellor stayed adamant, insisting that among everyone, no one knew how to live under the radar, as well as Castiel. But the blonde-bianthromorph didn't have to know that as long as he didn't go behind her back to convince Cullins to let him go to Novyslava all by himself until he agreed.

"Zella, please—" Carefully, he rested a light hand at Zella's side as if she were the only thing between him and falling into an abyss. Not even holding, simply resting his hand there. He couldn't bring himself to do more. He stared at her, pleading and earnest, for as much as he hated the idea of them going to Novyslava, he couldn't handle the idea of three of them going alone or, worse, Zella going all by herself. They were *good* people, and that was scarce in this world.

Something was infinitely more disturbing about how dull Zella's skin looked. How low her head hung. How emotionless and flat her voice came out, neither crying nor angry.

This empty looking Zella.

"Don't talk to me if you want me to change my decision about going to Novyslava." She flung his hand away, looking through him, signalling that she meant that with finality.

CHAPTER FOURTEEN

"You need to clean up your filth and get out of our country as soon as possible." The enlarged mammoth-like human snarled darkly as he scanned their suitcases, sharp eyes slashing back and forth between his team and the others. "Go back and rot in your prison as soon as you find the old hag."

Unlike the usual missions, they couldn't fly into Novyslava but instead enter the capital of Siberia via foot. If it weren't obvious, the auras of Zella, Castiel and Maia reached a new level of sour darkness in this hostile environment.

"These freaky breeds need to be wiped off from the face of the planet instead of playing soldiers and spreading more destruction." The second guard scanning them wasn't as gracious with his words as the first. He spat at them venomously in Siberian as soon as he recognised Castiel as a bianthromorph, reaching for the switch in a split second. Unbeknownst to him, both Zella and Maia were fluent in Siberian, having spent extra hours translating different papers in their Evolution and Biotechnology Advanced classes compared to the rest.

The human guards, seething with sheer disgust and hatred at the border, were nearly milliseconds from pressing the switches that controlled the chips of the anthromorphs and would have done so if it weren't for Caledon. His negotiating demeanour that put up with them even when they immediately pressed the switches controlling the RTFQ chips of the bianthromorphs as the latter pretended to wince in pain to not give away their act and land the anthromorphs in danger. Even if he feared to admit it out loud, the Cheetah-anthromorph nearly snapped back at the guards until Zella locked her gaze with his to signal that they had to tolerate through this and get to the safe-house arranged by the Anthromorphic Council instead of blowing things over. *Don't. Sylvain and I can take this.*

"Maybe someone needs to teach them how to dread their worthless lives until they kill themselves." The sneering words of the last guard in Siberian were like a relief which merely meant they could rush to their safe-house as soon as possible. "Make them realise the actual lives they have cost."

***

Zella only had one way to describe the safe-house set up by the facility; it was messy.

Well, compared to her own sterile dorm, it was messy. She could see both the living area and kitchen from the doorway, separated only by a little bar with barstools sitting at it.

The kitchen counters and table were covered in notebooks and papers, pens and notepads, what looked like flash drives and external hard drives, and some electronic squares covered in a dozen buttons that Zella hadn't taken a clear look at. Sitting in the only clear spot of the table were two different screens to monitor their perimeter and make up for the lack of their security system, which wouldn't be activated until they were actively attacked by the Siberians breaking their own protocols.

In the living area, there were take-out containers (only a few), but the coffee table was stacked with folded clothes and movies. The couch had sheets of lined paper covering it carefully, none of them overlapping. The ground had various trash cans overflowing with crumpled papers sitting in random locations in corners or the middle of the walkway. It was just a smokescreen tactic they used in the safe-houses set up by the facility, leaving traces of the previous teams who might have resided in this safe house.

The informant who had provided the intel for the previous teams sent to apprehend Delanna Jericho was supposed to meet them tomorrow. When he discovered one of the Allyson twins would be part of the new team, he refused to meet up with them unless they paid him a hefty price. It was pretty evident, this informant wasn't big on diplomacy, but rather as Maia phrased, '*He just needed to meet people who displayed the most brutal tendencies to scare it of him,*' clearly hinting at anyone except Caledon to be the best fit to meet up with the informant.

Caledon snorted, expression serious as he glanced at Zella to defend him as Maia laughed heartily. "I infiltrated just fine. Apparently, you just need someone who knows whom to flirt with, like an idiot."

Castiel couldn't help but steal glances at Zella, who seemed to feign no recollection over Caledon's story.

They hadn't spoken since that night outside the library, besides finding a temporary code to shut down all controls besides the tracker in the RTFQ chips of Caledon and Maia. 'BRAINWAVES' was only the key-phrase for gaining control over the chips of bianthromorphs which meant that neither could she concur a vial for the couple nor could he re-engineer the controls of the chips until they managed to get their hands on the control switches of the anthromorphs. So, that only meant Castiel would have to build a fake model for the switches until they were replaced by the real ones.

Castiel knew that he had no right to undermine her decision. Even if he wanted to clarify that, he just couldn't bring himself to do so, not with Zella acting apathetically unapologetic like the first time they had encountered each other in Zagreb. He couldn't blame anyone else but himself for that. After all, he had said the very words that he knew could push her away from him, hoping that she would back away from joining him and going to Novyslava.

Castiel was a fool. A ridiculous, idiotic fool. How could he act like this? He knew that she could take care of herself and cause greater havoc on them even without her energy surges, but they still outnumbered her to the point that they could easily hurt her.

But the moment he saw her raw, broken expression as her face paled, looking at him with eyes that screamed to hope that he would just say that he was merely joking and she had just misheard him. He felt as though he was agonisingly pierced with an endless array of ice shards, slowly but permanently.

Maia made a face of faux realisation. "Sleeping our way in," she gasped exaggeratedly before playfully jabbing Castiel to break his train of thoughts. "Why didn't we think of it before?"

"Who's sleeping around?" He asked, utterly confused by the direction of this conversation.

"We'll infiltrate Jericho's supposed security system by sleeping our way in," Maia teased as if they had just made a major breakthrough, knowing the icy apatite-coloured eyes had been zoning in and out of the conversation. "It's perfect! Almost poetically amusing!"

"I fail to see the find the amusement in this plan?" Castiel asked, expression pulled down in disapproval as Caledon and Maia burst out in laughter.

The window exploded.

Living area, window, gunshots, bullets.

Castiel lunged forward the short distance, grabbing Zella and twisting until they both hit the ground, Castiel laying on top of her for a moment, as bullet after bullet sounded against the drywall of the safe-house.

The first bullet shattered the window, spraying Maia with tiny fragments of glass. She froze as two more bullets whizzed past her, they could hear the air buzzing as Caledon, and Zella swiftly reached for each of her hands to pull down vigorously before the next three projectiles flew past her ear.

Too close!

"Guns!" Zella hissed, hitting Castiel's chest to get him to move and get on her feet.

"We're on the second floor of the safe-house," Maia snapped, staring at Zella, only inches from her face. "That's gotta be a sniper—We can't take that out without our energy surges unless they've also got some firearms hidden in this safe-house."

Caledon shook his head. The lightbulb above them shattered, and Zella dropped over Castiel, once again, covering his face with the length of her arms as tiny shards of glass rained down. She was just hoping it didn't get into his eyes-

As Caledon tackled her to the floor, he started to notice that one of the bullets had pierced her right arm, spraying blood on both Zella's and his shirts as Maia looked to the side, gasping and grimacing in pain. Caledon covered Maia with his body until the bullets stopped flying. Castiel threw a towel towards Zella before giving her a slight nod.

She wasted no time in getting his message and tied it around Maia's arm, applying some pressure and then making her hold the towel.

"We're compromised," Castiel said into Zella's shoulder, not willing to move and drop the glass on her back onto the boy under her. "Do you have any sort of survival—"

He knew that the amber-eyed bianthromorph definitely saw this coming, especially when—

The gunshots stopped.

Zella waited, holding her breath for only a moment before she swallowed. "Close your eyes, don't get glass in them," she ordered.

Adrenaline coursed familiarly as Castiel could finally stop thinking and worrying and just act on instinct and muscle memory.

He squeezed them shut tightly and moved quickly, rolling off and grateful that he was still wearing thicker clothing, unlike the others. The rest, on the other hand, were in sweats and bare feet. "Did you get your *Emergency Go-Bag*?" Castiel demanded, shifting carefully to avoid the tiny shards and keep himself below their line of sight.

"Bedroom, closet," Zella said, eyeing the glass around her. "Toss me the blanket on the couch."

He crawled along the ground, reaching up without lifting his head.

Several more gunshots, and he dropped to the ground, looking to Zella, who simply laid still, arm protecting her face as drywall rained from the walls.

The far wall of the kitchen was honeycombed with bullet holes. Castiel rolled up the blanket. "Catch," he said, tossing it. Zella caught it, carefully unrolling it, eyes focused and hands careful.

"Go," she said. "We'll be ready by the time you get out. Stay away from the window in the spare bedroom!" she said sharply, laying the blanket beside Caledon and Maia to roll over onto to avoid the glass.

Castiel nodded, crawling along the floor of the hallway.

He still heard bullets outside.

The room was dark, and Castiel didn't even bother glancing around, heading straight for the closet. Apparently, the humans were too focused on the living room because nothing shattered the window as Castiel found a little black duffle bag stuffed full, grabbing it and slinging it over his shoulder. He snatched a pair of Caledon's anthromorphic-prowess enhancing sneakers.

Back in the living area, the rest three of them sat with their backs against the side of the kitchen cabinets, out of sight and breathing a little hard as Zella picked a piece of glass from her arm that was bleeding slightly. Two more shards of glasses covered with blood sat by her side. His eyes were like ice again.

"Here," Castiel said, tossing the shoes towards Caledon, waiting in the curve of the hallway. The Jabatus-cruxawn began pulling on the shoes as the bullets stopped. Castiel slid beside Zella, grabbing the spare kitchen towel, tying it to her bleeding arm.

"*Merde!*" Maia gritted her teeth, staring at the rest of them with a cocked eyebrow. "Are we not supposed to pursue them?" She climbed up on the window sill and jumped out the window, her bare feet thumping down into the pile of glass that riddled the ground; the pain shot through her like a static shock, giving her a burst of adrenalin.

More bullets. One of them caught dangerously close to the cabinets Castiel leaned against. He flinched away, covering his face from the splintering wood. "Let's get out of here, then," he said, shifting forward. "I absolutely hate being a sitting duck."

Duffle bag in hand, the rest of them crawled to the door, avoiding the glass, and reached the front door. "Hold," Zella whispered, and Castiel waited, hand posed and ready on the doorknob. "We're going to have to sprint the whole way after getting Maia," She warned them. The boys nodded once.

The gunshots ceased. "Go," she hissed.

Castiel tore the door open.

Zella didn't glance back as they ran along the hallway, turning to the stairs at breakneck speeds, their legs matching pace, her eyes hard.

When she glanced back at Castiel, his eyes echoed the same. They burst out into the sunlight. He was glancing back at her, eyes trailing over Zella as if checking for injury.

"Lead the way," Caledon told her. "We'll watch your back. I will get the Maia. You two find the amateurs practically overdosing and shooting his snipper like a *damned* psychopath." He nodded for Zella to run in front.

Multiple snipers and only two people without any firearms to watch her six. And yet, Zella didn't hesitate, running in front and only sparing the boys a cursory glance before turning her eyes away and concentrating on watching her front.

People around her were screaming, running or dropping to the ground. Mothers grabbed their kids, and people walked alone, looking around to see what they should do.

A large catering truck blocked her view across the street for a moment, and when it moved, as the little green man appeared that signalled Zella to cross. She saw a man sitting at a cafe table across the street, sunglasses in place and a cap pulled down over what looked like military cropped hair, barely unfazed by the blatant shoot-out.

The man stared back at her. It was the last guard they had encountered in the Border-Control, and he was the one orchestrating the shoot-out.

Another gunshot rang out.

The shot came from behind her. Zella ran in that direction to the nearest shelter, a small abandoned alleyway, barely wide enough for her to fit, much less Castiel's wider frame. She risked a glance back to look at Castiel swiftly following her before Caledon rushed to find Maia.

The sunglasses man was gone.

Another gunshot and pieces of brick from their alleyway shattered and splintered in front of her. She jerked away, drawing the largest shard of glass (that she had picked from the mess in the safe-house) and throwing it accurately at the shooter shooting their alley. The glass pierced through the shooter's hand as he dropped his gun, clutching his wounded hand and yelling in pain.

"Engage or run?" Castiel asked

That second shot came from in front of where Castiel had been. Across the street, he had been prepared to cross, to reach over towards Caledon and Maia.

Multiple shooters?

So where the heck did she—

Another gunshot, but there was no chipping of brick or sound of a ricochet. Another shot, more distant, clearly not anywhere near their hiding spot. Were they just toying with them now?

Castiel quickly shook her shoulders and pointed his head towards the car coasting through the alley in front of them, squealing around the pavement as a burly masked man hung out the window, shooting towards their feet. They rushed straight towards the vehicle when Maia started shooting some foxglove-laced needle-shaped tranquillisers that they had been experimenting with using the foxgloves growing inside their Biotechnology labs and hitting both occupants.

The driver fell against the wheel, and the car glided off into the ravine at the other end of the lot. Caledon sped over towards the car and ripped the door off its hinges, seizing the driver, but he was knocked unconscious, a perfectly placed pint-sized hole at the base of his neck.

He looked over at the passenger seat, only to find it empty, as the guard who had arranged this shoot-out was already crawling away from the car. Before he could move an inch further, Maia yanked him towards her, placing her foot on the back of the man, leaving a bloody footprint from the cuts on the soles of her feet as she pushed down harder to stop him from squirming to free himself.

"P-please, don't—" the man begged, "I-I have a family, I was just s-scared. This was just supposed to injure you. I had no intention to kill you. These can't permanently harm—"

By this time, Maia was seething too much to think clearly, "You should have thought of them before acting on your fear." She said, merely trying to threaten the person making him believe his worse fears, before knocking him down, unconscious.

"Maybe, that's why you might understand my actions, for I need to protect my team."

Zella looked over to see Maia, with her hand aimed to pierce another needle into the driver's neck, clutching it tighter in her fist.

"Another dose might kill him," Zella warned, panting silently, advising Maia to not do what she had been controlling herself from doing. Knowing the full effect of the dose that they had concurred in the lab, together.

"I am aware of that. It's just a small dose of the antidote."

Zella merely nodded in affirmation to clear her mind from her own negative thoughts as Castiel looked through the pockets of the guards for his tracker and immediately hid it before Caledon or Maia could catch any glances of it.

"Good, head back and clean the cuts of your feet. I will join in a while after looking through the compartments of this car, clean our fingerprints, and park this car around the alley after dragging him back to the seat." Castiel said, pointing towards the man near her feet.

"I will help you with the clean-up. We need to destroy the security cameras." Zella offered as Caledon swung

Maia's free arm over his shoulders to steady her balance, taking her back to the safe-house.

"Just shoot the cameras with the hacking chips. I will rewire the footage as soon as we head back." He nodded, waiting for the couple to disappear back into the safe-house before destroying the tracker that could alert his team to send more back-up. The humans had broken the protocol, so even if they decided to send any back-up, the security system of the safe-house would already have been activated by the Anthromorphic Council.

"I have the actual switches controlling the RTFQ chips of Maia and Caledon," Zella said quietly, barely in a whisper, not knowing that he knew that already, assuming that he must have been searching for the control switches. "I picked the guard's pocket earlier during the check-through."

"I know," he nodded, not looking back. "I needed to destroy the tracker he had set up to disrupt the security system of the safe-house. He bit the bait." Castiel smirked back at her, knowing that she had purposely irked the guard in Siberian to watch if he would end up acting on it without any fear of breaking the protocols.

"You knew?" She asked, stunned anyone else had her quiet jabs besides the last guard.

"This is the only way we could get to activate the security systems of the safe-house," he shrugged his shoulders, wordlessly knowing her motives, picking up on her micro-expressions since the beginning. "They would have ended up ambushing us, later and without our energy surges, we are sitting dock. It's better to get it activated as soon as possible."

"It came with a price." She gnashed her teeth as guilt reflected in her amber irises, that averted away from his gaze. He wanted to say more, hand reaching out to her shoulder in an attempt to assure that Maia's injury wasn't on her but rather the humans who chose to harm them while they were unarmed. He held his hand back as she swallowed, fists clenching in anger of not predicting that they might be ambushed right away. *If she had warned them, this wouldn't have occurred.*

"We handled it well. We are alive. It's a win." he said firmly, slowly, picking each word and syllable carefully. "You couldn't have predicted this accurately. This is not on you." It was a mere preamble of biting back what he really wanted to say to her; *'Would you stop running around your own head and listen to what I am actually saying, rather than blaming yourself?'*

***

Inside the living room, Caledon was taking out the bullet from Maia's arm when Zella dashed back in, bending down towards Maia, as Caledon clutched her hand in panic, "I removed the bullet, but her condition is still worsening." Maia was struggling to keep her consciousness as the skin around her arm was already beginning to grey. "The bullet must have been laced with succinylcholine. It's fatal for any breedling, especially Canis breedlings."

"There has to be an antidote to this in my suitcase," Zella said before rushing to get the antidote and pushing the abandoned towel back on the wound and looking down at Maia as her veins began to blacken.

"They sent us completely unprepared. Cullins pretty much sent us to a slaughterhouse—" Caledon snapped, burying his head in his hands and shaking like a leaf feeling no comfort in Zella's sad attempt of an assurance grin as she broke down in cold sweat, still trying to process the pace of the events before things took a worse turn.

Castiel broke the tense atmosphere by muttering as Zella carefully injected the needle into Maia's neck, dispersing the antidote into her. "The security systems are activated now. Nothing can penetrate through the protective dome, and neither can anyone enter in the perimeter besides the four of us." He didn't bother fixing the system controlling the cameras in the safe-house, partially relieved that the humans had damaged it for good.

Caledon tightened his grip around Maia's hand as she woke up with a jolt, taking a long-pronounced breath.

She glared at the ceiling, jolting in a mixture of pain and relief before watching Zella falling back in relief and dropping the empty syringe from her hands. She seemed lost in thought for a while before looking over at Zella's face, portraying the same expression of being scared, just like the rest of them.

"*Zut!*" Maia gulped down some air, out of breath, when Caledon pulled her into a bear hug, sighing in relief.

"I need to clean the wound." Zella sighed with relief, masking her small smile with a stoic expression as she poured alcohol over another swab, as she extended her other hand to a frantic Caledon to hand her the bandage before trying to leave to give the couple some space.

Caledon caught her hand immediately with a warning glance, "You are not going anywhere until your wound is dressed up."

MAIA EMERSON

CHAPTER FIFTEEN

astiel and Zella wordlessly cleaned up the place after the anthromorphs had resorted to their rooms, letting the absolute shock of the events tire them to sleep.

Zella didn't fall asleep that night, except for an hour or so at about five in the morning. She remained sitting in the dim kitchen light until the natural sun began to pour through the kitchen window.

She felt worse than usual, and she felt numb and exhausted and just so shitty. But she had no way to remedy any of the things making her feel this way, so she simply stood, chugged the entirety of the water bottle she had left untouched, and slipped on her shoes as she went about searching the kitchen for coffee.

She sat at the empty seat at the kitchen table, nursing a hot cup (it was a weak off-brand, but Zella wasn't in a position to be choosy) and plotted out the concentrations for the next batch of her antidotes on the spare notepad placed on the kitchen counter. She didn't mull over anything, too tired to really contemplate her position, and simply stared off. It was nice, in a way. Almost like she could pretend her life wasn't falling to shit, for the past eight years ever since her mother was diagnosed with Stone-Man syndrome.

She expected the rest of them to sleep until noon, but it was only 8:01 when she heard the door down the hall open, bare feet tupp-ing down the hall, and Zella didn't look to see Castiel enter.

Castiel stared at Zella.

The air between them was palpable and thick, like the tense air outside. It wasn't tense, though, just viscous with knowledge and unspoken words.

The past weeks were off-balanced and strained. The fear of being caught by Cullins never ceased, and it mattered not that they were still reeling from a confession that clearly revealed their desires of protecting each other despite their hesitation, holding back. For the world had never been kind about what they wished to protect, snatching it away from them at every opportunity.

Their lives continued on, catching up on their classes, missions, preparing for their stay in Novyslava, relaxing during their combat practices by expelling their pent-up frustration, creating new gears they might never use until they get rid of Cullins' watch.

Preparing contingency plans to meet up with the slimy informant that revealed the exact location of Delanna Jericho and ensuring that no one would ever be able to hack their security systems if the Siberian humans decided to attack them when they were unarmed. They worked tirelessly to prepare everything that could increase their survival chances in Novyslava, especially without their energy surges. Cullins seemed pleased that the RTFQ chips of the missing seven teams merely informed them that they were still alive.

Cullins branded them as fruitless, emotional, and weak for not completing their missions.

The whole thing was enraging and unbelievable. Not weak, Logan Sian, their Forensic Chemistry's Professor, had tried to dilute the Chancellor's words quietly during the entire facility's outrage against the latter's colourful choice of words; *Weak'**er,**' but not weak.*

Zella looked uncomfortable the entire time, using willpower from every fibre of her body to hold herself back from ripping Cullins' throat. Every time she was prompted to open her mouth to inform Cullins about their preparations for Novyslava, she seemed almost vaguely ill.

Nothing, in all their lives, would ever prepare them for what was about to occur within just the following months.

"Are you alright?" Castiel had asked, looking oddly concerned.

"Yeah," Zella responded quietly. "I have faced worse wounds just merely sparring during Combat Practices."

Castiel looked almost looked tormented by hearing those words.

She knew that Castiel was different now.

Everyone was shifted from the time they had gotten back from the Allysons' Manor, but she could tell from Castiel's eyes that something had taken him and shaped him. Remoulded.

She didn't know what or how exactly, but she knew that the way they stared at each other now was not the way they stared before, five months ago.

And there was only one thing that had changed between those two times.

They were still ruthless to themselves. Aware of their own faults so deeply, it was all they could see at times. Even when they ended up caring for people, they couldn't help but hide it in every possible way instead of bearing the pain of watching it get ripped away from them all over again.

But one thing Castiel was, was perceptive. And he knew that the Zella Rune had never made any attempts of ever-changing people around her, being unapologetically protective of all around her, even when the shorter Allyson twin held malice against her true identity.

But he was facing the distinct feeling that Zella was someone who needed mere days to shift anyone who was as constant and reliable as an old oak tree.

He felt something curling in his gut in discomfort as he stared at her bandaged arm. He had seen worse, faced much worse, but this was something neither of them could afford. He was used to strangling weakness with his bare hands before allowing it to root in him and letting it be exploited against him all over again. Still, he wasn't used to someone being violently stubborn of staying by his side whenever he let it sprout or smiling victoriously whenever she got a chance to stomp over those who exploited him, along with him.

He just wasn't used to it. He hated that he couldn't find an ulterior motive in her actions.

Zella had not been avoiding him; she found that it was cowardly and childish, unbefitting of herself.

But she wanted to fool herself into believing that she had been caught up in their assignments, that Cullins never chose to spare them from, and she had not had time for anyone unless she was working with them.

Conveniently, any work that Zella may need Castiel for could be handled by another. In fact, that's how it had always been five months ago, and Maia was willing to act as her go-between, unknowingly.

But, if there was one thing that Zella knew, it was that every action you made caught up with you eventually. Cowardice would catch up with you; immaturity would catch up with you.

Castiel merely caught up faster than most.

And so, Zella stared at Castiel.

Castiel gazed back, the picture of calm and collected, dark eyes and composed countenance as he watched Zella freeze at the kitchen counter, her pen stalling on the page and creating a sizeable inky dot.

Zella was not afraid.

But she had no desire to hold a conversation at the moment. She lowered her eyes back to her paper as she heard Castiel close the door of his room slowly.

"What?" she asked crisply, ignoring the inky dot and writing around it. "I'm trying to catch up on making the next batch of the antidotes we would need—"

It was nothing uncommon for Zella to request. Castiel knew that she liked being lost in her space whenever she worked, and he was always careful to keep their meetings quick when they were pressed for time.

However, several seconds passed, and Castiel had said nothing.

Zella refused to look up, pausing her writing to check one of her calculations before filling in another space.

"You have been avoiding me."

Zella expected the question, and her pen did not pause, her voice even and guilt-free. "I have not been," she replied smoothly. "Maia got shot and poisoned, and I need to ensure that we have antidotes to recover if that does happen again. I cannot stop and chat until everything has been taken care of."

"You have been avoiding me."

Castiel was always too quiet, and Zella didn't even hear him before a hand was plucking the pen from her grip and placing it back in its holder.

Zella glared at him in annoyance, Castiel's own dark gaze meeting her without flinching as her fists curled on the counter.

"I'm not in the mood for games, Castiel," she warned. "I have to finish—"

"You and I both know that you must have gone through them at least a hundred times. You are punishing yourself, exactly like you do whenever anyone gets injured during the assigned missions." Castiel accused calmly.

"I am not fragile. I know what we were forced to face out there for the past five years."

The statement was absolutely meant to cut, but Zella never meant to say it.

But she did. And she watched as Castiel's jaw clenched, something hardening in his eyes as his lips thinned.

"I'm sorry," Castiel confessed quietly. "I shouldn't have doubted your decisions. I promised to have your back, and that shouldn't leave a *gateway* for any doubts."

Zella could not deal with snapping at Castiel for the ridiculous attempts of sacrificing himself to prevent the others from going to Novyslava. She had tried doing the same. It's like both Caledon and Maia decided to heighten their stubbornness to deflect either of the bianthromorphs' attempts to reconsider their choice.

And Zella also knew that he knew that.

And she knew that they were resorting to their jerk-selves.

But, like the dutiful, ever-faithful wolf bianthromorph that he was, he took the blame without question.

Zella's jaw clenched as she snatched the pen back. "You aren't going to come up with an excuse to justify your actions?"

There was a long silence. He didn't move. She could still see him standing near the counter.

"No, it doesn't change the fact I shouldn't have done that."

"You're placing too much importance on yourself," Zella said darkly, writing too hard, smearing the words. "I don't have time for this back and forth game, Castiel, unless you have something actually relevant to say—"

"Do you really care for me?"

Zella's pen tip snapped off against the page, spilling black ink across it.

She froze like prey caught in a lion's jaw, hoping that if it didn't move, it might be released.

And then numbness turned to icy fear coursing through her blood as ink ran off her page.

"Those," Castiel continued on quietly, voice low and deep, "were the last words you told me before I decided to be an imbecile and decide things on my own."

Zella's heart had never beat so fast. Never.

"Why do you *care?*" she asked as if each word was not another shovel of dirt on Castiel's grave, "You said it yourself; you can't afford to care. So, it doesn't matter that I do. I will deal with it on my own."

She still stared at her page, watching the thick paper soak up the blackness. Her hand still held her useless pen.

"I am not even sure if I know how to."

Zella slowly set the pen down. Her hands did not shake, surprisingly.

"I know that I am not unsure, but I can never tell. I don't want to drag you into that."

Zella thought of several paths of escape at once: Knock him down for a few hours. Say that she resonated with his words. Shove him to get into her room, lock it, and never emerge again.

Because what else could she do?

She could not lose Castiel. Not like this.

Castiel was level headed. He was capable of being the voice of reason. He would never allow something like this to happen. He would set her straight after such a violent display of uncontrollable emotion.

"Zella."

She hated that she was starting to get used to the familiarity of picking up on his tones. Familiar. The kind of familiar that only *you* could draw comfort from.

But now, Zella felt only dread. She still did not look up, her fists curling as her tongue tasted of ash.

"If you were expecting me to guide you through an assurance, especially with this," Zella pressed darkly. "Then, you have come to the wrong person."

She saw him move around the counter until he stood a few feet from Zella's chair.

Castiel would not be a coward. He would not whimper and try and bury his mistakes like a dog hiding its last bone.

If Castiel were removed and scorned, he would not do so while cowering before Zella. "I am not going to drown you with my fears. I would never."

Her head snapped up as he stood from the chair, expression twisting until she and Castiel stood inches apart, dark eyes meeting like a black hole swallowing stars.

"Then, what do you expect?" she demanded, practically spitting the words with venom dripping like acid from them. "What exactly do you plan to do, Castiel?" she spat, almost a taunt.

He waited for Zella to lose it at the intrusion to shove him away, to break his arm, to suddenly find the nearest kitchen knife to finish the job with. Zella just stiffened into the stone beneath his touch as Castiel held her firmly, giving her room to draw away.

Zella had never been the person that would not spend her last moments afraid. She was the type of person that would spend her mistake staring Castiel down. Until, at last, she would never feel fear.

Castiel suddenly fisted a hand in the sides of Zella's turtleneck, and her hands both leapt up to grab at it as he yanked her forward, Zella's hand dropping to strike at him.

Castiel's lips claimed Zella's before she had even managed to form a fist. Her fist fell flat as she pressed a hand against his chest and clenched her eyes shut.

It felt like placing the cramped muscles of overworked limbs under running lukewarm water; tauntingly slow for each moment, it brought relief as Castiel tugged her closer, both of their lips moving almost frantically in a dance that Zella had never thought them capable of.

Zella suddenly shoved him back, hard enough that Castiel stumbled, catching himself on the wall with a startled look.

Zella glared at him, her entire heart cursing Castiel's existence as she brought one hand up to nurse her injured arm with anger, breathing far too heavily.

"I will not be a stand-in," Zella spat venomously, everything in her yelling for her to wring Castiel's neck as betrayal set in her skin.

"What the hell are you talking about?" Castiel demanded, looking confused and affronted at the violent rejection, fists clenching at his sides.

"I will not stand here and act as your mannequin," She snapped dangerously, eyes narrowing like knife blades. "I don't care what sort of feelings you are conflicted with, but you leave me out of your experimentation, or I'll break every bone in your body."

Zella felt humiliation, the likes of which she never had.

And betrayal she had never known before.

Uncertainty was something ugly and dangerous that she refused to feel. It was fickle and stupid.

She did not feel uncertain over what she felt for Castiel and to show him how vast, how endless it grew, until Castiel could do nothing but stare out into a sea of blind faith, like the oceans that once covered everything on earth. To be able to physically show him how easy it was for him to sit by the shore of it, merely dipping his feet in and letting it cool him at ease. Or for him to leap into it with nothing but his eyes wide open, how easy it was to take a single step and suddenly be drowning in it. How quickly it filled his lungs and eyes, choking him with fresh air and cleared blindness. How she wished she could show that to him.

But she felt humiliation and betrayal at the thought of being used as some sort of experimentation in the hopes of reaching a conclusion. Because Castiel had never looked at her like he looked at him now.

She felt the urge to punch him. She didn't want her feelings to be toyed with all over again, just like Pearl had.

Castiel still stared as if Zella had struck him across the face.

"What—Did you listen to nothing I said?" he demanded sharply. "Even if you don't trust me yet, you know that I would never reduce you to that—"

"That says nothing for your own feelings!" Zella snapped, fists clenching. "And I don't care—"

"Do you really think I would ever imagine doing that to you?"

"How should I know?" Zella hissed viciously. "I don't read minds—"

"My anger isn't because of the fact that you would doubt me, especially after everything we have been through," Castiel said darkly, something in his eyes tightening. His voice suddenly dropped, "But do you truly believe I would attempt to use you like that?"

Zella felt a knife to her heart. She couldn't speak. Didn't trust herself to.

He continued to stare, his jaw tightening as if his own sensation of betrayal had gripped him. And despite her anger, Zella felt the urge to soothe it, to ensure that trust was still held.

But how could she, when her own trust was bruised?

"I may be messed up in my head in more ways than I can even think to count, but I am not a liar," Castiel said, something dripping from his voice. "Do you truly think that I would ever attempt to use you like that? Treat you as some sort of experiment—"

"What else am I supposed to think?" Zella snapped, angry and defensive and once more out of control. "When you're suddenly attempting to kiss me out of the blue without any sort of preamble—"

Her stomach clenched the longer Castiel stared as if she had violently missed the point.

His lips thinned like they did when he was holding himself back from snapping.

"I gave you a preamble," he said, infuriatingly calm.

"For what, exactly?" Zella demanded, seconds away from storming out of the room, just to save her from further humiliation while speaking about this.

Castiel's lips thinned further, his body stiffening. "I fear that my feelings for you might attract even more unwanted chaos towards you, but I don't *fear* the feelings I hold for you," he said slowly as if she were going deaf, "And it's ridiculous for you to think so."

And even though Zella had often been amazed by Castiel's disgustingly calm demeanour, she had forgotten how infuriating it was to be on the receiving end of the real thing.

Castiel's dark eyes stared silently at Zella for several moments. She almost cut him off. Her nails dug into her bruised palms.

"Would you stop looking at me like that?" Castiel suddenly demanded, eyes narrowing dangerously.

She stiffened.

"I am not about to add to whatever fear is swimming in your eyes," he snapped, "Would you stop running around your own head and listen to what I am actually saying, rather than whatever twisted version you're creating?"

Zella, instinctively, almost snapped back.

This had almost become their tête-à-tête, to stand against the parts of each other that couldn't stop fighting, even among their own team.

A hand caught her arm, and Zella raised her other hand in defence, ready to strike.

Castiel stood beside her, one hand wrapped around Zella's forearm, his eyes no longer sharp and dangerous.

They were stern and dark. That same look that Zella had gotten so used to seeing as she was torn out of her own head, the eyes of the person she had almost come to care for, the one who understood her darkness and somehow managed only to see her fierceness through it.

And she stared at Castiel now and felt fear in her heart. Fear unassociated with death.

This fear was firmly rooted in the fact that he was staring at her with familiar eyes, and Zella felt her entire body screaming for her to run because those were the eyes that brought out her confession.

Terrifying, exhilarating, never knowing if you were lost or right where you were supposed to be, outrunning something, running to something, her blood racing and her mind flying, her feet nearly coming out from under her.

Those eyes, the ones that dragged her up and held her there firmly, they were the ones that challenged hers to find solace in them if she dared to doubt herself.

But all he could do was catch Zella's face in his hands, knowing that Zella knew of that ocean's existence because he had built a castle of blind faith on its shores.

A massive, formidable structure with walls unable to be breached and doors that were always open, asking him to come in and to rest his head.

Neither of them could be fooled into thinking they were mistaken. "Stop running around your head," he murmured darkly, "Listen to me."

Really, Zella hadn't even known there were dots to connect, and so that simple statement, given so lightly and without bitterness, was possibly the most jarring reality check she had ever experienced. She stared at Castiel and tried to take on an expression of annoyance. Like all, this was just an inconvenience.

Castiel's grip was not removed as he stared at her sternly.

"Your presence keeps me grounded," he said darkly. "Even when I began to understand you all over again, your motivations, your reasons… How startlingly different and familiar it is to the person I had known when we were ten."

Zella wanted to tear herself away.

Instead, she simply clenched her jaw. "We have no use for daydreams, Castiel," she said, cruel, despite her own thoughts on the subject.

Once again, she felt guilt.

"They were not daydreams. Merely realisations. I understand that there's no way to undo what's been done," Castiel assured her. "The winner writes the history of the storyboard. I will unapologetically ensure that I stay beside you while you write yours."

"Why?" She asked quietly. Every single moment of suffering was nothing more than a moment where Zella had failed.

Society always had a desperate desire to define everything and confine its limits because if someone didn't fit those confinements, their chapters are pretty much doomed in existence.

Castiel was quiet for a moment. He lifted a calm eyebrow that was coloured with sarcasm. "I already gave you my answer."

"I still don't know what the hell that was," she sighed with frustration.

"I told you what it was."

"Stop it," she muttered, trying to be sharp but merely coming out desperate. "Stop the games, Castiel. I am too tired for this. I have too much running around— Stop playing with me." She tried to hiss weakly.

Zella turned away, putting the pen back in the holder and walking swiftly around the other edge of the counter, away from Castiel.

A hand caught her arm again, and Zella didn't snap. She merely turned and glared, feeling the weight of her feelings reflected in his eyes as Castiel stared at her.

Also, perhaps a bit desperate.

She wanted to pull away again.

"I was not being purposefully obtuse," Castiel promised, voice quiet and level. "I thought I was making myself clear."

"Half-truths and phrases are not clear, Castiel," she muttered, the fingers around her arm practically burning.

"I see that now; that was unfair," he went on quickly, never losing that stupid calm from his voice as if he were not slowly dismantling everything. His grip loosened until.

Until it was almost gentle.

"You've never had the freedom to say what you truly feel for the past five years."

Castiel froze.

He couldn't run away from his misery and fears. It was bound to chase him until he was cornered to conquer it, and the toll that was inflected couldn't be understood by anyone else except for Castiel himself. All that sympathy and pity just can't comprehend that journey, and that was alright for only he needed to know the chapters of his battles and stumbles.

Because now, now his voice was taking on a tone that Zella had never heard since the last time they had seen each other in Salvador.

When even being firm was useless, and Castiel nearly resorted to begging. It was, quite possibly, the closest thing to gentle Zella had heard.

But this gentle was familiar. Not pillow-soft like neither of them could ever recognise. Not like the gentle sunshine and breezes that they had felt in Salvador.

It was familiar like the heat waves that flew through the air, uncomfortably warm but almost gentle when compared to the fire itself that stung and burned.

Not something gentle, but something gentler.

And it was familiar.

"Maybe, neither of us have… In the past five years," Zella amended. "But you, of all of us, have carried your feelings so secretly, even you couldn't see them."

"My point is that," Castiel murmured, "I care for you. These events did not suddenly unearth feelings we were unaware of. It's ridiculous to believe we were so ignorant. I feel the same exact thing that I have always felt for you since the very moment we met. Trust, faith, a desire to stay by your side, to help you, to keep you safe."

She watched as his fingertips skated over her forearms, tracing the worst of her scars with a feather's touch, gnashing his teeth, visibly upset by their existence. Castiel's hand slid from her forearm to her wrist, wrapped loosely.

His icy eyes bore into her without a hint of anger or sharpness within them. It felt like being paralysed, forced to sit and listen to her every fear laid out before her.

Castiel's grip on her wrist tightened past the stage of gentle to tangible, not restraining, simply holding. He paused for only a moment, eyes searching Zella's face.

"We may have fear," he said firmly. "At least, I do. But I won't let it rule over this." His gut filled with ice, "I care for you."

Castiel took a step forward, and with their minimal distance, it practically had them standing toe to toe. His free hand lifted, drifting towards Zella's face.

At that, Zella didn't flinch away, despite adrenaline suddenly surging at the realisation of what was happening, how they were standing, what it must look like.

Castiel's hand merely hovered, eye contact never breaking. In his concentration not to shake, he had laid his hand against the side of Zella's neck, cradling it with long, calloused fingers. He murmured, deep and low. "Even if we risk ourselves; Will you still stay by my side?"

Zella still didn't move, but she felt what felt like tremors in her body. Against all laws of nature and experience. Zella did not shove him away. She did not embrace him back. But she did not push them further away.

Their hearts were bruised, to say the least. Delicate and safely hidden away from everything for fear of what might happen to them.

Family.

Trust.

"I am not going to let us risk ourselves," Zella breathed, her lungs locking up as if knowing that she was about to take a plunge.

Castiel's expression didn't shift, as if careful not to sway one way or another. He trusted Zella to tether his mind down, to pull him back from the brink of self-destruction he had been caught in.

And it almost made him want to laugh bitterly because could anything they do ever be worse than those days?

Trusting her was becoming instinctual like second nature.

Castiel was closer, warm breath fanning Zella's face as her entire body stood still, every cell holding its breath. Her fingertips pressed into his shoulder tightly, making the other open his eyes.

"We need to tell them," she replied crisply, tilting her head towards Caledon and Maia's rooms.

"About what?" he asked quietly, conversationally, genuinely.

"The RTFQ chips, Cullins, everything."

"I don't know about Emerson, but the Allysons pretty much provide half of the funds that run all the facilities in the ECA," Castiel found himself whispering as if he had suddenly been seized by doubt. But it wasn't spoken in fear. "You think he is just going to work against Cullins?" he demanded lowly, glaring.

She saw the way his jaw clenched and his eyes darkened, and she felt something between them slot into place.

She sighed and stared at him for a long moment, looking exhausted after everything that occurred within the span of a day. She ran a hand down her face and straightened. "Out there, we are a team." Zella's stare narrowed. "If we fight as separate entities, then we are going to end up dead or worse captured for the rest of our lives."

"What if it ends up being the very reason that creates the division?" he asked, voice just the tiniest bit thick with emotions. "What they wouldn't know can't cause them any confusion."

"We will be living in a closed space for over two months; what do you think is going to happen when they figure it out themselves?" Zella confessed, eyes slightly wide as they stared at Castiel's apatite-coloured ones that gazed at her resolutely. "Betrayal always causes vicious damage that can't be salvaged."

"What if telling them causes them to pick a side that betrays our ultimate goals? They are not like you," he commented, almost obtusely. His eyes remained solely on hers, waiting.

"I trust them as much as I trust you," she murmured, purposefully quiet to avoid the risk of her voice breaking.

"If you think this is a good idea, then I will back it up," he nodded once and glanced away again, running his thumb along his jaw.

"You are backing down so easily? Why?" Zella narrowed her eyes, expression hardening. "This isn't like you."

"I am not backing down. All I am saying is that I trust your choice." Castiel corrected softly, and she bit back a reply that she would never allow it.

Castiel stared, and he simply saw Zella.

Zella, as she had always been: weathered and battered, but still standing. Still as strong and resolute as a marble structure amid an earthquake. Zella was mesmerising in every way unrelated to her looks.

He cared for her more than he could possibly ever bring himself to admit. Beyond trust, there was something in his chest that reacted as Zella's eyes bored into his.

As Castiel realised what step they had just taken. He could not lose her. To anyone. Not even himself.

"You trust me, now?" she whispered against his skin.

"Rune, I don't understand the concept of trust when it comes to people. The only family I ever knew, my own father, a person whom I trusted the most for over 14 years, threw me out without batting an eye just because of my genotype," he breathed, barely audible. It was an almost dangerous statement. Reserved for only their most trusted ears. "I have been chewed up for the past 5 years, barely scraping by to survive for something I can't control. But I do understand why trust is mandatory in a team—"

"I have your back." She assured, eyelids twitching as they remained shut. The answer to that, regardless of what it referred to, was inherent.

Castiel swallowed thickly, the air pressing against him like a physical weight. "I know. All I can guarantee you is that I've got yours," he swore.

Loneliness and trust are always intertwined. Once you lose trust, the heart inches towards self-inflicted loneliness because the choices no longer matter, but one compatible trust is enough to drive away that loneliness. People never choose loneliness as a preference, but they start submerging themselves in it when betrayal and abandonment suffocate them. And every choice seems like one with an expiry date.

It was an answer from both of them. More than that, it was a promise.

Zella saw it coming, and she closed her eyes, clenching them so tightly, when Castiel's lips claimed hers again, she was bracing for it but was no more prepared than the first time.

The hand around her wrist tightened as the hand by her neck crept back, threading through the hairs cascading over the base of her neck and pulling her closer.

Castiel's lips were chapped from the dry air, and the kiss was anything but slow.

Their minds had never once considered each other in this fashion. There was no meeting or failure of expectations. There were no expectations or preconceived notions.

There was just Castiel, as he had always been.

If there was ever a moment where Castiel felt the minuscule urge to simply let go, it was with Zella. And only with Zella did he feel as if four titanium walls were shielding him, allowing him the safety of shedding his weights.

He still did not. It would be too foolish. But even the knowledge that he could, that there was someone with whom he could unload those burdens, should he choose, was enough to make it seem as if he had already laid them down.

When Castiel parted, both of them breathing heavily, their dark eyes met. His mouth opened, perhaps to speak, but Zella suddenly grabbed him by the back of his neck, crashing their lips together, more active this time.

Rather than recoiling in surprise, Castiel pulled her closer, surprising Zella like he had with the embrace when he first arrived at the facility. She had never been held like this.

The kiss was not frantic and uncoordinated, but it was fast and deep, both of them too aware of their lives to try for something slower.

Zella had never thought about kissing Castiel, not even in her throes of realising that she felt something more;

Not more. Different.

But kissing him was startlingly similar to everything else Zella ever did with Castiel.

Grounding, guarding, a pillar to lean on, an inherent knowledge that there was something there to catch her should she stumble.

Zella kissed him like she had held him during those nights of his terrors. Something familiar, despite the newness of the action.

She hadn't realised that they had moved until the back of her legs hit the edge of the kitchen island, both of them parting with their breath stolen and the study suddenly seeming warmer and smaller than before.

Zella's slender fingers cupped his cheek, barely an inch between them.

"Football?" She teased him to lighten the weight of his words of not being familiar with teams as a bianthromorph and quietly asked him about his time as a human after she had headed back to her home in California. He looked up, blinking, and she caught his eye with an impish grin, playful and bright for the first time since he had met her in Zagreb. Castiel let out a truly earnest laugh, shaking his head as his lips twitched. Perhaps it did feel freeing to have someone who knew about his past as a human, despite the danger that it brought.

It was a startlingly desperate promise. Similar to the first one they made when they built their first hesitant truce. It was not just a promise to guard their hearts. It was a promise to guard everything. Everything around and between them.

Castiel swallowed, his lips stinging from the kiss, staring at Zella in a light he had never used before.

"Under-16 Nationals." He said with a soft chuckle as she beamed back at him.

They were promises they had made before. Those had not changed.

They simply covered an extra area. One they had always protected but left unspoken. It wasn't unspoken anymore.

"Really?" She smirked, tilting her head and scrunching her nose, trying to tease him further as the back of his neck flushed.

"Ice Hockey? Really?" He asked, pushing his tongue against the inside of his cheeks, raising his eyebrow.

"H-How do you know?"

Castiel suddenly picked Zella up by the hips, sitting her on the edge of the island without caring for the utensils that were pushed aside. "Caledon talks. Are you even surprised at this point?"

Zella caught his arm with a sharp, warning look. "Do not get cocky," she warned at the manhandling, even as her grip remained on him, refusing to let go.

Castiel, for one of the few times in his life, ignored the statement, kissing her again, stepping between Zella's legs and tugging her close.

Close proximity was one thing they had never had, never outside of physically restraining each other. Perhaps, they might have sat nearby when they had sleepless nights too scared to fall asleep, but nothing like this.

Never had Castiel's hands ever pulled her closer, not out of concern, but out of desire. And never had Zella felt the urge to hold onto him without insanity at her heels.

Everything was so familiar but completely different.

And she trusted him enough, implicitly, without thought and without fear, that when he pressed forward, forcing Zella's head to tilt back, her lips parting as Zella's tongue ran alongside his.

"I don't wish to give you a reason to slit my throat by trying to rationalise my excuses." Even when his words held an amusing lilt to his tone, they both knew that he meant it, especially with how close Zella actually came to doing that during their combat practices while logging in more hours to prepare for Novyslava and would have succeeded in doing so, if they weren't practising with plastic swords.

And when breathing became an issue, and Zella pulled away, both of them breathing too heavy into each other's mouths, she rested their foreheads together, neither of them shying away. "Perhaps, you are starting to know me well."

Castiel's hand was careful against her cheek.

It felt like being vulnerable. Because he knew that she could see everything in his eyes.

Everything.

But Castiel's eyes fell closed, and his fists in Zella's clothing tightened as he released a quiet breath. Something turned almost desperate. "I hope to."

Trust was always an asset. It was—

It was a fantasy. It was a statement for that other world, with safety and no risk of death and loss. It was a best-case scenario that they would never be afforded. That held nothing but the truth. Raw, tested, worn-out truth. Maybe they had been trusting each other from the moment they met. Implicitly and without fail.

If they crossed the line, they had drawn. Could Zella trust Castiel to protect her, given the greater risk? Could he trust her to protect their delicate, battered hearts from the strain they were putting on them?

The two of them stood in some sort of limbo.

Neither pushing nor pulling. Neither fearful nor content. It was as if a boulder was shoved off a cliff, and they were quietly waiting for the moment it hit the ground.

Chapter Sixteen

"These are smoking," Caledon said, as he slightly jumped in between his steps, admiring his new anthromorphic-characteristic-enhancing friction-proof shoes.

"I just added a few tweaks to it according to your genetic makeup that Zella shared with me," Castiel said, voice tight with awkwardness, absent-mindedly looking out for their informant, actively looking through the sea of people passing by, trying to find the person who fit the descriptions. "I think we are closing in on him." He said, fixing the cap over his head.

"You do know that cap won't do any good in hiding your long hair, right?" Caledon chastised, blatantly raising his eyebrow, with a lopsided grin as he adjusted his cap. Castiel merely ignored him when he couldn't disagree with the breedling's words before he spotted the man who fit the descriptions of their informant.

"Why is he going into a book store?" Caledon asked, peeking over the blonde's shoulders as they hid behind the edge of the wall, which led to the turning of the next alley where the bookstore the informant was entering into was located.

"Careful, there is more than what meets the eye. He could have his back-up hiding in plain sight." Castiel said, trying to sound as possible, knowing that his tense expressions only made Caledon jumpier and hyper-sensitive to the slightest sounds, especially after last night's events. Novyslava was just an abyss of nightmares enveloping them. *He was just used to being comfortable with the quiet and understanding aura he had with Zella.*

"Why don't you try viewing it in infrared mode? We can at least know how many spineless asses we need to kick if they decide to ambush us." Caledon said, looking around a little frantically.

"Way ahead of you. I have already covered that."

"Then, it looks like we are the only non-humans within the range of fifty miles beside him," Caledon said, looking through his own lenses in infrared mode, as the blonde glared at his feet skidding against the ground and hoped they wouldn't draw any unnecessary attention. "Why the heck are we hiding? It's two against one; we can take him down, get the information from him and just get the job done."

It didn't sit well with Castiel that the informant was alone, but why was he here all alone? They watched him from their spot, just lazing through the glass panes of the tiny book store, when he anxiously tugged the top of his hood to hide as he tried to look for someone anxiously. It seemed like he was being paranoid of something waiting to pounce on him behind his back or his sides. It seemed more like he was running away from something.

"He is running away from something," Castiel said, making a clear conclusion on his actions.

"That's good news for us, right? I mean, as long as he doesn't spring an attack on us in fear or just run away."

"Not necessarily. Whatever he is running away from can't be good for us." Castiel said, quietly signalling for Caledon to reconsider his desire of confronting the informant right away. He wasn't used to watching the Jabatus cruxawn be on edge, but unlike him, Caledon just wasn't unpredictable attacks while being at ease. Unlike Caledon, he was never at ease. "Whoever is tracking him might end up gathering unnecessary attention towards us."

"Take off your jacket," Caledon said, as Castiel looked back at him if he was suddenly feeling hungry and was losing his mind due to the hunger. "I am fast. I can place the tracker on him without being noticed in case he decides to flee. But I can't do that without your blonde hair giving us away, especially with that ridiculous cap which is doing a pathetic job of hiding your long hair." He rolled his eyes before taking off his jacket swiftly before handing it over to Caledon and replacing it with the anthromorph's hoodie immediately as Caledon pulled Castiel's jacket over his head. "So, switch your jacket with my hoodie and try to get him more jittery than he already is."

"Fine, try to be as discreet as possible," Castiel said, with a clipped tone. This was the last time he was dragging the hematite-grey eyed breedling along to any situation that demands the slightest notion of discretion and blending in.

"Aye, aye captain," he said, before throwing a wink as they both walked into the open-cafe beside the bookstore to keep a closer eye on the informant before approaching when the crowd thinned out after Castiel stopped glaring at him for his playful gesture.

"Wow, he is really agitated," Caledon whispered stiffly, leaning to his right to get a better look at the informant, who was pulling down his hoodie and tapping his feet impatiently as he frantically surveyed his surroundings after they took their seats at a table for two.

A woman walked out, carrying two drink carriers. A man in a dark suit left while talking on the phone. A pair of teenagers entered, chatting obnoxiously. A redhead walked out, a sweet looking caramel drink in hand.

Castiel kept glancing around to find a target who could be gullible enough to cause the distraction they needed until he found a pair of eyes staring at him.

Found it.

"Cullins' carelessness for this mission is beginning to get on my nerves. It's like a direct mockery to the wealth and connections Pearl and I will be inheriting," Caledon said, with a slight snarl evident in his tone.

"Is there any field your parents aren't doing business with?" Castiel asked, trying to change the subject away from Cullins, knowing he might voice out his not-so-colourful remarks on the Chancellor in front of the wrong person. *This wasn't Zella.* No matter how much he tried to wrap his head around accepting that, the Allysons could possibly have connections with every major business sector in existence. It still caught him off-guard.

"Food." He replied with a grave tone, genuinely sulking for a second. It's ironic. How Caledon's parents didn't deal with any business involved with food, considering how much he loved food more than anything else.

As soon as the same pair caught him looking back right at them, they looked away immediately as if they were a deer caught in headlights, as their cheeks turned red. The owner of the pair of brown eyes was most definitely a human roughly in their early or mid-twenties with severely curly blonde hair highlighted light green at a few sections, tied in a loose ponytail, as she fiddled with the ends of the apron over her outfit. "Are you even listening to me?" The Jabatus-cruxawn whispered loudly as Castiel took another look at the informant to check if he was still there in the bookstore behind his menu-card, before looking for the curly-haired waitress.

"May I take your orders?" said a voice above Castiel's head as he looked up to stare at the same waitress he was looking for. He just hoped he could use her flustered state to make her clumsy enough to cause a noticeable distraction.

Castiel gave her a small practised smile out of courtesy as his eyes locked with hers, noticing her cheeks turning warmer. *This might just work.*

"Yeah, I will take a matcha latte with half condensed milk and half almond milk," Caledon said politely, legs crossing leisurely, as she immediately jolted down his order in her notepad, throwing him a quick smile out of courtesy before quickly sparring him a glance and immediately shifting her gaze to the ground and her cheeks tinged a slight pink.

"And you?"

"Anything you would recommend," Castiel said in a monotone.

"I am not sure if our tastes would match," she said, smiling widely, looking back at me for a second. "I don't wish to disappoint a customer due to my poor services."

"So far, I doubt that could happen." The blonde bianthromorph said, offering a small smile politely before she nodded back in acknowledgement.

"Okay, would you like some key-lime pie with it? It goes great along with the drink." she said, the glee in her tone unmistakable "It will be on the house!" she said, a little bit excited when he hesitated for a second to agree with her recommendation.

"Alright, I will trust you on that." He nodded before she walked with a slight bounce to her steps.

"It's not going to work without the hair on display." Caledon snickered, trying to bite back his laughter, pretending to be suddenly interested in the menu card, as he openly smirked at it. Castiel stared, jaw tight as he tried to figure out the best course of action.

"Will you shut up and just get ready to do your job so that I can drop the act?" He said, snarling at Caledon to dismiss the notion, not bothering to hide the ice in his voice at all as he glared.

"Come on, it's just some meaningless flirting, plus it can't be that bad. I mean, you have to admit she is cute," He shrugged, raising his eyebrow. "You must be used to this attention, even if people pretend to be stuck up in their orthodox asses."

"I am seriously regretting my decision of agreeing to bring you along with me." Castiel snapped under his breath, lips curling in disgust.

"Yeah, but even you can't deny that I am the fittest for this task. So, suck it up, Sylvain." The auburn-haired breedling laughed, slapping the table. "Tell me, are you admitting that you wouldn't have spared her a glance if you weren't looking for an excuse to create a distraction?" he asked, making no attempts to slide that teasing grin off his face. He knew that all canine anthromorphs were demisexuals. Castiel was a bianthromorph whose human gene was bound to the genes of both a wolf and a coyote, heightening his demisexuality even more than canine anthromorphs, to know that the answer to his question was a stark 'No'. However, he still wished to amuse the atmosphere around them.

Even if the bianthromorph had confirmed it himself when Charm had asked him flatly after one of their assigned missions in the Rome MPA, the auburn-haired breedling still needed a distraction from letting his mind rethink last night's events. It wasn't like he was unaware or immune to the hatred against breedlings, but they were never attacked as a target when they weren't in direct contact with humans.

Castiel sighed heavily, knowing extremely well, Caledon wouldn't drop it unless he answered him properly.

"No, I wouldn't have."

"Why? Not your type?"

"No, I don't have time for that," Castiel said, gritting his teeth and looking over at the bookstore to check the informant's location once again.

"That would sound more convincing if you didn't have a simpering look whenever Zella walks away." Caledon got all the answer he needed when Castiel glanced away, not correctly responding to being called out so blatantly. He felt the tips of his ears heating up, and it didn't go unnoticed despite trying his best to avoid Caledon's shocked look and gasping as if taken aback. "You have come a long way from biting remarks to openly declaring your feelings in gibberish. I mean; You. I'm never going to let this go even when your golden locks lose all their shine." His voice held an unwavering teasing lilt to it.

According to Scott, it was barely twenty minutes before his fifth combat practice with Castiel. The two of them were sitting in silence as the senior turned the knife over and over in his hands, leg bouncing agitatedly before Castiel warned without even glancing at him, voice flat. "Bounce your leg again, and I'll cut it off,"

"Shut Up." Castiel sneered, hoping that Caledon would drop this. "You truly have a knocked-up definition of *discretion*."

All these circles. All these talks. All these emotions.

Caledon was quiet, hands folded tightly. "I don't like leaving emotions so tangled," he admitted.

"I never asked you to touch mine!" Castiel spat.

"Oh, I never need to be asked," Caledon assured him as if that should be obvious. "I'm so nosy; my friends can't stand it sometimes. But I think emotions are like muscles."

Castiel actually rolled his eyes, but Caledon didn't even seem to notice. That apathy to his annoyance was familiar. And uncomfortable.

"You have to work them properly to know how to use them," he explained gently. "And when they're overworked, they hurt. And when they're never worked, they're atrophied. And when they get all tangled up in each other… it's like a knot in your shoulder. It hurts to work it out, it hurts to massage it away and straighten it out, but you have to. It's only healthy to—"

"Why should I care about your poetics?" Castiel snapped. "They affect me none."

Caledon closed his mouth for only a moment as if silently scolding the Bianthromorph for interrupting. "I have always liked the minor psychology classes offered by the facility," he said as an aside. "My point is that I grew up, and to this day, I'm surrounded by people with emotions that are overworked and underworked and tangled beyond recognition, and I wanted to help that."

"I don't want my emotions untangled," he hissed. "You stupid—"

"No one does," Caledon assured him. "But I've gotten some pretty tough skin against the people who yell at me for prying."

"So, in short, you're annoying," Castiel declared in affirmation, glaring at him.

"Most definitely." He said, having no intentions of ever letting this go.

Castiel's fists clenched. Caledon was suddenly infuriatingly calm. As if he thought he was in complete control of the situation. The bianthromorph couldn't see the situation clear enough to know how much control either of them really had.

"I don't know why I actually agreed to tolerate your loud, talkative ass that can't comprehend the meaning of keeping a *quiet profile*." Castiel groaned in defeat as his grin grew impossibly wider.

"Here you go," the waitress said, arriving with their orders before Caledon could come up with another clever remark. "This might seem out of line, but I just wanted to say that you have stunning eyes." She added, after placing their orders at their table

"No, it's quite alright. Thank you... I really like your hair." Castiel said lightly, not fazing his words to chop the awkward air around them and make it look he was not saying it just out of courtesy.

"Really?"

"Absolutely, the green streaks really bring out the colour of your eyes." He offered calculative, not paying explicit attention to her hair or her eyes, as he studied her actions to look for any signs of clumsiness.

Caledon chuckled at his clipped tone going unnoticed as he mouthed, *'You are lucky, your hair saves your analytical tone, at least put some effort in your poor attempt of flirting back,'* using the Menu Card as a shield to prevent her from reading his lips.

"Thank you, I actually had a hard time deciding whether I should go for this look or not." She explained, her careless grin fading slightly before righting itself as she straightened.

The conversation had gone too long. Castiel straightened. "Well, I am glad that you did. It suits you." He said, giving a polite smile, glaring at Caledon to shut up, as the hematite-grey eyed cruxawn hid his face behind the menu card to stifle his laughter when she looked away for a fleet of a second smiling at her feet.

"Are you here on a trip? How long will you be staying here?" she asked, recognising that his looks certainly didn't scream Siberian.

As she stepped closer, he quickly rolled the stone under his feet towards hers, making her lose her balance, immediately grabbing their table cloth for support. The table cloth just worsened her balance as it flung in the air along with their cups and plates. Castiel quickly glanced back at Caledon, giving him a signal to follow the informant actively after checking at the informant frantically rushing towards a deserted alleyway after hearing their commotion.

The food and drinks fell on the unfortunate bald man sitting on the table beside them while the waitress fell flat on the ground with the table cloth over her head.

Castiel quickly rushed to her side as if he wasn't expecting this to happen and severely slipped out of his hands, crawling under the table cloth to ask, "Are you alright?" when the bald man started screaming in a fury. He helped her to back on her feet, as her cheeks turned red, resembling crimson flames when the bald man continued yelling about suing the entire cafe.

"This is so embarrassing." The waitress mumbled, biting her lower lip from crying as her fellow colleagues rushed towards the bald man to apologise repeatedly to help him calm down and prevent the other customers from leaving due to the disturbance.

"No, it's not your fault. It was just an accident." Castiel said, feeling extremely sorry for using her like this as he pressed her shoulders lightly to console her before bending down to pick the broken pieces of the cups and plates.

"N-no, it's okay. I-I will pick them up." She said, rushing to help him with trembling hands. He held her hands immediately in an attempt to stop her as he slightly forced her to sit on his seat.

"Careful, you will hurt yourself." He warned this was the least he could do for intentionally dragging her into this mess.

Caledon appeared back at his spot, standing behind his chair as if he hadn't moved an inch in the first place, throwing Castiel a 'He-isn't-spilling-I-need-your-help' look. He turned to the bald man still yelling about his priceless shirt and whispered lightly in his ear. Caledon quietly slipped the promised amount into the man's hands as he stopped creating a commotion immediately.

He turned towards the staff, who looked at the anthromorph as if he was miraculous being for making the bald man shut up and walked towards the man wearing the tag of the MANAGER, on the front pocket of his shirt, who was busy glaring at the innocent curly haired waitress for creating this mess in the first place.

"It really was an accident. I will pay for the damage as well as for my order as long as she doesn't end up in any trouble-"

"You don't have to do that, sir. She should have been more—"

"I insist," Caledon demanded, with a tight smile, before paying the manager after he nodded nervously. He and Castiel wasted no more time in running out of the scene as soon as they could.

"I am the worst person to partake in a negotiation." Castiel deadpanned after following Caledon into the abandoned alley.

"No, he started yelling like a clown diving his head into the mouth of a hungry, bad-tempered lion," Caledon said sharply, sighing when the informant tried to flee again. "I don't think he isn't going to crack under negotiations. We could use *your* tactics."

Before the informant even made it to the more well-lit street, an arm was around his waist, and a hand was covering his mouth tightly.

The informant barely even had the time to process screaming as he simply froze as two pairs of arms dragged him back into the small alley between shops.

The kind of fear he'd never felt before.

They were enveloped in darkness as the informant, a hare anthromorph named Roy, was slammed roughly into the brick wall, Castiel's face suddenly only an inch from him. His dark, dangerous eyes stared at Roy's terrified ones as his knees shook.

The informant was breathing frantically, but not a noise escaped his mouth as he stared at Castiel, silent tears beginning to already form in his eyes. The bianthromorph's face didn't twitch, glaring at Roy dangerously.

"We are not going to hurt you," Caledon murmured lowly, barely a whisper into the space between them. "But if you fight us, we are not going to have a choice. Understand?"

It sounded like a threat, and Roy's vision blurred as he nodded as best he could against Castiel's hand, practically smothering him.

"Tell us everything you know about Delanna Jericho," Castiel demanded quietly, dark and looming over the dark-haired lanky Lepus-timidus cruxawn dangerously.

The fingers covering his mouth parted barely enough for sound to escape, still tensed and prepared to snap closed if Roy made a scene.

"U-Ural Mountains," he whispered hoarsely, not really able to articulate an answer aside from that. "I can send you the exact coordinates, but nobody has made it past her security systems."

"Are you sending us on a wild-goose chase?" Caledon asked, almost a bit taunting. As if he didn't actually believe that the informant was capable of doing it.

And he was correct.

Roy shook his head minutely, blood still icy in his veins as he stared back at Castiel's intent eyes.

He couldn't quite tell what emotions were held within them. They were hard and dangerous but didn't seem particularly angry.

"Are you going to kill me if I do?" Roy breathed voice shaking and chest stuttering against the arm across it.

Probably not the smartest question, but the informant's attention was currently focused on staying alive. If the bianthromorph was just going to kill him anyway, then he'd rather take his chances with screaming. Even if Castiel and Caledon found the proposition absolutely ridiculous, the latter knew they could use it against Roy to get all the information he had on Delanna Jericho.

But Castiel's eyes flickered across the informant's face slowly, as if trying to read into something, trying to notice something, trying to decide.

"That depends," the bianthromorph murmured, glancing back at his feline anthromorphic friend and having a wordless conversation. More analytical than angry. "Common sense says I should-"

The informant tensed, swallowing thickly.

"-But," Castiel stared the informant in the eye, intent and dark. "I'd really rather not have to kill you. Especially if you give us all the details about her security systems."

It still almost sounding like a mere threat? The words were almost comforting, but the tone was still chilling.

The informant felt sick. "Are you going to kill me or not?" he breathed, pressing further into the wall to put another inch of distance between them.

"That depends."

"On what?" he whispered agitatedly, bracing himself when Castiel adjusted himself slightly, straightening and standing another inch taller than the Lepus breedling.

"On you," Caledon said lowly, voice as inky black as his eyes that didn't shift. "We can't let you go until you tell us everything."

"A bianthromorph has me pinned to a wall." The informant whispered, lips shaking as he tried to glare. "I think only one of us is in danger."

Castiel's jaw tightened, eyes dragging back to Caledon's face purposefully as something in his eyes shifted before he nodded.

"If he backs away, will you not scream?" Caledon asked, carefully throwing a bait, though there was still a clear threat.

The informant wanted to ask if the bianthromorph was going to strangle him if he screamed. But he figured the answer was pretty obvious.

He nodded shakily, holding his breath as Castiel stared harder, searching for lies.

If cooperation meant that Roy got out of this alive, he didn't have a real problem with that.

"Know that we are tracking your blood pressure and body temperature," Caledon said stiffly. "You know that the pulse point of a Lepus breedling gives away their true intentions almost better than a lie detector. As long as you cooperate, you'll leave unharmed, Roy, understand?"

The line between false hope and threat blurred, but it didn't really matter. The hare anthromorph nodded, brain fuzzy with fearful static. Castiel waited another moment before stepping back and loosening his grip, still keeping his hold on the informant.

He took a deep, shaking breath, feeling his eyes burn as the blonde bianthromorph continued to stare at him, and none of the danger in his eyes had faded. The informant tried to knock Castiel's loosened hold and tried to flee, but his knees betrayed him, giving out after the first step as it felt like all of his muscles were trembling.

Hands caught him in a firm grip from behind, and Roy yelled, not quite a scream, but involuntary and much louder than intended as he slapped at Castiel's hands roughly, stumbling away.

Caledon's hands grabbed at the informant's arm, his patience snapping away, especially after his fear for Maia spiked a whole new level since last night, and Roy breathed rapidly, stumbling back as panic built.

The informant was suddenly yanked forward, a hand back over his mouth, and this time he wasn't able to hold the tears back, hot drops of fear racing down his cheeks as he stared at the bianthromorph's hardened expression as he was held chest-to-chest firmly, to keep him from breaking away.

The Lepus breedling stopped struggling, just staying numbly in Castiel's grip as he cried silently.

He hadn't meant to scream; he wasn't trying to run; he was just fucking scared.

The blonde bianthromorph stared down at him, completely merciless, and the informant was so sure he was about to get at least one of his bones broken.

He stared at his eyes, almost more afraid of the hardening edges than of the wicked knife peeking out of the inside his jacket.

"We are not going to hurt you," Castiel murmured, his grip on Roy loosening until he was barely holding on. "I don't want to hurt you, but I am really not in the mood of entertaining whatever game you are trying to pull with us."

He sucked in a pathetic breath as more tears spilt over the bianthromorph's hand, his entire body frozen.

Castiel's hand loosened over his mouth. "I just want to explain to you," he promised, voice low and firm. "If you don't conceal anything, you might know about her whereabouts; everything will be okay."

The informant didn't know what "okay" meant because there was still a hand around his wind-pipe that was seconds away from squeezing the life out of him.

The bianthromorph finally released him completely. "Let me explain," he warned, the final remnants of darkness seeping into his icy irises.

"If you are working for Cullins, then you can forget getting through." Roy breathed shakily, not bothering to wipe the stupid tears away as he stared at Castiel, waiting for him to go back to that anger. "I-If she hates anyone on this planet, then it would be Cullins' minions. She would most definitely hate you more than the humans here—"

"How would she know who we are?" Caledon asked though it sounded like a curious question rather than a threat. "What could she possibly have against Cullins? He pretty much works for the Council that she built."

And that, that more than any threat of violence, made the informant hesitate.

He drew his hands to his chest, glancing at the mouth of the alley, his entire body screaming for him to run, sprint, never speak a word of anything that had happened this day.

Forget that the Felis-breedling and his watchdog had ever been passing people in his life.

But Roy's legs wouldn't move as he looked back at Castiel, who simply taunted in the invitation for the hare anthromorph to go.

Would this bianthromorph truly not just attack him from the back for trying to leave?

"I-I don't know her reasons. She hates all anthromorphs, regardless." The informant whispered, voice shaking at his own helplessness for not already running.

The bianthromorph stared at him blankly, almost calculative, trying to check his tracker to pick up if he was lying.

"All I know is that the humans hate her less because she keeps Cullins' minions away." he pressed quietly, jaw tight. "You are going to disappear just like the previous seven teams he sent before."

There was a pause, Castiel simply glaring, and the informant was sure the next thing he would see would possibly be strangled to death.

But his Felis-breedling friend merely sighed quietly, as if regretting something, shoulders falling. "You are still hiding something. Your temperature is spiking way too frantically to not give that away," he responded slowly, eyes locking on the informant's teary ones. "But if you hesitate to spill it out, then why I don't just let my bianthromorphic friend murder you in cold blood for my own convenience, it would be better to spill all that you know, faster."

Part of Roy felt bitter at the statement, the hematite-grey eyed cruxawn talking as if killing him was something regrettable.

Okay, so maybe being really viciously rude was different from murdering someone. But it was clear that he couldn't exploit them for money, especially with a deranged bianthromorph in play. Who wouldn't hold any remorse for killing him? The humans wouldn't care for his death and would probably be silently grateful to the bianthromorph for killing him. *Since when was Cullins recruiting bianthromorphs into his facility?*

The better part of the Lepus-breedling, though, was still frozen in place.

He swallowed thickly. "All I know is that she pretty much invented the technology on reading brainwaves, so she uses an unidentified source to determine just how blindly you are devoted to Cullins," he rasped, hands shaking where they pressed against his own chest defensively before handing over the coordinates, as his temperature dropped back to normal. "This is the closest to her location. I can't infiltrate her security system to know her exact location."

"Leave," Caledon replied crisply, with slight annoyance on his face, before the informant fled as fast as he could, not needing to be told twice to do so.

"You were right. You are the only one who could have pulled this off." Castiel said with a satisfied grin, removing the hood falling over his head. He really wasn't expecting the playful anthromorph to threaten the informant to get what they needed, assuming the Felis-breedling to have his goody-two-shoes cut off the circulation to his brain to even consider this. Or even wordlessly trust him to go along with his tactics to use force, to get what they needed.

"Oh, I know." He smirked before his expression fell as he sighed. "Since, when did this become a rescue mission? I thought they would have sent a larger team to rescue the seven teams? We have no way of confirming that with the facility. He really sent us into this mess, blind. Moreover, our odds don't stand a good chance either."

Maybe there was hope that Allyson might not just blindly side with Cullins.

"We still need to maintain Radio Silence, but once I hack through her security system, using the drone set up by the Council. We can pinpoint her location from these coordinates." Castiel's jaw was still tense, eyes boring into the wall behind him, something waiting in his expression like he wanted to say something. All that mattered was that it brought him closer to some answers, behind the blurring lines between the CULT and the Anthromorphic Council, from someone who knows the entities inside out.

CHAPTER SEVENTEEN

M aia heard a sharp breath, a soft "Shit," as Caledon came into her vision. "Stop sitting in creepy places," he muttered, scrubbing at his eyes.

She glanced his way slowly. He had changed into an oversized t-shirt and looser sweats that were blue this time. His hair was a ruffled mess.

Silence stretched before them. Caledon's mouth was dry. He felt like he had missed a step in the dark, his lungs locking up.

After Castiel and Zella had spilt their entire plans and re-engineered the controls of their RTFQ chips permanently, Maia didn't hesitate to agree with their plan just like Castiel had predicted. Even if Zella and Caledon were the only ones left with a human family to worry about the consequences of their actions harming their human relatives, like a chain reaction, it still didn't waver the obvious fact that out of all of them, Caledon had the most to lose if he strayed out of the mission. It didn't matter if he agreed that *'Cullins just wasn't subtle with his actions'*.

Caledon stopped at the counter, staring at the half-filled coffee pot. He frowned at the brown mug clasped in Maia's hands. "What number cup is that?" he asked.

She looked at it. "Three? I think."

"Jesus Christ," Caledon breathed, taking the coffee pot off its holder and dumping it down the sink. "You're going to give yourself a fucking heart attack."

Maia narrowed her eyes as he poured out the only thing keeping her awake. "I was drinking that," she muttered.

The bianthromorphs had every right to believe that Cullins had to work for someone higher up in the Anthromorphic Council instead of settling for a lower position in running the main facility of the ECA. *But they didn't know him like Maia did.*

"Not anymore, you're not," Caledon said firmly, going to the fridge and pulling out some orange juice. "God, tell me you're not back to drinking that much caffeine on a regular basis." Maia only shrugged as Caledon grabbed a glass and poured juice up to the brim. "Just thinking about drinking that much coffee kills my stomach."

"That's what happens when you don't sleep," Maia replied.

"You are going to end up having insomnia, once again," Caledon muttered as he stepped up to the table, sliding the glass towards Maia and going for her coffee mug. Maia pulled it away, glaring. "This is currently the only thing keeping me conscious," she told him.

If Zella was taken aback by Maia's unfazed reaction to discovering that she was a bianthromorph, she didn't let it show. The Latrans cruxawn understood Caledon's hesitation, but he definitely didn't understand what was on the line considering the intel Castiel and Zella had collected. *She hadn't expected Cullins to get this far.*

Caledon rolled his eyes, making a quick grab at the mug with one hand as the other wrapped around her wrist, finger digging swiftly into Maia's wrist.

She cursed, letting go at the pressure point being pressed, a sharp pain shooting as Caledon whisked the mug away and shoved the juice at her, not looking triumphant but serious. "Drink it," he ordered. "Maybe you wouldn't be almost asleep if you actually ate something to give you calories to burn."

She could empathise with Caledon's frustration of hating that his sister blindly took Cullins' side, no matter what. But if they were on different sides, either one of their choices might end up costing the lives of their parents. When the cheetah-breedling joked about questioning whether his twin was even related to him by blood, Maia had stormed away from him without any explanations.

There was a tension they were unaccustomed to. She had never bothered to watch her step around Caledon, but she suddenly felt like she was standing in the middle of a live minefield.

Maia almost got up and fought for her goddamn coffee, but for god's sake, she was so tired. She grabbed the stupid juice, sipping it and cringing. "You want me to drink pulp?" she choked.

He glanced over his shoulder, delicate eyebrow lifted. "Do you get the part of the orange that actually provides nutrients? Yes, you do." He turned back and began rummaging through the fridge. "You're not turning into a vegetarian, are you?"

Maia swallowed hard, wrinkling her nose at the acid taste. She hadn't had orange juice in a long time. "Why would I start being a *vegetarian?*"

Caledon paused his rummaging but did not turn around. "A simple '*no*' would have been enough," he sighed, grabbing a box and pulling out a little single container of a serving of instant fried rice.

He didn't know what it actually meant to suffer from being connected to bad blood. Maia wanted to tell them all, she owed them all the truth if they had any chance of getting through this, but she didn't know where to start.

It was like trying to make yourself throw up when there was nothing in your stomach. Like a hiccup sitting in your chest that just wouldn't fucking come. It was like hanging over the edge of power but unable to fall.

It was naive ignorance to believe that the source of her shame wouldn't end up following her to the point where she had to confront it. If anyone had to be nervous in the agony of spilling the truth, it shouldn't have been the bianthromorphs, but her instead.

Her eyes followed him around the kitchen as he grabbed a pot, some water, throwing the half-prepared rice in and grabbing some red pepper paste, tossing some in, staring at it before shrugging and tossing in some more. He laid out several spices and examined them.

She stared. "Have you ever cooked before?"

Caledon hummed, searching the array of spices laid out from the cabinets, probably packed in by the previous teams. "Not really one to cook my own food. But I don't think inviting delivery people over would end very well right now." He picked up some Pipian sauce and shook in a generous amount, putting a top on and nodding as if he had accomplished something.

Maia had been one of the very few breedlings whose anthromorphic genes had activated at the mere age of ten. It wasn't a surprise, given her diagnosis to possess traits to be assessed as a clinical psychopath just like her mother. Clinical-assessed psychopaths in the human world had higher chances of being targeted by the CULT, making their offspring a perfect candidate to be a breedling with accelerated anthromorphic genes. She had had enough of being placed in foster-care systems and having her file always be overlooked to the point that she had felt relieved for the first six years of being rescued by the facility. They were her *saviours*.

She was one of the very few naturally-born anthromorphs, inheriting the recombinant coyote gene of her anthromorphic mother and the human gene of her human father. It wasn't that she was unaware of the knowledge that she wasn't her mother's first child or that her first child was with an unregistered bianthromorph when she was merely sixteen before she met her father. But all Maia knew was that she wasn't permitted to ask anything about the whereabouts of her half-brother. Back then, she was merely five to question or revolt against her mother's words. Still, more importantly, they were busy trying to survive through the anarchy of the riots that had occurred in the aftermath of the formation of the MPAs in the ECA.

The facility had given her a purpose to save more people like her from the cold-human world. But her illusion was soon broken when she met her half-brother. Never had Maia Emerson wanted her entire life to be a sick lie until that moment.

***

She wasn't supposed to walk in through the prohibited doors located through the walls of Cullins' office. It was the first time she had encountered cruxawn-trafficking rings, and they had managed to rescue all except a wolf-coyote bianthromorph. Most of the rescued rogue anthromorphs were sent to the Berlin MPA, except the Puma-breedling rescued by one of the Allyson twins.

It was one of their very first missions, and if she were, to be honest, they had handled it well. She may have had a soft spot for the twins, but she had no intentions of telling that to their faces, besides the Panther-breedling still got on her nerves. Even if Caledon hadn't asked, she would check up on the victims, considering the unimaginable things they had faced for months. It was a miracle that they were still alive, physically, but they were hardly responding to anything besides external stimuli. So lifeless, reduced to being just mere shells.

If anyone was capable of bringing back a fraction of their original selves and giving them a purpose, then it had to be Cullins. He indeed was the epitome of the word 'selfless'. Despite being nominated to be the youngest head of the Anthromorphic Council, he had given that up to continue rescuing more lost anthromorphs to give them a sense of purpose.

It wasn't like her to ever walk through before knocking, she had more dignity than that, but she froze immediately hearing the words she least expected to hear before watching Professor Topaz swiftly slit the throat of the last rescued cruxawn with a shiv made up of a material akin to a hydrocarbon, before letting it bleed to death along with the rest. *Only organic-based materials could be used to permanently kill breedlings in an instant.*

"They can't be controlled if they are broken." The Chancellor said briskly as if he were to comfort Topaz for the heinous crimes that he had committed. "They are nothing more than loose ends."

"What about the bianthromorph?" Professor Topaz lowly, voice tight. "Do you really wanna forge her files as an anthromorph."

"She can still be controlled," Cullins promised fiercely, removing the jacket strained with blood and replacing it with new robes as if he were trying to set a new schedule for classes for the next semester. "Still fighting. So, just do as instructed. You know bianthromorphs like us can't be beaten down that easily."

"What about the other bianthromorph that escaped?"

"If he wants to be a waste rather than serve a higher purpose, then we can't waste our resources on that," Cullins muttered, scoffing, as he shook his head. "Concentrate on finding the mole that's wasting our subjects by selling them off to vile humans. Shut down the CULT's base that the mole belongs to. Hunt down all the trafficking rings and kill those humans who dared to exploit our kind."

Topaz nodded curtly without any hesitations. He acted more like an obedient mongrel than an actual breedling with his own mind. "What do you want me to do once we find the mole? Dispose of them like these loose ends?" Topaz asked, keeping his voice low.

"No, that death would be a waste." Cullins looked marginally irritated by these questions, his tone visibly strained with apathy. "They can still be controlled to be an asset."

"What do you want me to be about the eavesdropper?" He snapped, jerking away from Cullins to face Maia with strained eyes, a distasteful curl to his lips. Before Maia could break out of her shock and make an exit, the doors behind snapped shut, trapping her inside. No matter how hard she tried to pull the doors open, it was of no use. It had to be controlled by Cullins' voice command.

"Leave. It's about time that I spoke with Ms Emerson. She is family." He demanded sharply as Topaz dragged three bodies through another door before angling his head to take a seat in front of him as he watched her crush the screen in her fists. *Just how many fucking doors did this room have?*

That's when Maia completely lost it. Her expression strained, as if she were trying to push against some invisible force, her hands flexed open and tensed, "You kill innocent lives seeing them as nothing but loose ends?!" She yelled, outraged and livid. "How could you do this to other breedlings?!"

"Why don't you calm down before we have a civil conversation?"

"Calm down? You just killed them all in cold blood!" She snapped, throat catching. Her teeth bared, but no curse fell from her lips as her breathing grew heavy as her eyes flickered around the room, as if noticing how small it was for the first time, "You expect me to calm down?!"

"What kind of lives do you think they will have, even if I try to help them?" he demanded, gesturing around the remaining corpses, and scoffed. "They will be in more pain while living, rather than be to put an end, numb their pain and be graced with a quick death."

Her expression was twisted. Something pained and dark and betrayed and angry, "The fact that you are so calm about this merely proves that you kill lives that don't bend to your will."

"I have a larger goal to fulfil, far larger than your naive mind can hope to comprehend. But you need to learn, someday." He said firmly, leaving no room for argument before handing his screen-board that clearly held DNA results.

"You forged this to trick anyone who would stumble upon your true colours." She immediately burst into laughter, utterly bewildered reading through the results over and over again. But no matter how many times she tried to re-read them, they refused to change that she was related to Cullins. *He was her half-brother?*

"My *true* colours? Kid, you don't even know me," he smirked coldly, shrugging his shoulders. "But, I am aware that you excel in your Biotechnology classes, to know that you can easily confirm these reports and believe that we are family."

"I don't care if they are true." She said shortly, eyes blazing and voice continuing to rise with fury. "You weren't there when our mother died. You are not my family!"

"Your psychotic tendencies seem to say otherwise. I read all the reports to keep track of the assigned missions." He pressed, stoically, before his lips broke into a smug grin. "We are way too alike, *dear sister*. You can't run from your genes."

Maia breathed heavily, her chest feeling as if a weight was placed on top of it, every passing second, watching the actual colour of his obsidian eyes as he grabbed a control switch from the inside pockets of his jacket to fix the projected frequency of the colour of his irises back into the shade of sapphire. Coloured lenses were of no use to any breedlings. They did nothing to hide the true colour of their eyes. But one glimpse at his obsidian eyes gave away that he was indeed a bianthromorph. They were way too polished to be that of an anthromorph.

"Fine, then lemme do you a favour and arrange a family reunion by announcing my *brother's* murder spree." She prompted condescendingly, voice echoing in the almost empty room, her nails digging into her palms as exasperation and frustration burst out.

"You can." He finally cleared his throat, straightening, his face conveying no emotions whatsoever. "But I am afraid that it has to wait for a few years."

"Bad timing?" She scoffed, tilting her head.

"Let's put it this way. I don't care if you wish to join my goals or not. I have saved you from the cold human world to return my gratitude to our mother, but that's where my kindness ends." The Chancellor stared, not quite a glare, but something equally as disarming. "It won't make a difference if you go and tell people, but I am going to ensure that all the anthromorphs that you have interacted with in this facility meet the same fate as them." He threatened, and Maia knew she was one misplaced word from potentially ruining something.

"That's too big of a loss for you. You wouldn't dare—" Maia shouted, blood hot and racing as she stared at the despicable man, skin feeling too tight across her body.

"You are not wrong, so I am just going to place my bet on the twins." He prompted sharply when only silence followed. "I still need the flow of funds from their parents, so sacrificing one of them wouldn't come at a price."

***

She figured that if she were out of the picture, he couldn't use her to threaten anyone, but the moment she ended up reporting to the Anthromorphic Council and getting thrown into the isolated psych ward of the facility, only then could she comprehend just how far of a reach Cullins had in the Council and why he had given up his position in the Council, without any hesitation. Cullins really didn't handle her decision to choose her own fate, well. He pretty much tossed the twins onto as many risky missions as he possibly could after removing her from their team.

Caledon turned, looking content, and paused at Maia's expression. Maia's hand had found its way onto her hip. "What?" he demanded. "Do you cook?" he challenged.

If Maia had to pinpoint a starting point, perhaps this is how they had fallen in love. Maia had developed insomnia ever since she was released from the psych-ward. Realising that no one would believe her, her secrets began to eat her up from the inside. Even when Caledon knew that the older would probably never talk, he still quietly offered her food from his secret stash of packaged snacks every time he spotted her walking her aimlessly after logging in extra hours in Advanced Forensic Chemistry class.

Maia couldn't help but snort quietly. "Let's put it this way; I cook better than that."

"Lemme do it for you this time." Caledon pressed, straightening, unable to fight the smile on his lips.

"Cullins is my half-brother."

It was a whisper. Breathed into the air from Maia's hung head, her body tense but falling loose as soon as she said it, like the last pillar that was holding up an entire structure finally giving out.

Her words punched Caledon in the stomach more cripplingly than the decision awaiting him. He felt like his body had been frozen while the rest of time moved on.

He stared at Maia, his eyes wide and shocked at the sudden declaration. He felt like even his blood had stopped moving along his veins.

***

Castiel did not get startled at the sudden body pressing against him from behind. He simply ran a hand over the algorithms written across the screen board.

"This one is different from the one across your eye?" Zella's voice asked against his ear, cold with calculation, despite the warm hands wrapped around his lower torso. And she had continued to stand behind him, all of it seeming to lead to this moment here. This moment with Castiel's hands holding her and Zella's fingers traced his jaw where she felt something similar to a sliver of a scar from a knife.

He hummed, nodding slowly, getting used to the familiar weight against his back. "This is probably the most normal scar I have. I am oddly fond of it. I just got nicked while carrying the abandoned food cartons in the anthromorphic refugee camps in Zagreb."

Probably, why the ECA was in a continued economic downfall. The UNH was so focused on fearing the anthromorphs that all the exportation of products from the ECA often got wasted instead of crossing the borders. It was not surprising that they feared that the Anthropomorphic Council might have genetically enhanced the produces that could alter their genes when consumed. *They weren't. Zella knew that way too well.*

Zella's grip on him tightened imperceptibly. "I am glad to hear that at least the raiding of produces in ECA fell into the right hands instead of going to waste," she muttered darkly.

"Well, people like you ensured that," Castiel agreed, lifting his free hand to rest against Zella's on his lower torso, sharp eyes relooking over the information he had already burned into his skull.

There was a moment of silence. "I am neither a farmer nor a marketer, Castiel," Zella murmured, almost like she was hinting at something.

Castiel nodded, his chest tightening, before explaining, "I didn't recognise you just because of your scars or your looks." He released a quiet breath as one hand clasped Zella's tightly, her nose brushing beneath the curve of his jaw silently, almost comfortingly.

Castiel suddenly had Zella's back against the wall, a gentle hand holding her jaw, and the other curled around her wrist. "There were only a few times when the rogue anthromorphs that were captured managed sent a distress signal to warn the refugee camps from the facilities' teams flying over to their locations to capture the rest of them." His expression held no amusement, but Zella saw the challenge in his eyes. "When I broke off your mask, my gloves picked up the same frequency of a signal that warned the refugee camps," he confessed quietly, barely a whisper against her lips.

Maybe as humans, it might have been amusement in his eyes. But a challenge was almost just as laughable.

Her eyes narrowed. She flipped her wrist in Castiel's grasp, allowing her fingers to curl around his wrist and twist. Her other hand snatched the hand at her jaw and pulled it away, flipping it and shoving Castiel away with a knee to his leg.

Castiel stepped back quickly with a smirk, but she kept hold of his wrist, twisting and turning until his back was shoved against the wall he had pinned her to, Zella pressing against his torso to hold him there, allowing her to whisper in his ear. "Is that why you trust my choices?"

Castiel chuckled, low and deep enough to reverberate in Zella's chest against his torso. "No. That had nothing to do with this. I had my suspicions since the start, but I eventually confirmed it after picking up on a few things," he peeked through the long strands of his ragged blonde hair framing his jaw, dark expression still challenging in a way that only Castiel would ever be able to live after delivering. "You knew where the cameras were installed by heart, were the only one to come in contact with the captives before the clean-up. You were the only one who was summoned into Cullins' way too many times to interfere with the frequency of the intel sent."

His leg shifted back, hooking around Zella's knee and pulling it forward, making her knees buckle, off-balance.

"You're making an enormous presumption that I am not selfish enough to be unbothered by this." Though Zella caught herself and blocked the first hand, Castiel's other came from the side like a viper strike, taking her wrist and lifting as he twirled Zella almost like a dancer.

By the time Zella slammed her foot down to stop the movement, Castiel's arms were locked over her shoulders, her back pressed against the wall as his lips brushed her ear.

"I am not presuming anything. I know that you are not selfish," he murmured quietly, breath barely fanning her skin, "You were the only one who had a personal motive."

If it were a world devoid of wars, Zella might describe it as playful. Coy. But it wasn't. It was still dark and dangerous.

But not to Zella. She was starting to know him too well. Knowing the ins and outs of his voice too intimately, even before these moments.

Zella continued to glare. "I didn't know anyone from these refugee camps," she challenged, though it was decidedly less sharp than the previous dismissals.

"You were the only one who was affected by the state of the captives, considering them as fools for sacrificing their lives to fight and be captured by the facility. For harming humans," he assured her that there was no point denying it, now. "I have also seen you do this in person."

Zella was going to strangle him.

While Castiel was still the ever-present rock beside her, he was becoming increasingly comfortable when they had moments alone that weren't pressured by work.

If Zella would take a moment to examine herself, she'd see her own willingness and near-eagerness creeping out, but she very pointedly refused to self-reflect and self-incriminate.

Because being with Castiel in this way, it changed something.

Zella was loathed to use the word '*fun*' in any context, but there was an unexplainable solace in being with Castiel. In being with someone who saw through her worst, and in front of whom, Zella was learning to shed every facade.

When Zella sat in the study chair of her room and put her head in her hands, racing to find the contents nano-sized piercer atop the switch controlling their RTFQ chips, she was met with the same distance and cold, critical nature from Castiel as always. Ever since Castiel had discovered the untraceable feature of the switch, she knew that it held far greater purpose than just a mere unexpected glitch.

But when the night dragged on, still with no answers in sight, the cold distance would turn to warm proximity as Castiel told her to sleep with nothing more than a touch to her shoulder.

It was still leagues more than he had ever given before.

And at Zella's flippant refusals that were ingrained in her nature by now, the warm proximity turned to heated lips on her own, drawing her scattered focus onto Castiel like metal shards under a magnet.

Quiet whispers of figuring it out tomorrow, and low murmurs asking her to sleep, had replaced a helpless distance that Zella used to find too easy to utilise to her detriment.

When the roles were reversed, that distance was gone, and Castiel was becoming willingly vulnerable to Zella's gentle prompting that drew him to his bed.

Sometimes, with Zella lingering.

Sometimes, with Zella's staying.

And sometimes, with nothing more than a touch to his arm before leaving him to sleep.

Castiel stared down at Zella as their little power dance came to a halt.

Zella pressed a finger to Castiel's chest as his hands found her hips firmly. "What?" she demanded quietly.

He did not even blink. "Our last mission in the Lisbon MPA, last month." She couldn't help but let her mind run wild, thinking of all the possibilities someone else might have figured it out and might hold it as leverage against them. "Don't let your mind run anywhere; no one can figure it out. The only reason I could figure it out is because I was familiar with receiving those signs in Zagreb."

"What were they like? The Camps?" she asked, carefully torn between guilt and anger, imagining just how he must have lived for the past five years, dropping her head to his chest, pressing against it firmly.

She was not startled by Castiel keeping his tight grip, tugging her back against his chest.

And Zella did not stare, wide-eyed as Castiel's face was suddenly only millimetres from hers.

"Scared, angry, hopeless. I can't remember the time anyone in the refugee camps ever bothered speaking or knowing anything about each other besides deciding who raided the abandoned food cartons or moving to a different location whenever we were warned," Castiel said lowly, polished-apatite eyes locked onto Zella's like a hook. "Trust was a luxury that they just didn't believe in."

"Because they couldn't afford to care or be attached," she stared at him, gaze shattered, but he nodded along with her words. "Not when one of them could decide to throw away their lives by acting on their anger and attacking the humans."

"Most often stopping them from acting on their rage, ended up gathering the Council's attention to our location." He sighed, barely even audible, staring at Zella, so utterly earnest. His expression didn't shift from curious and dark. "Tell me to leave," he murmured quietly with a warm smile. "And I will."

That was always the precursor.

From both of them. Whether it was Castiel going to Zella's room when sleep avoided him too long, "Tell me to go, and I will."

Or Zella trying to coax Castiel away from work long enough to rest, "Tell me to leave, and I will."

Or if it was an evening while waiting for their screen-boards to process their data and they could do nothing but wait. The two of them were moving past hands and lips, "Tell me to stop, and I will."

That was their one condition. One that neither would allow the other to break. A system of checks and balances.

"Tell me to leave… and I will," Castiel murmured, lips brushing her ear carefully.

From her micro-expressions, Castiel knew damn well what Zella's response would be, and she could feel the almost self-satisfaction rolling off of him as she rolled her eyes, grabbing him by the back of his neck and slamming their lips together.

Zella had grown used to the warmth that flooded her, racing from her torso to her fingertips that threaded through Castiel's hair.

His hands were on her hips before pulling her bun as the length of her hair fell till her lower back, so they stood chest to chest, finally getting what he wanted.

Zella wanted to hit him for dancing around for so long, but then Castiel's hands tugged her closer, and thoughts of teasing him were lost in a quiet smile, making Zella's hand fall to his arm, holding on as her fingers curled.

This was what Zella needed.

Someone who was able to stand against the gales she produced. Someone who wouldn't crumble against Zella's fiery obnoxiousness. Someone for her to beat herself against and remain as sturdy as stone in her way.

Forcing Zella to slow down enough to think and realise.

"I just think that we are designed to be hypocrites. We often mourn the lack of any aspect unless it comes down to hierarchy," Zella muttered, hands pressed to Castiel's chest, feeling how they rose and fell beneath her.

The competition was bound to exist, whether it was to maintain a balance between two different species competing for the same resource or claims over territory, but when the balance was tipped off by the elimination of one species, there was bound to be chaos within the same species, a mere catalyst fuelling self-destruction.

Competition among the surviving species sparked more greed than unity within the same species. The CULT was merely exploiting that greed in the most vicious manner. For they failed to see that individuality wasn't an obstruction to harmony, but instead stripping it away is what had been shattering harmony for centuries.

He merely inclined his head. "I don't know why humans decided that the concentration of melanin determined one's worth. Ironically, in this aspect, the ones who possessed *more* were considered inferior and were expected to bow down before the ones who had a much *lesser* concentration."

If Zella was going to start something, she was going to finish it.

"The pattern continues even among anthromorphs, the presence of an extra gene, pretty much brands us as any executioner's favourite breakfast." She huffed darkly, dragging Castiel back down into a kiss that stung his lips.

Her response was enough for Castiel to pick her up by her hips, making her sit on the edge of her desk, and

Zella swatted at him in annoyance. However, she never parted from him, allowing Castiel to drag her to the edge of the desk until her legs nearly wrapped around his waist.

Zella didn't stop Castiel, like she might have, when his fingers dug into her hips and thigh, pulling her closer until Zella feared he might tug her off the desk.

She did not stop herself from plunging her fingers into his long blonde hair, parting thick strands and using it to direct the kiss deeper, signalling for Castiel to come closer.

When they parted, Zella, a little more winded than her pride would allow her, glared at Castiel, who looked entirely too content with himself.

Castiel straightened, still holding Zella against his chest, arms around her waist. "We should be getting access through the security systems of her perimeter within the next hour," He murmured as if he could read the very thoughts inside of Zella's head. "If Caledon backs out, then we might have to do this without him."

"It won't come to that," she murmured, not an excuse but an observation. A statement of fact.

Castiel hummed, the sound travelling through Zella's back. "We are already running thin, so we can't afford to go out there with one less person on our side."

Their words were tainted with experiences and fear and everything they had lost, everything they were afraid to lose.

It was twisted with fear they couldn't afford the time to feel and marked by emotions they were neither allowed nor able to experience.

But it was theirs, marked and sealed and owned. It was made individually theirs, with each colour of terror and trust that dripped like ink into water, dispersing and tainting as much as it showed who it belonged to.

Flavoured by fear but guarded by a trust that had tied to their very bond.

"No, we can't," she looked exhausted, sighing out low and long.

He hummed, scanning Zella's face carefully, eyes hooded, before wordlessly pulling her wrist gently onto the kitchen. "Maybe we should take this chance to fuel up before we head for the mission."

"I'm sure we have enough to heat up the porridge in the fridge," she smiled warmly, as gentle as she could manage. "I just suddenly remembered you always… talked about eating Pirão porridge. So, I made some to keep us awake during our turn to night-watch." Zella quickly set the lukewarm bowl in his lap.

Castiel stared at it like he didn't know what to do. She watched a teardrop roll down the swell of his cheek.

She dropped to his knees beside Castiel quickly as another fell, heart leaping to her throat in panic.

"Castiel, what?" she asked gently, not touching him. "What's wrong?"

Castiel shook his head, pulling the container of soup closer, wrapping his arms around it as if to protect it.

Zella stared, a little in awe, as Castiel looked up, silent tears on his cheeks, staring at Zella as more joined the ones already falling down his face.

"I—" Castiel choked off, dropping his head again.

Zella could only remember the few times Castiel reminisced about the nights when his mom said they would have Pirão porridge...

She had assumed it might hold good memories.

And Castiel's tears were not bitter this time.

"Do you... want me to eat with you?" Zella offered quietly.

He nodded without looking up.

Zella sat beside him as Castiel ate it with shaking hands, the first thing she had seen him eat since they started this, and when the bowl was finished. Castiel pushed it away with trembling hands.

"Was it... good?" she whispered, hand hovering near Castiel.

Slow, jerking nods as he curled around his stomach, a hand pressing against it. Like drinking a hot soup in the middle of winter and feeling it warm you to your core.

Zella didn't hug him, too afraid of crowding him in this vulnerable state. But she laced her fingers gently through Castiel's, holding his hand carefully.

Castiel squeezed her hand so tightly, it was almost painful, but Zella was silent as he curled around their hands, drawing their joined hands to his chest and clutching it there.

She could feel his rapid heartbeat through his chest, tears hitting his skin icily.

Zella swallowed thickly, her other hand resting on Castiel's arm gently. "Castiel," she whispered quietly, stomach twisting. "Are you... happy?"

Because this wasn't anger.

Nor frustration.

Nor fear.

Nor agony.

Zella didn't know what else it could be.

So when Castiel held her hand closer, fingers squeezing her hand tight, and he nodded jerkily, head hung so low his lips almost brushed Zella's lips as he cried-.

Holy shit, he was happy.

"You're happy…" Zella breathed, feeling tears spring to her own eyes. She couldn't help it. She leaned against Castiel, her free hand wrapping around his back.

Castiel choked on a sob, leaning into Zella so heavily, he almost knocked her over. Castiel practically tried to crush her as he buried his face in her neck.

Zella couldn't even begin to describe the sensation that started to swell in her chest, choking her and pressing against her ribcage. She couldn't describe her own joy at Castiel being happy; Experiencing happiness for nothing more than a bowl of food; maybe it was that simple.

They barely had time to react before Caledon and Maia barged out of their rooms frantically searching for their screen-boards, sighing in defeat. "Well, it seems the decision has been made for me," Caledon said, pinching the bridge of his nose.

"What does that mean?" Castiel asked carefully as if he were checking that Caledon was trying to communicate with the species residing in a different dimension.

"Well, we now know who helps run the CULT from within the Council," Maia explained, gritting her teeth more at the information she was aware of rather than the question.

"You have to stop beating around the bush and get clearer than that." Zella coaxed as calmly as she possibly could, her eyes narrowing, pressing her lips into a thin line.

"Check the news." The tallest breedling offered, looking dazed every passing second, before handing Zella her screen-board to catch up with reality. "They have stolen the nuclear codes of the nukes that the humans had set up in Iceland to blow up the entire ECA if the Council pulled something like this."

"What did they do?" Castiel asked, practically hearing Zella gnashing her teeth as he leaned to read the screen along with her. Kheprium. The compound that literally signified rebirth, even used in minuscule amounts, was absolutely fatal to pure human genes, but those small traces also acted as a detonator switch to burn the cells from the inside. The piercer atop the control switch didn't affect the breedlings when used by them because their RTFQs also acted as a neutraliser to the side-effects of Kheperium, besides electrifying their nerves that allowed them to control the energy around the air they came in contact with-

maximised especially, with the use of their kevlar gloves binding to the nerves at the tips of their fingers or merely dispersing in uneven surges when they were at their weakest state.

Most humans had an involuntary response to use the control switch while interacting with all cruxawns from the ECA unless they had kids who were cruxawns and accepted them for who they were. They had thrown a perfect bait in the term of protection, using fear as a ploy for their advantage. None of them had any idea about the UNH's fail-safe plan in Iceland, which only meant that the data wasn't meant for public ears.

Although none of them voiced it out loud, it was certain each of the four had a perfect reason to betray or bail, whether it was for vengeance, taking their family's side or protecting their family. However, they still had to risk trusting each other and completing the task at hand while staying under the radar.

"It looks like this explains how they killed off the 12,375 humans who work for the UNH."

CHAPTER EIGHTEEN

"Are you sure it won't be detected?" The taller asked, his voice low and hoarse, looking through the contents of the vial as the Latrans cruxawn circled her fingers for the concentration that would hit the jackpot.

"Zella and I may have started working on in the Biotechnology lab along while working on the vials, but we split up our work to cope with the pressure of our final terms and missions. No one would know." The jade-eyed blonde explained, promising resolutely that no matter which angle they might be monitored, they wouldn't get caught. "We are really doing this?" She asked once again to give a gateway for any doubts to back out.

"We need resources. We can't fight this by ourselves. By his regards, we are the two most expendable ones in every regard." The icy-eyed bianthromorph shook his head curtly, biting the inside of his cheeks, making the skin over his cheekbones even more hollow. "No funds, no connections. He needs them more than us."

"Do we have to go this far? I am sure that, even if they knew they can pull it off—"

"No, the security systems are going to get tighter. They will get caught." The reply cut off the alternative immediately.

There are certain truths known to the world to be absolute.

The sky is blue, the chances of Cullins letting them act on their will was rare, the earth revolves around the sun, and they had no other alternative. It wasn't anything personal. Nothing to get upset or jealous about. It simply existed as a truth to the universe: trees produced oxygen, and they had to play their parts, well.

"He suspects us, already, and now that all the acts have dropped, he won't be distracted by staging missions to put up a facade in front of the UNH." Of course, just because the truth was absolute doesn't mean it always existed. But just because you didn't know about the truth didn't mean it hadn't always existed. "So, all his attention will be on the breedlings in the facility and ensuring that they are all on his side."

"Exactly, we need him to be distracted." The sigh, although defeated, paradoxically held a smug undertone that couldn't be picked digitally unless they gazed directly at the icy orbs.

"They may never forgive us for this. You know that, right?" It couldn't be overlooked, but it was a necessity for adaptation. Adaptation not merely to survive, but adaptation to living.

"We don't have any other alternatives."

***

"I may have stumbled upon something else while breaking through the security systems. I found someone else besides tracking the heat signatures of the missing seven teams and Deanna Jericho... An unregistered bianthromorph. A bianthromorph possessing the genes of a falcon and a stag, under the name of Donna Jericho."

But according to their history, Donna Jericho was an embodiment of her mother's ideologies, stubborn in her beliefs. Unfortunately, that didn't harmonise well with the CULT's ideologies, which explained why Cullins felt the need to shut her up for good and put her in her current vegetative state.

Every personification of a breedling's unconscious anima and animus had dual aspects that channelled the prowess of the beast within. The lighter aspect of their animus archetype manifested the breedlings' physical strength to its maximum potential, while the anima archetype manifested the development of their will and limits. Meanwhile, the darker aspect of the breedlings' animus archetype personified the petrification of their conscious body while the anima archetype amplified the aura of ego to invade their consciousness.

The awareness of the manifestation of the anima and animus developments in their personality helped form a bridge between their *conscious reflection*, which represented the lighter aspect of their personality and the *unconscious shadow*, which was represented by the darker aspect.

Donna Jericho imagined a world of spreading the significance of possessing the key to control and exercise these complexes to be their best version of themselves, regardless of their gender, regardless of their genetic make-up. She wanted humanity to recognise the value of equality in a world void of inferiority, the pride to feel comfortable in one's skin and DNA and exercise their own choices.

It was a practical move in removing Donna Jericho from the equation; Especially when the latter had always been trying to change the original ideologies of the CULT that merely complicated Cullins' grand plan. His father had a far stronger hold in the CULT to let go of the so-called legacy of the CULT instead of focusing on building the ideology that they were created for. So, he had no choice but to create his replacements to entertain his father.

The co-leaders of the CULT were not only chosen according to their success rate of successfully transforming into a Bianthromorph but also according to the compatibility of their very first brainwaves in their foetal state, from the raw data acquired by the CULT members stationed in nearly every hospital of the world, which was required for analysing whether the human was 'developed' enough to transform into a full-fledged anthromorph.

After what seemed like hours of quiet walking, growing more anxious the further they went, uneasiness seeping out of them like invisible energy, enveloping them like a force field when they finally reached the coordinates.

The entrance looked like the opening of a cave.

"Caves?" Caledon asked, puzzled, with a questioning look at Castiel to confirm if they were in the right place. The blonde nodded curtly, harsh and sure.

The caves were dark and damp and plagued with the smell of mould and wet chalk. The walls were saturated with some sort of kinetic sand that dripped down off a rusted moss that clung to the stone and seemed to be growing down from the ceiling. The entire pathway through the caverns was thrashed as if something had eaten through the stalactites of the cave-like rust on iron and reeked of blood and sweat. The Jabatus cruxawn looked like he wished to take a sample of it to study as he looked at them with wonder but held back with the fear of causing catastrophic consequences if he sniped a piece off the cave.

All the stimuli were amplified by their heightened anthromorphic senses. It was nearly unbearable to be down here.

"What are you doing?" Maia asked shortly, pulling back Caledon by his arm when he tried to get a closer look at the walls.

"I am not going to touch it to know what caused this. I just need to get closer to get a closer inspection on my gas chromatography-mass spectrometry machine." He explained, pointing towards the minimised size of the equipment he took out from the rear end of the holster attached to the upper leg of his suit. "What? I have my hobbies too." He shrugged his shoulders when the rest looked over at him to give him a look to question when exactly he had the time to modify the equipment to pocket-friendly and why on earth was he carrying it around.

"I just thought you might be carrying a spare sandwich in the spare compartments." Maia teased, shrugging her shoulders as he examined the walls.

"I would have, but there weren't any in the fridge, plus it's not like we particularly had time to create sandwiches before coming here," he said nonchalantly. "It looks like the gas has sublimed into solid." He pointed towards the ivory-coloured solidified droplets on the stalactites. "It's not virological." he read out the results as the equipment took some time to analyse the sublimed droplets. "Cyanogenic glycosides, cardiac glycosides, the doses of vitamin E are also spiking through the charts…elderberry cuttings." his face paled instantly as soon as he uttered those last two words as if they were venom.

Maia knew that cyanogenic glycosides and cardiac glycosides were fatal to one's system. Still, anthromorphs had a stronger immune system and could cancel these out of their systems, and since both the Jerichos' genes were bonded to stags, they had a naturally stronger immune system. Cervidae cruxawns could easily flush out these glycosides out of their systems before they could cause any fatal damages to their body.

"What's the matter?" She asked, not understanding his panicking state.

"Normally, these fatal glycosides shouldn't cause major harm to any anthromorphs, especially Cervidae anthromorphs, but when mixed with elderberry cuttings enhanced with rat poison, it's a different story. Normally these breedlings are resistant to several botanical poisons; by default, elderberry is one of the exceptions. We need to hurry." He said before the rest nodded immediately, getting a clearer idea why the situation wasn't unfolding in their favour before running at their maximum pace behind him.

They ran frantically for a good twenty minutes down the corridors that looked identical to the twenty before the ones they had passed.

The humans in the UNH would probably put up with the Council's new absurd demands until they created a neutraliser for the traces of kheperium themselves. Perhaps, that's all the time the Council needed to implement their true agenda, using fear as the perfect distraction.

"Cullins doesn't care for the CULT's weird legacy to have only bianthromorphs lead them," Maia said in exasperation as they dropped their speed abruptly.

"But he does care for the one leading them, now," Zella said flatly, voice-controlled and bordering on teasingly emotionless. "The current leader does care about the legacy."

"As long as we are on your side, we are almost untouchable, and that includes anyone related to us, no matter how much Cullins tries to threaten us using their lives as stakes," Caledon's expression was the same thoughtful blank that it always was, but Maia could see the tension in his mouth as he stared off.

It was impossible to clearly distinguish one cave from another in their haste, to the point where they had to consider the possibility that they must have certainly circled back to the same spot no less than two times.

Before finally entering a massive cavern, it was almost like it was carved out of the rocks by a craftsman. The walls were mismatched and a little too weirdly shaped to be natural; it stuck out like a thumb that didn't have enough blood circulation coursing through it.

"Well, the pattern of forging their files as anthromorphs didn't start with Zella, but rather with him and Donna... so the odd gamble would be—" Maia prompted when Castiel hadn't moved a couple of minutes later.

"Me." The blonde bianthromorph completed her sentence with a clipped tone. No malice, no hidden knife. Just facts.

"What if they are dead?" Maia posed, giving him an expectant stare, reminding them of Cullins' strategy of eliminating obstacles that weren't *efficient* to him in any aspect. "I am not saying that they are, but it's merely the worst possible scenario, given Cullin's record. Donna is pretty much a vegetable to him, so it serves him no purpose."

"But her mother does. In his criteria, '*She is not a waste and hence can be controlled by using her daughter as a ploy*'." Castiel said pointedly, with no more emotion than a piece of marble.

"He is getting sloppy, and his patience might not tolerate Jericho openly standing up against him," Maia posed petulantly, staring at Castiel, silently demanding an answer to the alternative.

Stalactites hung from the ceiling, dripping a greenish-blue liquid into pools beneath their feet, making it slippery to walk on. At least the air in here felt less suffocating than earlier. Zella glanced over at Caledon as he felt around against the walls, working his way out to the centre of the cavern, his arms stretched like he was guarding himself against bumping into an invisible wall.

"It all depends on whether he views these three bianthromorphs as competition or as another experimentation to control for his gains," Caledon assured her, lips twitching.

The cavern shook as the floor gave out below them, each of them clutched onto the side of the wall nearest to them to steady themselves.

The chances of this being a dead trail were getting significant, but there was no way they could get out of Novyslava without getting Delanna Jericho. All their attempts for radioing in for any purpose would be rejected unless it involved calling in bringing along the stag-anthromorph back to the facility.

There was a huge gaping hole opening at the floor with several ropes hanging at the edges of the mouth, each immediately grabbing holding of one and using it to slide down to the bottom of the pit.

At the bottom was a puny room which would be a massive nightmare for a claustrophobe. The ceiling hung so low that they could barely stand up. Both Castiel and Caledon's heads were an inch or two away from scraping the top. It felt like they were being stuffed into an elevator-sized coffin as if the room was closing in on them.

"We need more light," Maia announced, breathing heavily. Zella pulled out a small pocket torch, threw it down on the ground, and backed up, bumping into Caledon. "Sorry"

"It's alright," he mumbled back with a small smile. The light emitted by the torch illuminated the area just enough to make out what was in the room, which was practically nothing.

"It's empty," Castiel picked up the torch and shined it against the walls. Everything was covered floor to ceiling in Latin and cave art that seemed to depict the timeline of the anthromorphs since their creation. Under normal *non-deadly* circumstances, they might have looked around in awe, running their hands along with the carvings, perhaps even taking their time to look up and down the wall turning around in a circle to admire it all. They had to be over fifty years old, at least. It was oddly beautiful.

"Not empty," Caledon sighed wistfully, soon noticing a section of the wall on the far south had a stag's antlers carved into the stone. It was painted gold with encrusted gems of many colours giving off a three-dimensional pattern along the edges. It swirled inwards to showcase the large fist-sized ruby that was embedded into the middle.

"A giant ruby," Maia said resolutely, running her fingers along the surface. It glowed a brilliant crimson before giving out. "Even with these suits, let's hope we don't get crushed by a falling boulder or something at this point." She took in a deep breath as she rested her hand on the forehead of the stag, covering the entirety of the ruby.

A faint crimson coloured outline circled her hand, and the rock's surface raised up a few inches. Maia turned the rock in a semicircle and pressed in, then backed up. The rock face opened up into three large chambers. It echoed through the room like a freight train was passing by. A wave of fog poofed out of the opening, hitting them with a blast of strong blowing wind.

"Is this really necessary? I hate these fog effects." Zella coughed, swatting the air.

"What exactly happened to her that she goes to such lengths to prevent people from approaching her?" The hematite-grey eyed breedling asked as the fog cleared, before quietly complaining about being in this bizarre

18th-century structure still existing in the year 2155, without their kevlar gloves to channel their energy surges.

"I think we can take a safe bet and say it has to do everything with her daughter," Castiel said, jaw clenching imperceptibly, trying to perceive which one of the three directions might lead them in the right path.

Neither of them had time to make a rational decision besides jumping through the nearest chambers, to avoid the gigantic boulder dropping from the ceiling above them and separating them into each of the three chambers.

This was going to delay their plans even further.

***

Caledon and Maia had lunged into the middle of one of the three chambers before the boulder crashed down on them.

"We need to get to the others." She declared, getting back on her feet immediately after wordlessly asking if he was alright.

"Wait, someone is here alongside us," Caledon snapped, pulling her back as the ground beneath his feet treaded with sparks due to the friction of his soles halting against the ground.

"It could be Delanna—"

"I don't think—" Caledon didn't even need to confirm his instinct that it wasn't her as they stared at the unfamiliar figures staring right at them. Hybrids, specifically invertebrate-anthromorphs who had certainly failed the conversion. The hybrids narrowed their vision towards the breedlings, their expressions turned vicious, cracking their necks in unison and looking down at the floor, then up at the ceiling as if thanking Satan and the gods for what was about to happen.

They were trapped.

"I feel I am going to throw up," Caledon said, imagining the lives that were ruined to create mindless beings who merely thrived on destruction. His eyes widened when one of the hybrids smirked and looked directly at him and the other at Maia as if declaring and choosing their opponents.

They barely had time to glance at each other before they were immediately separated as the scorpion hybrid circled Caledon. In contrast, the larger hybrid, whose animal gene Maia didn't have time to analyse over, sided around her before snarling and making the first move by swinging full force at her. The panther-breedling ducked and countered with a right hook to the hybrid's cheek, sending it backwards startled.

"Don't give them a chance to recover. We need to get over with this as soon as possible to find Jericho," she screamed at Caledon as she roundhouse kicked the hybrid in its face before leaning down and gripping the hybrid by a fistful of hair sprouting on its head and kneeing it in the jaw to pin its torso, and immediately stabbing the daggers at its upper limbs to nail it to the ground permanently, as the pained shrill of the bleeding hybrid filled her ears.

"I am trying... I don't fancy wasting my time over sparring with a scorpion hybrid which happens to have a tail that can sting to death with its poisonous venom." Caledon snapped shortly. *If they could channel their energy surges, they would have already been at the opposite end of the chamber.*

Before she could get back on her feet from the crying hybrid under her, the scorpion hybrid charged at Caledon, tackling him to the ground. It hauled off and punched the cheetah-anthromorph hard in the jaw, leaving a small gash across his lip within a fraction of a second. Neither the hybrid nor Maia even got time to react because in that instant, when he tasted blood in his mouth, it was like something inside Caledon snapped as he punted the hybrid off of him and rolled over to stand, throwing several swift punches and nearly breaking its neck.

It was certain that he was in a trance of all the anger of everything occurring swallowed him, with the pained whimpers of the bleeding hybrid lying near his feet riling him up, when he made no attempts of stopping as he keeled over the barely conscious hybrid, grabbing its mid-section. He didn't seem to care that he had already done enough damage and was in a drive to damage the hybrid where it was beyond the scopes of recovering like a heap of broken dreams, defeated, laying it out with a mixture of punches and kicks.

It wasn't until he drew back his fist and BAM! A bone-crushing punch right to the jugular of its neck, he could feel it break the moment his fist made contact. He was the only one among the four, who hadn't experienced going so far as wanting to kill any being or succumbing to his anger, his positive light uplifting his morale, lost for the first time as he fell back staring at the lifeless scorpion hybrid, as his entire body shook like an autumn leaf falling from a tree. "I k-killed it."

"You had no choice, Caledon. They are hybrids. It's either kill or be killed." She mumbled as warmly as she could, not knowing how else to comfort him, especially when they had to get to the others as soon as possible.

"They were l-like us… h-had lives like us… never got a chance to live its life, and I k-killed it, and that's not even the worst part… I wanted to kill it," he said, looking at his shaking hands as if they had sinned.

"Allyson, this is not on you. Their lives were already destroyed from the moment the CULT destroyed their anatomy… You had to survive," Maia held sides of his face frantically, deciding that shaking him violently wouldn't make him snap out of his gaze as his pupils dilated, slowing down her words and locking his gaze with hers. "All we can do now is prevent any more lives being robbed from how they want to live and who they want to be."

"The others… We have to get them. W-we have to—" He held her hand, framing his jaw as his eyes regained focus.

"Don't rush!" Maia yelled, racing in the direction he had run past when she couldn't longer see him anymore in front of her vision. They couldn't just rush through the collapsing structure that was bound to set up with more traps. She stumbled back on her feet and struggled to maintain her footing while trying to brace herself to a sudden halt.

If it weren't for Caledon swiftly grabbing the back of her suit to pull her and make her fall backwards, she would have ended up falling forward into the flooding boiling tar spread around the end of the chamber. Quickly giving her a hand to help her get back on her feet, as they looked up at the ceiling, which was barely holding on to the detached planks usually chained to the ceiling.

"How do we cross this?" Caledon asked, frustrated, anxiety eating both of them up as they tried to not imagine the worst. "How the hell does any living being live in a cave filled with boiling tar?!"

***

Castiel had jumped the fastest, into the left chamber, out of the three. He barely had time to access his surroundings before looking at the cybernetic creature that moved closer to his face, turning his head to the side as he felt the cybernetic's heated breath on his cheek. He started backing away from the creature resembling a gigantic rhinoceros overdosed with growth hormones, taking several quick strides backwards.

The creature made a bee-line towards his direction, and Castiel ran as fast as his feet could carry him away. He needed time to study its movements to take it down, calculate its weak points while he tired it down by making it chase him in circles, for it would be like giving it a free pass to crush it if he used his brute strength to tackle with it.

Castiel jumped past the creature, dodging its tail and running towards the direction of the other end of the chamber, once again.

He had no time to stop the pained cry reverberating through his vocal cords just as the cybernetic creature knocked him off his feet slammed its horn through his shoulder, nearly dislocating it from its socket; if it weren't for the suit, it would have separated his arm from his shoulder, tears of anguish slipped unconsciously through the ends of his eyes as he used his good shoulder to grab the cybernetic's horn, giving his all to stop it from plunging its horn into his shoulder, before the potential energy in the air around him dispersed to absorb the electrical energy from the creature.

The creature stumbled, feeling weaker but not weak enough to fall down unconscious on the ground. Castiel grabbed his dislocated shoulder and stood up on his feet, feeling severely drained of energy and could barely think straight because of the sheer pain that exuded from his shoulder.

He dropped his head in anger, feeling ashamed of being bested so easily. He leaned his dislocated shoulder against the wall of the cavern and rammed his arm into it to put it back in its place, biting the bottom of his lip to prevent himself from screaming in pain like a banshee.

That's when he noticed another cybernetic, shaped like a massive panther, perched upon the top corner of the cavern, barely making any movements as if it were waiting for its turn to tear him down. He merely rotated his shoulder for good measure to distract the larger creature's attention back at him.

Castiel looked at the creature charging towards him before he stopped it in its tracks. The potential energy surged in an outburst, nearly draining the core fuelling the cybernetic until the creature backed up, yowling in defeat.

This only seemed to anger the creature, as it shook its head violently before charging towards again as if he were its prey.

Castiel pulled out the two daggers laced with a compound, that only Maia and Zella could pronounce, having created all by themselves as one of their many experimental vials in the Biotechnology labs of the facility, from the closed holsters on his suit under his forearms, and slid under the creature ramming one of the daggers straight through its belly and slashed through another cut under its belly, and ripping through the metal as the fuel's contents splattered over his suit and the side of his face.

He could feel the ground shake as the creature fell on the ground with a loud thud, just a few inches above his head, nearly missing getting crushed by the massive cybernetic beast.

The panther pounced atop its immobile fellow inhabitant circling him, measuring the other up. Both had the same striking green eyes and precise, lithe movements. The cybernetic panther lunged first, but Castiel was fast, and he dodged the attack, slicing across the big cat's shoulder. It got him an angry hiss and the baring of large canines for his effort.

He was completely focused on the panther, waiting for it to launch itself again. And when it did, one of his daggers stabbed into its massive torso while a huge paw came out and sliced across his stomach, nearly ripping through the suit.

The bianthromorph didn't wait for the cybernetic to attack again. Instead, he quickly moved to straddle its back, his weight pushing down onto the dagger that only went in deeper. The panther struggled weakly, but it was clearly evident that its fight was gone. The blonde then grabbed it at the scruff of its neck and sliced through its throat before retrieving his daggers to carve his way out of the chamber.

***

Zella's first reaction to avoid the boulder was to throw herself into the nearest chamber in front of her, and so she ended up in the one to the farthest right.

The chamber walls split in between and separated like two doors of an entrance to reveal a large tunnel below. Several metallic alloy slides began to emerge from the corners of the separated walls, forming steps that lead down to the largest cavern.

At the bottom, the floor swayed slightly as if it were made of gelatin, Zella wobbled a little as she tried to gain her footing, but her feet started losing more balance the longer she stood there. She kept observing what was laid out before her as if she was lost in her thoughts, trying to concoct a plan.

An uneasy feeling started looming over her chest, the stray hairs at the back of her neck on the standing edge as if alerting her senses that something was about to happen.

Not so unexpectedly, the second she took the third step, a giant pendulum swung down from out of nowhere, cutting the air in front of her with a swift swoosh. She narrowly missed it by jumping to the side at the last second to avoid being cut in half and losing her balance.

"Shit!" Zella skillfully rolled to the land back on her feet, dodging the pendulum as it swung back a second time.

Zella got used to the timing of the pendulums and dodged several more of those gigantic swinging pendulums, swerving left then right in a patterned rhythm until she cleared the path. The moment she stumbled onto the platform at the end of the path, the swinging pendulums stopped moving and retreated back into the ceiling.

She gaped up at an extensive barbed wooden wall that rose from the ground and scaled up till the ceiling. It had to be at least thirty feet tall. There was no way any being could scale up that thing. Her best option would

be to manipulate herself under it through the tiny gap
at the bottom.

Her breaths started getting heavier as she kneeled
down and laid on her stomach, commando-crawling
under the barrier. She inched along for about sixty feet
before she was able to clear the monstrosity and stand
back on her feet.

"Aghhh," Zella let out a scream. SPIDERS! All over
her. She swatted them off, spinning around in a circle,
slightly panicked as they crawled up and down her
body, itchy little legs tickling her skin. She grimaced as
she flung the last of the arachnids from herself.

She dusted the back of her carbon-fibre suit and
gazed at the next obstacle: a series of planks, in
varying thicknesses, hovering atop a thick tar-like
substance.

Zella picked a small pebble from the ground and
threw it into the tar. It burnt up in a matter of
seconds, emitting a horrid, burning flesh smell.

Zella tested the first plank, pushing on it lightly with
her feet. The second her shoe touched it, it
immediately fell loose from the chains attached to the
ceiling, and steam began to rise, toxic black fog
ghosting around her like it wanted to end her life.

She coughed violently as she covered her nose, glaring
at the ceiling to groan at this *damned* place. The

second, third and fourth planks similarly disappeared into the tar, leaving only the last plank for her to cross on. As soon as she stepped on the plank, it began to spin like a blade of a helicopter at a much slower pace.

Zella had to compensate for the horrific situation by taking tiny steps, steadying her footsteps by moving along with the plank as it spun, turning to her side and creeping down the plank.

Moments later, Zella reached the edge of the tar and stepped down off the other side of the platform, taking deep breaths.

Zella trudged several more feet, weary of the foreboding darkness behind the thick, patchy fog and anything unpredictable that could drop down and crush her. She seemed to be wary of what might happen above her that she didn't keep track of what might be below her.

Zella quickly stopped at the edge of the next obstacle, an expansive rift that spanned the whole length of the room.

The thick mist that had been hovering in the background began to recede like someone was sucking it all out with a vacuum. Upon inspecting it further, there was indeed a ventilator at the top of separated walls, clearing the whole area and revealing the light at the end of the chamber-like tunnel.

The thick mist that had been hovering in the background began to recede like someone was sucking it all out with a vacuum, clearing the whole area and revealing the grand finale on the other side. There, standing across the way, was a cybernetic creature in the form of a snarling four-legged beast that stared her down. Its razor-sharp teeth looked like they could actually tear flesh.

Zella pulled the daggers from her arm holsters, grasping them in her hands as if her life depended on it.

She kept her gaze locked with the creature's, calculating what it might do when she was occupying the same space.

Zella was just one jump away from the jaws of the cybernetic. A mess of saliva and muck dripped from its pointed teeth, waiting patiently to rip any intruder apart. She looked straight at its hind legs, calculating what the cybernetic might do when she was occupying the same space. She had to be fast, strike hard, and not get ripped apart.

She backed up and took a flying leap, flipping up and over and landing behind it. The creature whipped around in a fury of confusion, locking its sights on her jugular. It lunged at her, snapping its jaws ferociously.

Zella swung the daggers several times but missed as it dodged each attempt. The cybernetic had already managed to access and read her movements.

The cybernetic grew tired of waiting. It roared out, lashing its tail and slicing Zella across her suit. Although it couldn't slice through the suit, the hit was strong enough to make her drop the daggers as she collapsed to one knee.

It lunged forward, charging at the amber-eyed bianthromorph. She jumped out of the way, turning quickly and extending her daggered hand. She sliced the beast down the other side of its metallic exterior, hitting a weak spot.

It turned to bound again as Zella dove for her other dagger. It whipped its tail sharply, catching her foot and causing her to land on her face, the daggers flying forward out of her grasp. She rolled over on her side, spitting out a mouthful of blood, jerking her head up just in time as the cybernetic leapt onto her, pinning her down with its needle-like claws.

She clutched the sides of its jaw between her hands, trying to stop the cybernetic from progressing downward and shredding her apart.

The cybernetic dug its claws further into Zella's shoulder as it attempted to rip through the suit and disengage its mouth from her grip. She felt a wave of fatigue hit her. A weird sensation of numbness travelled down her arms. It felt like they were paralysed, her grip loosening on the cybernetic's jaws. Her insides burned like they were turned to lava, the pain becoming nearly excruciating.

Zella shook her head immediately, trying to snap out of her pain and focus, snapping through another weak spot, and the cybernetic would shut down.

She backed up and took a flying leap, flipping up and over and landing behind it. The cybernetic beast swung its tail, but Zella rolled out of the path, retrieving the dagger from her back and landing it upright to the beast's side and slashing the second weak spot built in its metallic underbelly with one quick swipe. Before finally reaching the switchboard that had been lying under the cybernetic-beast and smashing it shut. The boiling tar began to get sucked in, and several platforms started to get locked atop it, but it barely did anything to get rid of the nausea-inducing stench.

"Where would you even get such a huge amount of tar?" Caledon asked, with an annoyed sigh, exiting out of the chamber that he and Maia had been trapped in.

"It's Novyslava," Castiel said, holding his shoulder as he walked out of his chamber, holding a gaze that screamed insane even by his standards before they heard gunshots raining down nearly fifty feet away from where they stood. This was the weirdest structure in Novyslava.

CHAPTER NINETEEN

The first time Charm's team laid their eyes on Delanna Jericho, a middle-aged woman dressed in all white clothing, a long flowy white gauze dress, and laced up white sandals, they barely had time to time to react before they were separated away from Cullins and her, with a forcefield surrounding the two. The young breedlings barely had time to process one of the significant figures in their history actually existed before they were separated by their Chancellor's forcefield. This was the last thing they had expected to get roped into after returning from their recruitment mission in the Oslo MPA.

Her jet-black hair was neatly tied in a loose braid, but most of all, her looks were oddly similar to someone: Charm, as if they were related. "Fancy." Pearl coughed after regaining from her previous shock. "She looks quite young for her age, even for an anthromorph. She doesn't look a day over late-thirties to early-forties despite being in her late sixties. A little over the top, but fancy."

"I can't be the only one who notices the similarities, right?" Lizzie whispered, looking back and forth between Charm and Delanna Jericho.

"There are over two hundred trained human soldiers waiting to attack your breedlings if you dare to make a foolish move." Even when she was threatening them, Lizzie couldn't help but admit that the stag anthromorph had an alluring voice. "They are young. They will be spared."

"You are siding with humans over your own kind? *Humans* who killed your daughter?" Cullins grinned, sharp as a knife against his skin. He almost looked maniacal, but his eyes were too coherent like everyone else he had met here. Too clear with understanding.

This wasn't anger and rage that blinded. It sharpened them. Focused them on a single target that they believed with everything they held deserved to be destroyed and suffer for what it had done.

"If nothing else," the stag-anthromorph said coldly. "Death is too good for you. I want to watch you shake in fear like you watched my daughter be reduced to a vegetable in Vienna."

It was so angry and bitter.

It was justified if everything was true.

"In your words, I was more like your child than Donna ever was. Have you forgotten *your* own words?" Cullins asked hoarsely.

She chuckled darkly. "I said those words to the boy who might as well be *dead*."

"That's why your own daughter chose the CULT over you." He spat hoarsely, heart palpitating as his muscles burned.

The stag anthromorph let out a gut-wrenching scream and ran forward. Cullins threw down the gun and sword and braced himself for the impact. It came in the form of Jericho's fist colliding with his jaw so mightily it had Cullins spinning around and hitting the floor, face first.

Cullins looked up at his mentor, whose verdant eyes were flashing, chest heaving with emotion.

"Get up," she snarled, fists clenched at her sides, and Cullins couldn't help but spit at the ground, thinking about her limited ambition, just like her daughter. The thought made his own anger flare again as he flew up from the ground and threw himself at his mentor, arms and fists blindly lashing out in a fury.

She didn't even bother blocking the few blows Cullins managed to clumsily land. Instead, she hit him hard in the ribs, and then another blow to the face followed that had him spitting out blood as he tried to stop the room from spinning long enough so he could stand up again.

He was on his hands and knees, one eye almost swollen shut already, wondering if Delanna had broken a few ribs.

She lunged forward, and Cullins dodged the daggered hand that swung at him, "You pushed her to her death!" he yelled, but she didn't recognise the voice of the bianthromorph she had trained. She should have stopped him from the moment she found him tracing the bases of the CULT.

"Don't fight it. It hurts much worse when you fight it," she took several swipes at Cullins, but he managed to evade each movement. Cullins felt nearly dead inside. All his energy drained. Was his pride more important than his goals? He was wasting precious time.

"I spared your daughter's life even when she tried to kill me. You just don't want to admit that your precious daughter wanted to join the CULT, more than I ever did." Cullins yelled, reaching for his arm, but Jericho took advantage and pinned him against the cavern wall behind him. He struggled to keep the dagger from being plunged into his stomach. It took every ounce of strength to push her arm away. If he was stabbed with the dagger and was unable to remove it, he would bleed to death; the hydrocarbon compound would poison the skin around the puncture, causing the healing process to halt.

"You are nothing but a pathetic kid *desperate* to please and prove his worth. Don't test me." She warned.

"You know that I never lie. She manipulated you!"

The blade inched closer to Cullins' abdomen. He could feel the cold, sharp point against the cloth of his shirt. He closed his eyes, trying to find the strength to fight back, but the woman was too powerful. His arms ached, about to give out. This was it. He was going to die right here on some random cave in the middle of the Ural Mountains.

"Lies!"

"If you don't believe me, then it's better that you join her fate—" he muttered, opening his eyes to stare at his mentor who didn't even have the decency to spare him a doubt, before shutting the forcefield separating him and Delanna from the breedlings of his facility.

With a sudden force, Delanna was violently pulled off of him. He watched with a smug grin as Reyna plunged her dagger into the older's neck, her blood misting his face. There was a reason why he had always trusted Cyclopedidae breedlings like her to finish the job without any questions. *He may not have been at best at combat, but the anthromorphs trained in his facility were.* Just like he knew his former mentor wouldn't dare to attack a young breedling, underestimating their prowess because of their age, just like she had underestimated him during that age.

The dagger fell to the ground with a clank, kicked aside as the stag anthromorph's body convulsed from shock.

"Achh...rrrg..." Delanna gurgled, failing to pull herself from Reyna's grasp, realising the dagger was made up of exitialium, the hydrocarbon compound Delanna had engineered, herself, to control breedlings in exchange for gaining the humans' trust.

Charm had never seen so much blood in his life. It was obscene. He couldn't be responsible for a team that would be associated with this *horrendous* moment.

He wanted to run. He couldn't move away from this place, partly because of shock and partly because he still had to uphold his promise to a friend, who predicted this as a worst-case scenario. If he cared to be stupidly loyal to still keep his words, after all, that he had just seen, then it had to be with this friend who was insanely loyal to a fault even at the cost of her own life. If she had seen this coming, then Charm was certain that she was going to be pulling something *crazier* than this.

Cullins seized the older by the hair and pulled her neck to the side so he could rip further into her neck using the dagger, "This is why I can't expect anyone but finish the job by myself."

She finally stopped resisting, and her body went limp moments later. Cullins expelled a canister of liquid into the older's temple, locking eyes with the rest of the breedlings as he dramatically let go of her body. All of them watched as she fell to the ground, lifeless. As hoards of humans started flooding in from the chambers, he turned towards the breedlings. "Kill every single one of them if you don't want your human connections to meet the same fate as her." *These humans must have held a deep respect for his mentor, to hold back like she had asked them to, and 'fight' for her even after her death.*

The roaring thoughts flew in time with the beating of their boots against dirt. They split up as they reached the very hollow centre of the cavern's underground base. Pearl not hesitating to slide a knife across the human's neck.

Pearl and Lizzie ran off down the opposite fork in the hallway. Pearl ducked a knife that came flying from the side. She drove her dagger into the man's ribs, even as six others ran from Jericho's hollow chambers in the cavern, shouting for them to halt.

She was suddenly shoved out of the crowd of humans, whipping around with wide eyes.

Lizzie didn't see the two humans stepping out of another chamber. She simply heard her fellow felis cruxawn, Nadia's warning call and dropped to the ground like a stone.

Nadia threw a blade that struck one in the throat, leaping over Pearl to duck the second one's blow and stab through her stomach with her blade, shoving him off and turning back to Pearl, eyes fiery. Nadia had every right to scold and lecture her. She simply grabbed Pearl by the wrist and hauled her up roughly.

Nadia saw something move out of the corner of her eye. And she knew Pearl saw it too, both of them turning.

She knew Pearl saw something by the way she stiffened, even if Nadia didn't see what it actually was.

But she threw herself forward anyway. Her torso was thrown over Pearl's, and Nadia felt the semi-familiar sensation of a blade striking across her skin. Rather than plunging into the person on the floor, though, the blade was knocked off course by Nadia's moving body, not even tearing the nearly impenetrable carbon-fibre clothing she wore.

It still hurt like hell.

Nadia cried out even as she threw her legs over, rolling over Pearl's battered body and coming up, standing with her blade held.

A human stood at the mouth of the chamber nearest to their left, wearing all black and a mask, like the suit they wore, but plainer.

The human charged forward.

"Lunge!" Pearl yelled. Nadia closed her eyes and lunged forward, thrusting the dagger out.

A hand caught her wrist, twisting it, forcing Nadia around. Nadia cried out, dropping the dagger, even as she slammed her head back, feeling something (most likely the human's nose) crunch beneath her skull.

The human dropped quickly, shouting violently as he clutched his bleeding nose. Nadia dropped quickly, snatching the dagger again, stumbling back, glancing at Pearl. She was sitting up, the human's blade held in hand and her face pale with the effort to move.

"Turn!" The amethyst-eyed breedling warned, jerking forward.

Nadia whipped around, already thrusting with the dagger she held with both hands. Another human leapt back, glaring murderously as he lunged forward. She yelped, jerking to the side, the man barrelling past her towards Pearl. But Pearl stared past Nadia. "Behind!" she shouted as the human collided with her.

Nadia whipped around, blood pumping so quickly, she was becoming dizzy. She didn't even turn completely before the hilt of a knife was slamming into the back of her head.

She had no other choice. No moment to fight. Not even a chance to try and get help. Not even a moment to make sure Pearl was safe. She crumpled like a can beneath a car, hitting the ground hard and her vision going black so quickly it was terrifying.

Pearl, and their team of forty, against hundreds of combat-trained humans was infinitely more terrifying.

"-Up, -dia!"

Nadia felt the urge to scream rise up in her chest, but she swallowed it, shoving it down beneath the pain pulsing along with her entire form, her cordierite-coloured eyes being covered by her chocolate-brown hair.

"Shit-stard, ge-the h-up!"

Nadia tried. She was trying. For god's sake, she was trying to get through the pain. Her hand twitched against the ground that her eyes stared at, half-lidded and unfocused. It was like landing on your back from a five-story fall, paralysed, and the breath knocked from her as she struggled just to breathe, just to move.

The cacophony around her died out. Her fingers curled slightly against the harsh grovels of the ground beneath her.

A hand slapped her face. It was hardly violent, not a human kicking over a dead breedling's body, but it jarred her, breath slamming back into her lungs as her teeth grit together.

"Nadia, if y o-on't look a-m-right now !"

She shifted her eyes towards the blurred noise, like listening underwater. Her ears rang. Pearl was lying on the ground beside her, and for a horrifying moment, Nadia thought she had been shot, but she met Nadia's eyes and breathed out a hard sigh.

"Jesus Christ," she muttered into the ground before lifting her head again, eyes harder but fragile. "Where were you hit?" she asked, leaning to try and see Nadia's back. She shifted over when Nadia didn't answer.

She didn't know. Everything hurt. Everything was fiery and numb, like a flame licking at the skin until all your nerve endings were burned off. Her entire back could be riddled with holes for all she knew.

Careful not to rise above the ground, Pearl moved over, lifting herself up onto her arms to peer at Nadia's back.

She felt a sort of dull pressure, like poking at memory foam, here and there and. The cry that left Nadia's throat was neither voluntary nor expected, tearing from her chest as it felt like a sharp blade was stabbed into a spot just at the dip of her waist on her back.

"Shit," Pearl hissed, dropping onto the floor again. "Okay, that's a lot of blood, we need—"

Bullets cut her off, and Nadia's eyes slammed shut against the loud noise that seemed to vibrate even the blood in her veins. Pearl was cursing loudly beside her.

Nadia felt tired. And if she passed out, she likely wouldn't feel all of the pain currently running along each of her nerves. Her leg twitched, making her physically bite her tongue to keep from crying out again as it moved the muscles in her back.

Silence. Where were the bullets?

"We need first aid," The amethyst-eyed anthromorph muttered, shifting onto her elbows. "Stay—"

"Stop," Nadia bit out, trying not to move as feeling and sensation slowly filtered back into limbs. It was better when she couldn't move. "You don't have to act nice to me because of your guilt towards Rune." Even if Rune was mostly apathetic, she was very clear with her words and feelings. She even responded back with nearly friendly nods, almost always checking up on her if she got injured during their missions after Nadia stopped having expectations that the amber-eyed girl would hopefully change her mind later. She was clear, unlike Pearl. Honestly, Nadia preferred apathy over someone toying with her feelings. But she was still a fool.

Holy shit, her back hurt.

Pearl stared at her for a moment, not understanding. Almost everyone knew about the fallout between Rune and Allyson, although they had no idea about the cause.

"Take them out first," Nadia demanded between her teeth, sucking in a sharp breath that filled her lungs and lifted her back, which hurt like hell.

"You'll never be able to treat me while they're shooting at us."

"They are hundreds of them, and all I have is a stolen handgun," Pearl reminded her, and Nadia wished she could see her face instead of her shoulder, but she couldn't even shift her eyes. "I am not that good with my mark."

"There are going to kill us. If they worked for Jericho, then their bullets must be made up of exitialium." Nadia took small, short breaths. "You can fire those shots, can't you?" Maybe it was teasing. It was hard to make out through the hissed breaths and blood she could feel slipping down her skin.

"That's downright insane!" Pearl snapped before fishing through the compartments near her waist for spares. "I need to put pressure on that wound—"

She began to move, and Nadia's hand jerked forward a couple of inches. She didn't even touch Pearl, but the other froze as if Nadia had her chained down. Nadia swallowed, and her mouth tasted metallic. "You can't let any more of us die," she said icily.

"*Any more?* No one is going to die—"

"Pearl," she croaked as loudly as she could, the pressure flexing her muscles, and she had to take a second to breathe through the pain. "They outnumber us. We can't let them gain the upper hand. Your parents' are humans too. If we lose, their lives are at stake." she reminded her roughly. "Stop the threat. Take them out."

"I don't even have any cover!"

Nadia's fingers curled into a loose fist, handing her two more handguns fallen near her feet. "Then you'd better make your shots count."

It was stupid. It was suicidal.

It was their job.

But man, did it hurt enough to make her bite her cheeks to bleeding to stop from crying out with every pulse of blood shooting through her veins. Her head spun from the pain. Nadia wanted to ignore the gunshots. She wanted to succumb to the pain and just let go, but she clung to the edge of consciousness like she was hanging over a cliff. It was easier with one thing on her mind: live. Live through this so that her human connections don't get blown up. Their team needed to take these humans out.

Sounded like they were plenty of the breedlings who were going to die. Or maybe that was the bullet wound talking.

Nadia's breaths caught in her throat, tearing out in carefully hidden noises that still escaped. Composure was hard to keep when each breath shifted the metal inside her.

Pearl cursed lowly, breathing harshly, before huffing. "Fine, you are such a noble *saint.*"

Nadia almost demanded that if they were making any progress as Pearl took down twelve more humans, but all she did was shift closer to Nadia, expression grim. "Brace yourself," she warned, and that was all Nadia had time to do as she pressed the spare piece of cloth against her back.

For a moment, Nadia just blacked out. Her vision cleared as she panted, sweat dripping off her forehead and a searing throbbing in her back.

"I can't stay hold it down, but you're bleeding too much to leave it open," Pearl said, voice coming from the end of a tunnel as she pulled away before shooting another in his shooting arm, leaving a light pressure against the fire on Nadia's back. "Hopefully, it'll keep debris out of it, too."

All of this was happening too fucking fast. Could it slow down just enough for Nadia to get her breath back?

Nadia's hand was forced open, the handgun pushed into her palm, and her fingers closed around it, shaking from the pain beating with every pump of her heart. "If you bleed out while I'm dealing with these assholes, I swear to God, I will never forgive you," Pearl hissed, pulling away.

It sounded different to Nadia.

"What—"

"Shoot as many as you can to ensure that we win," Pearl said, and from where Nadia laid, she could see crawl along the ground, and the chaos continued.

Her leg twitched again, and the knife-agony shoved between her ribs was almost enough to make her blackout. She felt weak and wanted to know just how much blood she was losing. Her nerves were shot, random parts of her twitching and jarring her muscles that screamed for Nadia to just pass out.

Nadia made one, weak, valiant attempt to pull herself forward, to get a shot at another human shooting at their team, and it ended as well as could be expected, black creeping into her vision and locking her lungs up as she hissed a curse, a pained gasp ripping through her teeth.

"Nadia?" she heard Pearl call from her left.

"'Fine," she snapped, fingers tightening on the gun. She hated this whole thing.

Anger. Yes. Anger was better than fear. Fear paralysed. Anger made you move. Even if Nadia couldn't move either way.

"We are going to win through this," Nadia piped up; speech made it hurt so bad. Every twitch and flex of her muscles burned and shot pain. Nadia was sure she would have passed out long ago if she hadn't built up some sort of pain tolerance, but that didn't mean it didn't hurt like hell.

Spraying bullets were easy to slip between. Calculated shots aimed at your one opening were not. Pearl would never be able to get up to shoot before they got her first. The stupid assholes, aiming for their fucking chance of a lifetime.

"To your right," Nadia croaked suddenly, voice cracking.

"What?" Pearl asked, shifting her stance.

"They have figured out that Charm is leading the team," she said, louder, words stuttering as her lungs locked up and released. "They're aiming for him—You need to cover his back." It would buy him only seconds, but it were seconds they currently didn't have.

"You can't expect me to rush to his side and fire before they shift their sight five feet to the right and shoot you instead," Pearl hissed.

Nadia was silent for a moment, trying to breathe through a knife in her upper back that lodged there.

"Nadia?" Calm but panicked.

"Gimme a second," she wheezed, swallowing thickly, forcing the words out because they were wasting time and blood. "The—" her breaths cut her off. "You've gotta try. If he dies, then Cullins is going to declare our mission as a failure."

Pearl cursed rapidly, more shifting, muttering to herself that Nadia almost didn't hear. "I hate all this bullshit. Give me one thing and then try and tear everything else away—"

The world was beginning to spin slowly. "Stop playing a martyr here," Pearl muttered, and it sounded angry and bitter and fed up.

They didn't have time for that. They didn't even have time to argue about it. They only had time for crazy and reckless. "You've just gotta have his back."

And worried. Not scared. But not a meaningless statement that she didn't actually believe. It was as strong as she could make it, which was pathetic, really, but Pearl stopped shifting. "We—" She swallowed, teeth almost breaking as she gritted them. "We did not make it through everything else—We did not survive through all those missions, just to die in shitty Novyslava at the hands of maniacal humans with guns. I owe you dinner when all this is over," Pearl spat, voice shaking slightly.

Nadia would have laughed if it hadn't made her pass out. "How does me—hell—getting shot equate to you owing me dinner?"

"You just better show up!" Pearl snapped, and even if her voice was shaking, Nadia knew her hands weren't. "I owe you after two years, and you better not skip out!" *You better not die.*

Nadia swallowed, her eyes stinging. It was different. Having someone who cared if she lived or died. "If you can make five more shots without dying, I will definitely let you take me out to dinner after all this is over, Pearl."

They didn't have the luxury of heartfelt goodbye and tearful reassurances. As much as Nadia felt like they were needed, she kept them shoved back to the bottom of her throat. They could not afford thoughts of 'this is the end' or 'this is it.' Life did not gift them that luxury. There was only survival and getting through this alive. At any cost.

"Stay conscious."

Nadia huffed, and her vision tinged yellow-green. "Pearl, I might pass out," she said, tongue getting heavy in her mouth. She tried to breathe through it, eyes closed tightly against vertigo.

"Don't you dare," Pearl snapped, shooting another human taking shots at Charm from behind. "You better not, Nadia. I'm not kidding."

Well, what was she going to do about it? The darkness was inviting for its lack of pain but terrifying for its lack of awareness.

Nadia breathed as best she could, ignoring the spinning. "Then you'd better hurry up," she whispered, something like fear settling in her chest. She didn't want to fall unconscious, didn't want to be ignorant to what Pearl was doing, what was happening.

"Okay," Pearl whispered. She probably said it at full volume, but Nadia's ears felt like they were full of cotton. "Three."

A throb of pain with her heartbeat.

"Two."

Nadia swallowed, opening her eyes but closing them when her stomach rolled with the spinning room.

"One."

Through cotton ears, she heard a single gunshot nearly hit the breedling behind her.

Another shot from Charm. Two, three, four, five.

Nadia's heart was in her throat as she breathed in the scent of dirt and blood in the ground.

Chaos. Nadia blinked, and when she opened her eyes, half her vision was tunnelled. She could hear her heartbeat. Nothing else.

"Pearl?" It wasn't loud enough. Not even if Pearl had been right next to her. She felt like she was being shoved underwater. "Pearl, did we win?" she rasped, trying to be louder, the pressure in her chest chasing darkness into her eyes.

Cullins removed his jacket and threw it to the side, cracking his knuckles. He held up his hands, questioning if the last two humans standing were man enough to take him down, challenging someone forward. They dropped their guns and removed their jackets, both stepping up to their Chancellor, confident they could kick his ass and make an example out of him. They both attempted to pounce on him simultaneously and crashed into each other as Cullins quickly moved to the side. He took the opportunity to disarm several dead humans, taking the guns and shoving them straight through their chests. Their organs splattering on the floor made the breedlings hesitate to voice their anger back away, frightened.

"Who's next?" Cullins taunted, looking at the stunned faces of the last team he had sent over to Novyslava to finish this job. His half-sister looked downright murderous, having watched him kill the humans in cold blood. But it was the blonde bianthromorph who made the first move.

Suddenly, Pearl was dropped down in front of Nadia, making her jump violently, jarring her back, and making her cry out, breath hissing between her teeth, her ears ringing loudly like a siren blaring.

The bianthromorph swung at the Chancellor, but Cullins grabbed him by the arm, manoeuvred himself behind him, and snapped his arm backwards. Castiel yelled out in pain. His screams echoed off the stalactites, sounding like the soundtrack of a horror film. *Pearl had sparred against him several times to know he was hurting himself on purpose rather than Cullins actually besting over him.*

Castiel lunged forward, but Zella stopped him with a hard kick to the chest. He flew back but quickly recovered before aiming the semi-automatic revolver, fallen from the clutches of one of the corpses, at Cullins. "If you kill him, then you are going to get locked up. Your life will be ruined!"

"This is my goal! Killing the bastard running the CULT!" Castiel snapped venomously, paying no heed to her warnings.

Zella used one of the boulders as a shield, drowning out the screams of the breedlings behind them as the bullets penetrated the limestone. Zella pushed Cullins to the ground and ran to pounce on Castiel, slamming him to the ground. "I am not gonna let you throw away your life, Castiel!"

'That stupid bianthromorph! What the hell is he trying to pull? He is going to get Zella killed." It was like hearing through plastic. Pearl was talking to her. Yelling above her. Nadia couldn't hear.

"Castiel is right. I am not signing off to be someone's slave just to kill lives at his beck and call." Maia dashed towards Cullins, brandishing an exitialium dagger laced with succinylcholine. Her words had clear stuck a nerve with all the breedlings in the cavern, which hadn't hesitated to kill the trained humans working for Delanna Jericho.

She took several swipes at Cullins but missed each time as the Caledon forced the Chancellor to duck. Maia punished Caledon with a roundhouse kick to the chin, dropping him to his knees. "You think you are going to be spared if you kill him?! You don't have the upper hand in this, Maia."

She scoffed coldly at his words. "I don't want him to use me like a puppet until I am foolish enough to watch him kill my human relatives right in front of me like he killed all these humans today."

This angered the cheetah-breedling, and he became irrational, hindering any cognitive attempts at fighting. Maia loved when they reached this point because most feline anthromorphs could not focus through anger, not like she could. Maia wielded her anger like a weapon. She thrived off of it.

Charm had always been good with experimenting with frequencies. That's the reason why Zella had approached him before her mission to Novyslava. *"You have to promise me that you will be the only one responsible for clean-up in Novyslava if you get this frequency."* He didn't bother asking her questions, knowing that the amber-eyed girl wouldn't spare him with explanations, especially when she wasn't sure of a situation occurring with certainty. He also knew that he would be assigned to the next team to Novyslava if his friends failed to apprehend Delanna Jericho.

When Zella warned him about craziness, he wasn't expecting to receive a signal in a frequency that only he could perceive. At the same time, he watched four of his friends fighting against each other, separating away from their sight and Cullins, as Zella and Caledon tried to hold back Maia and Castiel from killing their Chancellor.

What the hell were they trying to pull?

"Should we help them?" Lizzie asked in a confused daze, trying to help their Chancellor get back on his feet, as she watched the four ruthlessly attack each other, utterly lethal with their hits, disappearing into one of the chambers.

"Who are we supposed to help?" Reyna asked matter-of-factly, slightly terrified of the sheer animosity radiating of the four.

"Let them be," Cullins ordered with a smirk. "They are going to end killing the ones who can't stay loyal to us."

Pearl immediately knew that the Chancellor wanted Castiel and Maia to be eliminated rather than deal with the possibilities of them rebelling against him. No matter how good Zella and her brother were in combat, Castiel and Maia matched them off well. Heck! Maia had basically trained the twins. The outcome could also end up with Zella and Caledon getting killed. Anger could easily overpower love in a split second, and she wasn't waiting to see which pair would end up getting favoured by the chances.

"What if Zella and Caledon fail to hold them back?" Charm asked in a clipped tone.

"There is forty of us. We can take them down if Zella and Caledon end up losing to them," Cullins shrugged as if he didn't care who actually ended up getting killed, as floods of older anthromorphs, most probably in their mid-40s, swarmed them, more particularly Cullins. A few hundred of them were adorning the uniforms of the Council and few others merely slate-grey suits, the CULT.

Charm knew they didn't stand a chance to fight against Cullins at this moment, so he did the only thing he could possibly think of as soon as he heard Caledon's scream echoing through the caverns. He grabbed a frozen Pearl and hauled her to her feet using the back of her suit and racing towards the direction that the four had headed off to.

Only to be frozen by the sight in front of him, Caledon looked like an ashen log sitting beside Maia's lifeless body. Before either Charm or Pearl could rush off towards Zella, holding Castiel back from using the canister containing a similar-coloured liquid that Cullins had used on Delanna Jericho. Charm really couldn't tell if Zella was holding Castiel back from using it on himself or if Castiel was blocking her from using it against him.

It all happened too fast when Cullins joined them along with a few members of the Council, and Castiel fell lifeless just like Maia, as Zella muttered with pure hatred, her tears falling to the ground, still holding the empty canister in her clenched fists. "I hate you."

Pearl couldn't hear either of their heartbeats. Castiel and Maia were dea—

It was like they were frozen in time, in this horrendous moment, until one of the Council members declared.

"They are dead. The RTFQ monitoring their functions is completely inactive, shutting down their trackers."

"Good, I believe the leader of this team should clean them up along with Jericho and the rest of the humans." Cullins barely acknowledged his words with a curt nod before dismissing them to prepare their departure from Novyslava along with the rest of the breedlings in the facility and members of the Council as well as the CULT. "So, that Ms Rune and Mr Allyson could get it out of their system and leave Novyslava with the rest of the humans."

***

Caledon and Zella wordlessly helped Charm and Pearl drag the lifeless bodies of Maia and Castiel onto the pile of other corpses.

Neither Charm and nor Pearl know what to say either of them or even ask. No matter how much the panther-breedling had wanted the Brazilian bianthromorph to get locked away, she felt shattered to actually watch him die. Even if she absolutely hated him, he was a good friend to the rest. He was a good person. And Maia—

Charm looked at Zella as if she was finally losing her sanity while holding Castiel's paling body and not dragging him away to the other corpses but rather injecting him with an unknown vial while Caledon did the same to Maia.

"They are dead. They have no heartbeat." Charm didn't understand what Novyslava might have done to these two, but they were never this sadistic. To harm people that they loved, even after killing them. "Let them go."

"Played well?" Caledon asked Zella flatly as he watched the EMP fields shut down after Cullins left the scene along with everyone, except the four of them and the anthromorph flying the last chopper that would fly the four of them out of Novyslava.

"We don't have any alternatives," Zella repeated the very same words from the night before when Caledon had asked if Charm could ever forgive them for toying with him and not warning him of the stunt they had just pulled.

This was the only way to completely deactivate the RTFQ chips of Maia and Castiel permanently and not just fry its external functions but also its internal monitoring functions. They had to fool the chip into believing that the life systems they were attached to were inactive by putting them into a catatonic state for exactly 30 minutes by making it look like their heartbeats had stopped.

Confidence was the perfect antidote to conquering over one's insecurities until the former tipped over the scale. For over-confidence ends up being the ignorant veil that fails to check the consumption of caution by the reformation of those very insecurities in an unrivalled form.

They needed Cullins to hallucinate through that very ignorant veil so that he would never doubt that he couldn't take down Castiel or Maia if they had decided to actually fight him. They needed him to neglect caution and leave behind the '*emotionally*' affected by the deaths for clean-up. Until they got their head back in the game.

As soon as Maia's antidote started to take its effect, their blood started warming to their body temperature, bringing back Maia and Castiel to regain their consciousness.

Before Pearl could shriek in horror, watching corpses coming back to life, Maia rushed to cover her mouth, eyes fleeting between her and Charm, who was slapping himself to wake himself from this sick joke.

"We can explain," Castiel said carefully, as Zella and Caledon looked at him with sheepishly guilty eyes, and that's when that Charm knew this illusion could be very, *very* real.

It was official. Charm Chang was losing his mind.

To Be Continued...

Map of Terra Firma - The Year 2155 AD

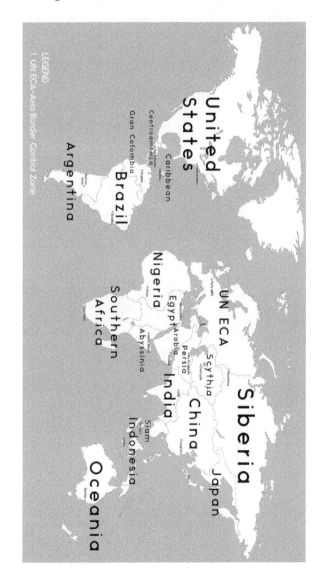

Also Available in the US Edition

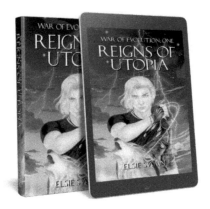

Milton Keynes UK
Ingram Content Group UK Ltd.
UKHW011940240823
427419UK00001B/7